PRAISE FOR TIJAN

"Nobody writes like Tijan. With addicting storylines and unparalleled prose, she's always an auto-click author for me."

—#1 *New York Times* bestselling author Rachel Van Dyken

"Tijan knows how to create addictive, fun, and exciting stories that you simply cannot put down!"

—Elle Kennedy, *New York Times* bestselling author

"I can always count on Tijan to write an action-packed, intense, emotional story that will have me invested until the very last page."

—Helena Hunting, *New York Times* bestselling author

"Tijan delivers on the fun, edge, and angst. Her books never fail to please!"

—Kylie Scott, *New York Times* bestseller

"Tijan delivers a power-punch with *Anti-Stepbrother*—angst, tension, and an emotional conclusion that'll have you glued to every page. The characters jump straight from the story and claim your heart. You won't be ready to let go."

—JB Salsbury, *New York Times* and *USA Today* bestselling author on *Anti-Stepbrother*

"One of my TIJAN faves, with a hero to die for and a heroine you'll want as your best friend."

—Katy Evans, *New York Times* bestselling author on *Anti-Stepbrother*

"5+ RIVETING Stars!!! The chemistry between Dusty and Stone was OFF-THE-CHARTS ELECTRIFYING. I was completely absorbed from the first page to the last. Tijan didn't just get a touchdown with this story, she won the Super Bowl!"

—Beth Flynn, *USA Today* bestselling author on *Enemies*

"Obsessed from page one! *The Insiders* is yet another addicting read from Tijan."

—Jennifer L. Armentrout, #1 *New York Times* bestselling author on *The Insiders*

"A whirlwind of high-stakes suspense."

—*Publishers Weekly* on *The Insiders*

"Hello, book hangover! With captivating, unique characters, this story is so much more than an epic sports romance. Redemption. Friendship. Unconditional love. And that ending! Hands down, my favorite Tijan book!"

—*USA Today* bestselling author Devney Perry on *The Not-Outcast*

"Blaise is the perfect rich prick to fall in love with! One of my fav reads in 2020!"

—Ilsa Madden-Mills, *Wall Street Journal* bestselling author on *Rich Prick*

"Emotionally tumultuous, angsty, and beautiful. *Ryan's Bed* is a new Tijan favorite and a must read for anyone going through loss!"

—#1 *New York Times* bestselling author Rachel Van Dyken on *Ryan's Bed*

A *Hateful* NEGOTIATION

OTHER TITLES BY TIJAN

A Dirty Business

Mafia Stand-Alones

Cole

Bennett Mafia

Jonah Bennett

Canary

Fallen Crest/Roussou Universe

Fallen Crest Series

Crew Series

The Boy I Grew Up With (stand-alone)

Rich Prick (stand-alone)

Nate

Aveke

Frisco

Other Series

Broken and Screwed Series (YA/NA)

Jaded Series (YA/NA suspense)

Davy Harwood Series (paranormal)

Carter Reed Series (mafia)

The Insiders

Sports Romance Stand-Alones

Enemies

Teardrop Shot

Hate To Love You

The Not-Outcast

Young Adult Stand-Alones

Ryan's Bed

A Whole New Crowd

Brady Remington Landed Me in Jail

College Stand-Alones

Anti-Stepbrother

Kian

Contemporary Romances

Bad Boy Brody

Home Tears

Fighter

Rockstar Romance Stand-Alone

Sustain

Paranormal Stand-Alones

Evil

Micaela's Big Bad

More books to come!

TIJAN

Published by Montlake, Seattle

www.apub.com

EU product safety contact:
Amazon Media EU S. à r.l.
38, avenue John F. Kennedy, L-1855 Luxembourg
amazonpublishing-gpsr@amazon.com

ISBN-13: 9781662524868 (paperback)
ISBN-13: 9781662524875 (digital)

Cover design by Hang Le
Cover image: © Wander Aguiar Photography; © ed2806 / Shutterstock

Printed in the United States of America

To all the readers who enjoyed Trace, Jess, Ashton,
Molly, Jake, and Sawyer.
I hope you enjoy Creighton and Blake!

CHAPTER ONE

BLAKE

Eight years old

I looked up at the house. White paint. It had a green door. I liked that.

"Okay." Mr. Nathan was sitting beside me. We'd come in his car, and he had some stuff on his lap. He was looking through some papers while he was huffing and muttering under his breath. I learned long ago that was just what Mr. Nathan did. He was in charge of me. He brought me to these homes, left me, and would come back later to ask how everything was going. I learned after the first home it was better if I always told him everything was fine.

I was fine.

He would ask. That would be my response, except some of the times, I wished I could ask if he could sneak me food. Sometimes there were no places to hide the food, but I was good at finding places. It was just making sure you hid your treats in there when no one was watching, and also getting them out. You had to be real sneaky.

But I hadn't asked Mr. Nathan for the extra treats, just so my tummy didn't growl. It bothered my last foster brother, and he'd punch me to make it stop.

I didn't want to make him angry, but I couldn't help my tummy. Punching me never stopped my tummy, so my foster brother would be angry all day long. That would make his real mom in a bad mood too. She didn't like when her real son was angry.

It was my fault.

The last time Mr. Nathan came to see how I was doing, I didn't need to say anything. He looked at me and started shaking without saying anything. I started to get worried I'd done something to make him mad, but he gave me a small smile and said we were going for treats.

Treats! I was a sucker for treats.

"You go and get your bag packed, Blake. Okay?"

My face hurt from when my foster mom had gotten angry at me, but I couldn't hold the smile back. I kept my face tucked down so my foster mom or brother wouldn't get mad at me again. Though, in my defense, I knew that they were just angry people. They wanted to hurt others, and I was the one in front of them. They were those kind of people.

I got to the stairs when Mr. Nathan called my name again.

I froze, scared he had changed his mind. I looked over my shoulder, and he was giving me another one of those nice smiles of his. I liked when he gave me that look. It meant everything was fine. That I hadn't messed up.

He gave me a small nod. "Pack all of your items."

My eyebrows shot up.

Did that mean . . . ?

A new sense of excitement rushed through me. Oh boy, oh boy. We were going for treats, and he wasn't bringing me back. That meant I'd get so much food that my tummy would hurt, but I liked when it was that hurt. Too much food was never a problem for me.

I didn't look at my foster mom and brother, though I could feel how angry they were.

That was how we were here now, in this driveway.

"What do you think, Blake? You think you might like living here?"

I looked at him. He was always so tired. He was a nice man, but he needed to learn how to comb his hair. Maybe I could give him one of my combs. I tended to get a new one each year for Christmas from the Salvation Army. I really only needed one, so yeah. I'd give Mr. Nathan one as his Christmas present from me.

We hadn't even gotten to Halloween yet, but that meant it was three holidays away.

I nodded to Mr. Nathan. "I like the door."

He paused before lifting his head. His eyes widened, and his mouth curved up in a smile, a real smile. "Oh. Yes. Well, look at that. Maybe they knew you were coming? A green door for a Miss Little Blake Green?" His eyes were twinkling now.

I giggled, but more because Mr. Nathan seemed actually happy. It wouldn't last, but I still liked it when it happened. "You're teasing me."

He chuckled. "I am. You're such a smart little girl." He relaxed back in his seat, and I swear his smile got a little bit bigger and his eyes shone a bit happier. That made me happier. "This is a good home, Blake. Miss Marcie is a good woman. Now, there's going to be a lot of other kids in there. So if you're uncomfortable with anyone or scared, I want you to tell me."

Some of my smile slipped.

"I mean it, Blake. I really do want you to tell me. Will you promise to tell me if there's anything or anyone who scares you?"

I nodded, but I didn't like that he was making me promise that. He didn't know what it was like sometimes, not having anyone want you or love you. The other kids in school all had mommy and daddies. They liked their kids. I could tell when they picked them up after school.

I didn't have that. Maybe one day. That would be amazing.

"You ready to meet Miss Marcie and your new foster brothers and sisters?"

I gave him another nod, though I never liked this part. I liked the part that we just did, when we sat in the car looking at the new home and I could pretend for a moment that my future family lived inside. It was the best, but then we'd actually go inside, and I always knew that they never really wanted me there.

Mr. Nathan got out of his car on his side, and I got out on my side, shutting the door.

He circled the front of the car, reaching for my hand.

I took it. My tummy started to twist. That had nothing to do with the candy Mr. Nathan let me have on the drive over.

He led the way to a back door and pushed the doorbell. He squeezed my hand. "It'll be fine, Blake. I should've brought you here first. It's just that Miss Marcie's always filled to the maximum. Still, she said she'd meet you. We'll make it work. This will be good for you and maybe her. She's not had a little girl in so long. She's been asking—"

There was a pounding of footsteps on the other side of the door.

"I got it—"

"*I* got it!"

"You—"

"BOYS!"

A bunch of boys were fighting on the other side of the door until someone hushed them. The door swung open. Oh, boy. All the boys! There were so many. Three right in front of us. One of them had flung the door open. He stood before us, his hand still on the door. He was older than me, and he looked me over before his nose wrinkled. "What? No way. We got another girl?"

One of the others shoved in front of him and pointed at me. "What happened to your face?"

That made the other boys start laughing before one shoved his elbow into the other's chest, and that one wrapped his arm around the boy's neck, yanking him down to the ground. Soon, all three were wrestling.

"Boys!" that same voice from before barked. "Take it outside or into the basement. And if someone gets hurt, you know what'll happen."

"Yeah, yeah," one of them whined. "We have to eat *all* the *vegetables* that the others don't finish. *Ugh.* Broccoli!"

"Exactly. Death by vegetables."

I wanted to hide behind Mr. Nathan, except as I began inching behind him, a woman moved in front of the door. She was big and tall, almost as tall as Mr. Nathan, and she was wearing the most colorful dress. Her skin was dark, darker than mine. Her hair was up in braids, wrapped around her head.

She looked like a goddess.

She was *beautiful.*

She was taking me in, too, and she knelt down, a smile on her face. "Well, hello there. Who have you brought me this time, Nathan?"

Mr. Nathan patted my shoulder, gently. "I've brought you a special one."

"I can see that." She was still taking me in, lingering on my face, and I knew she was seeing the bruises still there. "What's your name, sweetie?"

I couldn't speak. She was that beautiful.

"I'm Miss Marcie." She held out her hand. "What should I call you?"

Oh. Whoa. This was a serious thing. I stepped forward and put my hand in hers.

Her smile was almost blinding as we shook, and I said, "Blake." My voice came out as a whisper, and that was embarrassing. I ducked my head down, starting to inch back again.

"That's a beautiful name."

I stopped and lifted my head again.

She was still smiling at me. This time she looked at Mr. Nathan, straightening back up. "You don't play fair, Nathan."

"I know, but . . ."

She waved her hand at him. "You hush." She moved farther away from the door, an arm sweeping inside. "Come on in. You got her bag in the car?"

"I do. I didn't know—"

She laughed. "As if there'd be any question with this one."

"You have room? I know you're stretched as is—"

She made another of those hushing movements with her arm. "We'll make room. We got one that barely spends his time here as is."

They did the adult thing. Talking. Laughing. Then talking in hushed tones. That's when I knew they were talking about me or talking about something they didn't want me to hear. Mr. Nathan had me go to the car to grab my bag, and when I was coming back, a boy was sitting on the back doorsteps, staring at me.

He was different from the ones inside.

Bigger. Taller. Older.

He was pretty.

I'd never seen a boy as pretty as him, but he was hard. Tan skin. Blank eyes. Black hair. He had a bruise on his face too. Just like me. But he was hard on the inside. He might've looked like another boy, though he was so much prettier, but I knew he wasn't like other boys. His eyes gave that away, that he was different. If Mr. Nathan asked me what I meant, I couldn't explain. It was only something I *knew*.

"You're living here now?"

I got shy again, the nervous flutters in my tummy again, but this time those flutters were moving all over me on the inside. I couldn't talk again. Most times when I got like this, I looked away. I could pretend I was alone, and the flutters would go away.

I couldn't do that this time. I couldn't look away from this boy.

I didn't know why. I just couldn't.

"What's your name?"

"Blake," I whispered.

"What's your last name?"

I couldn't answer, but I looked at the green door behind him.

He shifted, looking where I did.

He rotated back. "Door?"

A giggle slipped out, and aghast, I clamped a hand over my mouth. That was embarrassing too.

His face didn't change, but I thought maybe he softened.

I shook my head.

"Green?" He grinned.

I bobbed my head up and down.

"How old are you?"

"Eight."

He didn't say anything after that, still taking me in.

I moved forward and reached up.

He went still, letting me get closer to him, close enough until my fingertips touched his bruise.

"This?" He was eyeing the bruises on my face. "I'm thinking I got mine in the same way you got yours? Someone got mad at you?"

I nodded, feeling sad.

He gave me another grin, but this one was a mask. Adults did that a lot. Smile when they didn't feel it. They were faking, but with him, it felt like it was just something he did all the time. I didn't feel he was trying to lie to me. Like it was his mask for the world, so others didn't see the real him.

Did that work? I couldn't tell.

"In my case, I deserved it. And I finished it. There'd be nothing you could do to give someone a reason to do that to you." His smile faded. His mask fell, and I knew this was the real him. "You want me to hurt them? I'm good at that sort of thing. The ones who did that to you?"

My breath hitched. He was serious.

He leaned closer, dropping his voice. "You don't have to decide now. You think on it. If you decide you want me to hurt them, I will." There was movement behind the door. The sound of voices was nearing. He sighed and stood up. "Don't tell them you met me. Okay? Miss Marcie would give me a whole lecture on top of the normal lecture I know is coming my way."

I frowned.

Catching my look, he stepped around me, now standing on the cement, and he was *so tall.* He looked down at me, reaching into his pocket. He pulled out a cigarette, lifting it to his mouth. He didn't light it, still just holding my gaze. "Listen, this is a good place. Miss Marcie is a good woman. I'm sure she already creamed her pants at seeing you. No doubt she's going to treat you like a princess, but by the looks of it, you deserve it. You been through a rough one. We all have been." He lit the cigarette and took a drag before motioning to the house, stepping farther around me.

I moved with him, my back now to the house. "What's your name?" My voice was still a whisper, but I got it to sound stronger. Like an adult.

He was inching farther and farther away, but his eyes didn't waver. He stopped now. One more step to the side and he could disappear into the neighbor's backyard. He lowered the cigarette. "They're going to tell you things about me, but it won't be true. It'll be true for others. Not you. A promise from me to you. You never have to be scared of me."

I got warm all over. He meant it. It was one of those sacred promises made. A rare one that was meant. I knew he meant it. I just felt it.

I whispered back, "You don't have to be scared of me either."

He just continued to stare at me. "I know."

The door started to open behind me.

The boy said, "My name's Creighton. You can call me Eight."

"Blake?" Mr. Nathan was in the doorway, frowning. His gaze swept behind me. "Were you talking to someone out here?"

I looked again, but he was gone.

CHAPTER TWO

BLAKE

Fourteen years later

I needed to rub my eyes because I couldn't be seeing what I was seeing.

So I did.

I looked again.

And yep. I actually *was* seeing this beautiful brownstone.

Something wasn't computing because there was no way this was where I'd be living for my senior year at Faulkner State College. This place was amazing. This was where rich people stayed. Like, millionaires and billionaires. Not college students that were poor, very poor. Like me.

There was a mix-up. There had to be. Granted, this brownstone was on the edge of campus. According to my new living packet, they'd put me in a graduate student dorm.

It had ivy running up the side. The stairs were almost grandiose, in gray bricks. The number of the house was engraved on a sign by the door. **4818**.

I almost didn't feel worthy to climb the stone steps to the door. I didn't have much with me, but what I did have were some of my more precious items. Most of them fit in my backpack. Sad, but true.

I tightened my hold on my bag's strap, slung over my shoulder, and trudged up the stone steps.

I rang the doorbell, but no one answered. There was a keypad, so I put in the code that was in the packet that the housing office gave me.

The door unlocked, and I stepped inside.

With a staircase in front of me, to the right was a small living room. Beyond that was the kitchen in another room. Behind the living room looked like another room. I could see the corner of a couch. A small hallway was on the left side of the stairs, so I assumed there was a room back there.

Already this place looked like a fun maze. Lots of different rooms.

"Hello?" I called out.

A thud came from upstairs.

I looked up. My heart picked up. I was nervous. I didn't know why I was nervous, but yeah. Totally a little scared to meet my new roommates.

Here goes nothing.

I went up, the wooden stairs creaking underneath my weight. When I reached the second floor, there was a narrow hallway to my right, and I came to a doorway. Glancing around, I didn't see another door, so I reached for the doorknob. It turned easily and swung open. Inside was what looked like the entryway to another apartment. A small and quaint-looking room spread out in front of me to the window. Another narrow door was to my immediate left, and if I stepped inside a few more feet, around a corner was a small kitchenette area. There wasn't a stove, but there was a sink. A microwave. A Keurig along with some cupboards that held dishes, mugs, and plates. It was cute and modern. Chic. All the colors were cream and a slate gray.

I loved it.

On my other side was what looked like a closet. I nudged the door, and it pushed inward. I slid it open, showing a small area for coats. Some snow boots were on the floor. Just inside was another small bench where a couple backpacks were sitting.

The sound of footsteps sounded from on the other side of the closet wall. Approaching.

A clicking sound.

"Oh!"

I stepped back, seeing a girl who had come from a bedroom. As she now stood in another doorway, I saw a bed behind her, and my interest was piqued. How big was this brownstone?

"Hi." I gave a small wave.

Before I could introduce myself, she said, "I'm hoping you're my new roommate and not a stranger that Heath and Marshall let in?"

"Who?"

"Oh. Wait. First. You're . . . ?"

"Blake. Your new roommate." I held my hand out.

She shook it before stepping back again. "Oh, good. You *are* who I thought. Heath and Marshall are two of our roommates, or housemates, depending on whatever terminology you want to say. We all live in this place together. There's another roommate on the main floor, but chances of you actually meeting her are slim. Niko. She moved in recently, too, and I've only met her once. We had someone else in her room, but Moira suddenly had to go home. Her mom got sick or something. Anyways, Niko's like a vampire. I swear. I'm Palma Beauregard, and this is our place." She indicated the room, then gestured to the ceiling. "The guys live on the floor above us. I'm sure you'll meet them tonight."

She gave me a rueful grin.

She had hazel eyes. A round, tan face. Reddish hair that could be considered brunette in darker lighting, but burnt-red tints shone from the light she was standing under now. She was pretty in a wholesome, pageanty way. Her hair had some blond highlights in it as well, and her skin could've been from a tanning booth or self-tanner. She wore makeup and seemed like the type who put it on as soon as she was awake. It was her armor for the world. Plump pink lips. She was my height, five seven, but she held a little more weight on her frame than myself.

She looked good. Healthy.

She was taking me in as I was doing the same to her.

Her eyes lingered on my bag with the frayed edges. My hand tightened on the strap again, feeling a little self-conscious. It wasn't fancy. I came from nothing. Had no one at one point. I needed to live in strangers' homes, made do with hand-me-downs, or what the state gave me, and it was obvious from the name-brand jeans, heels, and off-the-shoulder sweater she was wearing that we weren't the same. But as soon as that feeling reared, I stuffed it back down because I would not feel bad about where I came from.

"I can't wait," I said.

Her eyes were still tracing over my face before dipping down to give my arm and hand the same scrutiny. My nails were bare. If I ever got them painted, the nail polish chipped off within a few hours. I'd learned it was pointless to try and keep pretty colors on my nails.

I knew my nails didn't look like hers. Hers were exquisitely done. She wore a couple sparkly rings on her fingers, matching bracelets around her wrist.

I tucked my hands away so she couldn't keep staring at them.

"You are stunning." She blinked, as if she wasn't aware of what she'd just said. Retracting her hand, she straightened herself up, tucking some hair behind her ear. "Like, holy shit. Your hair is so sleek and black. And long. You have literal almond eyes. Sorry. I'll get myself under control. And I'm not coming onto you, but you are really beautiful." Her eyes grew distant before snapping back into focus. She laughed. "I'm straight. Palma. That's my name, which I already told you." A nervous hitch came next from her. "I'm totally messing this all up and you're probably scared of me. I swear I'm normal. Sane. Well, I don't know if I'm totally sane. Bad breakup recently. Like three days ago recently. We'd been together all through undergrad and he swore we could do long distance. I stayed, obviously. This is graduate housing. He went back home at the end of the summer to start working for his father's company. He lasted two days. Can you believe that? Two days back home before his dick was inside his old high school sweetheart. I want to call her something like Fanny Mae, but the bitch has a cool name. I'm not saying it. She doesn't deserve that.

"She totally knew about me too. And he's a piece of shit. I hate them both equally. Well, I hate him more. He didn't even tell me he'd cheated on me. One of her friends sent me a video of them. Can you believe that? A *video*? And it was *her friend* who sent it? Like, was it all a plan to break us up so she could get him back?" She laughed. Harshly. It hitched on a high note. "She's welcome to him. I'm sure they'll get married. Have kids. He'll cheat on her the whole marriage, but she won't care at first. She'll be set. My ex comes from serious money, so yeah, she won't care that he'll do disgusting things to his mistresses while she gets it missionary or the occasional doggy-style. And oh my god, I have to stop talking."

I was quiet for a bit, because, yeah. Processing. "What's his name?"

She snorted, rolling her eyes. "Ugh. That's the worst part. Brad Grundle, *the fifth*. It's the 'the fifth' part that I can't stand. Like they're royalty or something. Pretentious. We're all from the same town and we're in the south, and I don't know why I told you that either. Look at me. Whew. A bucket of TMI." Another nervous laugh came from her.

I dipped my head down. "New rule of dating. Only date a guy up to the 'the thirds.' Fourths, fifths, and anything beyond is banned."

Her eyes rounded on me before a laugh ripped from her. As soon as it did, another one followed. Deeper. More authentic. She kept going as tears came to her eyes.

My lip curved up.

"You—" She wiped at her eyes, her shoulders still shaking. "That's hilarious. Where were you when I started dating Brad?"

If they dated all through college and he'd graduated while she was now in graduate school, I would've been a senior in Cincinnati. A flash of blood, sounds of screaming, and the smell of burnt toast and sulfur clogged my nostrils.

I gave her a small smile. "Probably in high school and planning my escape."

She laughed, relaxing. "That's right. The email I got about you said you're still in undergrad? What's your major?"

"Senior year. Psychology. I decided I wanted a change of scenery for my last year."

"Psych. Nice. Feel free to analyze me. Maybe you can help me."

"No." I shook my head. "I'll just analyze myself. From what I hear, the license to analyze doesn't happen until much later. You know, when we're full of graduate school debt and need to hear ourselves talk."

She laughed again. "How'd you swing graduate housing? Do you have early acceptance for a grad program already?"

I didn't want to answer those types of questions. "Just lucky, I think? I had to leave where I was in the dorm. There was a situation with another girl on my floor. She—I'm sure the school is just scrambling, finding an open slot."

She tilted her head to the side. "Yeah, but . . ." A strand of her hair slid free from where it had been tucked behind her ear. She didn't notice. "You know, it doesn't matter. You must've won the lottery of housing because this is one of the best to get into. I should know. I've been gunning for a place here since Mr. Dollumn brought up being his grad assistant to me. We have the most space, with parking, and we're on campus. We're basically rock stars." She chuckled again. "Or that's how we're going to enjoy it until we have to go out into the real world and learn how to survive on crackers and ramen because we're suddenly poor. But that's the way of it, right?"

I gave her a weaker smile. "Sounds like. Yeah."

She gestured behind her. "Well, as you can see, this is my room." She moved past me, indicating the living room and kitchenette. "We share the house as a whole, so there's another actual living room and kitchen on the first floor, but we get this cute little sitting area and we've got enough space so we don't have to go downstairs for our first cup of coffee or snacks. Though, roommate request, please don't watch a movie late at night here. Keep it in your own room or use the first floor living room for that. I'm usually in bed by nine or nine thirty every night and trying to sleep by ten or so. Early morning sessions."

She moved through the sitting area, opening a door on the other side of the kitchenette, and stepped back. "Here's your room. You can claim the bathroom out here as your own. I have a little one attached to my room, so I'll keep to that." She indicated the door that'd been immediately to my right when I first entered the space.

She went over, opening it to show a tiny bathroom. A *very* tiny bathroom. "Still. Lap of luxury for us considering where we're living. Am I right?"

"I think it's nice."

She frowned at me before disappearing into her room. A second later, she emerged, sliding on a coat. She zipped it up, pulled her hair out, and flipped her long tresses behind her. "Anyways." She took two steps and opened a drawer in the kitchenette. A folder was inside. She handed it to me. "That's all yours. Wi-Fi information. Codes. Your fob. Not sure about a mail key, unless they might've just kept your mail where it was? There's other information in there. We have our own resident adviser. A Pete guy, but I've only met him once. I think he's a PhD student, so good luck getting a hold of him if you ever need him. I added my number, along with the guys' and our emails. Not sure if you need our socials. If so, we can share that later. I didn't include Niko since I don't know it myself."

She grabbed the coffee mug, pulling some creamer out from a little fridge on the floor, then moved to the closet. Reaching inside, she tugged on one of the backpacks. "Okay. I'm off. I'll be back this evening. Nine or so. You have my cell if you have questions. Text, please. If you call, I won't answer. And bye! Welcome to the house."

She left, and I was alone in my new place.

A queen-sized bed. A desk. A closet with a dresser inside.

A small window with a view of the next building's brick wall and fire escape.

This was all mine. I couldn't contain my smile.

CHAPTER THREE

CREIGHTON

"They're here, Boss." Levi pushed to my side, his gaze hooded, but I knew he was alarmed as he was focused on who was coming up the steps in my nightclub. Tristian West and Ashton Walden.

Best friends from childhood. Both came from Mafia families.

Their families used to run this city, along with a third Mafia family. The Worthing family. Then war happened between the Worthings and the other two families. People died. A lot of people died, and in the end, the best friends ran the city. They were the current kings of New York.

The entire place noted their arrival, moving aside to let the two heads pass through. One of my men led them up the stairs, and when he spotted me, I motioned to a booth in the corner. His head dipped down, a slight movement to let me know he understood.

I'd seen pictures and videos of both of these men, and I'd viewed each of them from a distance, but this was the closest I'd been to both. I was good at reading people. The closer I could get to them in person, the better my read was. I wasn't normal. I'd been diagnosed with having psychopathic tendencies, and I agreed with that psychiatrist to a degree. I didn't feel what others felt. I always knew this growing up. Not having normal feelings and emotions should've confused my ability to read into people. It didn't. It was the opposite. I was really good at identifying what others were experiencing, and I enjoyed assembling the puzzle of why they were feeling that way. When West reached out for a meeting, it's the reason I insisted they come to one of my establishments.

I wanted them here. Close. Slightly confused. It would be the best way for me to read them up close and personal. I was in their city, and I knew they did not want me here.

I was going to enjoy this meeting.

I began to go past Levi but paused to pat his chest. "I'm not only your boss, Levi. Don't call me that again."

He groaned, falling in line behind me.

I was tall, but he was even taller and bigger, lumbering almost like a giant. I knew what a picture we both made as we led the way to where I wanted to have this meeting. Levi once considered becoming a professional wrestler. In the end, he decided to stay by my side. He was one of our foster brothers, Blake's and mine. A few of our brothers were still with me, choosing to "work" for me instead of going legit how Miss Marcie wanted all of us to go. She never had hope for me, recognizing a lost cause the second she saw me, but the rest—there'd been a struggle for power between us. Miss Marcie ruled inside the house, and I ruled outside. It was up to the others to make their own choice. Some went to college, which was the route Blake chose to take. But some joined me.

Levi was one of those. Lassiter was another, who grew up as our neighbor, but because his dad was an abusive piece of shit, he mostly lived on Miss Marcie's couch.

Blake.

Though I would never love anyone, even Blake, she was the closest to someone that I could love if I was going to be able to have that feeling. As for my brothers—I wouldn't kill them as quickly as I would kill others.

Levi was aware of my sentiment.

The booth was in the far corner overlooking the club's entrance. It was set away from the rest of the club so other customers would be kept back. The music was loud so no one could overhear us. The lighting was also dark enough that no one could read our lips. I liked that as well, but mostly I just liked sitting in odd corners where I had the vantage point.

I liked watching, but not being watched.

Blake would say that was a control issue.

Of course it was.

I said to Levi, "Blake moved into her new housing today. Go and see her. Make sure she's okay where she is."

He instantly began shaking his head. "No. No way, Creight."

I narrowed my eyes on him. Most found this look from me unnerving.

It didn't work on Levi. "I am *not* getting between the two of you."

Tristian West and Ashton Walden had arrived, but Levi cut in front of them. There were three sides to sit in the booth. Levi shoved all the way to the inside of it. "You go and see her yourself. Of the two of you, make no mistake—I'm more scared of Blake than you. You're on your own Bos—" He cut himself off, then corrected. "You're on your own, Creight."

I didn't understand why I didn't like my foster brother calling me Boss. I shouldn't care, but I did. It made me want to shoot someone.

I motioned to his gun. "Give me that." I didn't have one with me because I had assured West that I wouldn't be armed when I sat down with him and his best friend. Of course, *they* knew my men would be and *I* knew they had sent their own men into the club earlier, all armed. They would have other men outside as well, but at this moment, I wanted to kill someone.

Levi went still before inching farther away in the booth. "No. You just want to shoot someone because I almost called you Boss again. You can't kill someone because you're annoyed."

My mouth curved down. "You've been hanging out with Blake too much."

A faint grin showed on his face.

He was right, though. There was that uncomfortable shifting inside of me. Blake was the one to identify that idiosyncrasy of mine. She was right. In the past I would've shot two men by now from the first time Levi called me Boss.

But she made me realize that it was easier to tell him not to call me that label.

Though I *was* Levi's boss.

Levi wasn't going to get involved between us, but he also knew that I couldn't go see her either. Blake and I had an agreement. I wasn't supposed to have anything to do with her. Mostly.

I wasn't supposed to visit her. I wasn't supposed to interfere with her life except for the one condition that I had someone watching her. That was my stipulation. It was for her safety. Her part of the agreement was that she wouldn't run from me.

I sent a text to one of my men who'd been instructed to keep eyes on her.

Me: Real time images.

Then I addressed the two heads that ran this city. "Thank you for coming to my nightclub."

Tristian West scoffed, a half laugh, while Ashton Walden looked like he wanted to kill me then and there. He probably did, but that was for later. Tristian West looked like a smooth motherfucker. He had the whole bit. High cheekbones. Square jaw. Six four. A little over two hundred pounds and I'm sure most of that was muscle. Hair slicked back like a lawyer. I'd seen other pictures where his hair was a little ruffled. He looked better with it ruffled and when he looked out of control.

Though, of the two, Walden was the one who'd more likely snap.

He was similar in body to his best friend, except there was an extra fire to Walden. Dark hair. Dark eyes. He used to model, and yes, he was photogenic. I could see it now in person.

"You're both very handsome."

They faltered, shooting each other a confused glance.

I indicated the booth. "If you'll have a seat? Before we get to business, please give your orders to my man. He'll taste the drinks in front of you, if you think I'd consider poisoning you."

"We're not here to have drinks, Lane." Walden growled. "This isn't a friendly sit-down."

"True. We're in a war." He was right, of course, but I'd hoped for some friendly banter before we got to the threats.

Tristian West cast a wary glance at his best friend, running a hand over his jaw before he moved into the booth first. Walden sat beside him. Both remained as close to the edge as possible.

I sat across from them.

Neither man was happy to be here, but we were still in the early stages of a war right now. This was the phase where they needed to pretend to play nice.

Neither asked for a drink.

I motioned for my man to leave. "Another person might be insulted. I offer you beverages and you refuse. Are my beverages not good enough for you?"

Ashton Walden expelled a harsh curse, jerking back in the seat. "My eyes can't roll as high as I'd like them because that's the biggest bunch of bullshit I've ever heard. You. Being insulted." He jerked forward, the movement so abrupt and threatening that I saw Levi's arm moving. If I'd looked, I was sure that I would've seen his hand on his gun under the table.

"Yes." I smiled at him. "West reached out on your behalf. He asked for a face-to-face meeting. I suggested my nightclub. Are we not here in one of my booths? Come now. There's dancing. Drinking. Music. This is a place for friendship. Maybe we could be friends?"

Levi shook his head next to me.

I knew what was to come when Walden had this look. I'd studied him enough. He was arming himself, getting ready to strike. West knew this and placed his hand on his best friend's arm. At his touch, Walden's eyes closed. He went even more still.

I frowned. I couldn't discern what was happening, so I asked, "Why are you so hostile toward me?"

West cursed, his head falling back.

Walden's eyes opened to slits. "You're fucking with me. Aren't you? I can't tell if you're incredibly calculating or incredibly stupid. Which are you, Lane? We're here because you've been making moves against us for a while."

"No. You're here because you helped someone try to hurt someone I care about." I was referring to a whole situation that happened prior to this meeting, when Walden had a hand in helping someone else kidnap Blake.

"That's not exactly how it went down."

"No? Explain it to me then. Maybe I'll understand it in a different way. You didn't get one of Blake's dorm-mates to befriend her? Lure her somewhere so that Jake Worthing could kidnap her?"

He didn't say a word. He couldn't because he couldn't argue against me.

He said instead, "You're here. In my city. Jake Worthing already opened up a door for you to take over the rest of the Worthing assets here, but if you think we're not aware you are recruiting men at an alarming pace, you must be stupid."

I smiled. "Jake Worthing. Yes. Let's talk more about Worthing." I leaned forward and lowered my head, as if I were sharing a secret with them. "Blake did a DNA kit on me for school, and guess who I found. A whole family I had no idea about. My cousin, Jake Worthing."

Walden's jaw clenched.

West kept glancing at his friend, but he responded, wryly, "Yes. We're aware."

"Ah. Good. Good."

I was younger than these men. They were in their mid-thirties. It was still a couple years before I'd hit thirty. West was married. Walden was about to be. West had children. Walden soon would. Both of their women had full lives themselves.

West's woman used to be a parole officer, a cop in my mind. She was now retired and had opened her own gallery to showcase her paintings, masterpieces that did very well, according to my investigator. Walden's woman continued to run her own bowling alley, and there were plans to expand. They already filed for a permit.

I leaned forward to study Walden. "You've banished Worthing from coming back to this city. Why would you do that to him? I thought you had a friendship, correct? You know his woman has family here."

I was fully aware that I was poking at him, trying to bait him.

Walden was still simmering, the violence building. He was like a volcano getting ready to blow. I was enjoying watching this. I wanted him to explode. I wanted to see what would happen then.

He bit out, "Funny. You talking about Jake like that. Acting like such a concerned, loving cousin. You *just* found out you're related to him."

I shrugged. "Family love can be instant."

"You've killed half of them. You took a hit out on Jake."

I waved that away. "It was a misunderstanding. I thought he was in the way of something I wanted."

"Which brings us back to here. You having a foothold in *my* city." Walden managed to gain control over some of his emotions, a concrete wall falling down over his face, but his eyes were still seething. He couldn't stomp out the rage there.

"Your city," I chided, amused. "I think I'm going to make it my city."

Walden lunged, hitting the table.

West cursed, also lunging but reaching for his best friend.

It happened in an instant because as soon as he went for my throat, I flicked my wrist and he froze, feeling the pointed edge of the dagger that I had under my napkin. Levi had left it for me when he first slid through the booth. Such a thoughtful gift from him.

I had it pressed against Walden's throat, and if he'd gone one more inch forward, he would've embedded it inside of himself. His eyes rolled down, but he could only see the side of the knife before meeting my gaze again.

I nudged him to the side. "Look."

He resisted.

"No." I tsked. *"Look."*

He did, slowly, and when he saw what I was referencing he drew in a sharp breath.

Levi had raised his gun, pointing it at the side of Tristian West's head. Only a few inches separated him from the gun's muzzle.

Walden cursed before slipping back to his seat, going at a slow pace. "You think we came alone? That we didn't send men earlier to infiltrate inside?"

"No." My body was buzzing by now. I loved this shit. "I know you did. I assumed you would, so we had each of them collected and disarmed. You'll find them outside, behind the closest dumpster. Some might still be alive."

Walden's eyes turned to ice. "You have the advantage inside. We have it outside. Thirty of our men have surrounded this place. One gunshot and they'll storm in shooting. You have civilians here. Customers. *You'll* be the reason why they're murdered. I'll make sure the police blame you for their deaths."

"Yes. I imagine you would be able to do that." I agreed with him.

Walden had quite a few police and administrators on his payroll. It was just one of the many strongholds they had that I was chipping away at. The last count I knew that he had was over a hundred, but thirty of them were now mine. If they weren't mine, they weren't breathing anymore. I considered that a win because those were thirty openings for someone I paid to fill.

I motioned for Levi to put his gun away and leaned forward, my smile never falling from my face. I looked between the two friends. West was watching me warily. He was the one who wasn't able to understand me. Walden wasn't even trying. He was too emotional. There was too much baggage still fresh in his mind.

Yes, it was true that I put a contract out on Jake Worthing. But I'd rescinded that contract, allowing Jake, his woman, and all of her family members to remain alive. What I got from that deal was Blake promising not to run from me. It'd been the precursor to our current agreement because she'd been the one to advocate on behalf of Jake and his woman. There were other details that surrounded those events, but it was more important to note that Jake Worthing had been someone Ashton Walden considered a friend.

Friend or foe, I wasn't totally sure. I hadn't fully figured out the friendship between them, but I knew there *were* conflicted emotions because at the end of the day, Jake Worthing gave me a whole host of assets and resources that his family still had in the city.

His family. Technically through my mother, I shared blood with them, but I would never consider the Worthings my family. I did not choose them.

I added, "But you're starting to slip, Ashton."

Walden's head snapped backward, and his nostrils flared. "Don't fucking use my first name."

I ignored that. "Just like your hold on the shipping yards. On the warehouse district. On the north end of the city. On Brooklyn." I could name more territories, but I didn't need to. The areas they never retained control over were now mine. I just mentioned the ones I'd taken from them, but there'd be more.

I was expanding. They knew this.

My battle tactic wasn't to kill their men. It was to take their men. They just didn't know how I did it, or how I *kept* their men as mine.

"We still have Red Hook's Marine Terminal. Plus the rest that you didn't name." His grin was icy. "Manhattan."

"You have *parts* of Manhattan."

"No. You have parts of Manhattan, but we'll be taking them back. It's only a matter of time. Especially the parts where your girlfriend goes to school."

"You already tried with Blake. Try again and see what I'll do."

"How about this? You stop recruiting or I'll kill your pretty little Miss Green." Walden lowered his head so he was equal with me, and he raised an eyebrow. Taunting. "How's that for a counter?"

How was that for a counter? I repeated his question in my head, but I never faltered. My smile didn't twitch. "That's the second time you've threatened her in a matter of minutes. Now you get to see what I'll do."

His eyes snapped to slits. He was glaring at me, and I knew I was letting him see the void inside of me. It had a certain *effect* on people.

"He's not threatening her." West placed a hand on his friend's shoulder and pushed. "We're not going there."

Walden resisted, growling. "Don't speak for me. I will threaten her all day any day."

"Stop," West snapped, shoving him now. "Move."

Walden remained in place until he pushed up and shoved past my men. West followed at a more sedate pace, standing at the end of our table. He looked at me, almost impassive, but I could see the tension clinging to his body. His face was rigid. He couldn't hide that. There were pinched lines at the corners of his eyes. He was keeping his jaw tight, and he forced himself to let it all go. He didn't want me to see his anger.

Interesting.

I didn't understand that.

I knew he was angry. Why not let me see it? Why try to cover it?

"You are taking what's ours. That's an act of war, but we've been at war for a while. Haven't we, Lane?"

I leaned back in the booth, continuing to study this man. He was fascinating. "You already made a move against me when you helped Jake kidnap Blake. Of course, all of that worked out in the end, but your best friend just threatened her again. Twice. She is someone I care about. Is this your way of 'smoothing it over'? Reminding me of moves I've made prior to coming into this city? That's just good battle strategy. You know this. You surround your enemy before you move in for the kill."

He went still at my words, at what I was suggesting. They surrounded my nightclub tonight, but I'd already surrounded their city.

He twitched. It was minimal and it was only at the corner of his eye, but I saw it. It was enough to show a crack, and now that I saw it, I could see the rest. I witnessed how his anger moved through him.

Even more fascinating.

I couldn't place which was the more dangerous of the two. This one who usually showed nothing but was ruthless at the drop of a hat or the other, who'd react with a killing blow like a cobra attacking. Both were intelligent. Both were ruthless. Each balanced out the other. Together, they were formidable.

I was very excited to war with them.

"My intention was genuine when I reached out. I said on the phone that I wanted to come to a compromise, stop this war before it escalates. I'm aware of how fast you overtook Cincinnati. That you've run the streets since you were sixteen and that you owned the politicians since you were nineteen. You're twenty-eight. That's a long time to operate an entire city. I'm also aware of your vast network, the magnitude of soldiers you have at your beck and call, and the questions surrounding them. How is it that you recruit so fast? The loyalty rate of them. That even if they're taken and tortured, when they break—because everyone breaks—they only give up lies. Makes you wonder if their loyalty is really to you or to others? Do you threaten their families like the cartel? Is that how you operate? Do you hang the heads of your soldiers' loved ones if they go against you?"

He was staring at me hard as he said all of this.

I could feel Levi growing restless, getting angry, and knew it was a matter of seconds before he did something that I'd rather he didn't. Breaking eye contact with West, which I was even more fascinated to realize that I was reluctant to do, I shook my head at Levi. Briskly and minutely.

Outrage flared over his face, but he kept his mouth shut, only letting out a small growl.

Tristian West observed this interaction between us, frowning before he continued, "Having said all of that, I have people I love. A family. So does Ashton. I did want to come to a resolution so the ones we love are not included in this war between us. I can see, now, you don't want to come to an understanding. I watched you tonight and I watched how you enjoyed playing with my best friend. Baiting him. Seeing him react. He cared for Jake Worthing, and you used that against him. Me, though. I don't give a fuck about Worthing, but I do give a fuck about my best friend. Ashton threatened someone you care about. I know you're not going to let that lie, but keep this in mind when you make your move: We're *also* aware of your weakness. Whatever you do against us, we'll answer it threefold. Do you understand me, Lane?"

My smile widened. "Perfectly, Tristian West."

He began to leave but faltered at my words, glancing at me again. Studying me. After a moment, his gaze shuttered and he trailed behind his best friend.

One of my men came over to check the booth in case they left anything behind. A listening device. A bomb. Either was possible. When we got the all-clear, Levi asked, "Why don't you just kill them?"

I continued to watch the front entrance, but I was notified both slipped out through a side exit. A second alert came through, notifying me that their men left with them. They'd already collected the other men from the dumpster.

"Because sometimes in battle, you can't move too fast. They're too strong right now. If they hit back, *when* they hit back, I need to have my defenses built stronger so I can withstand the hit."

"But you are going to do something. They keep fucking threatening Blake. That was three times in this meeting and I'm not including their involvement before we even fucking got here."

No Mafia family would sit back and welcome an invasion by a rival. Their anger was expected. I was aware of this, aware there would be repercussions. I was *taking* from them. Taking their streets. Taking their business. Taking their money. But Blake wasn't to be touched. Ever.

"Of course I'm going to do something."

"*Good.* What are you going to do?"

My phone buzzed. I opened it to see the images I'd requested of Blake.

She was walking up a stoop to a brownstone.

Going inside.

The rest were through a window as she was shaking hands with another girl.

I smoothed my thumb over the last image.

Blake was smiling as she was looking at a room.

That smile.

I imagined the smile on West's and Walden's women's faces and answered.

"I'm going to take their smiles away."

CHAPTER FOUR

BLAKE

Third grade

The other kids were playing in front of the school.

I paused on the sidewalk, my insides turning inside out.

"What's up, Little Blake?"

My head snapped up, then a big smile stretched over my face. A group of boys were coming down the sidewalk behind me, Creighton with them.

"Eight!" I waved, shuffling aside as his friends kept going. Creighton stayed behind, ignoring how his friends all looked back and moved farther away to wait for him. He stood beside me, facing the school with me, and cocked his head to the side.

"New school for you, huh?"

I sighed, looking down. My hands went back to the backpack Miss Marcie gave me. I was pretty sure it had belonged to one of the other foster kids in the house. My fingers tightened on its worn straps. I swallowed nervously. "Yeah."

He glanced down, side-eyeing me. "Always the new kid too."

Something about his tone, as if he understood. I tipped my head back so I could see him better. He was so tall. Then again, he went to *high school.* I didn't know why he was here with me. His school was on a whole different block. "You too?"

He didn't answer. His eyes flicked beyond me to where his friends probably were before coming back to my face. He studied me a second, all serious. "You've known me for a bit now, haven't you?"

My forehead wrinkled. "I guess." I'd been at the house for a few days, but Creighton was cool. He was older. There was something different about him. The guys adhered to whatever he said. The girls his age were always around him. Even Miss Marcie, who was the best foster mom I'd ever had—and it was still early, but even now I knew she always would be—listened to him. When he walked into a room, she talked to him like he was her equal.

"So you know that I might know a little something about being new, right?"

I wasn't sure where he was going with this, but I nodded, just happy that he was talking to me. I always felt safe when Creighton was talking to me. Eight. He told me I could call him that, but I was only going to do that in private, even though I slipped up and said it in front of his friends just now. I needed to remember. A couple other times when I called him that name in front of some of the other foster kids, they all gave me nasty looks. One of the girls cut up my favorite shirt.

They were jealous.

"Okay then." He knelt down so he was facing me, real serious.

I turned to face him too. We were almost equal height this way.

"This is what you do. When you walk in there, you walk in already knowing that you belong there because you belong anywhere and everywhere you go. You hear me?" He gently tapped under my chin. "Head up. Shoulders back. You own your space. No one takes that from you. And if you think you don't belong somewhere or the other kids don't want you there, fuck 'em because you do."

I reeled a little inside, but didn't show it. Creighton had said enough bad words at the house, so I knew it was just how he spoke, but I couldn't believe he got away with all that cursing.

I wasn't going to correct him.

He stood, still watching me, still all serious. "You got it?"

I nodded.

He chuckled softly before knocking his fist to my shoulder, softly, before going past me. "You got this, Little Blake. Have a badass day."

I watched as his friends greeted him and the whole group kept moving, jostling each other and joking. A few glanced back at me until they turned the corner.

"Bye, Eight," I whispered to myself before I did what he said.

Head up. Shoulders back. I was going to own my space, whatever that meant.

CHAPTER FIVE

BLAKE

Cognitive psychology. Was. *Awesome.*

I'd known within the first week it was going to be my favorite class and that realization never changed. It only strengthened. Learning about the mind and how it affects thinking, problem-solving, and how people learn new information was fascinating to me. Granted, I had a personal stake in understanding the mind, but it was still such a complex study.

I loved it.

"Blake?"

We'd just finished for the day, finished for the week actually, and I was packing my things away when the professor called my name. "Yeah?"

Dr. Langen motioned for me. "Do you have time for a quick chat?"

"Oh." I frowned. There were very few adults I was comfortable around and even fewer that I enjoyed. I'd begun to enjoy this professor, but I knew that could change at the drop of a hat. I was loath for that to go away, and talking with her one-on-one was a window opening for that to happen. I'd only met two adults who turned out to be stand-up through and through. My first social worker and Miss Marcie. I doubted this professor was also one of them, but with a tight smile, I gave a nod. "Sure." Standing up, I grabbed my bag and shrugged it on.

She was a thin woman, with short black and gray hair, cut similar to a boy's haircut. She had a propensity for wearing thick red glasses, long baggy skirts, and sweaters. The sweaters and skirts were always brightly colored, and they never matched. Today she was wearing a green neon skirt that went all the way to the ground with an orange fuzzy sweater. A brooch was always pinned to the top right corner of her sweater. A metallic unicorn with some diamonds attached. It was pretty, but odd looking. Though, I was starting to enjoy her various outfits. I knew some of the guys laughed about them, and I'd heard a fraternity had her different outfits made into a drinking game. I didn't know the details. I didn't want to know.

She motioned for the door. "Walk and talk with me?"

That made me even more tense. "Uh. Sure."

She waited until we stepped out into the hallway. "I've been impressed with the papers you've turned in so far."

"You have?" My head popped up. "I mean, that's great." We'd only turned in three smaller ones. She might change her mind when our midterm paper was due.

"And I'm sorry." She paused, touching my arm. "Can I go personal with you?"

No.

That was my automatic answer, but I just smiled tightly again and prepared myself. "Sure."

She relaxed, her own smile widening. "Good because I wanted to bring up your entry essay. I read it."

My stomach dipped. "I didn't know faculty could read those."

"We can, if we request to see it. Sometimes we do if we think it might give us further insight into a student. Which is why I asked to read yours. I meant it when I said I've been impressed with your essays. What you have to say, the insight you have, it's postgraduate-level work, to be honest. I wondered if you had personal experience in some of the things you've been writing about, and I read that you were in the foster system."

"Yeah . . ." *Please don't ask me to talk about it. Please don't ask me—*

"The reason I'm bringing it up is because a colleague of mine received a grant for a community center. They've recently opened. It's supposed to cater to general youth in the area, but a unique opportunity has been brought to her attention. They're going to offer one of the lounges only to youth in the foster system, and also foster parents."

"What?" I wasn't sure if I was hearing this correctly. I was hoping I wasn't because she had no idea the ramifications that could come with that.

She nodded, brightening. Eager. "Yes. Doesn't that sound wonderful? The idea is that it's there if a foster kid needed an additional place to spend time for whatever. Homework. A place to get away that's safe. It'll be supervised, of course. And there'll be resources available. A few computers. Art. Books. The other idea she had was that if multiple foster parents knew about it, there could be an opportunity to see previous foster kids or parents that they don't get to see anymore. My colleague is a foster parent herself and has mentioned how she misses some of her past kids." She lowered her head, stepping closer. "The reason I'm bringing this up to you is because she needs some staff to help supervise that room specifically. Previous foster children would be the best qualified, don't you agree? It wouldn't be a paid position, but you could use it as an internship for an independent study. I'd be overseeing you as the professor, but she'd be your on-site internship supervisor. This would be a great experience for you, especially if you want to continue on to graduate education. You're majoring in psychology, so that's a good avenue for you to keep in mind. There isn't a lot of entry-level work for a bachelor's in psychology. You'd need to go onto a specialization or for your master's or a PhD program."

This was my last year in college. I hadn't considered doing more college, but she was right about this particular degree. I should've been thinking of the future, but just to get into college was an achievement for me. To graduate college was almost mind-blowing. I used to live with the motto that you lived life in the present. You survive the present and worry about the future when it got here. I'd adopted that mantra for my psychology degree as well. I'd worry about it when I needed to do something about it. Right now, being here, being in New York, being away from someone was all I could focus on.

"You transferred from Cincinnati, right?"

I got even more tense. "Yeah."

What was she going to say? I didn't want to talk about growing up in the foster system, though I'd been able to stay at Miss Marcie's for so long and was grateful for her. But I also didn't want to talk about anything or *anyone* from Cincinnati. When I came here, I wanted to get away. I wanted to be free.

"I assumed you transferred here because of our postgraduate opportunities. If that's the case, this opportunity really is a great experience for you, if you choose to do it." Her phone buzzed, and she glanced at it, her forehead wrinkling. Distracted. "Okay. I have to get going, but how about you think on it? I'll have my secretary email you the center's information and you can look into it? Let me know by tomorrow?"

"We don't have class tomorrow."

"End of day. Let me know. Or I can have Lucinda reach out to you. That's the secretary in our department. I'll leave a note for her to do that and for her to notify me as well. If you decide to pass on this, I'll need to let my colleague know so she can fill that position. But also, you wouldn't be the only one supervising. There'd be others. You'd all work together." Her phone buzzed again, and she began walking away. "I'll look forward to hearing from you. Give it a good thought. Yeah?"

She hurried down the hallway, quickly being swallowed up by students, and I just stared after her.

I didn't understand this world sometimes.

I came from the foster system. Survived it. Survived other things, and now I was being asked to return to it? Just in a different capacity.

I wasn't in school for social work. I wanted to learn more about cognitive thought patterns, how the brain worked, why certain people had not-so-good tendencies or why they were apathetic toward others' suffering. I wanted to help fix someone. That's why I was majoring in psychology. Not social work.

That's not why I came to college. But feeling a tight burning sensation spreading under my sternum, I couldn't get her words out of my head. A center where foster parents and kids could see each other. That was a need; that was a good need in that world. The good parents, of course.

Miss Marcie was one of those for me.

I wasn't going to take the job. Nope. That's not why I came here, but the longer I stood there, I-I needed to change my thoughts.

I'd come a long ways, and I could, in a way, appreciate it.

The new brownstone I was living in.

Just a few train stops away was Times Square.

Now I was being offered the type of job that wasn't a job, but it was wrapped up as an "opportunity" for a world beyond just my bachelor's degree. Me. People like me didn't get offered "jobs" or "opportunities." We had to beg, borrow, plead, and sometimes steal for every rung we needed to climb up. And now I was getting offered a position.

A sudden bubble burst out of me, half sounding like a bark and a laugh. I didn't know what it was, but it was something unreal because this world—a year ago, I was planning my escape. Two years ago, I was just trying to keep going. Three years ago, I was a fish out of water. Four years ago, I wanted to crawl into my own coffin and pull the lid over me.

How did I get here?

My eye caught on a student farther down the hallway, leaning against the wall, his head tipped back, watching me, and I came crashing back down to Earth. No, this wasn't my new life. This was just my reprieve. Anger lit in me, and I took a step toward that student.

I didn't know what I was going to say to him, but it wouldn't matter. My problem wasn't with him.

His head tilted forward, but he didn't move from his leaning stance. His arms were crossed over his chest. He was the image of cool and relaxed, and other students were taking note. This was always how it was with these guys because this wasn't a student at all.

There was an extra air to them. They came from the street. They were dangerous. They gave off this whole "cool" air, but it was only because they didn't give one fuck about anything or anyone around them. The others around were able to sense this. I'd seen it time and time again. The only thing these guys did care about was their job, to watch me.

My problem wasn't with him or the others that had come before him and the others that'd come after him. It was with their boss.

This was one of Creighton's guys.

CHAPTER SIX

CREIGHTON

I loved technology.

Or I loved that the guys I employed could do almost anything with technology, including getting my own fob for Blake's townhouse. Using it on the back door, I let myself inside.

She was on the second floor, but it was four in the morning. The last of her roommates had arrived home an hour and a half ago with their light turning off forty minutes earlier. Everyone was asleep, and that meant I was free to peruse the interior.

I could've done this during the day. The house sat empty for a longer period of time during the waking hours, but I would've missed out on my favorite part of this entire expedition.

I wanted to see Blake.

In her bed.

Sleeping.

Without her walls.

Where she was vulnerable.

The kitchen was to my left. Moving through it, I took in the mugs hanging on the wall. The schedules on the fridge. The marker board. The messages scrawled there for other roommates. I recognized Blake's own handwriting, a message not to forget to grab more coffee creamer.

I frowned at that. She knew she could utilize my men to do her shopping. She could save her money. I had more than enough for the both of us, but no. She had her pride.

She was such a stubborn one.

I grinned faintly, proud.

I moved into the living room and idly scratched at my chest. Fourteen years I'd known Blake. And fourteen years I'd been feeling emotions. I still wasn't used to them. Half of my life had been spent not having these sensations. I should've been used to them by now. They were only getting worse, more intense, the longer I knew Blake. They were uncomfortable at best. At worst, they made me vulnerable, but that was the name of the game.

Vulnerability.

Blake was mine. Too many people knew it as Blake grew up and as my power rose, so I flipped it. I had to or she would've ended up dead by now. If anyone touched her, hurt her, considered even a negative thought about her, they were snuffed out immediately.

Blake herself gave me the rules that I used to live by. No one good. No one innocent. That's who I couldn't harm except if someone hurt her. They would pay. That was rule number one for me.

I moved through the rest of the main floor, opening the door to the girl's bedroom on the first floor. Niko. When she slept, she slept like the dead, so I wasn't worried about her waking up.

Still. I didn't go through too many of her things while she was in the room. If she woke up, she'd raise the alarm and Blake would be even more incensed by me.

I'd go through her things later, when she was out of the house.

I avoided the stairs that would squeak under my weight and bypassed the second floor.

I wanted to spend the longest time in Blake's room, with Blake, so I went to the third floor.

The two guys had a similar layout to her room except the boys' sitting area was much messier. A cereal bowl sat on a counter with mold growing over it. Weights were left haphazard by their couch. I went through the one boy's room. Marshall Finch. He looked like an angel sleeping with some drool pooling on his pillow. The framed pictures on his desk matched what I read had been his childhood. He was from a two-parent household. He had two older brothers. He was the baby. They all looked similar, with chestnut curls on top of the head. Brown eyes. Athletic physiques.

A literal picket-fence type of home he grew up in. His parents were still married. There was no history of secrets within the family. No infidelity. His mom and dad both owned a realty business, with his mother being the Realtor. The dad did the books and was the broker. They had a good setup. They were flexible, the mom being home when the boys had hockey practice growing up. The dad rotated in when she had to show a client a home. They were a team. All three boys played hockey. The other two played in college. Both graduated with MBAs. Marshall was the only one who didn't play hockey in college and now he was in graduate school for biology.

I moved on to the next boy. Heath Nogoskeski. This one I knew.

He didn't look like his brothers, except he had the same dark blond hair and a full sleeve of tattoos. His brothers were much taller, bigger in build too. They were almost giants compared to this one, but Heath wasn't little. He was just shy of six feet, and I could see that he kept himself strong.

He slept how he operated during the day. Guarded and on edge. He was frowning in his sleep, one of his hands curled into a fist.

My eyes fell to the bulge under his other pillow and knew what was there. Interesting. I thought his brothers picked up that habit because they worked for me, but perhaps it originated from their home.

His two older brothers pledged their lives to me. Both were good soldiers. Fierce. Ruthless. Loyal. So I would use this connection. There were two reasons I had Blake placed in this house, and he was one of them. The closer he was to Blake, the more rewards I would heap on his brothers' shoulders.

I moved around his room. Looked through his desk. Rifled through his bag. His wallet.

I was tempted to take his phone, but instead I put mine next to it, the one my tech team gave me. It beeped quietly as I began to clone. If he reached out to his brothers about me, I would be privy to that conversation. While the phone worked, I moved to the head of his bed.

I reached under his pillow, touched the end of a handgun, and pulled it out.

He was a true Nogoskeski. He kept his weapons close when he slept.

I could respect that and put the gun back.

The phone quietly beeped again when it was done, and I put it into my pocket, leaving his room.

Going to the second floor, I stepped into Blake's area. I wanted to go right to her, but forced myself go through her floormate's room first. Palma Beauregard. As soon as I stepped inside, I didn't like how she slept. Open. Naked. Her blanket was thrown to the side. She was splayed out, a perfect victim for another monster.

This was not good. If she were going to have the honor of being Blake's floormate, she would need to be smarter in how she operated. That included sleeping. She should be on guard, like the Nogoskeski boy.

I didn't enjoy being in her room. Her perfume was too heavy. It made me want to sneeze, so I left without going through her things and moved to Blake's room.

As soon as I touched her door, I felt her. The connection grew clearer, stronger, and I pushed open the door to see her.

She thought I was obsessed with her. *Am* obsessed with her. Yes. That part was true, but it's more than that for me. It's always been more than that, though I've never told her exactly how much. If I did, the pressure she would feel resting on her shoulders would be too much. She was already burdened by so much because of me. I felt it happening inside of me how it happened the first time I saw her get out of her social worker's car.

It happened then. The click inside of me.

Something that had been missing was unleashed inside me.

I'd been leaving to kill someone that day when the car turned into our driveway. People knew not to park in our driveway. That was for Miss Marcie, no one else, except a little angel stepped outside of the new vehicle.

I knew it instantly, right then and there. She was good. All good.

My errand was forgotten, and I returned to the house when she came out a second time. She was the reason I was on those stairs, and she was the reason I hadn't killed the man I was supposed to that day. It hadn't mattered. He still died, except not by my hands. As it also turned out, he ended up rescuing someone that day. Another little girl was almost run over by a car, but he'd been there, and he pulled her to safety. If I had kept going when I left the house, he would've been dead. That little girl would've been run over.

It was another reason I looked at Blake with different lenses.

She was meant to be in my life.

I enjoyed this moment when I was with her again.

Just like this.

No walls.

No hostility.

No guardedness.

Beautiful.

She was perfect.

I took my time going through her room. A certain satisfaction went through me when I saw the books she had lined up on her shelf. Each one I bought her; some of them she chose from a trip to the store with me. A few pictures were set up.

She was still using the laptop she used in high school. She would need a new one soon.

I grinned when I spotted the stuffed quokka on her desk.

A list on her desk caught my eye. It was a list of tasks she needed to accomplish. Laundry. Groceries. I frowned, reading *Check out foster center. Not sure yet.* And at the bottom was *Need $ now!!!!!! Job needed. Can't rely on ykw.*

I didn't like that.

YKW. You know who. A.k.a. me.

She made a little mewling sound, and I turned to her.

There was a chair in the corner of her room, so I sat. I leaned back, relaxing, and pulled my phone out to check. There were two texts waiting for me.

Levi: Ready. Waiting on your order.

I clicked on the other one first.

Lassiter: We need to talk.

He'd sent it three minutes ago.

I glanced up once more, taking in the sight of how peaceful Blake was resting.

I was remiss to leave, so I changed my notifications so it wouldn't buzz and turned down the light as well. The volume was all the way down already, so only a low light would flash when texts would come through.

Me: About what?

Lassiter: I'm in NY. Tech guys didn't want to bother you so they sent me something they found a few days ago. I came to explore it. Now you gotta get looped in. Has to do with the rival team.

I barely grinned, enjoying his horrible code.

Me: Give me an hour.

Lassiter: Meet at the nightclub?

Me: Yes.

Lassiter: You need to give that a better name than The Nightclub. You have three nightclubs in this city. What are you going to name them? Nightclub 1, Nightclub 2, Nightclub 3?

I knew Lassiter was genuinely annoyed by this. He wasn't teasing in his text.

Me: Stop being grouchy.

Lassiter: Stop being boring.

My grin widened. He, Levi, and Blake were the only ones who could talk to me like that. I enjoyed when they talked to me like this.

Me: Where are you currently?

Lassiter: Ignoring my other text, I see. Fine. I'll retitle your clubs myself.

Lassiter: I'm with Levi. They're waiting on your orders to do the things you wanted.

The things I wanted. Yes. I'd been waiting for this.

Tonight was the first time I launched my direct attack, except after my meeting with West and Walden, I altered my plans. They threatened Blake too many times in my presence. That would not go unpunished.

I wanted to be in Blake's presence, whether she was conscious or not, when my orders would be carried out.

Levi wasn't the only team on standby for me tonight. I checked in with the other two, and when my phone buzzed back that they were all ready, I sent out a text to each of them individually. It said one word only: Go.

CHAPTER SEVEN

CREIGHTON

We were supposed to meet at the nightclub, but I changed our locations. When I arrived, Lassiter was waiting outside of one of my warehouses for me. He grew up with us, on our street, so we considered him one of us. We being myself, Levi, and Blake. Lassiter never did. He worked for me, but he was the one who reminded us (if we said anything) that he was not one of us. He was only a neighbor.

It was bullshit.

He was one of us.

His hands were in his pockets, and he was leaning against the warehouse wall. He'd always been skinny, almost a petite physique, but in ripped skinny jeans, a white Henley with a black zipped sweatshirt pulled tight over his frame, he looked like he'd lost weight. He didn't have much to lose, but I knew not to comment. He'd bristle and get pissed about it. Instead, I'd mention something to Levi, who would become a nagging mosquito in Lassiter's ears, and he'd continuously bring food for him.

Lassiter had a pretty face. Blue eyes. High cheekbones. A narrow chin that worked on him somehow. He liked to keep multiple earrings in his ears, sometimes an eyebrow ring, sometimes a nose ring. Tattoos went all the way up his neck. One was a giant black hand that surrounded the back of his neck. He kept his dirty-blond hair similar to a Viking style, with two thick braids that ran from the side of his skull and to the back, falling loose. Tonight he wore a dark-gray stocking hat, pulled low.

"I thought your agreement with Blake was to stay away from her?"

There was no judgment in his voice, but there was something else there. I couldn't quite place it. "I have, as far as she's aware."

He snorted, shaking his head. "You've taken over the neighborhood surrounding her school. She's going to find out, and she's going to be pissed."

I didn't comment. There was no reason because yes, I had. Was I going to stop? No.

He laughed shortly under his breath. "You tasked me with looking for any incoming threat coming our way. We got a potential problem." His hand came out of his pocket and tossed something my way.

Catching it in my hand, it was a USB drive. I held it up. "What's on here?"

"Plans for a bill being introduced that's going to allow new security measures such as AI and plans for a research study where they're going to use drones for surveillance."

Drones with artificial intelligence. This wasn't good. I gave the USB a considering look. "Those drones are coming here." It wasn't a question. I already knew this was why Lassiter was even in town, otherwise he would've remained in Cincinnati, overlooking the city for me. "Who's in charge?"

He indicated the USB. "It's there."

"Save me time and tell me yourself."

A hard grin flickered over his face, but it didn't match the rest of him. His eyes were dead. "You need to read the information for yourself. Tell me what you want me to do with it."

A scream sounded from inside the warehouse.

Lassiter pushed off from the wall, glancing behind him at the warehouse because just on the other side of that wall someone was waiting for me. "I'll keep a watch on the bill and the study, but what our tech guys are telling me is that it's happening."

A second scream came.

"Have fun with that. I'll keep in touch."

I watched him go. Change was inevitable. I was proof of that because of how I recruited and took over territories, but Lassiter was alarmed enough for him to make a visit in person. When a third scream sounded, I pocketed the USB and headed inside.

I had work to do.

Two of my men straightened upright when I stepped inside. They moved away from the man tied up, with his feet barely touching the floor from where a rope was holding him in place.

Ashton Walden.

His head hung down. Blood dripped out from one of his sides.

I gave a nod for my men to leave and began rolling up the sleeves of my own Henley.

I took hold of his hair and pulled his head up so he could see me, but also to surveil the damage already done to him. One black eye. A split lip. His cheekbone looked smashed, but for torture, that was the prerequisite. Even Ashton Walden himself would agree. A certain amount of maiming was necessary for a good torture session to be had.

"I was told on the way here that it was remarkably easy for them to take you. You really should always travel with your guards, Walden. Especially now when we're at war." My tone was chiding. Taunting.

He tried to glare at me through one of his eyes. The other remained shut. "Fuck you."

I punched one of his good ribs and heard a crack. I flashed him a grin. "Satisfying, right?" I hit him again, and yep. A definite break. That rib was broken for sure.

He would've doubled over if he could've. Instead, he just tried to jerk away from me. A hoarse curse that was half of a scream ripped from his mouth. "I swear to Go—"

"Now, now." I placed a finger against his mouth, hushing him.

He tried to bite my finger off, and I stepped back, grinning.

A different man would've been concerned about the emptiness he just saw in one of his employees' eyes, someone who grew up with him. He would've been disturbed by his own stalking tendency and his disregard to break into a home and violate it, walking through it to watch a certain woman sleep. I wasn't that man. But this, causing pain, I felt *this* emotion.

I fixed Ashton with a hard look. "You like torturing. Correct? That's what my research says about you. You like to enact the pain, while your counterpart is the planner, and I'm not talking about that woman of yours. I'm referring to your best friend. Tristian West is the thinker. He thinks long-term. You're the doer, but that research is shortsighted. Isn't it? If it came down to it, if I really hurt someone Tristian West cared about, I bet he would enjoy enacting revenge. Wouldn't he? I wonder what I would need to do to enrage him enough?"

Picking up a knife, I went to him.

He swallowed at the sight, his eyes skirting between the knife and my face. "He'll gut you, you know. You won't even see him coming."

"Maybe." I trailed the tip of the knife across his chest. "That's a cute little fiancée you have. Molly Easter."

He paled again, but my words invigorated him. He tried breaking free from his restraints. I caught his chair, holding him in place. He tried swinging out at me, but it was a futile attempt. He could've hurt himself in the process, but I didn't see that stopping someone like Ashton Walden.

His head reared back up, and he snarled, "I'm going to fucking kill you, Lane. If you touch Molly—I swear to Go—"

He wasn't hiding his emotions anymore. He was letting them out, and I was reveling in it. I wanted to see everything he felt inside. I wanted to understand the inner workings of this man.

I gave him a moment. That was the usual thing to do? Blake would've known. I was guessing here. I was doing my best. After a few minutes, I leaned forward and dropped my voice, "You probably need time to process your emotions. You're upset. I can see that."

I waited, letting him work out his aggression.

He was relaying how much he wanted to flay my face open while I was alive. That would be interesting to witness. There were a few other threats that intrigued me. He wanted to disembowel me. I wasn't sure about that one, though. He kept sputtering away until he began coughing up blood.

I frowned. That would cut our fun in half.

I cut him off in mid-threat of putting my balls in a blender and how he would feed them to Blake when she was starving. That—that made me pause because I wasn't sure if I was mad at that threat or impressed. I considered it and decided that if he did do that, he would have Blake to fear once she found out. I was going to add that threat to his already mountain of debt.

"Walden, shut up. I'm here to tell you things, things you need to know before we finish."

He drew quiet, coughing more blood.

My men had done more damage than I thought before I got here.

Others would wince at how he looked.

Not me. He looked like a masterpiece. He was bloodied, with different bodily liquids sticking to him. Bruises were coloring all over him. They were fresh, but the speed of how they were appearing promised me how beautiful he'd look by the end of our session together.

"What are you talking about?" he rasped out, more blood being coughed up, then trickling out of his mouth.

"You haven't asked the basic question every captive asks."

He frowned before giving that question thought. "Why the fuck am I here?"

I smiled. "See. Was that so hard?"

He looked at me as if I suddenly turned purple in front of him. "I'm here because you're a piece of shi—"

I held up a hand, stopping him. "I apologize." I motioned between him and me. "Normally I would enjoy the back-and-forth. That's part of this dance we do. I'm sure you'd agree." I grew serious again, letting a little of my mask slip. The one I wore so others only saw my dead eyes and didn't see the real monster I could be. But we were having a moment, and if you couldn't be yourself when you were torturing or being tortured, then when could you be yourself? Really?

His eyes widened, and a deeper emotion flared in his eyes. Fear. I inclined my head and lowered my voice. "I had you kidnapped because . . ." I raised my knife again. "You see, Ashton, there's a lot you don't know about me. Yes, yes." I reached up and began using the knife to cut at the ropes he had holding him up. The ropes were thick, and the knife was dull, which was on purpose, so it would take time. I talked as I cut. "I enjoy fighting. I enjoy this whole thing we're doing. You, me, your best friend. I like matching wits against wits. You see, I operate under a specific set of rules. Do you want to find out what they are?" I paused in my cutting to see if he was starting to understand.

Sweat rolled down his face. His one eye was dilated, and the side of his mouth was pulled back, as if in a perpetual grimace. That could've been from my jostling. He was probably in a lot of pain.

I liked pain. I also liked pleasure. Torture and sex. Now those emotions, I could feel.

"I mentioned your fiancée for a reason." I cut through the last bit of rope and *snap*. He went down like a sack of potatoes.

He tried to rally against the pain and began to crawl away.

That was funny to watch, to think he had a chance.

I moved forward and put my foot down on his hand.

He screamed, his entire body coming alive. He tried swinging on me, but I was ready and merely brought my knife down so he impaled himself on it. Another guttural scream strangled from him.

I liked hearing that sound.

I could say that I hadn't stabbed him. Technically he stabbed himself.

I left the knife in his hand, because if he tore it out, I'd let him use it against me. He would've earned that. That's another reason why it was dull, though. In case it was used against me. The other reason: the duller it was, the more work it took to wreak havoc. Win-win-win as far as I was concerned.

I squatted in front of him.

His chest was taking in deep breaths, rising and falling. And he was calculating. I had no doubt he was making more promises in his head, what he'd do to hurt me.

"Ask me again why you're here, Ashton." I said it softly, almost tenderly.

He cringed against that sound from me. "Why am I here, you fucking psychopath?" He spat out those words.

I heaved out a sigh because he'd listen now. We were finally getting somewhere. "Normally, I would just slit your throat and be done with you, but we're in a rather delicate situation here. Aren't we?"

I pushed him back down, putting my foot on his throat this time. He could swing on me. I was letting his good hand free. If he did, I had another plan on how he could hurt himself. Ashton remained lying there under my foot. He didn't swing on me again.

He was learning. Good boy.

"*You* helped in having Blake kidnapped. So that's why I had *you* kidnapped."

I removed my foot from his throat.

He was lying still, but the next part would fill him with fire.

I was looking forward to that, but again, I wasn't stupid. I whistled, and the door opened. My men filtered back inside. I motioned for them to come forward. I'd need them to hold him back.

"I'm going to let you live, Ashton."

His eyes jerked to mine. He didn't believe me.

I squatted at his head again. "No. It's true. After I tell you the rest, my men will take you back."

I took hold of his hand, the one where my knife was still embedded. He hadn't used it on me, so I was going to take it back. Another day, though. Another battle. I held his hand, took hold of the knife, and waited. "The other reason I had you taken? One of my rules is that once you hurt onc of mine, I return it tenfold. So because of that, when you get home, you're going to find out what it's like to have someone of your own hurting. I hurt you physically, but the most enjoyment I get is when I hurt you here." I touched his chest where his heart was located. "Your woman runs a bowling alley, right?"

He froze.

"She bought it. Renovated it. Put her heart and soul into it." I met his gaze, wrapping my hand around the knife's handle again. "Too bad it burned down tonight."

His body coiled to spring, but I ripped the knife out of him and backed up.

He sprung up, charging me.

My men were there. This time I let them hold him back.

He couldn't fight them, not in the state he was in.

I had one more item to share. "Tristian West was also a part of gathering information on Blake."

"I'm going to kill you. Slowly and one limb at a time," he vowed. He meant it too. I could see he did, and I paused to take in this sight of him. Enacting revenge for what they did to Blake, that was my job.

That was *my right.*

"His woman is a painter, right? She's doing well. Has a new gallery with all her pretty new paintings. New masterpieces that sell for thousands."

He cursed under his breath, but he stopped fighting my men.

"She has a new show coming up in two weeks." This time, I smiled, and this time, I meant it. "They'll have to find a new location. Both the gallery and your woman's bowling alley burned down on the same night. All those paintings. All ash now." I stopped smiling, though I still relished the pain on his face.

His fight had left him, so I motioned for my men to let him go. They did.

He didn't try crawling away this time. He only watched me, his eyes blazing, ringed in agony.

"Think about that the next time you insist on threatening one of mine. Do you hear me?" There was a new burning in his depths. Yes. He got it. I could see it in his eyes.

I stood and motioned. "My men will give you a ride home, unless you want a trip to the hospital first. The Presbyterian, right? That's considered 'your hospital'?"

I didn't wait for his answer, turning instead and motioning for my men to deal with him.

It was their turn now.

That's how it went in wars like ours.

CHAPTER EIGHT

BLAKE

Seventh grade

There was a commotion up ahead in the hallway.

My gut sank because I knew. I just knew. It was a full *knowing* feeling that whatever was happening up ahead was right by my locker. Leaving the library, I only had a few minutes to grab my books, and then I needed to get all the way over to where my Spanish class was, which was up on the fourth floor.

I never thought I'd miss sixth grade, but I did at this moment because back then our classes were all grouped together. We went from room to room as a group, and there were teachers in the hallway. The supervision was stricter in that school, but here we were, in junior high. Everything was different.

And I hugged my books to my chest, nearing the crowd. These just weren't the right books.

People were yelling.

Crash.

Punch.

I stopped in my tracks as one guy was shoved violently into the lockers. The crowd cleared to get out of the way, and crap. I was right.

They were exchanging punches in front of my locker. Like, right there. It was my locker that they hit, and they weren't moving away, still trading punches.

I didn't even know these guys. Maybe they were eighth graders?

They didn't seem to be stopping.

I couldn't see any teachers either. No one was going to wade in to stop this anytime soon.

It looked like I was going to be late for my class. I was irritated. Why couldn't they—"Look out!"

Hearing someone scream, I looked up.

The guys were hurtling right at me.

"Fuck!" a guy cursed behind me. "No. Not her—"

I tried to get out of the way, but it happened too fast. Too quick. A part of me froze and—*crash!*

Pain erupted over my face. It erupted again from the back of my head as I was slammed into the locker. The two guys crushed me, and more pain engulfed me in the middle. I felt like I'd been hit by an oncoming bus, multiple times.

My legs weren't working. I was trying to slide away, or crawl away, but the two guys wouldn't stop fighting. It was as if they didn't know they'd hurt someone else, but suddenly a rough hand grabbed my arm. I was yanked to the side. At the same time, the guys were gone. They were thrown to the ground, and immediately a group of six others were kicking them.

I couldn't make sense of what was happening, but oh my god, I was in so much pain.

A face got in front of me, a guy who was bending down to talk to me. I recognized him. He was a junior, and he was the one who'd pulled me out of the way. He was holding me upright. "Where are you hurt?"

I was dazed. "What?"

He cursed, paling a little as he was assessing my injuries. He looked down, pausing on something there. "Did they get you there too?"

"What?" I was having a hard time hearing him.

He cursed again, stepping away, and then he was speaking on a phone. His face was all rigid and pissed off, and this wasn't good.

". . . She's in shock, I think."

Shock. That would make sense.

I'd been hit before, but this interaction came at me so fast, and it had nothing to do with me.

Other hands were touching me.

The guy snapped at whoever that was, "Don't fucking touch her! This is—do you know who this is?"

I grimaced, knowing what he was going to say. I didn't want him to say it.

"She's Lane's. Those guys are dead."

He said it.

"What's going on here?"

I sagged back against the locker when a teacher finally showed, my knees buckling, except I couldn't fall. That guy was still holding me upright. More of his friends came to stand around him, all grim, and all focusing on him as they were inspecting me with their eyes.

"What happened?" The same teacher's voice got louder. More firm. "Hello. Anyone going to fill me in? I was told two boys were fighting out here. Where are they?"

"Uh . . ." Someone spoke up.

The guys by me whipped around. One took a threatening step toward the speaker. "Don't say a word."

The voice belonged to a girl, who gave him a nasty look. "They have cameras. It'll be on video."

He took another intimidating step her way. Fear flashed in her eyes, but she jerked her gaze away from him. "Will Proguesly and Hector Smith were fighting. They knocked into her."

"And where are they now?"

She hesitated again, sinking away from completely narcing on the rest because what I found out later was that when I got hit, Creighton's guys were notified. They were in another hallway. They tore into the fight, beating the crap out of the two guys.

I was in seventh grade, but everyone already knew. No one went against Creighton Lane.

I had a black eye and bruises all over, but I was fine. Will and Hector had mostly just knocked the wind out of me, but them—Hector's elbow was what had given me the black eye. He came to school a week later without a hand. And Will, he was the one who was blamed for the fight in the first place.

Will never came back to school.

Will never came back at all.

His face went up on a missing persons flyer, but everyone knew what happened to him.

Creighton killed him.

CHAPTER NINE

BLAKE

A pile of books dropped beside me on the table.

I jumped from the suddenness of it, and at the same time two chairs pulled out from the table.

My guy roommates both dropped down into the chairs. I still hadn't met the girl who lived on the main floor of the townhouse. Niko. That was her name, but Marshall and Heath, I'd met them my second day there. They'd originally met each other because they came from the same fraternity, which was also how they met Palma because she was in the sorority that they partied with a lot. Marshall beamed at me while Heath glowered from across the table. And this summed up how they viewed me.

Marshall liked me.

Heath very much *did not*. I didn't know what his problem was. I thought maybe that was his default setting.

It wasn't.

He was gentle with Palma.

He was friendly with Marshall.

I hadn't witnessed him with anyone else, so as far as I could tell he had a problem with me. Or maybe new people? I hadn't spent a lot of time with my roommates because turns out, being graduate students, they were busy. They were really busy. Between my own studies and looking for a job, the time when I'd been at the house had been spent alone. I heard Palma come home a couple times, but our paths rarely crossed during the day. And none of them had been around last weekend.

"So." Marshall whistled. "I think we need a housemate hangout. You've been living with us for two weeks now, and we've barely seen you. Come out with us tonight."

"I don't know," I started to say.

He added, "It's Palma's birthday."

Well. Fuck.

"Palma said you're cool. You look cool. I'm thinking you're cool. Come out with us tonight." He flicked a finger under my book, shutting it. "You're in college. You got your whole life to study. It's Palma's *birthday*. Eh? Eh? You're coming out, aren't you? I can see the wheels turning. You're totally coming."

Going out with people?

I used to daydream about what it would be like to be normal. It never happened for me because I was a foster kid first. Then I was Creighton's, just . . . Creighton's. When I came to New York, there'd been a time period where I'd just been Blake Green. No Creighton shadow over me.

I loved it. It'd been glorious, and I tried having the normal friend thing.

It hadn't worked out.

I wish there wasn't a flutter of anxiety in my chest. I really did, but there was. Creighton's watchdog was sitting at a table a few over. He didn't quite have his back to me. His clothes blended. He had a backpack. A coffee. A textbook and notebook spread out on the table. He looked like a college student. Except he wasn't.

And suddenly I was pissed off because fuck Creighton.

If I wanted to try and be normal, and going out with college friends was almost as normal as I could imagine, then I was going to do it.

"You know what. Yeah. Let's go out tonight."

The guy lifted his head, his eyes flicking to me. He reached for his phone, and I wanted to jump up, grab that phone, and bash it to pieces because I knew who he was notifying.

There'd been a line outside the club where Marshall told me to head. I needed to study, and they went ahead to pick up some of Palma's friends, so I arrived later. Nightclub 1. It was a new club that Palma wanted to check out. I laughed a little at the name of the club, seeing the owners had put a lot of thought into it.

I didn't see Palma or anyone else in line that I knew, so I bypassed it for the door. I didn't know if this would work, but they might've given my name to the bouncer. I was right. He whisked open the door almost right away, nodding to me. "Go right in, Miss Green."

A few people grumbled that were still waiting to get inside, but the other guard raised his voice, "Shut it!"

The first guy nodded again to me, reassuring. "Go ahead. Go on inside."

Loud hip hop dance music blasted me as soon as I stepped inside. The place was packed, but I weaved through the crowd, seeing Palma at the edge of the dance floor. Their group had claimed two tables. I skimmed over the others but only recognized Palma and Marshall. I didn't know the others. I'm sure Heath was there, but I couldn't see him. I wasn't exactly going to go looking for him.

Nearing the group, Palma saw me coming. She squealed, ran over, and wound her arms around my neck. "Ahh! You came. I'm so happy."

Her cheeks were rosy. She looked happy.

A couple of her friends came up, asking her a question. As she let go of me to answer, I caught a flash of movement against the far wall of the club. A certain head of dirty-blond hair that was moving fast along the periphery of the bar, and my heart stopped.

No.

I considered the possibility, but no. No way.

The guy was gone now, disappearing past a door, but how he moved, the side profile of his face—he looked like someone I'd grown up with. Lassiter. But there was no way. Last (what we called him for a nickname) wouldn't be here.

He never left Cincinnati.

He was Creighton's number two.

But if it *was* him . . . The only reason he'd be here would be—my stomach dipped again.

No.

No, no, no.

My vision grew blurry at the edges. I tried to shove down my alarm, scanning the room.

If that was Lassiter, and that was a big *if,* then the reason he'd be here was if he were here to see Creighton. And if Creighton was here, he would've already known I was as well, and—horror started to creep inside of me.

I . . .

My stomach was a mess.

Palma was still talking to her friends. I put my hand on her arm, interrupting her. "Hey. Uh." The room began to sway around me. "Did you leave my name at the door?"

She leaned in closer to hear better. "What?"

"When I got here, the men at the door let me in right away. Did you leave my name?"

She blinked, her head lifting up. "I—no. Unless Heath did?" She began to turn, looking for him.

No. Not Heath. I put my hand on her arm. "Never mind. That's okay."

Heath wouldn't have given the bouncers my name. He didn't want me here.

And just then, the door where I thought Lassiter had gone through opened again. This time, a different guy stepped out. It wasn't Lassiter, but the sight of this new guy still made my stomach drop altogether.

God. No.

I stepped from Palma, my hand falling away.

The guy was looking right at me, and there was an added kick to my stomach because there was no surprise on his face. He knew I was here. He was staring at me, guarded, which I didn't like because I knew this guy. I'd grown up with this guy, too, and he never used to look at me as if he were waiting for me to hate him.

I didn't know what excuse I said to Palma and her friends. It must've been fine because no one gave me an odd look when I made my excuses. I was only aware of pushing through the crowd until I stood in front of him.

"Levi."

His gaze fell to me as mine tipped up to his. We stood there, a moment, taking each other in.

He was here because of Creighton, which I hated, but a sudden well of fondness surged in me. I flung myself at his chest, wrapping my arms around him and squeezing with all I could. He was so big and so tall, my arms didn't fit around him. I was nearly five seven and I wasn't slim. I was still smaller than what was considered a normal size now for a woman, but I was strong. That's all I cared about. I was toned, but Levi always made me feel like a little girl next to him.

He hesitated a moment before lifting his big beefy arms to hold me back. He squeezed me, too, but a lot gentler.

My throat swelled up. Stepping away, I blinked back some tears and pretended to swipe some dust off his shirt. My voice came out hoarse. "Did you start eating people since I last saw you? I swear you've doubled in size. Is there another man inside of your tummy?" I poked it. It was firm, like the rest of him, which didn't surprise me.

For a moment, I just saw the sweet little boy I remembered, who I shared my potato chips with when we got them for a treat. And popcorn. He was always so shy, scared to talk when he first came to the house. I took him under my wing, in a way pretending I finally got a little brother, except Levi was technically older than me. In Miss Marcie's house, it was different. I had seniority over him, so in my eyes, he was always going to be younger than me.

"No people. Rocks. Boulders, maybe. No people." He winked. "I'd remember."

We shared a grin for the moment until my gaze trailed to the door behind him. To who I was assuming was somewhere on the other side.

His grin fell away. "Blake—"

I began to step around him, reaching for the door, but paused at my name.

He didn't say anything more. The slight flash of the little boy I used to share chips with was gone, and he had a stark expression over his face now.

I didn't know what that meant, seeing that starkness on him. The hairs on the back of my neck stood up, but I shook my head. "I know."

He quieted.

I touched his arm, feeling how rigid he was. "He puts his office in the same location no matter where he is. I know where I'm going. You can stay here. Those are my new roommates and friends over there. I don't want anything to happen to them."

I heard his swift intake of breath.

If Creighton wanted one of them hurt, Levi would be the one he'd send. I just put Levi on notice. He'd have to choose whose orders to follow. Creighton's or mine. Most of the time he would adhere to Creighton, but there had been moments when he chose me. The real secret was that Creighton secretly loved when Levi chose me over him, though he never let anyone know.

Levi dipped his head down in an acknowledgment, stepping back and letting the door shut between us.

I headed upstairs, not needing to focus on finding his office.

If Creighton was within the same vicinity, I always knew where he was. I could feel him. And like those times, I let my body follow the internal beacon inside of me.

It led me straight to him.

CHAPTER TEN

BLAKE

It wasn't fair.

That was the first thought that crossed my mind as soon as I opened the door. There were no guards outside. None in the hallway, but I knew. I just knew he'd be behind this door. I hated and loved this beacon I had for him. Like the man himself, who still looked like a pretty boy.

He was still hot. I'd had a brief stint away from him, and seeing him again, having that time away, he washed over me. I hadn't been ready for this, how my body wanted to go to him, but I *couldn't.* I just couldn't.

His face was sharper, if that was possible, but it was sharper in a more chiseled cheekbone sort of way.

Fuck. He could be in one of those elite magazines. His jawline was more pronounced somehow. His black hair was short on the sides with a little extra on top for him to run a hand through. And those gray eyes of his. They were usually bland, looking dead, but not today. Today they were pinned on me, and I could see the intense satisfaction in them.

It wasn't fair that he could look like that, like a preppy college student, like a fraternity brother, like an Instagram model, and *yet* have the mind that was rivaling two other Mafia heads in this city. He was a fucking chameleon, and he shouldn't have been graced with those blessings. Not him. Of everyone, not him.

I stepped inside, a bolt of electricity going through me because being this close to Creighton always made me feel everything. Good or bad. Everything was intensified to the umpteenth. That was part of him too. Creighton was a magnifier for those around him. He brought out whatever was hidden underneath. If someone was trying to shove something below the surface, it would always rise to the top. I'd watched so many people not understand why they were having the feelings they were having. I didn't understand it, but I'd seen it enough to know it happened.

And Creighton would watch it all and be amused by it.

It pissed me off.

Lassiter made a choking sound from the side. I swung my gaze over, taking him in too. It *had* been him downstairs. His head swung between Creighton and me, but I didn't have time for him. My eyes returned to Creighton as Lassiter half-laughed, "Hey, Blak—"

"Out," I growled.

Creighton moved to lean on the edge of his desk. He raised his eyebrows as Lassiter left the room without protest. I followed to lock the door behind him. As soon as it was just him and me, the tension ramped up. The anger was there, swimming in me in waves. It doubled. There were other emotions underneath, ones I wasn't ready to acknowledge.

I didn't take a step toward him. It felt safer to stay across the room, and I adopted a similar stance to his, except I leaned back against the wall beside the door. "What are you doing here, Creight?"

His eyes dimmed a little. He cocked his head to the side. "Prefer the other name you have for me."

Fuck. I felt that disappointment in me.

I bristled.

I gritted my teeth, ignoring the warring emotions in me. "Yeah, well, I don't give a fuck right now." I wanted to push off from the wall, stalk toward him, but I held myself in place. As far away from him as possible right now. "We made a deal—"

"Yes, we did." He shoved off his desk.

I held my breath, but he only took one step toward me before stopping.

I ached. I wanted him to come all the way, and I bent my head because why did I want that? I had a stupid crush on him growing up, but it was just that. A schoolgirl crush, one that I never should've had. Creighton was six years older. He didn't look at me like that.

He never had. Obsessed, yes. Just not in *that* way.

I didn't think. Right?

God. I was so confused.

My heart pounded in a frenzied staccato, and I lifted my gaze again.

He was watching me intently, his own head bent a little as if to see me better. His hands were shoved in his pockets. He spoke softly, "The deal was to stay away from you. If I did, you wouldn't run again, but I'm allowed to have someone watch you. It's the only way I know you're safe."

That wasn't true. The thought was in the back of my mind. We could feel each other. He always had been able to, but it felt more now.

Why?

Why now?

I tore my gaze away, my thoughts getting cloudy. I needed to think clearly again. What had he been saying? "This is your place?"

He didn't answer. He didn't need to.

I was nodding to myself, putting together the pieces.

It was a new club. Not far from campus.

My gut sank.

It made perfect sense, a new club that college students would want to check out. That Palma would want to check out.

"You set a trap for me. You renovated this nightclub into a place that you knew college students would want to hang out in. You knew it would eventually bring me here."

He drew closer. "I don't see the problem here. I don't have stipulations about where you can go, remember? I want to see you."

A shiver went down my spine.

I could feel his heat. He touched underneath my chin, lifting my gaze to meet his own. And as it did, he moved in. His hand fell away as his head inclined over me. "What's the problem here, Blake?"

I ignored the tingle where he'd touched me. "The problem is you." I placed my hand to his chest and shoved him back. "You don't want me to run again?" I moved to him. "Stop. Fucking. Killing. People."

A storm brewed in his gaze. Those dead eyes that looked anything but right now. They were ominous. Lethal. "I will always protect you—"

"No!" I shoved him again, my control snapping. "I told you—I told you—no one innocent. No one good." I shoved at him again, moving with him. My body was heated. "I'm sick of worrying about guys who simply talk to me, if you're going to have them killed. I'm sick of being responsible for your lunacy."

He was done being pushed.

I started to shove him once more, my hands rising, but I saw the flash of death and stopped. My hands fell back to my side as his words cut into me. "You *insult* me. You think I kill senselessly? That I have no boundaries?" He moved into me, his chest grazing against mine. His breath was hot on my neck, and I couldn't suppress the tremor that passed through my body. "You are my boundary, Blake. You. I don't kill anyone good, anyone innocent. Only bad. Your words, your rules. I adhere to only you, and you accuse me otherwise."

I angled my head back to see him again. "But the two guys three years ago—"

"One tried to drug you. The second was making plans to fuck you with his friends."

God. His eyes pierced me.

He gave an inch, moving back from me. "I have never broken your rules."

I trembled slightly, feeling as if we'd gone a thousand rounds instead of just one, but this was how it was with Creighton.

I whispered, "Eight." I broke first.

He softened. His hand lifted to cup the side of my face, his thumb brushing over my cheek before he let me go once again. "You can date, Blake. But if he or she is going to hurt you, then . . ."

Right. *Then.*

He'd do what he did.

My throat swelled. A lump formed there. "Promise me."

He frowned. "Promise."

His eyes were fierce again. I knew he'd follow his promise.

I jerked my chin up, abrupt and awkward. "Okay." I could take a deep breath now. "Okay." I felt better. Lighter.

Creighton moved in again, and his thumb swept over my cheek before he went back to his desk. "Your roommate. Nogoskeski."

I frowned. "I don't know their last names."

"Ah. The boy. Blond. Tattoos."

"Heath." I had a feeling I wasn't going to like whatever was coming next.

"He's from North Fairmount."

"Wait. What?" No. That couldn't be. Then . . . Oh, shit. North Fairmount was a tough neighborhood. He was from Cincinnati. And that meant—he knew me. If he was from where Creighton said he was from, then he definitely knew Creighton.

"He has two brothers who are mine."

Creighton meant that they'd joined his army. I hated them, his soldiers. They were more like Creighton's followers. Once they vowed to follow him, their sense of loyalty became like a cult. No one understood how it happened. They thought there was brainwashing or blackmail. There wasn't. In the beginning it was just money.

As soon as someone made an oath to Creighton, they began earning *fast.* That was one thing about Creighton. He didn't care about money like most might've. It wasn't the reason he did what he did. I knew he had money. He had *a lot* of it, but he only took a small percentage of it. The rest was shared with his army. The longer someone was loyal to Creighton, the higher their percentage grew, and that type of money ensured loyalty. *A lot* of loyalty.

I was dazed that Heath knew me. "But Heath's not? Not one of yours."

"No. The file I have on him said he's mostly estranged from his brothers. He barely talks to his mother. He left for college and has not been back since. He spends his holidays with the male roommate that came with him tonight."

A belated thought crossed my mind. What an odd way to refer to Marshall. "Uh. Yeah. That makes sense. They seem close."

Creighton's phone began ringing, but he ignored it. His attention, like all the time, was centered only on me. It used to make me feel like the most important girl in the world. I don't know if that was where my crush originated from, but I'm sure it helped fan that flame.

My throat swelled again.

Creighton saw me.

He always saw me.

I felt myself melting. It was innate. It just happened when I was in his presence because that was just how it was with Creighton. He had a part of my heart, and I'd long ago accepted that I'd have to be okay not ever getting that chunk back. It was his. His alone. Whether he knew that, though, was a different story. For how ruthless he was, I—no. I couldn't finish that thought.

It wasn't right.

"You seem to be enjoying your new place."

My gut flared. "You got me in there, didn't you? It's the only explanation for how an undergrad got placed in one of the best graduate residences."

He didn't reply at first, then when he did, he spoke slowly, as if cautiously, "You ran from me, Blake. I *never* want to experience that again. And how I found you—I never want to experience *that* either.

You want me to be a certain type of man, but I am not. I am not a good man. I've always known that about myself. I am who I am. I'd rather you hate me and be alive than be a nice guy and you be dead." He didn't blink.

His phone began ringing again. He ignored it again.

I cursed and crossed to where it was on his desk. I answered swiftly, mocking, "Felonious Creighton Lane's phone. One moment please. I'll transfer you to his current location in his demonic lair line. There might be some screaming in the background, but pay no attention. Beeeeeeeeeeee—aahhhhhhhh—noooooooo—don'tkillme—eeeeep. Here you go." I shoved it at his chest as I reached for the door.

He stopped me just as I opened it. "Blake."

I was still boiling, but I waited.

"You remember our agreement."

I was confused. "Wha—" I remembered.

Our agreement was that he would stay away *until* I went to him. After that, it was considered null and void. I'd agreed in that moment because I hadn't considered he would trick me like this, but Creighton didn't adhere to "that's not fair" or "you tricked me."

The facts were that I came to him.

Lead filled me.

The agreement was done.

"That means I can come to you."

CHAPTER ELEVEN

BLAKE

The guy doing my interview gave me an incredulous look when he met me at the front door of Octavia, right before introducing himself as Spence. It was another nightclub in the area. I needed money and fast, and working in a bar or club was what experience I had. I knew Creighton would pay for anything and everything if I let him, but I had my pride. I would stand on my two feet.

Tips would be good. Plus, I was good at food and beverage work.

We were toward the end of the interview when the guy pushed back his chair, turning away from his computer, and he stared hard at me.

He didn't speak for a moment.

I frowned, shifting a little in my chair. "What?"

He was young, maybe a few years older than me, but there was an older aura of maturity that surrounded him. If my life were different, he would've been someone I'd be interested in. He was cute too. A lean athletic body. Maybe he wasn't dressed in what someone might have worn as a club manager, in jeans, a hoodie, and sneakers. I glanced down at his feet again and amended that they were nice sneakers. The kind that people waited in line for outside the store when they first released. He had a similar face to Creighton's too. A younger looking face. Pretty. But he had brown shaggy hair, and it looked as if he ran his hand through it on the regular, a frustrated motion that was habitual. He wasn't quite clean shaven. Some facial hair remained, like he'd forgotten to shave and he was currently running his hand over it before he expelled a sigh, his hand falling back to his lap. "Are you shitting me?"

My eyebrows went up. "Uh. No?"

Because, no. But the way he said it, I almost questioned myself.

I sat forward. "I need a job. I'm used to this industry. You can see my work history."

His eyes fell on my résumé, but he didn't pick it up. "Why here?" He fixed me with intense scrutiny.

I was confused.

He leaned forward abruptly. "We looked you up. I know who you are. I have to imagine that you know who we are."

Another flat stare.

He *was* talking about who I thought. "I know who owns this club."

He leaned back in his chair, his hands pushed into the front pocket of his hoodie. "And again, we know who you are. Creighton Lane has his own establishments. Why aren't you employed at one of them?"

I deflated. He really did know who I was. Okay then. I wasn't going to bullshit with him. "This club is owned by Cole Mauricio. He's from another Mafia family, and this club is considered neutral territory. I'm not one of Creighton's soldiers, and I don't want anything to do with the fight going on between him and the other two families in this city. I'm a college student. I want a job, and I want to make some money. That's it."

An unnatural stillness came over him before he shifted in his seat. "We have an understanding with the West and Walden families. They're allowed to be in here, as long as they're here as patrons *only*. No violence. They're not allowed to operate here. This club is owned and run by Cole Mauricio. Only Cole Mauricio. Lane has not reached out for the same agreement, but I've got a feeling that if I hire you, he'll be on the phone within the hour. He's not allowed to enter until he has an agreement with my employer. I'm sure he'll be aware of that condition. He's a smart prick."

My own mouth twitched.

I liked the no-nonsense attitude from this guy. I also liked that there wasn't one iota of nervousness about Creighton. That was the best part.

He was eyeing my résumé again. Still wary. "If I hire you, there's no fucking way I'm putting you on the floor. You're applying to be a server or a shot girl." His gaze lifted to me. "You'll bartend, and you will keep your ass behind the bar, you got me?"

Was he . . .

"What are you saying?"

"Lane will not be allowed to recruit here. Patron only. Anything else, he's out. We do not give one fuck how scary he can be."

I frowned. "Wait. Are you saying—"

He heaved a deep breath and held out his hand. "You're hired if you're okay with a bartending job?"

I shot to my feet and shook his hand, trying not to pump it from how happy I was. "Yes. Yes, si—"

"God. Just Spence, please."

"Yes, Spence. Mr. Spence—Calloway. Thank you for this."

His face went dark. "One slipup from Lane and you're out of here."

My throat swelled up, and I swallowed, thickly. "Understood."

"Then welcome to Octavia."

CHAPTER TWELVE

CREIGHTON

She went to Octavia today. She got the job.

She was sleeping now, but she didn't come to me for a job. She went to a foster center too. That was perfect for her. I didn't know if she would love working there. She was always torn about her experience being a foster kid, but I knew Blake. Her heart wouldn't let her not work there. The second she saw one foster kid who needed help, she wouldn't be going anywhere else. It would be cemented for her. Whether she accepted it or not, it's where she's supposed to be.

She'd be running it within three to five years.

I stood over her. She rolled to her side, presenting the side of her face, her smooth skin. I couldn't help but graze the back of my hand over her cheek.

She didn't think I knew about her feelings for me, but of course I knew. She considered it a crush growing up. Maybe it had morphed into something deeper? Maybe it was time to give it oxygen? See if the fire built.

I knew I'd been holding mine back, and it was damn near combustible by now. I was tired of holding myself back from her. I was tired of pretending these feelings weren't here. Yes, there was my obsession, but I wanted her.

I was tired of not having her.

Her head moved, her nose twitched. I lifted my hand away, not wanting to wake her. But I couldn't bring myself to leave either. Why would I?

Settling down in her chair, I sat back to watch her sleep.

Tonight she slept contentedly. I wished she always slept like this, but I knew she didn't. There was darkness lurking in the back of her mind, and sometimes it slipped out, infecting her dreams, turning them into nightmares. I'm sure some of it was because of the things I'd done in the past to protect her, but it was always to protect her.

Things would change.

I glanced to her desk and saw her note about her new work schedule. She was making her own moves. Octavia. The foster center.

She was finding her way, so I would find my way with her. I would move alongside her.

I had missed her.

My phone lit up from my hand, and I turned it over to see who texted.

Lassiter: Someone's reached out for a meet. Can you come?

Lassiter would never text unless it was someone I needed to see.

Me: On the way.

CHAPTER THIRTEEN

CREIGHTON

Lassiter's directions brought me to the alley beside Cole Mauricio's nightclub.

The man who called for this meeting stood just outside Octavia's side door. Lassiter, Levi, and a few of my other men stood between me and him. They stepped aside so I could better view him. Some of his staff also lingered in the alley. I noted their guns and knew these weren't just Octavia's staff. They were Cole Mauricio's men.

This was Blake's new boss. A young manager running a nightclub in New York City for Cole Mauricio.

He was younger than me, and on the outside, we looked similar.

I knew without a doubt that Blake would've found him attractive.

"Spence Calloway."

His nostrils flared at my greeting, but he masked the hostile expression before attempting to smile at me.

I motioned to his eyes. "Those give you away."

He swiftly inhaled. "Excuse me?"

I took a step closer so he could see my face better. The light was better. I gestured to my eyes. "You're trying to mask your hatred for me, but it won't work. You also don't need to do that. I expect people to hate me before they meet me, then hate me *more* after they meet me.

You can show your hate. It's fine. You're not like me. You don't have to worry about appearing a certain way. I act to appear normal, but you, you *are* normal." I gave him a more considered look. "You're not a lamb, but you're not a wolf either."

He glared at me, showing me his teeth.

I smiled.

"I shoul—" He reached for his side, but I moved quickly. My hand went to his wrist, and as he started to bring out a knife, I twisted his wrist, applying enough pressure so he made a gasping sound, forcing him to drop the knife or I would've broken his wrist.

As the knife slipped from his hold, I took it, stepping back.

"Boss!" Levi and Lassiter both moved for me.

I held up a hand.

They halted immediately, and I offered them the knife that I'd just taken. When they didn't automatically reach for it, I snapped. "Take it."

I could feel their hesitation.

I fixed Levi with a glare. "We'll discuss your slip later."

He was confused until he got it, and he tried giving me an appeasing look. "Sorry, Bo—"

I growled in warning.

"Creighton," he corrected himself.

Lassiter was eyeing both Levi and me until he stepped to the side and studied Octavia's manager instead. I couldn't place what he was thinking as he watched the other man.

"Did you call this meeting to attack me?" I motioned toward my men, ignoring his men. "That wasn't well thought out. A bit shortsighted. No?"

Spence Calloway drew back a step and raised his head, trying to regain control over himself again. "You recently came from Chicago?"

That was also interesting. "You hired one of mine. Cole Mauricio has an agreement with my enemies. I wanted to be sure of her safety." I grinned again. "There are rules, are there not? Rules on how to operate within Cole Mauricio's club, or to be more specific, rules for how not to act. I have the same agreement he has with West and Walden." I was trying to figure out his reasons for this meeting. It wasn't a necessary meeting. "I am permitted on these premises as long as I am without a weapon. Though, I'm wondering if that's necessary in this alley. If someone is standing on one side, it's easy to shoot across the imaginary line. Too close together. The other side belongs to Ashton Walden. You're aware he owns that building?" I gestured to the side.

Spence's eyes widened.

He hadn't known that fact. I wondered if his boss had.

I made sure to turn and smile at the security cameras that were attached to Walden's building.

Both cameras were blinking, so they were active.

I was about to press this new fact when there was a screech of brakes. Shouting was next. Gunshots. Then a pair of headlights swept through the alley.

A vehicle barreled right at us.

Levi and Lassiter got between me and the vehicle while my men began shooting. Tristian West was driving, with crazed eyes, white knuckles on the steering wheel, and most importantly—he was alone. There were no guards with him.

My body hummed.

Spence was gone. I wasn't done with Octavia's manager.

Irritation beat in me, a steady drum as I turned to focus on the impending arrival.

The vehicle suddenly stopped, and I stepped out from behind Levi and Lassiter, my hand in the air to halt my men from shooting him. "Don't." The front door flung open. Tristian West shoved out of the vehicle, a gun in one hand and a wrench in the other.

I paused at that.

A wrench? I expected the gun. A knife at the very least. But a wrench? He could do better with a bat. A steel bat. I would gift him one, or send it to Ashton Walden's hospital room and have it addressed to "the best friend." I liked that idea.

"You think this is fucking funny?" He growled, advancing swiftly. The gun was raised.

He was going to shoot. I had seconds to react.

I moved at the same time he pulled the trigger. His shot went wide, hitting the wall behind me. I wasn't paying attention to anything else, just needing to disarm the threat. Personally I didn't like guns. They were a coward's choice of weapon. Anyone could hold a gun and pull a trigger, but a real monster was a weapon in themselves. I liked knives. Or machetes. Or any other weapon, to be honest, because they were just a tool. I was the weapon. How I used them was the weapon. Guns, they were like a cheat card. But because they were effective, I didn't like having one pointed at me, so as West's first shot missed, my men yelled from the street.

West turned.

Levi and Lassiter were there.

Levi moved in to block him, and Lassiter grabbed West's arm, disarming him instantly. West went still, seeing the odds. He was outnumbered.

He came here to kill me.

Levi shoved West hard against his own vehicle. It jarred him, but didn't stop him. He swung the wrench.

"Levi," I barked, yanking him back.

He shot me a look, but I ignored him. We both knew it wasn't because I was worried about him. Levi could hold his own. It was because I wanted in on some of this action.

"Fuck's sakes, Creight." But he moved back, and West lunged for me.

He swung again.

I stepped to the side, noting, "Was it the sight of your best friend that did this? You're not thinking clearly, West." When he swung a second time on me, it was almost insultingly easy to avoid that one too. "You're also not good at this either."

"At what?" he growled again, swinging backward. "And fuck you, Lane."

I'd taken his best friend, strung him up, and tortured him. I did to Ashton Walden what his reputation says he does to others. As for Tristian West, there'd not been much information on his fighting ability. I could see why there wasn't. There wasn't anything to report.

"Enough." I ducked one last time and twisted the wrench out of his hands. As soon as I did, I tossed it to Levi. He caught it and grabbed West from behind. He brought his own wrench around West's throat, using it to hold him in place.

Tristian West wasn't thinking clearly. That much was obvious. I took a step closer to inspect him. Between his wife's gallery burning down and what I had done to his best friend, *had* I put him over the edge?

I leaned in. "You are the steady one in your group. Your wife is not steady. Your best friend certainly is not. His woman, no. You are. That's your role. That's not what this is. This isn't who you are." I shook my head. "What were you thinking? Why didn't you send your guards?"

"Because you would've killed them."

"They're guards. That's their job."

"Not mine."

This was perplexing.

He was a king that felt his fall coming, but most kings ran to survive. They tried to become king somewhere else. He wasn't going away. He came in place of his men. I sought to hurt him and Ashton Walden where it would do the most damage. I didn't go for their men. Their businesses. I went for their heart.

I hurt their women.

My men were going through his vehicle. It was as I suspected. No guards. No other weapons.

"I am your enemy." I pointed to the camera set up on Walden's building. "You came for me because you knew my location, but this?" I motioned to him and his SUV, shaking my head again. "I am within my right to take your life. You came at me. I *should* kill you because *that's what we do*. You sent someone after my woman." I ignored how Lassiter went still at those words. "You threatened her, multiple times in one sitting. You came after me like *this*. You—" I didn't like it. I didn't like it at all. I motioned to his SUV again. "At least have a bomb on that machine. That would be a good move against me. A last move of yours, but a move that I would respect. This—" I motioned again to him. Disgusted. "Your man will heal. Your woman can paint more masterpieces. You can build a new gallery. Walden's woman can build a new bowling alley. I am the fox that threw a firecracker in a chicken coop. I expected your team to react, scatter a little, but not this reaction."

He had paused, his chest heaving up and down, but he never stopped glaring at me. There was a white line around his mouth. "I will kill you—"

"Yes!" I got back in his face, some of that uncomfortable feeling began to dissipate. Thank goodness. I smiled again. "I am testing your team to see how you react, and *I am not impressed.* Sending my own cousin to kidnap Blake, that was a move that I respected. I was furious, but I respected it. You are the brains. You see the big picture." I moved even closer until my chest was grazing his. "The planner. This was not a planned move. Your loved ones *will* recover from what I did to them. Come back with a better move."

I was done with this. It was a glitch. That's what this was.

I had hoped, but no. Both of these men, West and Walden, were not like me. They loved. They felt.

They were normal.

I'd been mistaken.

I turned and began to walk away.

"It was me or him."

I looked back.

West was still glaring, but there was some defeat in how his shoulders slumped down. He was rubbing at his throat, where Levi had been holding him. "Ashton was going to come after you. I came so he couldn't."

Understanding dawned. That made more sense.

I dipped my head to him. "I respect that. Perhaps you won this one." I still wasn't going to kill him. Not yet. It was too soon. I wasn't ready to move onto the next stage in our fight. So far none of the main players had been killed. There was a sense of teasing still in this stage. A kind of foreplay in the air. I liked this phase. I wanted to prolong it as long as possible.

"You are psychotic." Tristian West's voice was dumbfounded.

I kept going. That wasn't anything new to me, just to him. He'd learn.

My men inspected our own vehicles for bombs because maybe I underestimated Tristian West after all. That would've been a gamble, but a good move.

It turns out, I had.

There were no bombs, but they found a tracking device.

CHAPTER FOURTEEN

BLAKE

Someone was in my room.

I woke up with a gasp because *someone was in my room.* They shifted. I could see their silhouette, sitting in the chair that was in the corner of my room and then, Jesus Christ. I automatically relaxed because I knew that silhouette.

But wait.

I jerked upright.

"What are you doing here?" I hissed, my hands fisted in my blanket because I had half a mind to jump out and lunge for him and the other half was remembering I was only in my sleeping top and underwear. My very skimpy top. My *lacy* underwear. Underwear that was sexy and I didn't think anyone would see because I hadn't bought these for someone else to see, not yet anyways. These were just for me. Now I was dying a little of embarrassment because Creighton was in my room at four in the morning. And I was dying from something else, squirming in bed, but I grabbed tight to my blanket and ignored how I suddenly felt flushed.

He didn't respond, but I knew it was him.

"Creighton?"

He still didn't respond. I grew concerned. My voice dropped to a whisper, and I pushed my blanket aside, only focused on him. "Eight?"

He jerked alive at the nickname, but he didn't move. "They aren't like me."

I frowned. "What? Who's not like you?"

"I thought they'd be like me. That's what the rumors say. How cruel they are, but they aren't like me. They're like you."

I still didn't know who he was talking about. "Eight?" I was going to regret this. "Come here."

He only lifted his head up.

I patted the bed. "Come here."

He stared at me, and I felt that stare. It was long, intense, but somehow I didn't feel he was even seeing me.

Creighton was lost, and that was never a good thing on any day, but Eight being lost just hurt my heart. He always knew what to do, where to go, who to maim. I didn't like this version being in my room, more so because it was confusing in *uncomfortable* ways too. "Please."

The please did it.

He got up from the chair, and the bed depressed under his weight. He kneeled, but waited because I knew the routine. And I was heating up for those same other reasons because us being in bed together used to not be so uncommon, but that'd been when I was a kid. When I was sick and he stayed to watch animal shows with me. Or if I had a nightmare and he was just there, even when he wasn't in the house anymore, but somehow he always knew when I woke up silently screaming with tears soaking my face. He was there, and he would sleep next to me, and it worked. I calmed. His presence and the weight of his body beside me, touching my shoulder, and I fell back asleep.

Grief rose up in me, mixing with this new inferno inside of me as well. I'd missed this time with him. These moments.

But this was different. Time changed us, changed this.

I was suddenly *very aware* of our close proximity and how muscled, but lean, Creighton was. The power of his body, every movement he made. And his smell. God. I'd missed it. A manly pine tree musk. There were times when I'd wear his hoodie to school and I'd bury my head into his sweatshirt, breathing deep. His smell settled me.

But the routine tonight was making me aware of him, aware of how his gaze lingered on my underwear, and gah. I was hot all over. I liked my beds against the corner so I scooted up against the wall. He was on the side of the bed closest to the door. We lay on our sides, sharing a pillow.

"You're attracted to me."

"Creighton!" I was dying. I covered my face with my hands and wanted to shrink farther down in bed.

He said that so clinically, as if he wasn't affected either. Wait. Was he?

I lowered one of my hands and peeked at him. He was still watching me, that ever-present emptiness in his eyes, but he was tracing over my face.

I wished he was normal. I knew he wasn't, but in that moment, I wished I could see a little something.

"I don't want to talk about that."

He said, "You're twenty-two. Long past the age of consent now."

I was back to squirming. "Creighton, please. I'm still . . ." I grasped at something out of desperation. I was still mad at him, but all of that was pushed to the back of my head because he was right. I was attracted to him. Fuck. Fuck! What did I do with this now? I had enough on my plate dealing with Creighton. I did not need to add sexual chemistry, and yep. So squirming. "Can we—uh—why are you here?"

He was silent beside me, and I could feel him studying the side of my face. "You don't want to talk about this attraction you have for me? Your body is getting hot, and your pulse is spiking. It's hard to ignore this. I think we should talk about this."

"Please stop," I hissed, back to covering my face with both of my hands again. "I'm fucked in the head enough as it with you and our deal and ugh, everything that's you. You're hot. You know you are. It's late at night. I'm straight, and yeah. This is a normal reaction. Don't get a big head about this. I'd feel this way about any—" I squeaked because suddenly my hands were ripped away from my face and he was looming over me.

"You don't talk about another man when I'm in bed with you," he growled. Savagely.

Oh, god. That was even hotter.

I whispered, "Creighton."

He continued to stare down at me, his eyes now flaring and growing dark. Molten.

Holy shit. Holy shit! He wanted me too.

No way. I mean . . .

Did he?

I began panting, my chest heaving, and that inferno spread through my entire body because he was letting himself look at me. All of me. From my eyes, and he moved the blanket aside so he could see the rest of me, my breasts, my waist, where my underwear rested on my hips, my thighs, all the way down to my toes and back up again. He shifted so he was holding himself up next to me and he grazed the side of my thigh with his hand.

Tingles trailed his touch, and I sucked in my breath.

I could see him, but it wasn't enough. I needed to see his face, see if he really was reacting the same as me. My hand trembled as I reached for the lamp above my bed.

He caught my hand, knowing what I was doing. "Don't."

"I want to see you."

"I don't want you to see me right now."

That hurt. "Oh."

"Not because I don't want you—"

Seriously! Creighton.

He continued, "That's not why I'm here tonight. I . . ."

He drew in an audible breath and lowered himself all the way to my side. He reached out, his hand rested on my stomach. He moved a finger, smoothing back and forth, and more tingles shot through me.

But this touch was comforting as well as exciting. I wasn't sure what he intended here, but okay. I meant what I said. My mind was truly too fucked to deal with this new development between us, and gah. I was fully admitting to this development. That was insane. Attraction. Me and Creighton.

What had I done in a past life to have all this craziness with someone like Creighton? I must've been a jail attendant for babies or something. But I laced our fingers and held our hands to my chest.

I reminded myself that he sought me out. He came here. That meant he needed me, and Creighton wouldn't have done this to hit on me. No. He'd do that when I was awake and could face him squarely on my own two feet. He'd probably make it some form of challenge to me, because he loved that sort of shit.

So messed up.

But, man. I cherished moments like this from the past. I shoved that away. I focused on the here and now, and right now, I didn't have someone scary and dangerous in my bed. The outside world didn't exist beyond this room. It was just the two of us.

I traced his fingers with my own, and asked, "What happened tonight?"

"They love like you do."

"Who? What?"

He sounded disappointed and perplexed at the same time. Who . . .

It hit me. Was he talking about the heads of the West and Walden families?

But why?

I sucked in some oxygen, held it, repressing all the other bad feelings that swept into my body when we referenced that world. No. I didn't want those feelings or thoughts in here. Not right now. Not this time.

I'd missed Eight. Weird attraction aside, I missed this version of him.

The image of him touching my neck flashed in my mind, how I could arch my neck for him. To give him better access—*Really, Blake?* I chided myself.

Creighton came to me. He was never vulnerable. He could be raw, but I hadn't realized how hungry I'd been for him.

I really had missed him.

I kept tracing his hand.

I shouldn't love that he was here. I knew I shouldn't, because of what he could do in my name. My heart pounded.

I didn't want him to leave.

I stifled a groan, lying here next to him because he wasn't even only in my heart. He was behind my heart. He got in there at some point when I was eight years old, and I don't think he'd ever left. This connection—whatever it was, I wouldn't have it with anyone else.

I didn't know if that was a beautiful thing or just bleak.

"Were you hoping they'd be like you?" Did that mean he was lonely somehow? Looking for others like him? But that wasn't how it worked for someone who had his affliction. Was it? Maybe it wasn't so black and white? Perhaps there was some gray in someone like Creighton.

I began tracing my fingers over the back of his hand.

"No." He sighed. "I just thought maybe they were."

"No one's like you, Eight. No one understands you."

"You do."

I lifted my head. He was watching me intently. "You understand me."

I don't think I did understand him.

I looked away because I didn't want to see if he was looking at me with those dead eyes or if they had an emotion, because sometimes, when he looked at me, there *was* emotion there. I thought I saw it tonight, but maybe I hadn't. Maybe I just saw what I wanted to see, and that's why he stopped me from turning the light on.

That was probably it.

I could think and think and think to infinity and still never have him figured out, so tonight, I wasn't going to do anything. I wasn't going to get mad he was here. I wasn't going to be embarrassed either. Scooting down in the bed, I rolled to the other side.

He didn't say anything more, one of his hands resting on my hip as he settled in behind me.

I didn't let go of his other hand. I should've, but I didn't.

CHAPTER FIFTEEN

BLAKE

He was gone in the morning.

He came back the next night, crawled in with me.

We didn't talk. I rolled toward him, and he held my hand. I fell back asleep, and he was gone in the morning again. The third night was a repeat.

It kept happening.

I didn't want it to stop happening.

CHAPTER SIXTEEN

BLAKE

The train screeched to a halt, and when the doors opened, not many got off. Instead, a whole slew of guys got on.

Over the years, I'd begun to recognize Creighton's army. It wasn't all guys. Girls joined as well, but he tended to use the girls for different jobs. They were recruiters. Scouters too. Girls got overlooked, so Creighton used that, utilized them in areas where he wanted them to be overlooked. Guys, though, they looked like these guys. Youngish. Always dressed to blend in. Some wore jeans. Some wore joggers. Sweatshirts. Baseball caps. They could be teenagers or thirty-year-olds. They took care of themselves. Kept themselves fit. Clean shaven (generally), and their hair was cut with a fade on the side and a little extra on the top.

Nothing to stick out.

Except their eyes.

If they came to Creighton without hardened eyes, they got them soon after. Then again, the type of guy or girl who would sign up to work for Creighton generally already had those eyes. Most came from the street.

Like Creighton. Like me.

I counted twelve that got on. They were Creighton's. I knew without a doubt, and just before the doors were going to close, the man himself stepped onto the train.

Conversations ceased. Eyes went to him.

It's just how he affected people, his own army and strangers. They knew he was *someone*, and I was remembering so many other times when I was on the bus or on a train and I'd be alone. Creighton would show up. He'd watch me as I would watch him. We'd share a smile because no one else mattered except the two of us. He only had eyes for me, and though I would try to fight against his pull, I would only have eyes for him too.

He'd sit beside me, sliding into my seat, and turn to me. The world would be boxed out. It was more effective on the bus, but it had the same effect today. He touched the pole beside my seat and indicated the spot beside me. An eyebrow quirked up.

I slid over, making room.

He pivoted around the pole and slid right in, all smooth.

I drawled, "Nice."

He smirked. "I've had practice."

I laughed.

He smiled.

And my heart fluttered.

I ordered it to stop and tried to scowl. "What are you doing here?"

He made a show of looking back and forth, leaning around, and looking again. "Wait. Is this not the subway? My bad. I must be using the bus. I didn't intend to use the bus. I'll have to get off at the next stop."

"Stop." I caught his hand, ignored how it jump-started my pulse. "You know what I mean."

"Yeah. Stop. The next stop."

I groaned, trying to hold back a grin. "Creight. You're being ridiculous."

He chuckled, getting serious, and nudged his shoulder to mine. "Made you smile."

I smoothed out that grin. "Barely."

He raised an eyebrow. "Oh? Is that a challenge?"

"You'rc bcing cxtra today."

"Well, you know. We're friends again."

"We're not."

"You're holding my hand."

I looked down at it and let his hand go. "Doesn't mean anything."

He moved in closer, his head bending farther to me. "I've been crawling into you—"

"Fine. Shut up. Friends. We're . . . friendly. We're friendly." I groaned. "I don't think I'd classify us as friends. Family. Mortal enemies. Either would work better than friends."

A genuine chuckle slipped free from him. "Where are you heading?"

I shook my head. "Why do you do that? Pretend you don't know?"

"Because you like the option of giving me the answer. We can switch roles. You can ask me where I'm going." He pretended to tsk me. "Always about you. Jeez, Blake. Why don't you ask me how my day is going for a change?"

I bit down on my lip, trying to swallow the grin. "Fine. Where are you going today? You and your friends? Church? Going to volunteer at a soup kitchen?"

He pretended to scowl. "Now you're just making fun of me."

"You're right. You're more likely going to rob the soup kitchen."

He barked out a laugh, and I knew that laugh would've gotten anyone's attention that wasn't already turned our way. It was commonplace growing up with Creighton Lane beside me. Stalking me. Prowling behind me. Leading the charge. Or doing what he was doing now, laughing with me and acting like the world didn't exist outside of us.

I used to love days like this.

Until I remembered the bodies. My smile faded.

"I'd never rob a soup kitchen." He saw the myriad of thoughts cross my face. "You'd never have that. A saint would tell you what I'd be up to. Before I'd even be able to leave with whatever little money they had, you'd be marching your way in and ordering me to put it back and then you'd make me write a check for triple what I tried to steal." He lifted up an eyebrow. "That sound right?"

"It did except for the saint part. If I could talk to saints, I would've told my social worker to skip Miss Marcie's house." I couldn't help myself, knowing that was meant to hurt him.

Did it? I watched him for any reaction.

He got quiet, and the small curve from his lip slowly lowered down. Those blank eyes stayed blank.

He murmured, "Point to Blake."

That stung, a little, so I looked away. "I'm going to the foster center."

"Mind if I walk you there?"

Some of the sting lifted. He sounded genuine, and I found myself nodding. "Sure."

He slid down in the seat, getting comfortable, and reached for my hand. My chest lifted and held still. My heart flipped over, and for a moment, one moment, I blinked back tears because I wanted this with him. A train ride. Him to be a regular guy. I was just a girl, traveling with her boyfriend, and he was holding her hand because we got to indulge in this very normal public display of affection.

I blinked away a tear and pushed aside that nagging voice to remember why I ran from him in the beginning because he was there, still behind my heart, and my fight was fading more and more.

I just didn't want to hear it.

Lassiter found me when I was working a shift at Octavia that night. He slid onto a barstool, saying, "You spent the day with him."

"Not technically, but a part of it. Yeah." I frowned at him, wondering why he was here and why he was bringing this up.

My coworker began to go to him. I waved him off. "I got him. I know the little shit."

Lassiter grinned, but it fell away right away. He wasn't a drinker, so I filled a glass of water and put it in front of him.

He didn't reach for it. "He called you his woman the other week."

His woman?

I shrugged, not wanting to focus on what he said. "Everyone knows I'm one of his."

He leaned farther over the counter, crossing his arms. "Not his woman, not like that. That's new. That changes things. Is that what's going on?"

I frowned, unease skittering down my spine. "I came here to get away from him. You know that . . ." Movement caught my eye. Spence was heading our way, watching us. Or, correction, watching Lassiter.

Lassiter noticed him and sat back on his stool. "He's here for me."

I frowned. "He's my boss."

Lassiter shook his head. "He's here for me."

As Spence closed the distance, coming to the end of my counter with two security guards behind him, Lassiter spoke first, almost blandly. "I have no weapons on me. Your bouncers know this."

"You're distracting my employee."

My skin grew hot because he was right. I should be working, not talking about Creighton. Moving aside, I began filling drink orders. We got hit by a rush, and by the time I got some semblance of a break, I glanced around, but Lassiter was gone.

I didn't think anything of it. I'd talk to him later or more than likely, Lassiter would find me to follow up on whatever he was concerned about.

Later, I was leaving the locker room at the end of my shift and called out to the rest still inside, "Have a good night, everyone."

"Bye, Blake!"

"See you."

"Have a good one." A few called back.

I enjoyed working here so far. The boss had remained away except for tonight. My coworkers were all friendly. For knowing the place had Mafia ties, it didn't seem like it. The whole nightclub felt like any other nightclub. It was run deftly. A good place. I always felt safe, knowing their security was active and involved.

Yeah. I liked it here. I was glad I'd applied.

I pushed out the back door. Creighton's watcher would be waiting for me in the front, where he'd trail me to the subway and take a seat a few back from me. It was our routine, so I went through the alley that would take me to the street.

Hearing voices that came from the alley, I didn't think anything of it. They were low, almost hushed. No one was stressed or upset. There was no reason to set off an alarm with me, but I'd only gotten three steps before I saw who was speaking.

Two men were talking, tucked against the wall of the building across from Octavia. One had his back to the alley, but I could see him from the side. The other was facing the alley, his face in shadow. There was a door behind him.

Both were businessmen. Both wore custom tailored suits, reeking of money.

I didn't think much of the exchange until one guy reached inside his suit jacket, lifting it to reveal a gun that was holstered against his hip.

I still didn't think anything of it. Guns were common in my life, but then the guy pulled out a thick envelope and handed it to the man, who took it, tucking it away instantly. He turned to leave, saw me, and stopped short. *"Fuck."*

I didn't know this guy, but he was looking at me as if I were an inconvenience to him. Like a gnat.

I started to say something, probably a retort because it was late at night and I didn't care one iota who this guy was, but the other one, the guy who'd handed him the envelope, stepped out from the shadows.

I stopped in my tracks, swallowing thickly. Him, I did know. Though I wished I didn't.

It was Ashton Walden, and his gaze was pinned right smack on me. Yep. He fully knew who I was too.

The bottom of my gut fell to my feet. This was so very *very* not good.

Walden's mouth flattened, and he took a step toward me. "Well, Miss Green. You are not supposed to be here. Of all the little girls to walk down this alley on this night, at this hour, it had to be you. You must have some bad luck."

I almost snorted because he had no idea.

A scrape sounded from behind me, and before I could respond or react, something was shoved over my head. The world went dark. I felt a prick as a needle was jammed into my neck.

I gasped, my legs shifting into a fighting stance automatically. But I was too late because the world began to tilt, and I was going down.

Strong arms caught me right as I realized what was happening.

Shit. I'm being kidnapped.

CHAPTER SEVENTEEN

BLAKE

The covering was whisked away, and there, as my hands had been tied behind my chair, two fuckheads stared down at me. Tristian West and Ashton Walden.

I growled because no fucking way was this happening to me again. No way in hell. I began working, trying to get one of my hands free right away. I probably should've been scared. I knew this, but right now, I was *pissed.*

These two assholes.

Walden's face was bruised. I got a better look at him since there was light in the room, and he looked as if he went three rounds with a heavyweight champion, and lost. West wasn't too much better. Both were heavily bruised, and both were scowling at me. They were livid and looking at me as if I was the cause of whoever pissed in their cereal.

Wait . . .

Oh. Oh, man.

I got it then, and I probably should have gotten it before then, but I was probably partly to blame for whatever had pissed them off.

Creighton had been fucking with these guys.

I drawled, my hands still working on the knots behind my chair, "Am I to take from the silent reception that I'm the recipient of you fucking Creighton back? Is that why I'm tied up to a chair?"

I sounded frustrated and on edge, but my insides were more than torpedoing in somersaults, blasting and bouncing all around me. I couldn't let them see that side of me. More so because I didn't want to give them the satisfaction that yes, a part of me was scared here. A small part.

Okay. Maybe more than a small part, but I wasn't going to indulge. I might do that later, when I was in the shower, and no one could hear me crying. Yes. I'd plan a sobfest date with myself, but later. When I was safe and free.

Ugh. I was so mad that I was in this situation.

Think, think, think, Blake!

I felt the slack on one of my hands. *Yes.* The rope fell loose around one of my hands, but I caught it so the rope didn't fall to the ground. I needed more time. A few more minutes as I began working on the other hand, and this one would go faster. Scanning the room, I began looking. There was always an escape route. A wall I could tear through, a window I could slip out, a side of a building I could climb down. There was always a way. I just had to get free first, then find the escape route.

There were no windows.

There was a table. Two doors. A panel in the ceiling. A camera pointed my way. Plastic sheets had been spread out underneath me, and I wasn't going to ponder on their existence.

"I'm feeling a weird sense of déjà vu, like I've done this before," I bit out, sarcastically.

Walden was the one who stepped closer. His eyes were hard. His face was harder, like granite. My eyes widened. He was more furious than I was. What *had* Creighton done?

I felt the slack behind me. The second hand was almost free.

"You've not been kidnapped, Miss Green," the West guy spoke up. Hazel eyes. Wide cheekbones. He was rugged, but handsome at the same time. I was placing him at six four, maybe two hundred and fifteen pounds? That was a guess. His hair was slicked back. He was a lot more put together than the other one. He shot Walden a look, who shuddered when he saw it and visibly shook before he stepped back. Okay then.

West was the spokesman.

"Really?" I said. "My tied-up hands say otherwise."

"You're here because we have questions."

I glanced between the two. "So this has nothing to do with the other guy I saw in the alley?"

West pinned his Walden with a glare. "What is she talking about?"

Walden shrugged. "I don't fucking know. She's a liar, like her boyfriend."

"Boyfriend?" I ignored the kick in my chest.

"Ashton."

He glared at West, his jaw clenching. "It doesn't matter and not in front of her."

"Fine." West indicated the door. "Hallway. Now." He stalked off.

Walden glared at me again.

West shoved open the door and barked, "That wasn't a request." He let the door slam shut behind him.

I held Walden's scowl. "I think your boyfriend wants to have a talk. You've been a bad boy, Ashton Walden."

"Keep fucking talking. Your boyfriend enjoyed torturing me. What do you think he'd do if I returned the favor on you?"

I shook my head, seething inside. "You don't get it."

His eyes narrowed to slits. "What don't I get?"

I leaned my head forward, as far as I could, and said softly, taunting, "I am not like your women. You won't have to worry what Eight will do to you. I'll handle you myself. I don't have the same moral code as your best friend's cop." I saw the surprise in his eyes and laughed, an edge to my tone. "Yeah. I did my research, too, dumbass. When you find yourself getting kidnapped one time, you educate yourself on who might do it a *second fucking time*. Thanks for that, dickhead. But I know your woman, too, and I don't need to wait for my switch to get flipped like she does. I'll come out swinging with a gun in one hand and a machete in the other. *That's* who *I am*."

The door opened behind him. A sharp command, "Ashton!"

He was quiet until, "Eight?"

I'd messed up. I hadn't meant to let that slip, but I continued to glare back at him. "I like machetes. I have a favorite back in my room."

He scoffed before he left.

I went back to finishing the last knot on my left hand. One last tug and the rope fell away. I didn't need to catch this one. I let it fall because it wouldn't matter. By the time they'd come back, I wouldn't be here.

I sprang.

First course of action, I took the chair to the camera, climbed up, and angled the camera so it was looking away. After that, I tried the second door. It was locked. That wasn't surprising, so I took the chair under the panel, removed it, and began to climb up. Once I was high enough, I nudged the chair aside so it wouldn't be so obvious I had climbed up. I didn't want it to fall and make a loud crash, but there was only so much control I had over that. Some things were more important, like getting out of there. When it fell backward on the plastic sheets, which cushioned the fall so it was only a muted *thunk*, I said a quick thank-you to the universe.

I put the vent back in place behind me and began crawling. The venting system was big enough for me and sturdy enough so I wasn't too worried when I heard shouting behind me.

They knew I was gone.

Turning the camera would give me some leeway. I was hoping they'd assume I had gotten through the second door and relocked it before concluding I was in the vents. Yeah, going through the venting system was almost commonplace in movies, but not in real life.

Real life, they'd think about windows and doors first.

I was hoping that would give me enough time to find an exit door for wherever they'd brought me, so I stayed calm and I kept crawling.

As I did, fury and tears began to build up in me.

This was Creighton's fault.

Again.

I was hearing their shouting underneath me, behind me, ahead of me. They were all over, and here I was, moving my way through whatever type of building this was, and I was *livid.*

A tear from frustration slipped down my face, but I wiped it away and kept going because that's what I did. I kept going. Like always. My throat closed up as emotions were beginning to pile on top of each other.

West and Walden. They weren't happy with each other right now, but their closeness was there. It was so thick that it was visible. They were family to each other.

I didn't understand normal families. They were an anomaly to me. Two months ago I was kidnapped, which set off the chain of events that led me back here, but through that situation, I met a family. A real family. Aunts. A mom. Cousins. They loved each other. I could see it in front of my eyes. It was palpable.

I hadn't understood it then.

I'd heard Palma on the phone with her sisters one night. She *wanted* to talk to them. She was laughing and giggling. They talked for over an hour.

That perplexed me.

It was the same with Marshall. I heard him on the phone with his mom the other morning. He laughed at something she said, and I froze. I hadn't meant to eavesdrop and overhear, but he was in the living room, and I was coming down the stairs to go to the kitchen.

I hadn't been able to leave. My legs ceased to work, so I sat on the stairs, listening to his entire conversation.

I couldn't say what they talked about, but I'd been rocked by the love I heard in his voice. It was real and authentic. In his mom's, too, as I could hear her speaking through his phone. She *adored* him.

Those were the types of relationships that I started to think didn't exist. They were the unicorn relationships.

No one wanted me. It's why I was in the foster system. I was just a foster kid.

Except Creighton wanted me. We were family. Him. Levi. Lassiter. Me. We were fucked up. And right now I was back to contemplating potentially gutting Creighton, but he was family. I loved all of them. So yes, I did have a family, but we weren't normal. We were still so very messed up.

And I was in this mess because of those family members.

Dammit, Creighton.

I kept crawling through the vents, and I was a shaking mess.

Anger. I'd focus on anger because it burned the most right now. It was the easiest to process, and I let it overwhelm me until every inch of me was pulsating fury. I was a literal fucking phoenix crawling through these stupid vents.

Creighton was like an infection.

If I cut him off, would this type of life go away? Would I stop being kidnapped? Being tied up. Being drugged. A girl could only be threatened so many times before she actually picked up a machete. I was nearing that point.

I was done.

So. Done.

Tears were burning my eyes by the time I found an exit to this building. I got to it, and paused, my chest hurting. I had no idea where my phone was. My wallet. My keys. I groaned quietly, pressing my mouth into my arm as more tears slipped free.

I rested my head against the paneling behind me and drew in gaping breaths. My chest was still hurting. A hollow ache was there, and it was so empty. It felt like there was no end to how empty I was feeling.

Life sucked sometimes.

Wiping my face on my shoulder, I shifted to my butt and lifted up a foot. With one heave, I kicked out the last panel. Looking out the side of the building, I gulped. Whoa. I was probably up on the seventh floor, and that was still a long way down. But there were grooves on the side of the building. They looked big enough to get my feet in them, so I needed a minute to collect myself. Calm my shit, and focus. All was not lost. I'd deal with the toxin in my life, but right now, I needed to keep my head about myself or I'd slip and fall.

I reached down, testing to make sure my fingers could wrap around them. They could! The grooves went all the way down, so okay then.

I'd done this before. It was an old hat.

I just needed to take my time. *Keep* my head clear. And climb.

Could a person survive a seven-story fall?

I was about to find out.

CHAPTER EIGHTEEN

BLAKE

I got to the street after climbing down, and realized they'd only taken me to the building next door. Honestly. I was more insulted by their lack of effort. Or maybe they thought the genius was in the simplicity, but yeah. Next door to where I worked was where I'd been taken.

I decided to be insulted, but the benefit was that I knew where I was.

I didn't care what happened to my watcher. He must still be alive because Creighton didn't seem to know that I'd been taken. I could see that as I was in the shadows now, and I was the one watching him this time.

No phone. No wallet. No keys. I walked to Creighton's club, and a part of me dared anyone to try and mess with me on the way. No one dared, sadly. I could've used an outlet for some of my fury. Alas, I was able to get there safely.

So here I was. In the shadows of his nightclub. Nightclub 1.

Watching him now as he moved around the edge of this nightclub, one that was catering to some very wealthy and elite clientele, the kind that liked the after-hours of the after-hours type of club, I enjoyed this role reversal.

He knew I was here. I could tell when he paused, his head inclined as if he were trying to suss out where I was, but I wasn't letting him. I kept to the shadows, noting where his cameras would be and staying in their blind spots. He didn't know where I was, not my exact location.

Good.

I wanted him on edge. Uneasy.

I wanted to have the power. To be in the know. Where he didn't know.

I wanted there to be an imbalance between us.

I was breathing hard. My pulse was pounding. I was surprised others couldn't hear it over the music blaring.

How was he getting away with running this club? At this hour? I almost snorted at myself because of course, he'd already have cops on his payroll. Duh. Creighton moved so fucking fast when he made the decision to take over an area.

I wanted to run from him. I wanted to hurt him, but damn him. Creighton knew I would want to run again. It's why we made the deal we had. He stayed out of my life, kept a watcher on me, and I wouldn't run. But that agreement was over because he tricked me into violating it.

This motherfucker.

I should run again, just to make him feel *something.*

Creighton was walking away from the last table of businessmen. He took a few steps, stopped, and seemed to rotate exactly to the direction where I was standing.

He probably had the same inside compass. A Blake compass, like I had a Creighton compass.

Right now I hated it like I hated him.

He was facing me, but I was still in the shadows. He frowned, just slightly, and moved forward. A step. Two. He was getting closer.

Jesus. He really did have a compass.

I waited, my breath held and frozen. My heart began thumping in my chest. The anger in me was a volcano, and it was close to erupting. I needed to make a choice. Right now.

Leave, make him hurt, or . . .

It was too late.

I was rooted in place as he stepped into the same shadow that was hiding me. I knew the second his gaze lit onto me. A wave of awareness thundered down on me. Dammit. I sucked in oxygen, feeling as if I were breathing the wind that would rush off of an ocean wave crashing onto the beach. It was big. It was powerful. It was all-consuming, and it was threatening to completely knock me off my axis.

Goddamn. I just described Creighton. He was a storm sent by Mother Nature herself to knock out everyone and everything in his path. Except me. Or *especially* me because I was knocked over, just from how he was looking at me right now.

His eyes darkened.

He grew eerily still, and I knew it was because he was reading me.

He didn't say anything. I was seething at him, wanting him to say something. Anything. Because then I'd react. I didn't know what I would do, but it'd be something.

Anything.

I had to do something.

I couldn't keep on this way.

I closed my eyes. Sucking in some air again, because *fuck* him. One look and he knew. I didn't know what he knew, but he just knew. He knew more than I knew myself. He understood me more than I understood myself. Why him? Why did he get this power over me? No one else could read me as seamlessly as he could. Another freak of nature power he'd been gifted.

A tear trickled down my cheek.

He tracked it, his eyes growing fierce.

He'd just been shaking hands and schmoozing with businessmen, and I could see the cut of their three-piece custom suits. They were powerful men. They were *someone* in this city. And they were here, shaking hands with Creighton, and enjoying themselves in his establishment. I don't know what they saw when they looked at him. He was in a suit of his own. He looked so good. He rarely wore them.

I'd seen him in everything by now.

Jeans and a hoodie. A ball cap. That was my favorite look.

Jeans and a leather jacket.

A business suit.

Shirtless and bruised and bloody.

Shirtless and in gray sweats. Barefoot. Like what he wears when he crawls into bed with me.

I suppressed a shiver.

He was gorgeous in every way, and someone that didn't look altogether human. Maybe it was his dead eyes? Or the mix of how pretty he looked? The extreme cut of his jawline? If I brought him home with me, Palma would die from how hot he was. Marshall would die because he'd know he couldn't compete against Creighton. And Heath would just die, because Heath knew who Creighton really was.

Creighton wouldn't take the risk that he'd make me feel uncomfortable in my home. He wouldn't care that it'd been Heath's home longer. That he knew Palma and Marshall much longer than me. He'd just care how Heath's reaction would make me feel, and he'd do something about it.

I didn't know I had continued crying until he closed the distance and his finger touched my cheek, soaking up another tear. He held it away. "Who do I kill for this?"

I reached out, without thinking, and took hold of his wrist, keeping his hand in front of me. My finger moved over his vein. "You'd have to kill yourself." I waited, feeling his pulse spike as my answer registered.

He let out a soft sigh, closing the distance between us until his chest was softly grazing against mine. He brought his finger to his mouth, and he tasted my tear, his tongue sucking on his finger.

I was still a mess inside, churning and twisting and *raw*, but it hit me with the force of an F5 tornado. This desire for him.

I wanted him.

Now.

My hand stayed wrapped around his, and it brushed against his jawline, feeling the roughness that he hadn't shaved away that day, but I didn't pull away. I didn't want to.

Everything was twisting inside of me.

I hated him.

But fuck him, I couldn't kill him.

I couldn't walk away from him.

What did I do?

He was torturing me.

I was so tired of the destruction that came along with Creighton.

I was doomed.

"Blake," he whispered.

I growled, savagely, and my hand grabbed hold of his shirt. I fisted it.

I needed . . .

I licked my lips.

What did I need?

A voice in the back of my head told me to make him pay.

His eyes were glittering. He was smiling. And staring at me, still so close. He wiped away the rest of my tears. He leaned down, his forehead resting to mine, and he breathed out, "You have such hate in your eyes. What is wrong?"

I lifted my other hand, circling his wrist as he was holding my other wrist in place. "You. You're what's wrong." And because I was suddenly burning up, I shoved his hand away from me, tearing my other wrist out of his hold. When he fell back, I moved to the side, slipping out. "Stay *the fuck* away from me."

CHAPTER NINETEEN

CREIGHTON

They took her tonight.

My inside guy said he helped to run interference when she escaped. Said he tied her ropes looser than he normally would have, but it wouldn't have mattered with Blake. She would've gotten out of them. She was a fighter and a survivor. It's what she did, so yes, she would've been fine no matter how tight he made them. But he helped stall West and Walden from finding her.

I failed her. I hadn't stopped them from taking her, and I hadn't gotten there in time.

Blake never needed me, not for her physical safety. It was just my pleasure.

She saved herself. Over and over again. I just wished she'd realize that she didn't need to. She could do anything. She could be anyone. She could get anyone to love her. I just hoped she never did, because if she truly decided to leave me . . . I didn't think the world would survive my desolation. Except tonight, she came to me.

To. Me.

My inside man sent me the video of her climbing down the side of Walden's building. She was truly magnificent.

She told me to stay away, but I couldn't. She didn't understand. She'd been taken too many times from me, and tonight the hunger was on her face. She knew it was there, and for a moment, I thought she would act on it. She looked ready for it. Ready for me. Finally. Maybe she did mean it when she told me to stay away, but . . . I couldn't, not now that I saw she was ready to act on that ache on her face.

It was a different ball game now. New rules. New stakes. New opponents.

I eased myself down into the chair in her bedroom's corner and sat back to watch her sleep.

Sleep, Blake. Tomorrow everything changes.

She wasn't alone in this new battle because I knew things were changing for me too.

I was changing.

CHAPTER TWENTY

BLAKE

I woke up, and in a second everything came back to me. I gasped and rolled over, then deflated.

Creighton wasn't here. I thought . . . I woke during the night and thought he was here. It should've enraged me. I just slept better.

I groaned, falling onto my back, and raised my hands. Balling them into fists, I pressed them to my forehead.

What was I doing?

I told him to stay away, but fuck. Fuck! How he looked at me and how I looked at him.

I wanted him.

I'd felt this need for him the first night he came to me, and it'd only gotten worse each night after except fear accompanied it. Fear because good Lord, that would change everything. Was I ready?

Except last night, I hadn't cared. I'd been two seconds away from doing something about it. Yanking him to me. Pressing my mouth to his. I'd had such a physical and visceral reaction to him. It took *everything* out of me not to lunge at him, and he saw it. I know he saw my reaction.

Creighton and me.

I blew out a breath.

That was nuts.

And yet I couldn't deny the ache that was building in me again at merely remembering last night.

I was lying here, more upset about my lack of control with Creighton than I was about being kidnapped. Fucking. Kidnapped.

Again.

A soft sigh left me.

I'd been so furious last night, blaming Creighton, which was valid. Everything was his fault, but dammit . . . My head was swimming.

Okay. New plan.

Day by day. I'd figure things out as I went and hopefully find a solution so I could . . . I didn't know, but my body was heating up and calling myself a liar. I was trying to delude myself.

Was that what I was doing?

I got up out of bed, heading for the door, when a pile of things on my desk caught my eye.

My heart stilled, and my mouth opened an inch.

A phone. A wallet. A set of keys. All mine. Like, not new items. They were mine from when I'd been taken last night.

I was *staggered.*

Creighton left them.

That meant he'd been given them.

He knew. Had he known the whole time? Before he saw me? After he saw me?

I snatched my phone up and googled for the crime report for the area where I worked. When it came up and I scrolled through it, tension eased in my chest. No shootings. No bodies found. No fires.

Creighton hadn't retaliated yet, but he would.

God help us when that happened.

I sent a quick text to Spence.

Me: Effective immediately, I quit.

CHAPTER TWENTY-ONE

CREIGHTON

I was in an SUV, staring outside at an older woman leaving a house with a younger man. He was younger than her, but he had a hardened look to him. Black curly hair. Face hadn't been shaved in a couple days. He had a thick upper lip. Very intense dark eyes. His face was a little boxy, too boxy to be considered handsome, but there was a ruggedness to him. Some women and men would like that hard look on him. He had her purse in one hand and his arm up so she could use it for balance.

I knew this woman.

The man was a surprise, and I wondered why he hadn't initially been included in my first round of reports on my enemies. This was Tristian West's mother-in-law. Judging by the same chin, similar bone structure, and the fact they both walked the same, this was the brother-in-law as well. "This is Isaac Montell?" I asked Lassiter, who was watching them with me.

He glanced my way, his eyebrows pinching together. His Viking braids were hidden underneath a black ball cap. I couldn't read him either because his sunglasses hid his eyes. "You're more on edge than normal. Something happen with Blake?"

I pressed my mouth together. "Why would you automatically assume there's something wrong with Blake?"

He laughed. "Are you serious? She's the only thing that affects you."

Thing.

I wasn't amused. "She's not a thing, Last."

He got quiet. "You know what I mean. What happened?"

I ignored that and said, "Show me the other two." I gestured to the file on his lap.

He handed over images of two more individuals.

I knew these faces. I'd seen them before, and I shuffled through the information in my head until I placed their names to the images. Pialto Rodriguez and Sophie Iriston. They were employees and considered "like family" to Ashton Walden's woman.

Good. I liked these prospects.

I gave the file back to him and nodded toward West's mother- and brother-in-law. "Take them."

His head jerked up, taking me in for a moment before looking back at the window. Jess West's mother and brother were now getting inside a car. Two other men were tailing them at a decent distance. Security.

We could always get around security. I had enough men to literally swarm the guards, stalling them, and the mother and brother could get snatched up.

"Who?" Lassiter clipped out.

I nodded toward the car that was now passing us. Both occupants didn't look at us. They were oblivious. Their guards followed in a second car, and they saw us, both of their eyes widening.

Lassiter cursed but pulled out from our parking spot. He gunned the engine as three more guards came running from the house. They jumped into two trucks.

I had my gun out, but I didn't think it was needed. I held it against my leg, ready. Just in case.

Lassiter was on his phone, relaying information to my tech team, who would then find my closest men. They would intersect anyone coming after us. We traveled three more blocks. The two trucks were getting closer, but more vehicles suddenly appeared. They swerved to get between us and them. Those were my men. Lassiter raised a hand to one of the drivers.

Three more blocks and West's men turned back. We were too close to my territory.

We went to Nightclub 2.

Levi was at the back door. When he saw us, he broke into a wide grin. Shoving his hands into his pockets, he began heading our way.

"I'll organize the kidnapping," Lassiter said, reaching for his door handle.

"I want all of them."

His hand pulled back. "All of them?" His face went slack. "Easter's two close friends and Jess Montell's mother and brother?"

"I believe she goes by Jess West now."

"I don't care. All of them? An older woman who's fighting cancer and two coworkers."

"They took Blake." I was in his face in a second.

He went still. "They took Blake?"

"The fun is over. Blake's fine, but *I'm* not. Take them. All four of them."

"They saw us. They're going to ramp up their protection."

"So get creative."

He clamped his mouth shut tight, turning away from me. He didn't like my orders.

Lassiter didn't usually care.

His eyes darted to mine. The tightness in his face softened. "I don't want to take the Pialto guy. He's gay."

I understood. He was like Lassiter. "I don't care. Take him, take the girl, and take the mother and brother. Then *take care of them.*" I smiled, letting him see my real smile, the one where there was no question if I had a soul or not. I didn't. "It's a precursor for what life will be like if anything happens to Blake. If she's gone, nothing will tether me in place. Do you understand?"

Levi was waiting, watching us through the window, chewing on his lip.

Lassiter clipped out, "Why? Why them?"

"Is this because of Pialto—"

"She has cancer. They're innocent. Blake wouldn't want you to hurt them. Why not go for Blake's counterpart? Go after their women themselves?"

He was right. I waited to make sure he was done, and I dropped the smile. I closed the window and adopted the facial features of someone normal. Who felt. Who sympathized. Empathized. I even made sure my voice was almost gentle. "Because I want to hurt their women, and this will hurt them *more*. And before you ask, I want you to do it. It'll be more humane if you do it."

Blake would care about that.

CHAPTER TWENTY-TWO

BLAKE

Marshall and Heath were waiting for me when I left my second class for the day. Both fell in step with me. Marshall put his arm around my shoulders. "Roommate."

I said back, "Housemate."

Heath glanced at my books and grunted. "Ironic."

I shot him a look and hugged my ethics of law textbook closer to my chest. It was an elective and my second class. Cognitive psych was next.

Marshall's eyes flicked down, only making a humming sound. "Yes. Anyways, as I was saying—"

Heath added, dryly, "You only said roommate. You didn't say anything else."

Marshall gave him an aggrieved look, his arm tightening around my shoulders, and he leaned a little bit on me. He raised his voice, ignoring Heath. "As I was saying, *roommate*. There's this thing tonight. A fight night at a local place. Heath has the hookup, and one of our buddies is going to fight, but we sort of need a date to get in. It's a whole policy they have in place. I think it's to make sure enough women get in, though they said there was no stipulation on the gender of the date.

Turns out, I need a date." He flashed me his most welcoming smile and wiggled his eyebrows. "How about it? Fun excursion on my arm? Take pity on me, roommate."

Dear god, he had dimples. He was flashing me dimples.

I held up a hand. "Please. Stop."

Heath burst out laughing before coughing, spasming at his own involuntary response to me.

Marshall ignored him, his head perking up "You'll go?"

"I—"

He cut me off, grabbing my arm, and tugged me in for a hug. "Great. We'll leave tonight. It's a late-night thing, so we should be there by eleven. Dress for a nightclub. This will be awesome."

I had no idea what I didn't agree to just now, but Marshall was already off, focused on his phone.

Heath had gotten over his coughing fit. He lingered, a slight twitch to his mouth before he left, following behind Marshall. I was certain I heard him utter under his mouth, "This will be interesting."

Interesting.

Wonderful.

I did the time math in my head and winced. I'd be cutting it close after my shift at the foster center.

I stayed an hour after the lounge closed because one of the foster kids' pickup never showed. Volunteering to take him to their home, I only left once I was certain that he was actually safe. He reassured me. The foster mom and dad also reassured me. Some of the other kids who were still awake—some were doing homework, a couple others were watching a movie—all reassured me, too, but I didn't move from watching the house across the street.

The mom kept apologizing, saying that she forgot and her phone died. Maybe. I'm sure someone in the house had a phone she could've used. My gut still rolled over and over again until the side door opened. The boy I'd brought home came out, along with one of the older girls. They hurried across the street, coming to me.

"Miss Blake." The boy was a little out of breath, running as fast as he could toward me across the road. I searched his eyes, but he wasn't haunted. At least not tonight. "I'll be fine. I promise. Miss Sherry isn't like that."

He knew that I knew what he meant. When he and the others in the center met me tonight, I'd shared with them my history. All of them visibly relaxed. They got it. I was one of them. Had been one of them. *I* got *it.*

He nudged the girl, who rolled her eyes, but added, "What he said. Sherry's forgetful. She's a ditz sometimes, and this one forgets to save our numbers in the phone he has so he doesn't know who to call. And he won't because he doesn't want to be embarrassed if he accidentally calls someone he doesn't want to call."

He huffed. "Everyone's numbers change. It gets confusing."

She nudged him back, a fond expression on her face. "So just change the number the next time you get our new numbers. It's better to be able to contact us than not. Next time, Miss Blake might not be working and be able to make sure you get back safely." She glanced my way. "Thank you again. He told me a little about you, explained why you were still watching the house. He's fine. I don't know if he ate at the center—"

"He did."

"I did! We made spaghetti. They let us use the kitchen. It's real nice. You should come next time, too, Cap."

Cap had that fond look on her face again. "Maybe." It went away when she said to me, "Anyways, thank you. Malik will be there again, I'm sure."

They returned, with Malik giving me a small wave over his shoulder. Cap bent down, saying something to him, and he giggled before both disappeared inside again.

My phone buzzed.

Taking it out, I saw a text from Palma and one from Marshall.

I didn't even want to check the time. I knew I was so late.

Palma: Where are you??? We're here. There are so many hot guys here. You need to come, woman. Come. As in literal and well... The other literal way too. Okay. Just kidding on that one. They have these purple drinks that are deadly. They're delish. You'll see when you finally get here. Get here!

Marshall: I was able to get in without a date, but are you still coming?

It was almost eleven.

I did the math in my head and knew my lateness would be ridiculous. That was if I took the subway. Uh . . . I did have an alternative option for traveling.

I glanced to my left.

A guy unglued himself from some shadows and approached. Footsteps sounded deftly on the sidewalk.

It was Creighton's watcher, and I waited as he stepped close enough to scan my phone screen, seeing the text messages.

"I can have a vehicle here in five minutes."

Of course he could because Creighton's army was literally anywhere.

Worrying about Malik and keeping old memories at bay had taken a toll on me.

"Thanks."

I gave in.

CHAPTER TWENTY-THREE

BLAKE

We arrived at a warehouse titled Warehouse A, and I instantly understood how Heath had the hookup. Because one of his real-life brothers was in attendance, and the reason his brother was here was because he was *running the whole thing*. I knew this because the guys at the door said to head for the bar to check in with Nogoskeski.

Because he'd been put in charge of it *by Creighton*.

This was Creighton's warehouse.

How was this happening all over again?

I told him to stay away from me. He responded by showing up in my bedroom and giving me back my things. Now this.

As I was let inside, I got there in time to see Heath's brother coming down some stairs. He skimmed the group, saw Heath, and went over to hug him.

I felt like I was in a different reality because as I headed their way, Heath began introducing his brother to the rest of their group. It was Marshall, Palma, some of Palma's friends from the other time we'd ended up at Creighton's nightclub, and a few guys that I guessed were the friends Marshall and Heath mentioned.

Palma saw me and squealed, coming over for a hug like the night at the club. Marshall saw me and gave me a nod but remained at the bar. He was talking to a girl and, from the looks of it, had no intention of leaving her anytime soon. I snorted to myself. I could see now how he got in. Needed a date, my ass. He had a date.

Seeing me, Heath came over. His head lowered an inch, and he grabbed at the back of his neck. It was a whole "awe shucks" and sheepish mannerism. He gestured behind him. "Marsh saw my brother's text, and it spiraled from there. I'm sorry."

I wasn't sure what he was apologizing for because we hadn't acknowledged the common thread linking us. Technically. But I was guessing that's what he was referencing, apologizing for not giving me the heads-up?

"What's up, little Green?" His brother came with him, standing just behind him. He was tall enough so he had a clear view of me, and he put his hand on Heath's shoulder. "I didn't know you knew my brother."

I didn't comment on that. It was what it was. I did note, "Guaranteed my presence here has already been called in, but you should still let him know yourself. He might have separate orders for my friends."

He gave a nod, his face and eyes blank. Guarded.

Palma frowned. "Him who?"

We were getting looks. From the other door security, who mostly seemed like all-new recruits, but also from others in the bar area. A lot of them were with my housemates. If we kept talking, they'd start having questions.

No one responded to Palma.

"I'll let everyone know who you are." Heath's brother was referring to the rest of Creighton's men.

I sighed. "I'd rather you didn't."

He grimaced. "Have to. Sorry. Boss's order is to take care of you first. Always. In case something happens, you'll be protected."

That was the last thing I wanted. To be treated like a princess piranha, in a school of one.

"Awesome. I need a drink."

I wasn't ready for my two worlds to implode against each other, but it seemed that's exactly what was going to happen. I'd only taken three steps for the bar before Lassiter seemed to materialize out of nowhere.

He stopped. Stared at me.

I stopped. Stared at him.

I didn't care about my housemates' friends. I honestly didn't, but I did care about my housemates, and Palma had waited for me. So had Marshall. Heath moved around me, going to the bar. He raised two fingers in the air for the bartender as he kept glancing over his shoulder to me. All of them were watching me, as was Lassiter.

Well. Crap. This was going to happen.

Lassiter drew closer. "He's not here, so normally you'd be fine. Except—" He cringed, just a slight one, but I saw it, movement behind him. A second later, my name was being yelled. Loudly.

A giant-sized mastiff puppy in a human's body was barreling my way.

There was no going back.

"BLAKE! Blakey. Blakester. Blake, where is she . . ." The crowd parted, or to be more accurate, half of them were shoved out of the way as Levi pushed forward. His eyes lit up, seeing me, and a wide smile took up half of his giant face. *"Blake!"*

Lassiter took a step to the side just as Levi closed the distance, almost not seeing him. He picked me up and twirled me around. "Blakester. Blake. You're here. You came to one of our events, willingly." He was bursting with excitement. And he was still twirling me.

I patted his shoulder. "Put me down, big guy."

He did, but he took my hands, and we were going in circles still. He danced around with me. This big giant of a man was dancing, and he was beaming. He was so happy.

I melted.

Even Lassiter was trying to hide a grin but couldn't. As Levi stopped pulling me in circles, he shook his head. "I'll have them clear out the top loft for your group. Drinks are on us—"

I stopped him, my hand on his arm. "That's not necessary."

The corner of his mouth lifted up in a rueful grin. "Okay, but girls are drinking free tonight. It's a part of the whole promotion. Free drinks bring girls. Girls bring guys. We want more guys here for the fights. Means more bets. Means more money. So, sorry, but that means free drinks for girls."

Palma was close. Marsh came over from hearing the commotion. Heath remained at the bar, and it looked as if he had no intention of leaving before he got another two drinks.

I dipped my head down. "That's fine. I'll—"

Levi wrapped an arm around my back, tugging me against his side, and turned us to face Palma and the rest. "Introduce me to your friends. I've been dying to meet them. I'm Levi." He clasped me against his side tighter, bouncing me. His chest puffed out. "Blake's brother—"

"Foster brother."

He frowned, just slightly. "Yeah. Foster brother, but basically her brother."

Lassiter started laughing, walking away before I could say something. Or hit him.

Palma's own eyebrows were arched high, but at Levi's words, she thawed. Her smile relaxed. She drew even closer, which she needed to do because the inside of the warehouse was packed. There was no way they weren't violating fire safety and health code for how many people were packed in here. Then again, this was an underground fighting ring, and it was organized by Creighton's men, so I shouldn't be surprised.

"I had no idea you had a foster brother, or that he was here. I thought you were from Cincinnati?" She held her hand out, taking in all of Levi. "I'm Palma. Blake's roommate."

"She is from Cincy." He dropped his hand from around my shoulders and took hers in both of his, pumping it. "Let's talk about you, though. Wow. You're her roommate?"

Marshall gestured to himself, Palma, and toward the bar where Heath was still standing. "We all are. Me. Heath over there. There's another roommate, but good luck seeing her. She could be a vampire."

Levi started to shake his hand before the words registered. He stopped, doing a double take at what Marshall just said, along with seeing who Heath was. Confusion crossed his face. Alarm was right after. Then more confusion.

He gave me a questioning look.

I shrugged. "That's between me and—you know." I nudged his arm, indicating Marshall again. "Technically, I'm supposed to be here as Marshall's date."

Levi had begun to reach for Marshall's hand to shake, but at my last statement, he doubled over in a coughing fit. I did not do the nice thing and pat him on the back. I let him suffer. When he stopped, he fixed me with a dark look, but I caught the amusement too. "Right. I'm not seeing why you—never mind." He took Marshall's hand and gave him a brisk nod. "It's nice to meet you guys. Have you met anyone else from Blake's life?"

I cursed out a half laugh, half hiss. "Subtle."

He just blinked at me, still grinning.

"No. Why?" Palma's eyes were wide, leaning forward.

Levi's arm came down around my shoulders, and he tugged me once more into his side. "Lassiter, the little angry-looking blondie who seems pissed at the world. Him too. He has the braids in his hair, tattoos all over. Though, if you call him our foster brother, he'll get pissed. He was more like a foster neighbor. Grew up on the same street with us, but don't let him fool you. He basically grew up on Miss Marcie's couch."

Palma turned to look, and as she did, Marshall asked Levi a question. Soon the two began conversing. That was when Palma sidled up to my other side.

Holding her drink close and stirring the paper straw, she said quietly, "I didn't know you grew up in foster care."

I searched her face, trying to see if that was a problem. The reactions were always varied. They either looked down their nose at me or began to view me as some sort of threat to them. Positive responses were rare.

"I did. Yes."

I held my breath, waiting to see how Palma was going to react.

A sheen shone in her eyes, and underneath was kindness, mixed with respect? Was I seeing that correctly? I almost wept. I reached for her instead, hugging her. She was not someone I would have to say goodbye to, at least not right now.

Her face stuttered before she tried to give me a smile. "I'm sorry."

Sometimes, with some people, they may say something similar, but they didn't mean it. Palma meant what she said. It made a difference. A big one.

She playfully nudged me. "So. A foster brother *and* a foster neighbor? You got any more foster siblings around here?"

Oh, boy.

CHAPTER TWENTY-FOUR

BLAKE

Palma fell into the seat beside me, flushed and a little sweaty. "Your foster brother is hot." And a little wasted since I was smelling a good amount of rum from her breath. She ran a hand through her hair, dislodging it, frowning down at herself. "Shit."

Placing her drink on the table in front of us, she used both her hands to redo her hair. It'd been hanging loose earlier, but after an hour moving around and yelling at the fights, she put it up in a clip. She was redoing the clip. I was envious how seamless she made it look. Two seconds and voilà, done. Insta-beautiful.

"So." Palma raised her eyebrows at me, waiting for a response.

I hid a grin. "You're talking about Levi, right?"

"Of course Levi." She exhaled a dramatic sigh, grinning at me, and her cheeks were getting more red. "I'm interested. He's hot. And he has the goofiest, but dreamiest smile. I don't understand why I keep looking at it." She groaned, slinking farther down in her seat.

I was enjoying this side of Palma. Not sure about her being into Levi, though.

He'd been doting on us the whole night. He would disappear to do whatever Creighton needed him to do or whatever his job was to do here, but then come back. He'd make sure our drinks were full. Offer to get us food. He'd sit with us, tell some funny stories about us growing up together. He was keeping Creighton out of them, which I was thankful for. I wasn't ready for my roommates to find out about him, not yet.

Until then, Levi was being charming.

"He loves that you're here." Palma poked me in the arm. "He's mentioned that like eighteen times."

I made a *pfft* sound. Eighteen was a bit high. It was more like twelve.

Shrugging, I reached for my drink. This was a delicate balance of what I could say here, but I was going with the option of not speaking at all.

Marshall had taken to hanging out by the bar with the other guys in their group. There were a lot of them in the corner of the loft where we were sitting. From their angle, they were able to watch the fights below. Some of their dates were dancing with each other in front of them as well. A few of the girls came over to sit with us just as the crowd parted around us.

I expected to see Levi coming our way, but it was Lassiter.

He approached, his top lip lifted in a hostile little sneer at me.

I raised my chin up, challenging him. He didn't scare me. He was so opposite of Levi, who was happy and joyous and smiling every time he came around. Lassiter was growly and pissed off. And absent. This was the first time he'd come over since I arrived. I was a little nervous he was about to tell me Creighton was on his way.

I wasn't ready for that disaster.

He continued to glare at me before his gaze fell to my drink. "How many of those have you had?"

I made a face at him. "None of your business."

His eyes narrowed before he turned to one of the girls. "You're with number 97?"

She jerked upright. "Um. Yeah. He's fighting tonight."

"I know. Where is he?"

"Oh." Her face flooded with color. She looked around. "He was just here. I—" She began to stand up. "I'll go and find him."

Lassiter jerked his head toward the fighting ring. "Tell him to head down. He's third up." He handed her a piece of paper. "There's an area in the back where he can get ready, get his head on straight. You can accompany him, if he wants."

She started to rush off, but he blocked her. His eyes were chilled. "We'll repeat the rules down there, but just in case: no weapons allowed. To win, it's KO or if he's too incapacitated to fight back. Or death."

"Death?" She gulped, swaying on her feet. "KO?"

"Knock out." He stepped to the side, motioning for her to leave. It was an almost callous dismissal. "Go and find your boyfriend."

Lassiter was done with her, so he turned his back on her as he flicked me a glance.

I steeled myself for whatever he was going to say.

He said nothing, disappeared. The crowd swallowed him up.

Levi appeared right after and clapped his hands. "I'm supposed to lead you to the prime viewing spot for the fight." He did a funny little shuffle, turning to the side and holding out an elbow.

Palma thought that was the cutest thing ever. She hurried out of her seat to link her arm with his.

I stood at a slower pace because where was this prime viewing spot and who else would be there?

"Ready?" Levi was asking me.

Marshall noticed we were on the move and zipped around his friends as Levi began leading us into a back hallway.

"Where are we going?" Marshall leaned in, his forehead bumping my arm since he was trying to take a drink at the same time. And walk. And talk. So he stumbled into a wall as well.

He was drunk. He'd been drinking steadily the whole time.

I chose to save my breath.

Levi continued moving, now going through a door and into a hallway on the second floor.

Palma glanced back at us and mouthed, "So. Hot!"

Marshall frowned at her. "What'd you just say?"

She bulged her eyes out at him before looking ahead again.

I slapped Marshall on the chest.

"Ouch." He touched where I'd hit him. "What was that for?"

I shook my head. "Just because."

He was still rubbing his chest. "Well, that hurt."

I was on edge. Again. I'd been watching how much I drank once we got here because if Creighton showed up, I knew him. Everything would be about him. And he wouldn't hardly do anything. He'd just have to walk through the room, but this place was full of his soldiers. Or followers. They would know he was here. The air in the room would change.

I ignored the pinching in my chest, reminding myself it was because of the last time he and I spoke.

The "prime viewing spot" was a private balcony above the fighting ring. No one else but our group was allowed.

My knees almost shook from the relief.

Levi noticed my reaction, shaking his head. I couldn't help it. He was all in with Creighton. He also didn't know what it was like to have a conscience, so there you go. He didn't understand, but it didn't matter tonight. Creighton wasn't here. Their friend was about to fight soon.

I needed more drinks.

CHAPTER TWENTY-FIVE

CREIGHTON

I was rarely tired, even though I hardly slept. I didn't feel the stress of this life. Blake used to tease me and then complain how it was another attribute that made me not human.

I told her she was just jealous, but tonight I was tired.

West and Walden moved on Blake when she was at Cole Mauricio's nightclub. She was on Mauricio territory, so I was returning from a summons to explain my side of her kidnapping. Cole Mauricio shouldn't have that much power, but he did. He was attached to another formidable name as well, another Mafia family that ran an entire country and half of this one. They didn't run where I lived, but together they were strong enough where I needed to step carefully moving forward.

We didn't need additional Mafia families joining. The war was between West and Walden and me. They needed a couple name.

Walst?

Or Tristian and Ashton . . . Tristian was commonly called Trace.

Trashtan. Just Trash.

Team Trash. I liked that.

The Trash Twins.

The Trash Twins fucked up.

The war was between them and me. Not Cole Mauricio. The grievance happened on his territory, so he'd decide what he would want for repercussions. My guess was that Mauricio would want territory. If he did, it'd be inevitable that Mauricio would enter this war. They wouldn't give him what they were already fighting me to keep. And once I won, I'd have to turn my fight on Mauricio for that exact territory that Team Trash shouldn't have given away.

All of that was a big "if," but I needed to be prepared.

Cole Mauricio ran Chicago and had moved into running the Twin Cities with his new allegiance.

I needed to dispatch my recruiters to those cities and to start gathering information.

I'd just gotten back from my trip to Chicago, and I was tired. I just didn't know why. I didn't think my actual body was tired, so what did that mean?

My heart? It barely functioned except when Blake was around.

I didn't care about stress or responsibilities. I was more confused than anything else, but we arrived at the warehouse, and soon, all those questions faded.

My driver brought me to the back. There was still a line in front, people waiting to get in.

I gave this event to Nogoskeski to run. He wouldn't be able to help himself and would notify his brother. After that, sometimes a string would unravel itself and sometimes it wouldn't. This time, it unraveled, and a little kitty came to play with it.

I'd been notified Blake was here.

Slipping inside, my men stood back. Each dipped his head in a nod. I greeted them, but this night I had more important people to see. I would check in with my men later.

Lassiter was coming down the back stairs as I began to head up. He took me in, his usual scowl in place before his facial expression switched. There was a window, a brief one, but I saw inside before he masked it with a smirk instead.

Too late. I saw the pain he was hiding.

I hardened.

I was obsessed with Blake. He knew this. It had always been the way, even before he came. And Lassiter was obsessed with me. He didn't think I knew, but I did.

He stopped three steps above me. "She's here with her friends."

"And one of them is all over Levi."

He didn't ask who had given me the report. It didn't matter. I had thirty men inside this warehouse. They all reported to me.

Lassiter's hand tightened around the handrail before he jerked it free, stuffing it inside his pocket. "She doesn't want you here."

I moved past him.

He turned with me, hissing, "Leave her be."

No. "She came to me. The rules changed."

"Because you tricked her."

Yes. I did. I wasn't a good man.

He let out a frustrated sound and began down the last two steps.

"Last." I used his nickname.

He paused.

I was normally patient with him. He was family.

"When I go to her, she doesn't turn me away."

Hurt flared in him before he shoved out the door.

I *could* be patient, kind, to him. Just not tonight.

CHAPTER TWENTY-SIX

BLAKE

Junior year in college
Cincinnati

God, I was nervous. Really nervous.

"Hey, you." One of my roommates popped her head into my room. She whistled. "You look hot. Where are you going tonight? One of Creight & Barrel's nightclubs?"

That was her nickname, which wasn't a nickname at all, for Creighton. I must've made a face because she straightened up. "Uh oh. What is it? Are you two fighting?"

When weren't we? I just shrugged. "I'm not going to one of his clubs." I met her gaze in the mirror, letting my hands drop back down to my side. I'd been fussing with my hair. "I have a date."

Her eyes got big, really big. She sucked in her cheeks and let out another whistle. "Damn. Okay. I didn't see that coming. Crate'n'Barrel knows about the date?"

My jaw clenched. Everything in me tensed. I jerked up a shoulder and went back to getting ready.

"Who is it?"

"Tommy Pritsch."

Her eyebrows drew together. She was trying to place him.

"He's in my cross-cultural class. He's nice."

She still couldn't place him.

I relented, "He's on the football team."

Her eyes went big again. "Damn. *That* Tommy Pritsch? Didn't he date one of the cheerleaders last year?"

"Thought you're *my* roommate?"

She flushed. "Sorry. Yeah. You're right. What do you have planned for the night?"

I smoothed my hand down my shirt. I wasn't sure what to wear, but since it was spring and not that cold, I opted for a cargo skirt. A white tank top. Black bra with a bra strap that would show. I had a cute jacket that matched my skirt if it got cold. My hair was perfect since I went to the salon and spent the whole day waiting for a blowout. Sometimes my hair got frizzy, and it was that type of weather again.

Time was spent at the spa. Manicure, pedicure, and I learned how to do some fresh makeup techniques. I generally liked the natural and shiny look, but tonight I was going with the smokey-eye effect. Red popping lipstick.

I did look good. Was it too much? "Is this . . . ?" I turned and waved a hand up and down myself. "Okay? Too much? Maybe I should just wear jeans."

Jeans were a good idea. A better idea. Jeans were safe.

She blocked me. "No way. You look hot, like smoking tamale hot. My only thing is that, really? Tommy Pritsch? The guy's a player, Blakester."

"You don't think he'll be interested in me?"

She rolled her eyes. "Jesus Christ, have you seen yourself? You're too good for him." She gave me a reassuring smile. "You look good, and since when do we dress for the guy? We dress for us. Am I right?"

I smiled back, some of the nerves smoothing out. "Yeah. You're right. We do."

"He's damned lucky to have you on his arm tonight. Just have fun. Don't overthink anything."

"I will. Did you need something?"

"Oh! Yes. I have a Netflix and chill date coming over. Can I use the projector thing? Put the show thing on the ceiling?"

I told her where it was, and she left.

Then I sat and waited for my date.

He never showed.

He was found hanging later in the night.

CHAPTER TWENTY-SEVEN

BLAKE

I was drunk. And dancing, blissfully dancing.

After the last fight, the lights went low, and the music turned up. I let loose.

I couldn't deny that it was nice to be spending time with Levi again. He was wrapped all around Palma from behind. The two were doing a sexy slow grind that would make me uncomfortable if there was better lighting where I'd have to see them. Right now, they were more just a hint of what was going on with them.

It was even fun to see Lassiter. Even though he was usually an asshole.

The only one missing . . .

No. I shook that thought away. I was drunk. That was the only reason it slipped through.

Except, as if on cue, hands came to my hips from behind, and after pausing a moment, after I relaxed back into his arms because I knew, I just knew who it was, he pressed against me.

Tingles shot down my spine. My breath hitched.

Creighton was here.

A part of me melted. The other part had alarms blaring.

They were so far in the back and muted and fuzzy from the other warm feelings happening right now. I was with my family. Levi and Creighton, they were mine. These new people, Palma, Marshall, even Heath, they could maybe be someone to me. I didn't know. It was too soon. I'd gone through too much, so it took a long time before anyone got into my heart space, though Palma was working her way in there.

And Levi was all about Palma.

Palma was all about Levi.

And that made me happy. Maybe it shouldn't. Maybe I should be worried about the aftermath, if there was going to be an aftermath, or hell, of course there would be, so whenever that aftermath would happen, it would happen *then*. I wasn't thinking about that now.

I'd kept myself away, tried to keep away from Creighton, tried to warn him away. But I just wanted to give in.

I burrowed farther into his arms, my body heating, awakening. I *needed*.

I turned around, fitting myself against his chest, and with that desperation clawing its way up my throat, I reached for his neck, a mewling whimper tearing from my throat.

My mind shut off.

My body was operating on its own.

I was done fighting against myself. I couldn't remember why I ever had been.

As I reached for him, he bent down, and I lifted myself up at the same time. I didn't even want to be dancing anymore.

I. Just. Wanted. Creighton.

He stood, lifting me in his arms. My legs wrapped around his waist, my arms tightened around his neck, and I breathed into his neck, filling myself with the smell of him. A fresh coldness from outside along with a whiff of peppermint and forest. I didn't even know where any of those scents came from, but they were him.

He was moving with me wrapped around him like a koala bear. I was in a happy state, where I could either fall asleep or—I rocked over him and smiled as he groaned deep and low into my ear.

I rocked again. That felt so good.

His hand fell to my ass, grasping it. "Blake."

I wanted more. Lifting my mouth, I tasted his throat, and he groaned again. That sound was so blissful. A shiver went through me, making me tremble in his arms.

I didn't know where we were anymore, but he was moving us.

The music faded.

We were going up.

"What—" someone else started.

"Leave," Creighton clipped out.

A door clicked, closing, and it was quiet now. Peaceful. Except I was writhing inside. The dam had been building for so fucking long, and I let it shatter. Everything was rushing through me, making me feel like I was going to go insane.

I reached for Creighton's shirt and yanked him to me. I growled in his face. "You." I dragged his mouth to mine. I barely registered his eyes widening, but then it didn't matter because I was tasting him, this time on the lips, and things clicked into place inside of me. The right drawers suddenly found the shelves they were supposed to be in. All the madness cleared out of me. Lights that had been blinking in a frenzy all dimmed, all at the same time. A peace that I'd never let myself welcome wound itself through me, waking up every cell in my body, and just telling me that same message over and over again.

Home.

I was home.

And that was in Creighton's arms, with his lips on mine, and I let myself ride in my own boat right over that dam.

I fell.

He stiffened, pulling away. "Wait."

I panted. "Want."

He dodged my mouth, gripping the back of my neck. He angled his head to see me better. "How much have you been drinking?"

I cursed. This was stupid. I knew what I wanted. I moved for him again.

His hand tightened on my neck, until another whimper left me, and he tore himself out of my arms. I landed on a desk with a thud, and suddenly he was across the room, breathing hard, his hands on his hips. "How much have you had to drink?"

"What does it matter?" I snapped.

He snapped right back, "It matters. You matter. You're the only thing that matters, so yes, if you're in an altered state of mind, *it matters*." He heaved a breath, his nostrils flaring. "How much?"

I deflated.

Those words.

Jesus. Those words.

. . . you matter. You're the only thing that matters . . . I blinked back tears.

I knew Creighton's obsession, but to hear it in those words, the madness was coming back to my head. It was going to fill me up, and I was going to get all confused once more. It'd felt so nice being in his arms, giving in, and letting everything else filter out. My mind was quiet for once.

I wanted that back.

I snorted. "Why do you care now about—" I folded my arms over my chest, pouting.

Tomorrow I'd regret pouting. I acknowledged that, but I got a glimpse at what the world felt like in his arms. I got a taste before it was gone. I wanted that *back*. This need for him was in me, burrowing deeper behind my heart, and he was making himself comfortable there.

He ripped that away.

"I care about you." He jerked toward me, his words puncturing me. "I am not a man that cares about right from wrong, *except* when it concerns you. Only with you. Don't you get that? You're my barometer.

You're my compass. I know which way is right because of you. You're the reason why I'm able to function as a normal person. So yes, Blake, it's always going to matter *with you*."

My bottom lip was trembling, and my hand was shaking.

How could a girl function after hearing that?

My lungs were burning again, wanting to explode. The feeling was building, rising, growing.

I was drunk, but I wanted to give in. One night. Just one.

It was my excuse for why I could let myself get lost in him.

Hot tears slid down my face. I ignored them. "I can't be with you sober."

I heard his soft intake of air. "And that's the only way I'd have you."

Sober. Not drunk.

Well, fuck him then.

I glared at him, my eyebrows pulled low. *Fuck.* Him.

He looked almost normal at the moment. I sneered. "Look at you, having a conscience."

He barked out a harsh laugh, raking a hand through his hair. "Only for you. You *are* my conscience." He turned, going to a window that overlooked the rest of the warehouse. "I wasn't born with a soul, Blake. For fourteen years I walked around, knowing something was different about me, but I didn't know what it was. It didn't matter to me. Then one day a little girl got out of a car, and suddenly I had something in my chest. I didn't know what it was. I just knew something was there that hadn't been there before. So if that makes you my soul or my conscience, I don't care. I'll take it. But that only stays that way as long as I don't fuck up with you. Letting myself touch you when there's a chance you could regret it, that's me poisoning it. I won't do it. Not *that*. Not *you*."

How could he stand there, having done all the things he'd done over the years, the dead bodies that he laid at my feet, tricking me at times, and *now* he stood on some moral podium? "This was your chance, Eight."

He said, deadpan, "I need to be a better man to be with you, and here I am, being that man, but it's not what you want right now. Bit of a hypocrite, aren't you?"

I felt slapped.

A low simmer had already started in me. The heat cranked up, and my blood began to boil over. "You—"

"We have never talked about the option of you and me as in *you and me*. As in an us. Isn't that what you like to do? Talk about feelings? You didn't want to talk about it the other night. And tonight, we skipped right over that, and you're not even realizing that."

I blanched, because he was right. What did that mean?

My head was swimming again, getting all confused. I liked either wanting him or being mad at him because then I knew what I wanted. I knew what I felt. But this, it was making everything all cloudy again.

I whispered, "Eight."

"We've been doing this dance all our lives. You and me. It's always been you and me. My role keeps changing for you. Not your brother. Not your father. But I'm in your life. Provider." He laughed, a bitterness there. "If you let me. Protector. If you let me."

"You have no parameters." What was he doing here? Where was he going with this?

He suddenly stalked over to me. "I have parameters."

What was he doing?

I began backing up until I hit the wall.

And he was right there, in front of me, leaning over me. I could feel his heat from his body. His breath coated me, and I tried to suppress a shiver. It didn't work. He saw it, and he lowered his head even more.

He was so close.

The yearning was building again, taking me over.

I wanted to reach out to him. Take hold of his shirt, pull him to me, close the distance. There was hardly any air separating us, and then he closed the distance even more, bracing his hands on either side of my head. I was pinned in place.

My heart was thumping loudly, demanding his touch.

He watched me, his eyes so dark again. He spoke, his tone hollow, "I met a little girl when she was eight years old, and suddenly I understood the world. You gave me the world. You gave me everything. I use the parameters that *you* gave me. Don't you remember, Blake? No one good. No one innocent. Everyone else, fair game. You said those words to me. I've been living by those parameters for the last fourteen years." His head dipped down to my neck. I shivered, feeling his lips grazing over my skin. He was touching me. He was fanning the flames, but he wasn't doing anything to extinguish the fire. He was here. He was in my space, but he was masking everything else. I didn't like being able to read him. I couldn't see his face, so I slid a hand up his neck. He went rigid at my touch. My fingers went up to the back of his head and took a fistful of his hair. I wanted to yank his head back, but he closed all the distance between us. His entire body plastered against mine, and he trailed his hand down my sides, to my legs, and he hoisted one up so it wound around his waist.

I moaned, closing my eyes. My fingers slacked on his hair.

He ground into me.

Pleasure coursed through me. That felt so good. He felt so good.

My hand began trembling. I was losing the fight in me.

I wanted to feel his skin. I wanted to feel him inside of me, moving, sliding in and out—

Then he said, quietly, still against my neck. "You ran from me, and I stayed away. I have stayed away—"

Cold reality hit me, dampening my desire. I remembered why I ran. "I ran because of you. I left because of who you are and what you did to the last guy who tried to date me."

Goddammit. I needed to see his face, and I tightened my hold on his hair again. I tried tugging his head back, but he wouldn't move. He trailed his other hand down my back, from my shoulder, down my side, and wound around my waist.

I gritted my teeth. This was so typical of him.

With Creighton, he would always push for power. He'd always try to unbalance the balance because that's who he was.

Right?

Or was I wrong?

I looked away because my head was starting to hurt and I was getting confused all over again.

Maybe I was sobering up.

I needed to be away from him, as far as possible. I was tired of playing these games with him, and I shoved him back. He went, easily. My chest seized at that, too, because he wouldn't give me anything I wanted tonight, but he would give me space?

Fuck him.

Keeping my head down, I wouldn't make eye contact, and I went to the door.

"He didn't ghost you, Blake."

My chest seized. I stopped as I'd been about to reach for the door. "What?"

"The last guy you tried dating."

A bitter laugh slipped from me because really? "What? Was he another one looking to hurt me? Gangbang with his buddies to get back at you? Because how many times can those sorts of things happen to the same girl before it starts to look like you're searching for an excuse to kill them? You say I can date, but that's not the truth. You don't want me to be with anyone else. You won't let yourself be with me tonight. I'm tired of this back-and-forth, Creighton. I'm tired of it. Let me go or . . ." There was no point in finishing that because he wouldn't. I whispered, feeling something in me breaking off, falling into a void, "You won't let me go."

"No." He snarled, advancing on me.

I held up a hand, more out of instinct, and I half turned away.

He braked, drawing up short, but his words were harsh. He bit out, "I won't let you go. Not anymore. That ship sailed. You want me, so now I'm yours and you're mine."

"Just not tonight." I lifted my gaze and winced.

He was staring at me, hard. His jaw clenched. "No, not when there's a risk your mind is altered. But make no mistake, Blake. I wouldn't let some guy take you out on a date after railing three different girls that day. I didn't let it happen back then, and there's *no way* I'll let it happen now. The guy you were supposed to go on a date with wasn't planning on hurting you because of me, but that didn't mean he wouldn't have hurt you in other ways. He was just a typical sleazeball that wasn't good enough for you. That's where he messed up because you're *not* the fourth girl he's going to fuck in a day. Not you."

His words seared me. That's what happened? I choked out, "Are you serious?"

"You don't have the best taste in men." He gestured to himself. "Are you that surprised?"

I blinked some tears away, not understanding why they were there. His words sank in. "He was *careless,* and you hanged him for that?"

"He wasn't disclosing his sexually transmitted diseases to his partners. But I'll be very clear here." He stepped aside and I could see him from the light again. There was nothing on his face. His same dead eyes. He was a statue, a pretty, empty, and murderous statue. "If his diseased dick had gotten anywhere near you, I would've hanged *everyone* he loved."

A rattling began inside of me, but I couldn't face whatever this was.

I fled.

CHAPTER TWENTY-EIGHT

BLAKE

I got as far as the main floor, which was where Palma found me, launching herself at me. Her face was bright. Her eyes were glazed. Her hair was sweaty. She was having a glorious time. I looked for Levi but didn't see him. She wound her arms around my neck, squeezing me tight to her. "Hi. Where'd you go? How are you? HOLY SHIT! WHO WAS THE HOTTIE YOU WERE GRINDING WITH?" The smell of alcohol blanketed me from her breath, and I cringed, more from the question than from her screaming in my ear.

Before I could respond, Marshall came over and tapped me on the shoulder. Heath was behind him, his arm thrown around the shoulders of another guy. His brother was also there frowning at Heath.

Marshall was saying, "We're going to head out. Some of us were thinking about getting food—"

Palma lurched forward. "Yes! I'm hungrrryyyyy. Can we get food and then go to bedddd?" She hiccupped before laughing. "Oops. Sorry."

Marshall frowned at me. "What do you want to do?"

Well, right now I wanted to breathe. Palma was squeezing the life out of me, but I croaked, "Home. Bed please."

"Gotcha."

The music suddenly went up a whole decibel, and a wave of people swarmed past us, so Marshall leaned closer, yelling in my ear, "There's a diner a block over. We could get food there and take it back to the house."

I moved my head up and down to save my energy. That sounded like a good plan.

I looked around but didn't see the girl he'd been flirting with earlier. "Where's your friend?"

He gave me a weird look. "Who?"

I gestured to where he'd been standing at the bar. "The girl you were talking to before. You seemed into her."

"Oh!" He shrugged, ducking his head a little. "She took off with her friends. I think she had her eye on someone else." He gave me another assessing look. "You good? You look sober-ish."

I gave him a thumbs-up.

Some relief fleeted across his face. Alerting Palma on the arm, he knelt down and patted his back. He didn't say anything, but she knew what to do. With a squeal, she climbed on, and now she was the koala bear in the situation.

No.

I mentally reprimanded myself for thinking of Creighton.

If his diseased dick had gotten anywhere near you, I would've hanged everyone *he loved.*

I could not be with Creighton.

I couldn't be with someone like that. Other feelings were coming up. I shoved them all down because none of it mattered. The whole gate had lifted for Creighton, and the want and need and other feelings were still there. They were potent. Knowing someone was capable of and perpetuated cold-blooded murder needed to be a lust-destroyer.

I needed to shut it down.

Following everyone as we left the warehouse, another shiver wracked through me, this one heating me again, and I hated that.

Tears suddenly pricked at my eyes.

You're my conscience.

He made me feel alive.

I was so screwed.

An extra-loud whistle screeched behind us.

Everyone winced.

"What the hell, man," someone grumbled.

"Wait up!"

My head fell back, and my eyes closed. The sound of a herd of elephants stampeded our way. I couldn't stop a grin from tugging at my lips. Levi blasted past me, bumping my arm gently. He whispered as he continued past me, "Heya, Blakey." His voice boomed a beat later, just in front of me. "Gimme, gimme. I give great piggyback rides."

Palma tipped her head back, her hair falling so close to the ground. "It's Leviiii. Where'd you go before? You dsispeared? Dissperead? Dis-a-p-peard on me."

Levi chuckled as she climbed onto his back. He ducked his head toward hers, and she moved her own, inching closer to him. They were whispering together.

Heath was farther up in the group. His brother had relinquished him to some of Marshall and Heath's friends. Seeing he was taken care of, Heath's brother met my gaze once, giving me a brisk dip of his head before he went back inside. Marshall noted the exchange, the corner of his mouth falling down, but as he fell in step next to me, he didn't comment on it.

I had a feeling all those questions would come later.

A toned arm suddenly draped over my shoulders, and I tensed instinctively but then relaxed (slightly) when someone chuckled beside me. Lassiter had joined us. He was only a few inches taller than me, so it felt almost intimate when I looked up, meeting his gaze. His head was tipped toward me, and he held my look, a wry tug coming to his top lip.

"Hey." I stepped into him, my hip bumping his.

"Hey." He bumped me back.

I tried to smother a grin. Tried and failed.

His matching grin told me he noticed.

"LASSITER!" Levi noticed him and swung around. Palma shrieked, burrowing her face into his massive neck. He held his meaty arms out, walking for us. "You're joining us tonight?"

Lassiter's arm tightened a little around me. "For a bit."

"Nice." Levi's smile stretched from ear to ear. His gaze went to me and turned calculating. "You think we could get Cr—"

I coughed. *"No."*

We were almost to the street.

Lassiter cut in. "Turn around, Levi. You're about to get hit by a car."

Levi's eyes widened, and he swung around, then cursed and braked to a sudden stop as a bus went past him. His laugh was a little uneasy. "Thanks for that, man. You just saved my ass."

Lassiter chuckled softly next to me.

Marshall moved farther away from us, catching up to Palma and Levi. Because Lassiter seemed like he was being nice tonight, I reached up and laced our fingers together.

He glanced down at me, his eyebrows raised.

I lowered my voice. "I know how you feel about him." I ignored the sudden tension in his body. Maybe I shouldn't bring it up, but knowing Lassiter, there wouldn't be another time like this. He so rarely lingered, and here he was, walking with me. I wanted him to know, and if this was the only chance I had to talk to him about it, I was going to take it. "I'm sorry."

He didn't reply, but he also didn't pull away. Half of the group broke away, going a different direction. Our small group with Levi, Palma, Heath, and Marshall continued moving forward.

Lassiter's mouth curved down. His arm felt like dead weight around my shoulders. "It doesn't matter. He'll only be obsessed with you, and I'm aware of that."

I tipped my head up to meet his gaze.

A dark and slightly sad understanding passed between us.

I tried suppressing a tremble that went down my spine, tried and failed.

Lassiter felt it, his eyes questioning.

My breath caught in my chest. I held it a moment before I said, quietly, "I'd be with him in a heartbeat if he wasn't . . ." If he wasn't who he was.

Lassiter bit out a bitter laugh. "And I want him any way I can get him."

A bell rang ahead of us as someone opened the diner's door. They ducked inside. When it was just me and Lassiter, I held him back. "Last."

My heart ached at hearing what he said.

He avoided my eyes. "It doesn't matter. He wants you. I know you're going to fight tooth and nail because you're the good one of all of us, but at the end of the day"—his eyes flitted to mine—"you love him too." He cursed before lowering his forehead to rest against mine. He hugged me to him with his one arm still around my shoulders. "Don't feel any sort of way for me, Blake. He's never been quiet about his obsession for you."

"Things have changed. Recently. It wasn't always this way."

His laugh was soft. And sad. "Wasn't it?"

Oh, god. That hit me deep. "Does he know how you feel?"

He stepped back, his arm falling away. "I don't know. Knowing Creight, probably. It doesn't matter." The side of his mouth tipped up. "Look at us, having a moment."

I snorted, playfully punching him in the chest. "You mean, look at you. You're not being an asshole for once."

"Yeah. Well." He reached for a packet of cigarettes and took one out. He held it up. "Go on in. I need a smoke."

"You're going to join us?"

He held my gaze, and I saw it then. He wasn't. He was going to leave, and who knew when I'd see him again.

I didn't know why he decided to walk with me tonight. It was out of the norm for him, and now that I'd said what I said, now that I addressed some of the awkward undertones, he was going to cut and run.

I said, "I've missed you."

He tipped his head back, his grin transforming into a smirk. He masked everything else inside of him. "Don't be such a fucking stranger then, hmmm?" He nodded behind us to the diner. "It's like Levi lost a nut, the way he's been going on about not being able to see you. The whole agreement you have with Creight fucks the rest of us as well. You want us to stay away too?"

I pffted at his words. "You're the one who usually stays away. Not me. And besides, it doesn't seem to matter anymore."

"Do Levi a favor? Let him be around you. He's one of Creight's, but you're his sister. He's like a giant teddy bear without his stuffing when he can't see you. It's weird to see. Pathetic."

"I don't think you need to worry about that. That boundary's been blown tonight."

There was another shriek from inside. I grinned, recognizing Palma.

"Get in there. I'll stay put for a bit before heading back."

It felt like there was more to say, but my head had exploded from everything that happened tonight. With my two worlds combining in a big way. With my fight with Creighton. With the feel of being in his arms—with this very rare gift I just got with Lassiter.

I kept trying to keep all the different parts of my lives separate and in their own lanes. I was trying to control everything, but I couldn't. I *kept* trying to control everything. Maybe that was the problem? Maybe I should stop trying to think, trying to control, and just let life happen because at the end of the day, that's what was going to happen anyways?

My thoughts were all muddled as I went inside, and once the door swished shut behind me, it took a second before I looked up.

I went still, oxygen freezing in my lungs.

Three masked men had guns in the air. The rest of my group was on the floor. I skimmed over everybody, taking in what I could. Marshall and Heath had their arms around Palma, who was silently crying.

Levi was the closest to me, and his hands were in the air, but he was glowering at them. He met my gaze, and we shared a look because *fuck*.

The one closest to me shoved his gun to my head. His hand grabbed my shoulder, and he shoved me. "Get the fuck down, bitch, and empty your pockets."

We were being robbed.

CHAPTER TWENTY-NINE

BLAKE

Being scared would be a normal response to a situation like this.

"No." I wasn't normal.

He surged toward me, raising his voice at the same time he raised his gun. "What'd you say to me, bitch?"

I flicked a glance toward Levi. He only lifted his eyebrows up at me.

We were literally one block from one of Creighton's buildings. Lassiter was just outside. It was inevitable that his men would be alerted, so the only real thing I needed to do was not get shot before Creighton would end this. What I actually did was start thinking about the aftermath because I already knew how this would play out. I didn't know the exact details or specifics, but once Creighton knew what was happening here, he'd send the alert out. Whichever of his guys was closest would bust in here. It would probably be Lassiter, and if that was the case, he'd come in shooting. After that, the robbery guys would be educated on their mistake, and they'd either shit their pants or they'd be smart and run for their lives. Either way, the robbery would be interrupted. Now, what happened beyond that, I didn't know. It'd be contingent on a few factors, and none of them I could predict.

"Oh, shit! SHIT! Fuck no. Oh—fuckingshityouguyswe'resosfucked." The third robber had pulled out his phone and was looking down at it.

I started laughing.

"Blake!" Palma hissed, horrified.

I shook my head. I couldn't stop laughing.

"Dude." The second robber went over to his friend.

The first one got in my face. "SHUT YOUR MOTHERFUCKING WHORE MOUTH, DO YOU HEAR ME?"

"Phil—NO!" the third robber screamed.

The first one, the one screaming in my face, stopped and twisted around. "What do you—"

"*Shut up!* You have no idea—" The third guy moved closer, taking me in, and he visibly gulped. "We're going to die."

That was when the front door ripped open and Lassiter came in, gun drawn.

Levi and I moved at the same time.

Before the other two could turn on Lassiter, I rammed my knee up in the third guy's groin. He doubled over, a half screech strangling out of him while Levi punched the other one in the face. Both were incapacitated right away. After shooting out a camera set up in the corner, Lassiter went straight for the third guy. "*Put the gun down.* Now."

"Yo. I—" He gulped again but put the gun down.

Lassiter ripped off his ski mask. The guy was trembling, and he was as pale as a ghost. His hands were shaking as he held them up. "I'm one of you."

"Fuck no, you're not." Lassiter motioned to the counter. "Sit your ass down." He turned, snapping his fingers. "Levi."

"On it."

They got to work. Lassiter produced zip ties from his pocket, and there was no comment about why he would have zip ties on him because of course he would. They used them on the other two guys. Their ski masks were left in place, but I knew it was because they'd be pulled off at another location.

Palma was still crying. There were no other customers, which was a small blessing. The only other two people were the cook and a server girl. Both were sitting with the others.

I knew what was coming next.

I knew, but I didn't want to think it.

Closing my eyes, I began to dissociate. If I was outside of my body, it wasn't as if it were happening, but I was still there. All of this had been for nothing. I was witnessing it disintegrating before my eyes. My planning. My hopes. I tried. I really tried to have a normal life, but all of it had been for nothing because—the door opened again.

More of Creighton's men came in. I recognized my watcher, along with three guys who'd been acting as security at the fights. Lassiter motioned them over, pointing to the two that they had zip-tied. "Take them out."

"Wait. What are you doing?" Marshall started to stand up.

I flinched when Levi shoved him back down.

Marshall looked so confused. Heath wasn't.

Palma gasped. "What?" She was looking at Levi as if he'd grown three heads and turned green. "What's going on?"

"Just," Heath spoke up, then faltered. He cursed under his breath, shaking his head. "Just be quiet for a minute. Okay? We'll be fine. Just, shut up and don't say a thing."

Marshall made a protesting sound.

Heath whipped his head around. "I mean it. Not a *goddamn* word. You have no idea who—just shut the fuck up. There's no narcs here." His eyes lifted, growing hostile as Levi towered over him.

Levi gave Heath a smug look of approval. "That's a good little Nogoskeski." He put his finger in Heath's forehead and pushed him back. "You know the drill. I'll be sure to let big bro know how helpful you were. Both of them." Levi winked at Heath.

The other guys were picking up the two robbers and carried them outside. Doors were slammed shut a moment later, and the screech of tires sounded next.

"Whe-where are they taking them?" Palma shrunk down when Levi looked her way. She hugged her knees to herself, but she was still thinking. She was questioning things. She wasn't so scared that she ceased thinking.

It was a trickle. A small one, but I felt a spark of warmth start in my chest. It grew and stretched, and slowly, painfully, I was back in my own body. I hadn't dissociated from this situation for too long, and I gasped, silently.

Palma turned her head, her eyes widening. "Blake. Are you okay?" She tried scrambling toward me, but Marshall and Heath both reached for her, holding her down.

Levi had also moved to block her, standing between us, but when he saw the others were holding her back, he relaxed before stepping to me.

Lassiter was on his phone, standing by the last remaining robber. He was watching me as he continued typing on his phone with one hand.

"Blake." Levi dropped his voice so the others couldn't hear.

I ignored him.

I hated this next part. Hated it. Bitterness and resentment and regret all began to burn inside of me. Mix it with anger and loathing and *knowing* how this would change everything. It already had. Palma had been my friend. Or she could've been a friend. She was a roommate. Marshall. Even Heath. All of it was gone now.

They would demand an explanation. Heath would give it to them. A normal response would be to call the police. No cops were being called in this situation. Creighton would handle it, just like he always did. And in the process, he'd destroy yet another attempt I made at living some sort of normalcy.

By the time that door opened, and by the time the usual reaction happened whenever Creighton was present, I was beyond giving a fuck. I watched it all, barely staying in my body, but this time from my own fury.

Levi straightened, his cocky attitude falling away.

The robber snapped to attention, jerking to his feet so quickly that he almost fell.

Lassiter reached out, steadying him, his eyes going to Creighton, a knowing wariness there as well.

Heath turned away for a moment.

The only two other reactions I cared about were Marshall and Palma. Both were confused, but interest swirled in Palma's eyes. It was mixed with other expressions. Being scared. Nervous. Not knowing what was happening, but *knowing* that Creighton was someone.

A flash of attraction was there too. It was gone as quickly as it appeared, but I caught it. I even understood it. How could I not?

Then the last, recognition.

Her eyes darted to mine.

After that, I couldn't look at her anymore. I didn't want to see the accusation or the horror when she would realize my connection to these men. My stomach churned, and I forced my gaze away, accidentally meeting Creighton's, who was watching me.

He'd stopped, just inside the door. "Are you okay?"

I barely restrained myself from glaring at him, which Creighton read from me because he grinned, laughing softly. "You must be since you look like you want to murder me."

Levi shot me a grin. Even Lassiter glanced my way, somewhat amused.

I growled at them all.

He glanced over. "They touched her?"

"No," I said at the same time Levi overrode me, "He shoved her shoulder. She's fine."

I glared at him.

Levi shrugged at me, and I knew what he was thinking. Creighton would see it anyways. He'd look at the security footage before Lassiter shot out the camera. If he hadn't already viewed it.

"Blake," Palma whispered, trying to lean forward around Marshall and Heath. Both of them hushed her. She ducked her head down, looking like she was going to argue, but Heath grabbed her head and put his mouth to her ear. He was talking urgently to her, and whatever he was saying, she quieted.

I tore my gaze away. God. Why did I do this to myself? Try to make friends and then the inevitable would happen. Creighton would come in and destroy everything. Every single time.

I only had two options. Fake my death or give in. Pain seared me. I couldn't do either of them.

I'd be cutting myself in half.

Creighton spared me another look before going to stand in front of the robber. The guy was visibly shaking, and I wouldn't be surprised if he pissed himself soon. As if on my same wavelength, Levi, Lassiter, and Creighton took a step back from the guy.

"You're one of mine, I'm told."

"Ye-yes, sir. I joined yesterday." His voice pitched but then came out rushed, pleading. "It was my buddy's idea. He wanted one last score. He's set to go upstate on Monday. I didn't want to help, said it was against your rules, but he didn't care. He's been my buddy for fifteen years. I'm sorry, Mr. Lane. I-I-I didn't know. I'm so sorry."

I couldn't look. The desperation in his voice was too much.

He kept begging, trying to plead his case until Creighton was done. "Enough."

The guy stopped, though blubbering sounds still slipped out.

"You have others on your plan?"

"Y-y-yes, sir."

"Who's on your plan?"

Sometimes people came to Creighton because they had families to support. When they were plugged into his money system, that money could be allotted so it would go to those loved ones. It helped keep Creighton's people loyal even if they were taken by an enemy or caught by law enforcement. Once they joined, they began earning right away. The money flowed, and it flowed well. Creighton had a system for people who weren't loyal. I never stuck around to find out exactly what it was, but I knew it was so few. No one wanted to be cut off from the money they got working for Creighton.

The guy was still stuttering as he answered, "M-my mom and my sister. My sister's got a kid coming. They're not doing so well. Her old man, he's upstate, too, and a real piece of work, if you know what I mean."

The silence in the room was palpable.

My chest was tight.

"Blake," Creighton spoke my name, softly.

I heaved a silent sigh but lifted my gaze. I knew what he was asking. Should he let this man live or not?

I found myself wincing as I met Creighton's gaze, and my eyelids shuttered. I didn't want Creighton to kill this man. Not in front of my roommates.

He gave me a small nod, focusing back on the guy.

"Your name?"

"Craig, sir. Uh . . . Do you want my last name?"

"Craig, you came in here alone. Do you understand me?"

Relief hit me hard. Creighton was giving him a break. He wasn't going to kill him. He was giving him the story to recite to the authorities.

The guy bobbed his head up and down. Quickly. Eagerly. "Uh. Y-ye-yes sir, I did this alone. You're right, sir."

"Your two friends *did not* come in here with you. It was your idea. You were desperate for money to help your sister, her kid, and your mom."

"Yeah—yeah. That's why I joined your—okay. Yes, sir." His voice dropped. "I acted alone. It was all my idea."

"The security cameras weren't working. When the police arrive, you will confess. You'll be taken in. Are you okay with a public defender or should I send a lawyer for you?"

Craig's head popped up. "You're going to help me fight the charge?"

"No. You're going to plead guilty, but my lawyer can help with a plea deal. But that's up to you. Whatever your sentence is, you'll do the time. You'll be a good inmate. If you get parole or probation, you'll follow the rules. I will have men wherever you end up so you'll be protected. If you run into problems, you'll need to let us know. You'll take the fall for this, but you'll be fine. You'll continue earning so your mom, sister, and her child will be financially supported. Do you understand this? You were never here with your two friends. It was you and you alone."

He swallowed. "Yes, sir. I understand, sir."

"Good." Creighton seemed to inspect my roommates' faces before addressing the cook and server. He motioned for them to stand. "I'm sorry this happened in your place of employment."

"It's no problem, Mr. Lane." The cook jumped up and held out his hand. He and the girl had seemed shaky, but there was a lack of fear on their faces. He shook Creighton's hand, then Levi's and Lassiter's. Lassiter held out a wad of bills for the man, who took it before touching the server's back. She was more cautious, sending Creighton, Levi, and Lassiter furtive looks, but she and the cook left quickly. They knew the drill. Of course they knew the drill. They were a block away from one of Creighton's buildings. This would be considered his territory. Every business on this street was protected under Creighton's watch.

Police sirens could be heard.

Creighton stood there, his gaze returning to me.

I hated everything about this. That I was here. That my housemates were as well. That they witnessed Creighton in action.

The police were getting closer. The sirens were louder.

"Boss." Lassiter went to the door, holding it open.

More of Creighton's men were outside, waiting by an SUV.

"Levi, you'll stay behind."

"No problemo." He dropped down and crossed his legs, right next to Palma, who eyed him. She edged away.

Creighton came to stand in front of me, his eyes darkening. He lifted a hand, tracing a finger down the side of my face. It was such a light and soft touch, and I couldn't stop a tremble from going through me.

He saw it, his eyes darkening even more, but he didn't comment on it. His eyes went to my shoulder and held there. "He shouldn't have touched you."

CHAPTER THIRTY

BLAKE

The ride home was eerily quiet.

God. What had just happened?

They were going to kick me out, and I couldn't blame them. I didn't have that much to pack, so that was easy, but then what? Go where? Heath's and Marshall's phones were buzzing nonstop, and I didn't need a guess to ask who or what they were talking about with each other.

Our SUV pulled to a stop outside of our brownstone, and I looked at Levi. He'd been quiet ever since Creighton told him to go with us. He took up residence next to Palma, knowing I'd want space. He was multitasking. I always wanted space when my world imploded, but he was also acting as a barrier. Heath and Marshall couldn't get to Palma's ear as much, though they could blow up her phone all they wanted.

I was the first inside. My hands shaking, I went to the kitchen to pour myself a drink. I'd need one to get through what was coming next.

They were quiet, traipsing in behind me.

I couldn't look at them. The guilt was overwhelming. I knew an argument could be made that I wasn't Creighton. I couldn't be held responsible for what he did, and yeah, maybe they would've gone to the fighting ring without me, and yeah, they would've gone to that diner, and *yeah*, those robbers wouldn't have been stopped like they had, but this still came down on me, somehow. Later when I would be thinking clearer, I'd figure it out. Right now, the regret and guilt were like acid inside of me.

I could barely see straight.

"Are we going to fucking talk about this?" Marshall started it out.

Awesome.

I took a big drag from my drink and let the whiskey replace the burn inside of me.

Levi got comfortable at the table, his arm draped over the back of his chair as he was half turned toward me. The rest were lined up just inside the room. Palma's hands were folded over each other, pressed in front of her. Heath looked half blitzed. His hair was all askew. Marshall was pissed. His jawline was tight and clenched, and the look he was giving Levi was seething.

Levi clocked it, only grinning back at him. He winked. "This ain't my act in the play. I'm background support right now."

"Background support for who? You're here for *him*." His gaze turned my way, still seething. "And speaking of, who is he, Blake?"

I took another drag of my whiskey. My hand was still shaking. Shit.

I didn't want to lose them.

Sudden very real and clear regret ate at me. I hadn't had enough time to spend with them. I hadn't let them get to know me either, and that was suddenly all I wanted.

It was too late.

I needed to tell them what was what. I'd pack and go after that. I'd upended their lives enough.

"Living room," I rasped out. I couldn't look any of them in the eye. "Might as well get comfortable for this."

Levi positioned himself in one of the corner chairs, an arm and leg draped over the side and back of his chair, his big body turned toward the group, also toward the front door. He'd made himself a drink before joining us, and he rattled his glass to me. He was keeping a lazy expression on his face, but I knew it was an act. Catching my eyes, he lifted his glass, shooting me a look of support.

I tried giving him a tiny grin back, except my face was etched in rock.

Heath and Palma were on the couch.

Heath spread his legs out, and his head rested back on the couch. His eyes were closed. He looked as if he could fall asleep like that. Palma was in the opposite corner of the couch, a pillow clasped tightly on her lap. She was picking at the seams in a nervous movement. Marshall was just behind where Palma was sitting. His arms were crossed over his chest, and his scowl was directed right at me. He was going to remain standing. "Enough stalling. You need to clue us in to who the fuck you are and who the fuck that guy was." He raked a hand through his hair, almost savagely. "We deserve that, don't you think?"

Levi's head lifted. His lazy expression disappeared. "Watch how you speak to her."

"Or what?" Marshall's head jerked in his direction.

"Or you'll find out who we are in a whole different way. One where you might lose a few body parts." Levi didn't move, but the ice delivered with that threat was enough to have Marshall turning back toward me. Levi waited to see if he'd say anything more. When he didn't, Levi resumed his lazy facade again, giving me a wink.

It was my turn.

My stomach filled with lead.

I didn't give them the whole background story of Creighton and me, but I told them enough.

I met him in a foster home. Levi as well. We grew up together. The story of explaining Creighton and how he came to take over the streets and the city wasn't my story to tell. I didn't say anything about how Creighton had psychopathic tendencies, or how he tried to curb those so he didn't hurt innocent people. I didn't give them the long and sordid story of how Creighton's easy ability to end people who hurt me dogged my every decision since I could remember.

"Growing up under Creighton's shadow has been a lot. But he and I made an agreement. This was my chance to try and live a normal life, or as normal as a kid from foster care could get. Moving into this place with you guys, it's been a dream. I couldn't believe it. You've all been great. I know we've all been busy with our different courses and workload, but I've appreciated that you guys tried including me with your group. It's just—getting to know people takes a while with me." I was going to throw up. "I just want you to know that, and I'm sorry for anything that Creighton's done or if you guys end up as collateral damage. I'm sorry again."

I needed to go. Now.

The urge to flee was strong. I tried to restrain myself. Instead of running, I went upstairs with a brisk walk.

Hurt and panic and the ability to breathe was becoming increasingly hard. I pushed it all aside as I got to my room and started throwing things onto my bed. I upended everything in my closet. All my clothes. Shoes. My things for the bathroom. Grabbing some bags, I began blindly stuffing everything inside of them.

I was trying not to cry. I really was, but this one hurt more than the others. I didn't know why, but dammit. Tears were breaking free, sliding down my face. I had a suitcase I could use for my books. I realized that I was leaving with four times the amount of stuff.

How had that happened?

I always kept my items to a single bag. It was easier to cut and run if you only had one bag to grab, but here I was now with four.

"What are you doing?"

I jumped.

Palma was inside my door, pale, streaks of dried tears on her face.

"I—"

She jerked forward into the room, her eyes pinned to my bags. "You're leaving?"

I closed my mouth. My shoulders lowered. "You don't want me here. I thought you wouldn't want me to stay."

She scoffed, bitterness mingling in there. "Maybe give us a chance to say it? Because, Blake, we're not going to say it. I'm not. Were you going to say goodbye? How was this going to go in your mind?"

I winced, hearing the hurt in her voice. "Creighton is—"

"Your boyfriend is psychotic and scary, but guess what? He doesn't get to keep you for himself. You're my friend now." She raised her chin up. "I'm from the south, darlin'. Us Beauregards don't scare easy."

"Marshall doesn't want me here."

She snorted. "If you haven't started to figure Marshall out, what he says and does is usually the exact opposite. He acts all flirty and carefree when he's the most cautious one of us all." She picked up one of my bags. "Or he was until you. Pretty sure you got him beat for that award."

"What about Heath? He didn't say anything, but I know he doesn't want me here."

She took my bag back to my bed. "That might've been true in the beginning, but after a week of you being here, you're one of us. Heath's also the biggest baby of us all. You just haven't stuck around to figure that out either." She unzipped my bag and began pulling out my items. One at a time. "To my count, that sounds like you've still got some things to learn about us. That means you can't leave. Hmmm?"

Dumbfounded, I stood there. My chest was going to cave in as she walked around my room and returned everything back to where it'd been previously. She got a few things wrong, but it didn't matter.

She started working on the second bag.

"Palma," I tried to protest, reaching for it.

She caught my hand and squeezed it before pushing it aside gently. "I grew up blessed. Two good parents. I love my mama something fierce, and there's five of us girls from our household. I had one room growing up. I could fill it up with all of my things. Change the color on the walls as often as I wanted. Same house all my life, and I don't think it'll be going anywhere. I don't see myself ever not being able to go home if I needed to, so I have no idea what it was like growing up how you did. Not one clue. I'm not even going to try to imagine. I figure

I'd get it wrong anyways, so I'm just going to say this. Your time being scared to let other people in can come to an end with me. I get that's a tall order. I'm aware it'll take time. You gotta give me that time to show you I'm worth letting in." She put down the second bag. "The minute you told me not to date anyone with fourth or fifth after their name, I began looking at you like a sister I was just meeting for the first time."

I felt raw, so I jerked up a shoulder and looked away. "The whole name of it all. Brad Grundle? Who wants to become Mrs. Grundle? If someone wrote a poem about you, they'd rhyme that with bundle. You're meant for more."

Palma fell silent, staring at me.

She burst out laughing. "I have no idea what that means, but it's funny. Mrs. Grundle. Rhymes with bundle. A bundle of what?" She picked up the third bag.

I eased beside her and began to take my things from her. She pulled them from the bag. I put them away. "Bundle of dildos."

She snorted, taking a pile to my dresser. "Bundle of cock rings."

"Bundle of douchebags."

"Ew." She wrinkled her nose. "Why'd you go there? I enjoyed thinking about our poem. Oh, what life would be like as Mrs. Grundle. To wake up each morning, ordering enough vibrators so they'd come as a bundle."

"To become Mrs. Grundle the fifth, one would need to accept their new life as one for the bird . . . s."

She laughed. "A jaybird."

"A game bird."

"Password."

We shared a grin.

I said, "Swear word."

"Unheard."

"Preferred."

"Referred."

My grin darkened. "Absurd."

She barked out another laugh. "Just like this poem has become."

"This was a poem?"

We were down to my suitcase. She knelt and unzipped it, grabbing the first of my books. "One of the worst I've ever heard."

"And that feels appropriate for what life might've been as Mrs. Grundle the fifth."

We were still laughing when my room was back in order.

After placing my suitcase in the closet, Palma came over and sat on the end of my bed. We both fell silent. The air in the room shifted, the lighthearted moment was done.

I shifted to sit on the other end and looked at my lap. "He comes here sometimes. You should know that."

"Comes here?"

I lifted my head. "He sleeps with me."

Her eyes widened, jerking down to the bed we were both sitting on.

"Not—" I touched the cover. "Not like sex or anything. Not like that. Just—just sleeping."

"Oh." She relaxed but continued frowning at the bed. "Do you love him?"

I made a choking sound, hearing words that plagued me. I shook my head. "I . . . He's family." Because it was that simple, right?

I didn't tell her how I ordered him to stay away from me, then wrapped my legs around him the next time I saw him.

"But you . . ." She looked away before turning back. A new determination was over her face. "You don't love him like you love Levi."

I stared at her.

She added, "Levi's like family to you too. Right? Like a brother."

I couldn't respond, fearful where she was going next.

"It's not the same with him. Creighton doesn't look at you like that."

"He can't love."

She frowned.

"He doesn't have the capability to love, but yes, he's obsessed with me."

"And you're . . ." She hesitated before reaching forward to take my hand in hers. "He's obsessed with you while you're . . ."

She trailed off when I began shaking my head. Fervently.

Pain sliced through me, at almost hearing the words I couldn't admit to myself.

"I-I can't. He'd need to be a different person. He's a monster, and he'll never not be a monster."

"He's not a monster to you."

No. He wasn't.

"I think you're wrong."

I frowned at her.

She let go of my hand after giving it one last squeeze, the ends of her mouth lifting up in a small grin. A hesitant grin. "I think if he was a different person, you wouldn't have the feelings you do for him. Because then he wouldn't be *your* Creighton."

I didn't know how to respond to that.

My Creighton.

CHAPTER THIRTY-ONE

BLAKE

I was waiting for him the next night. I left the light off but moved to the chair in the far corner so when he opened the door, I could see him, but he couldn't yet see me. Watching him ghost inside, moving silently and lithely, I would never get over how he could move. Among everything, Creighton had some innate athleticism that in another world, he could've used to become a professional athlete in some sport. He'd been too vicious for football or basketball. Coaches knew not to give him a ball for baseball. Hockey was the best fit, but when he learned how to use his stick as a knife, he was quickly taken off the ice. I never heard those stories from Creighton himself, but the other foster kids loved to tell them at times. There were a lot of stories about Creighton. All of them had the same theme. He was dangerous and deadly.

And yet, I hadn't been able to get Palma's words out of my head.

I needed him to be a different man in order to be with him, but she was right. He would not be the man I . . . My heart palpitated. I hadn't argued against what Palma said, but acknowledging and saying those words to myself meant that I needed to accept what I felt for Creighton.

A tremor went through my hands.

I still wasn't ready. Not yet, but we needed to talk.

I couldn't stand aside any longer in this new war he was embroiled in. When he came into my room that night, I waited until he was standing over my bed, looking at the body pillow I'd put under my blankets.

I moved fast, knowing I only had the element of surprise for this to work.

I had a pair of handcuffs opened and in my hand, and as his back was turned to me, I pounced. I slapped one of the handcuffs around his hand and used my body to propel him onto my bed and lifted his arm so I could slap the other handcuff around my bedpost. As he lay there under my weight, momentarily surprised, I scrambled to do the same with his other hand. By that time, as I was lifting his other hand, Creighton had caught on to my intentions. I expected him to fight. He didn't. He let me lift his arm up, and he watched, almost amused as I finished the second pair of handcuffs.

I was out of breath, and my pulse was pounding from the buildup more than anything.

He tested the handcuffs. They held firm. I made sure that he couldn't flip over and bring his hands together because if he did, he'd figure out a way to pick the handcuffs. I knew he could because I'd learned how to do it from him.

I sank down over him, a little sweaty, and gave him a lopsided grin. "I can't believe that worked."

He only raised his eyebrows, his eyes slowly trekking down my body and lingering where I was nestled right over him. "I'm game to see where this is going." He lifted his hips, grinding up and into me.

I stifled a moan, not expecting the pleasure that coasted through me.

With him.

This was new to me.

Him. Me.

"So far I'm enjoying it."

I groaned before I growled, lifting up only to grab a pillow. I put that over him and sank back down. He couldn't grind against me as well with the pillow in place, but I still wanted to keep my weight on him, as if I needed that added way to hold him in place. It was probably a useless way of thinking, but it made me feel more in control. And it added an extra closeness for the conversation we needed to have.

He waited, but when I remained quiet, he inclined his head toward me. "Do you know what you're doing?"

I was a little lightheaded as I confessed, "Not really. No. It was more of an idea, but I didn't think it'd work. I'm kinda figuring this out as we go."

I rested a hand to his chest and tried to ignore all the feelings happening in my body.

I liked sitting this way on Creighton.

Like I could dominate him.

Like he would have to do what I wanted him to do.

The power was intoxicating.

Though, of course, it'd only work until the morning because he had an ungodly amount of followers who'd crap their pants if their boss was absent for longer than a night. One of his men would come looking for him. Probably Lassiter. He wouldn't care who he had to bowl over in order to check my bedroom.

Or Levi, who was still here. And was also trying to charm his way into Palma's bed.

I could talk Levi into helping cover for me, though he'd probably only give me another day. If Lassiter showed up, no way. The game would be up, but until any of that happened, I let myself relish the fact that Creighton was handcuffed to my bed.

"Usually when handcuffs come out, the other person tells me what they want from me. Information or . . ." He lifted his hips up again, and I squeaked a little because even with a pillow between us, I could feel him. And he felt good.

This felt good, the rocking motion he was starting to do.

I pressed my hand harder on his chest. "Stop."

A chuckle came from him. "Or what? You haven't told me the reason for this." He moved his left hand, rattling the handcuff.

I was getting all confused before remembering. "Answers." I moved my hand.

His head lowered, watching where my hand was going. "For?"

I'd started to lift his shirt up over his stomach. Flustered, I smoothed his shirt back in place and crossed my arms over my chest, glaring down at him, or more accurately, glaring straight at him since he was sitting up against the headboard. "Your war." My voice cracked.

We were so close to each other.

If I leaned forward and if he met me halfway, our mouths would touch.

My gaze fell to his lips. I was remembering what it'd been like to kiss him. To be in his arms. To taste him.

I swallowed roughly.

My blood was heating up.

"My war?" A faint hint of amusement was heard from him. As his own gaze fell to my mouth before lifting to meet my eyes, he was aware of the internal turmoil happening inside of me. I was getting distracted by my body and his body and the fact we were on my bed, at night, and no one would be interrupting us anytime soon.

Finding myself leaning forward, I groaned and closed my eyes. Slapping a hand to his chest, I shoved myself backward, imagining a bucket of cold water coming down over me.

"One of the last times you saw me, you wanted to murder me."

Murder him.

Right. Yes.

The robbery.

"I need to know what's going on with your war with West and Walden. You knew they took me."

He went eerily still. "You've always been able to protect yourself. I failed you."

"No," I started to say, but paused.

I sank farther back on his lap. Both of my hands went to his chest and began toying with the bottom of his shirt. "Wait. When did you find out?"

"I have an inside man with them. He was going to notify me, but the alarms went off. You'd already escaped. He ran interference, tried to help give you time to get away. Did they hurt you?"

That explained a lot. I shook my head. "They looked like they wanted to. Walden's unhinged."

He made a noncommittal sound, his mouth pressing in a flat line. "He deserved everything he got."

That attitude wasn't going to bring this war to an end. He was going to keep it going, and going, and going. "Creighton, if I'm going to make a decision about you and me"—my heart was suddenly trying to pound its way out of my own chest—"then I need to be read in on everything. Changes and compromises have to be made. Do you agree? I mean, if you do want a you and me thing, that is. Do you want that?"

Gah. I was doing this backward. People in real life hooked up, hooked up again and again, and after it was a pattern, they talked about maybe getting into a "thing" together. Creight and I hooked up once and boom, he was handcuffed to my bed and I was making him have the talk.

I had out-stalked my stalker. Mic drop.

He didn't respond, staring at me with his default setting. His dead eyes.

"If I'm staying here and if you're going to continue to be a part of this war, they're going to come after me again." I skipped over the other question. Because, embarrassing.

His eyes shifted, still not showing any emotion. "They took you from Octavia. In doing that, they included a whole other Mafia organization into this fight, but maybe that was the plan. I can't make a move against them until I know what decision Cole Mauricio has made concerning repercussions."

I was trying to catch up. "No. Wait. There was a guy. I forgot about him. I was leaving work when I saw Walden with the guy. That's when they took me. Maybe . . ."

"What guy?"

"A guy." I shrugged, relaying everything I remembered about the incident.

Creighton had gone still beneath me. "He handed him a thick envelope?"

I nodded. "He said that I wasn't supposed to be there."

"Walden said that?"

"I thought he meant because of Octavia. Because of the owner." I was suddenly terrified to ask. "Is Cole Mauricio powerful?"

"Yes."

My heart sank. "How powerful?"

"He runs Chicago. With Carter Reed, they run half of the Twin Cities too."

"That's in Minnesota?"

"Yes. Minneapolis and St. Paul."

My chest tightened again. "Who runs the other half?"

"Kai Bennett. They have a tentative truce."

My mouth dried. I didn't understand that part. "And how powerful is Kai Bennett?"

"He runs half the country."

"Oh."

"And Canada."

My heart dropped. "So he's scary."

"If I were to experience that feeling, yes." He was answering all of the questions with those same bland responses that were his default setting.

I swallowed a knot, remembering one advantage that Creighton had over his enemies. He wasn't ruled by emotions, so therefore as I studied him, I knew that even though he was using those words, he was doing it for my benefit. He was not scared of those men. It's the advantage he'd been extorting against Tristian West and Ashton Walden, and it'd been working so far. Which brought me back to the original reason for all of this. "I have people here that I care about."

"You're worried West and Walden would go after your friends?"

I held his gaze, knowing he could see my answer.

He didn't reply, not at first. He was quiet for a moment before he said, "I can put more guards on your friends, but I don't think they'll move on your roommates."

"I like them, Eight."

My hand was resting against his chest, and it was only for that reason that I felt his heart thump when I whispered that nickname for him. That was his only reaction. His face, his eyes, his tone, nothing else changed.

"I thought they would kick me out, but they didn't. Palma got mad at me when she caught me. I . . ." Could I have this hope? Could I have it and keep it? "I've only wanted to feel normal, and Palma gave me that. I think I could finally have that normal life, but that means your war can't hurt them."

I sank farther down on him.

That's what I wanted from him. I wanted to stay. I wanted to remain in these people's lives. And I wanted to not be a part of Creighton's war. Except that was unrealistic, because I was the one weakness he had. I would never be rid of him. I didn't think I even wanted that anymore. And Creighton would never stop being Creighton.

"What do you want?" I asked him.

He cocked his head to the side. That was his only indication he didn't understand my question.

I clarified, "At the end of the day, what do you want?"

"I want you."

God. Those words hit me in the sternum, sending vibrations through my whole body. They were intoxicating to hear. My blood heated.

"But other than me, what do you want?"

He considered my question for a little bit. "I can't live under someone else's rule. That's what you're asking, isn't it?" His eyes lingered on my mouth. He flicked back up to meet my gaze. "You want me to stop doing what I do. If I did, that would mean another gang or organization or family would rule instead. Where there is an opening for power, someone will take it. It's the natural way of things. Someone always rises to the top. We'd have to live under their rules and guidelines. I wouldn't be able to protect you. I can't do that. Where you go, I will always try to protect you. Even though you have proved over and over again that you don't need me."

My heart leapt. I whispered, unable to stop myself, "I'll always need you."

And just like that, all of the hope that I'd been too scared to let myself feel, all of it deflated right out of me. We were back to square one because if I had him, I'd never live any semblance of a normal life.

I wanted him, but not how he was. And he couldn't change himself.

I was being torn apart inside.

"Uncuff me." His eyes were suddenly heated, tracing over every inch of my face.

My arms were weighed down by cement anchors, but I did as he asked. As soon as one hand was free, his arm snaked forward, his hand cupping the side of my face. He smoothed his thumb over my cheek, tilting my head in his palm. "What did I say that made you so sad?"

Because of course he wouldn't understand. Maybe logically, but not emotionally.

I shook my head, my voice rough as I whispered, "It doesn't matter."

He leaned closer, now arching over me. "It matters to me." He kept searching my face as if the answer would suddenly appear there. It wasn't that simple. "What do you want me to do, Blake? Tell me. I'll do it. This one time."

I could've said so much, but the truth was that I wanted him to be someone else, and that would never happen. "I—" My whole body was hurting. All of it was one massive ache that was never going to leave me. This wasn't going to work. I needed to accept that.

I couldn't stay in this in-between stage. Where he and I were dancing around being together or not. I needed to try something different.

"Kiss me."

He studied me for another beat, his eyebrows pinching together, but then his face cleared, and once again, with dead eyes, he leaned to me. His lips found mine, and I gasped, because even though there was no emotion on his face, the fact was that his touch elicited all the emotions inside of me. I had more than enough for both of us.

Something had to change.

I was going to give in.

CHAPTER THIRTY-TWO

BLAKE

Creighton didn't hold back.

His mouth opened over mine, and I was helpless to do anything except cling to him. He was rough. There was a primal edge to his kiss, and something inside of me, deep inside of me, began to respond. Like there was my own monster in me and he was waking her up.

My whole body shook. *"Eight."*

He had one hand holding the side of my face, but suddenly both his hands were there. How he got the other free, I didn't know. I also wasn't surprised. He framed my face.

God. Those eyes of his. They were usually dead. They were black looking back at me, but I could see something stirring in them. There was a heat overlaying that, whatever was underneath.

A prick of fear stabbed me, and I shoved it aside.

He held still, still staring at me, and both of his thumbs swept over my cheeks. He tilted my head backward, dropping his mouth to my throat. A groan left me.

That felt good. That felt so good.

"Creighton," I gasped again, my hands grabbing onto his biceps.

His hands left my face and dropped to my thighs. He lifted me up, swept the pillow out from between us, and pulled me on top of him. I sank down, feeling how hard he was.

I pulled back and looked at where we met. We were both still clothed. I hadn't wanted to feel completely disarmed against him, so I stayed in my day clothes when I waited for him. Jeans and a sweatshirt. He came to me in black athletic joggers and a black sweatshirt. I loved this look on him. Always had. It made him look like an elite athlete, and sometimes I liked to indulge. I'd daydream about what life would be like if we were different people. If he was a professional athlete and I was his girlfriend. Or hell, maybe someone like the owner of a bookstore. *Notting Hill*, where neither of us were known.

But Creighton would turn those blank eyes on me, and the reminder that there was no point to daydreaming would return. Tonight, though, I could pretend. I could indulge. He tasted my throat, and another tremor went through me.

I was giving in. At least for the night.

I was letting myself be his.

A thrill burst in me as I rocked over him.

He surged up, his hands clamping over my hips, and as I began moving over him, he moved with me.

He kept tasting my throat, sliding to linger over my pulse.

Dark hunger amped up in me. I felt electrified and alive, and I didn't know how to handle all these sensations that he was giving me. They were big and strong and demanding to be met. Demanding to be faced.

I gulped. My head was beginning to swim. My vision was clouding.

One of his hands slid to my waist and slipped under my sweatshirt. He let it rest there, but the feel of his palm against my naked skin, knowing how close it was to where I was aching for more, another groan escaped me.

I didn't try suppressing how my body was shaking. Raking my hands up his arm, over his shoulders, up the back of his neck, my fingers tangled with his hair like in his warehouse. This time, though, I gave in to my need and yanked his head back.

He let me, his eyes opening to slits to meet my gaze.

This monster was mine. All mine. He was letting me do whatever the fuck I wanted to do to him. I was drunk on that power. A sudden impatience whipped through me, making me slide even closer to the edge. I was slipping.

I didn't give a fuck.

Creighton frowned, seeing the storm inside of me, but didn't comment.

I kept one of my hands holding his hair, kept holding his head back, and lifted up from his lap. I only knelt upward, my other hand making quick work of unbuttoning my jeans.

His hands moved to help me.

I growled. *"No."* Deep and low.

His hands fell away, but his eyes turned molten. He liked my commands.

When I got my jeans opened, I shoved them down. My underwear as well. My impatience had snapped. I was barely able to even think about what I was doing. I just wanted him, and I was done waiting. I didn't sink back down on him. Not yet. My hand moved to his pants, and I growled again, because I couldn't pull them down with only one hand.

I pushed my body against his, arching over him, and I hissed a low warning. "Stay."

The blackness in his eyes sparked, but he didn't respond. He stayed as I let go of his hand. Standing up, I shimmied the rest of the way out of my jeans and underwear. They were tossed aside, then I knelt before him. I yanked his pants down. My hand reached inside his boxer briefs and wrapped around his dick, finding it thick and long and hard.

I pulled his boxer briefs down the rest of the way. My hand worked him over.

His own groan slipped from him. He had moved his head enough so he could watch me. His eyes were hooded. For some reason, I liked that look on his face.

"Do you have a condom?"

His eyebrows lowered, just briefly, but he nodded. "Wallet. Pants pocket."

I knelt down to fish it out, finding the condom. I pulled it out and sheathed it over him, my hand smoothing over his tip.

His body shook. "Fuck, Quokk—"

"No," I snapped, glowering at him.

He bit his lip. Fuck. He liked what I was doing.

A part of me enjoyed that. It helped feed this wanton need that had risen to the surface, demanding to take over because I was so very tired of starving myself from him. Not anymore. Not tonight. I was going to have my fill.

I moved back over him and began to lower myself.

He caught my hips and squeezed. "Blake," he rasped out.

"No." I didn't know what he wanted, but this was about me and what I wanted. But some reality slipped in, and I remembered that I needed to make sure he wanted to do this. "Do you want me?"

His hands flexed at my question. "Always."

"Then I want this."

He started to say something.

I clasped my hand over his mouth, shutting him up. "I need this, Creighton."

He gently bit the inside of my hand, which sent tingles through my core. I was throbbing. After licking over that mark, he pulled his head back and murmured, "You're a virgin."

How did he—of course, he would know. "It's creepy as fuck that you know that."

He flashed me a slight smile but bent to kiss my hand again before taking it in his teeth, in a gentle hold. He raked his teeth over my finger before pulling back to say, "I need to make sure you're ready. Let me."

His hand slid to my clit, and he began circling there, massaging me.

Lust built and built the more he rubbed, then he slid a finger inside of me, stretching me.

I caught my breath.

He leaned in, his mouth finding my throat. He nuzzled there before moving up, kissing my chin, then my lips again. He spoke against them as he slid a second finger inside, moving both within me. "Your hymen is still intact. Are you sure you want to do this?"

I moved my head in permission, soundless.

He inserted a third finger, still stretching me.

I grunted. The pain was there.

He pressed a kiss against the corner of my mouth. "This will hurt."

I tilted my head, my mouth closing over his fully, and I was done waiting. I lowered myself over him. His hand slipped out, but only went to help align himself with me. His other helped guide my hips.

I tensed.

"You need to relax." His tongue slid inside of my mouth.

Need shook me.

He felt my body trembling. His one hand slipped to the small of my back, his palm splaying out, anchoring me. "Baby, are you su—"

I sheathed myself over him, feeling him entering me and pushing past that resistance.

It hurt. He was fully inside of me, but he waited, holding firm. He pulled my body against his and his mouth gaped over my throat. "Holy fuck. You're tight." His teeth skimmed my neck, but he still held still.

Both of his hands went to the tops of my legs, just touching me there.

I tried to move.

He pressed down. "No. Wait. You need to adjust to me."

I dropped my head to his neck and mewled against him, needing this pain to go away. I'd waited so long, and it was an annoyance. He wrapped his arms around me tightly. "Wait, Blake. God. Please. Fucking wait. I don't want to hurt you anymore."

Hearing his voice break, I settled, but then I was just gasping for breath. And suddenly, I needed him to be completely naked. I wanted skin on skin. Almost frantic, I pulled at his shirt. A desperate cry ripped from me because I couldn't get it off him fast enough.

He helped, then reached for my sweatshirt until finally, blessedly, I felt his naked skin against mine. There was a sheen of sweat that had worked over his chest. Feeling his heart pounding through his chest, it thumped against my own. He smoothed a finger up the side of my body, his thumb taking over, trailing up my arm, to my throat, to my chin, and he tipped my head to meet his. His mouth dropped back over mine.

"I *need* you."

He sighed in surrender, and began to move.

It hurt.

He continued going inside of me. The pain began to lessen as the pleasure began to awaken.

"Eight," I sighed.

Suddenly there was only pleasure.

I'd never felt anything as good as this. It was swirling through me and building and writhing, and I wanted more of it.

I pulled on his hair, as hard as I could, needing, just needing more.

He bit out a curse, reached up, and disengaged one of my hands. "You can scrape me up as much as you want, but I need my hair."

Right, I realized belatedly, but he was thrusting up into me, and I forgot all about what he said. Except the part where I could scrape him. My nails raked over his back. He trembled under my touch.

I liked knowing that I could make him react like that, so I did it again. And again.

He shook every time until he clamped an arm tight around me and flipped us so I was on my back and he was settled between my legs. He stayed inside of me, only paused once to make sure I was okay. My head fell back against the bed, and I moaned. "Fucking move. Now."

A husky laugh left him before he cursed. He took hold of my hip and used that for traction so he could thrust at a deeper angle.

I grasped onto the back of his head again, but remembered about his hair. I only tugged on him lightly, lifting his head so I could assert my mouth to his again. I liked kissing him as he was moving inside of me. "I'm not fragile."

"You'll be sore."

A sound of frustration rose from me. I scowled at him. "I want you to *fuck* me."

Something snapped inside of him. I caught my breath, seeing a glimpse at the monster I knew resided inside of him. He rose over me, yanked me down at a different angle, and braced himself against the headboard. He reared back only to slam into me.

Yes. *Yes.* This was what I wanted.

This was fucking. I didn't want anything smooth that might've resembled lovemaking. I wanted primal and carnal and animalistic, and this was what he was giving me. He pounded into me, no longer holding back for me. This. I shivered, my hands skimming his neck, to his shoulders, to his back.

This was what I wanted from him, and now that I had it, why had I waited this long?

He opened a door in me, one that went into something vast and deep and dark, and my body quaked from how addictive all of this was. It rose and climbed, and I opened my mouth, a silent scream caught in my throat. I hurdled over the edge, my walls clamping down on him. My vision went black, and I dug my nails into his skin.

I broke through, feeling something warm and hot trickle out.

It sent him over the edge, and he grew still, his release pulsating inside of me.

As the tremors began to wane, I lay there, trying to catch my breath because holy shit, what had that been? I met his gaze as he pulled out. He tugged off the condom, tying it up, leaving the bed and room.

He came back a moment later, a warm towel in his hand, and he used it to clean me. He left again. When he returned, he pulled on his boxer briefs and slipped back into bed with me. "You should go to the bathroom." He patted my hip.

I didn't want to move, but I knew he was right.

I slipped out of the bed, reached for his sweatshirt and put it on. It fell to my thighs. I hurried into the bathroom and tried avoiding the mirror because I already knew I would look a mess. I went through the motions of getting ready for bed before returning to bed. I snuggled in still wearing his sweatshirt. It smelled like him.

He moved to my side, curling around me, and one of his hands went to my stomach. He began to rub in slow circles. "You okay?"

A half laugh, half gurgle came out of me. "Is sex like that normal?"

His eyes flickered, some of the vast emptiness looked like it sparked a little. "That—" He expelled a ragged breath. "No, Blake. That wasn't normal sex. You're going to be sore tomorrow."

I grabbed his hand and brought it up to lightly bite his fingers.

He chuckled, letting me nibble on his hand. I didn't know why I was doing this. He'd woken something in me, and whatever it was, there was anger in me, mixing with a thirst that felt like it was never going to be quenched. It made me feel on edge, which was mixing with a deep feeling of contentment and being sated. I was all mixed up inside, and somehow, clamping down on his hand with my teeth helped take some of that edge off.

I moved my head so I was looking up and not at him anymore. I confessed, breathless, "I want to do that again."

He used his other hand to smooth some of my hair down the side of my face. "We will. We'll do it as many times as you want."

"Even if I'm mad at you? Because I'm mad at you a lot."

He sighed. "Even if you're mad at me."

"Even if I hate you at that moment and want to murder you?"

"Even then."

There was one more thing, and my throat swelled at the idea of bringing it up because we had never talked about other people before. "I don't want you touching anyone else." I knew he had used others in the past for his sexual needs.

His hand stilled on my hair before he continued running his fingers through my strands. "I will not let anyone else touch me. Just you."

I relaxed and closed my eyes, knowing full well that we both just skirted around the truth. That I had just claimed him as much as he had always claimed me. A shiver worked its way down my spine, but I ignored it. Right now, I didn't care what the consequences for this night were going to be.

I went to sleep.

CHAPTER THIRTY-THREE

CREIGHTON

Blake was sleeping. The house was dark, but I moved through it easily. It was second nature by now. She fell asleep in my sweatshirt, so I pulled on my pants and my Henley for this conversation. They had another roommate, one they barely knew anything about, except I knew enough about. She was awake, like she always was at this time of the night. It was her lounging time, so I found her in the kitchen.

She was dressed for bed. Skimpy black shorts. A black tank top. Her long black hair was loose. She was stirring something on the stove. I watched her a moment in the shadows where I knew she couldn't see me. She'd feel me soon enough, but right now, I was glad for her relaxed state.

I saw the dragon tattoo circling her entire arm, all the way to her shoulder where the dragon's tail would end just beneath her neck. Someone who didn't know better would think it was simply a cool tattoo.

"You're Yakuza."

She went still, her only reaction. Slowly, she turned to find me where I stood.

I stepped forward, and she turned the oven off, half facing me.

I didn't go any closer.

She knew who I was, just like I knew who she was. There was no fear in her eyes. Only awareness. She tilted her head up, her chin almost challenging. "I've been waiting for you to introduce yourself. You skirt around me the other nights, going to your girlfriend upstairs."

So she *had* known who Blake was to me. "My reports tell me that you are not here acting as a current member of the Yakuza."

"I'm here as a student. I'm getting my PhD."

"And when you're done?"

A warning flashed in her eyes. "When I'm done is none of your business."

"You are here. You are either a threat or you are an asset. Which are you?"

Anger gleamed back at me. Her nostrils flared slightly. She forced herself back so she was leaning against the kitchen counter and reached for her stirring spoon. She began moving it around her hand, her wrist flicking back and forth. She did it so naturally, as if she weren't aware she was doing it. She seemed contemplative before her face cleared. "*You* put your girlfriend here."

She was connecting some dots. I was interested if she could put it all together.

She commented further, "I'm the reason she came here." Her chest rose swiftly as she landed on some theory. She shifted to her side so she could stir her food. "Were you hoping I'd become attached to your girlfriend and use that connection to your benefit? I've not even met her. And I am not Yakuza. My family is. They will not give one fuck about your girlfriend, even if I had formed some sort of fondness for her. Which I haven't. If you were hoping to use me to grow some sort of alliance with my family, you are mistaken."

Ah. Yes. That would be a normal way of doing business.

"Your brother is second in command, along with your uncle and three of your cousins. They killed your father."

The stirring spoon halted abruptly; only her pinkie held it in place.

I continued, "His death was the penance received as payment so you could come here as a student."

"You're lying."

I almost smiled at that. "Psychopaths *are* known to be skilled liars."

The stirring spoon fell out of her hand, clattering to the floor. She didn't dare look away from me. Since this conversation started, she had a certain arrogance to her. She was cocky. Yes, she'd been aware of me, and yes, she knew when I skirted around her on the nights when I would go to Blake.

So many looked at my face and put their own judgments on me, and I was okay with that. It usually served my purpose, but it was important right now, for this particular girl, to have a full understanding of who I was.

I don't care if she thought I was lying or not.

"I know about you. I know you have only one weakness." Her eyes flicked to the ceiling.

"I should gut you for that threat." I said it casually because, well, it actually was a casual consideration to me. But I'd also learned that normal people tended to get nervous when I said words like that, as if I were asking if they had a pen I could use. Her chest paused and held, and there, right there, I saw a slight trickle of fear begin to show.

It was easy for me to read normal people. People were like paintings to me. Each emotion had a different color, and all of the many emotions woven together made up such pretty masterpieces. I had a certain appreciation for each normal human, and unlike other psychopaths, I had no interest in pulling apart each emotion in order to better understand where they came from.

Her pinkie finger began to shake. I didn't think she was aware of it.

Her eyes stayed wide and almost unblinking, glued to me.

I should get back to Blake. "I did not put Blake here to get to your family. I would never use her in that way. I put *you* here because you are an added shield. You and the Nogoskeski boy. I am in a war right now, and if anyone moves on her while she's in this house, your family could use that as a perceived threat against their organization. West and Walden will not want to risk another fight on their hands."

"So I'm a shield for your girlfriend?" she asked.

Funny. She had no reaction to hearing how I orchestrated her housing placement.

"Yes," I answered.

"And if they try to make a deal with my family and offer up your girlfriend to solidify that alliance?"

That could happen. It was a risk of war. Alliances would shift and adjust as the pieces would be placed and moved across the chessboard. But I just gave her a smile, knowing it was one that Blake would call my smile of death and promised destruction. "If that were to happen, I would enjoy peeling the skin from you that I would ship in a box to your brother."

She braced herself as far back against the counter as possible. "I should gut *you* for that threat."

That would be even more interesting. "Do we have an understanding?"

"Yes," she clipped out. Not happy. "All this is null and void if I move out."

That would inconvenience me. "You should not do that."

There was no heated warning behind my words, but I smiled at her again.

One of her arms shook, but she tucked it farther to hide it behind her.

The conversation seemed to be done. We understood each other.

I left, only veering to the smaller sitting room where Levi had taken up residence. He was awake, lying on one of the couches with a blanket tossed over him. He turned his head at my approach. I could hear his amusement. "You're like a giant fucking feral panther, and that was the equivalent of you dragging a hyena that you killed and bringing it to her doorstep as a gesture of respect. The problem is that she's also a hyena and you brought one of her family members as a gift."

"She's a person. She's not a hyena."

He expelled a half laugh, coughing to cover it up. "It's a metaphor."

"I like hyenas."

He laughed again, this time not trying to cover it up. "Of course you do. And again, it's a metaphor. I could've called her a leopard."

"Hyenas are misunderstood."

"Oh, Jesus Christ, Creight. Let it go on the hyenas. I'm just saying she doesn't realize that whole conversation was you trying to be *respectful* to her, since she was here first and you not only are making your presence known, but you also put one of your own in her house *because* she's here."

"I put her here."

He snorted. "Not making it better."

"Blake likes hyenas too. She likes most animals."

He settled further on the couch. "I know you don't give a fuck, but I'm happy for you. Mom and Dad are finally together." He laughed to himself. "Go to bed, Creight. Tomorrow's going to be interesting."

I texted Lassiter as I returned to Blake.

Me: Hold off on completing my order. The four gifts.

Lassiter: Taking or the other part?

Me: The other part.

Lassiter: Got it.

I sent another order to my IT guys.

Me: The night Blake was taken, she said Walden was having a meeting with another man in the alley between his building and Octavia. He handed him an envelope. Find out who that man was. Send me everything you can get on him.

IT Lead: Got it, Boss.

CHAPTER THIRTY-FOUR

BLAKE

When I woke, the night came back to me. I froze.

Creighton was always gone in the mornings, but last night was different. I lifted my head and looked over, and he was there. Relief flooded me, which made me feel embarrassed. I ducked my head, but I was happy he was here.

He was sitting up, back resting against the headboard, those dead eyes not missing anything. "I brought you coffee."

"Oh." It was on the nightstand. I sat up, sitting cross-legged so I was facing him. The coffee was hot. "When did you make this?"

"Earlier. It got cold, so I made another pot. I know you like your coffee."

I frowned. "How long have you been awake?"

"I never went to sleep."

I choked on the sip of coffee I just took. "What?"

"I don't need a lot of sleep. You know this."

I blinked a few times. "I mean, I knew that. But that was back . . ." When I was in high school. "I guess I just haven't thought about it. So, wait. Every time you came here, you didn't sleep?"

"A few hours."

I groaned. "I wish I had that problem."

"How are you feeling?"

I'd taken another sip, my eyes jumping back to him. Man. With no sleep, he still looked good. He was in his clothes minus his sweatshirt because I was wearing that. His hair was wet, so he must've showered. There was no emotion in his gaze, but he was watching my every move intently. "I'm . . ." I wiggled a little on the bed. "I'll be fine today."

He stared a little longer before motioning to the door. "Go to the bathroom."

I snorted. "Bossy much?"

"Yes." He was deadpan.

I suppressed a sigh. I'd lost my virginity last night. Some people lost it early in life, or during high school. Maybe I'd always waited because I knew Creighton's reaction to the guy that would've hurt me in that way, even though it would've been unavoidable. It wasn't the first time I wished Creighton understood emotions, but I really wished that morning. A part of me, where I was shy and self-conscious and feeling a little raw, wished that he would just know what to do for me. Like cuddling this morning. A hug. A forehead kiss. But I contemplated the mug in my hand as I slipped out the door. He made me coffee, and when the first pot went cold, he made me another.

And he stayed. He *was* taking care of me. In a nonviolent way. That was progress.

Palma's door was still closed when I went past. Checking the time on our kitchenette's microwave, I saw it was a little after six. Everyone would start getting up soon.

After using the toilet, I hopped into the shower. I didn't look in the mirror until I was brushing my teeth, and I paused.

Had I made a mistake last night?

Did I look different? I had sex for the first time my senior year of college. Did that make me normal? Abnormal? It was a big moment.

I'd no longer be someone who hadn't had sex. After today, I was like everyone else. Right?

And I lost it to Creighton.

My hands shook as I rinsed off my toothbrush. Putting it away, I went through the motions of getting ready for the day, but my mind was racing.

Was it all a colossal mistake?

Would he be *worse*?

Would he kill anyone who even breathed wrong in my direction?

My hands shook even harder.

I couldn't let that happen. Who was I kidding, though? No one controlled Creighton. I came the closest, but there were limitations to that control.

He hadn't moved when I returned. He tracked me as I moved around the room, slipping on some clothes. I pulled his sweatshirt back on. I was loath to part with it.

It was Friday so I had three classes to go to today.

I didn't bother with socks or my shoes, sliding back into bed with Creighton.

There was a new mug of coffee on my nightstand. I reached for it, feeling it was warm. "You made a third pot?"

He just continued to watch me with no emotion. "I want to make sure your morning is good."

I paused, taking him in for a moment. Warmth filled me. I left the coffee where it was and moved to him, cupping the side of his face.

He reached for me, pulling me to straddle his lap.

I was suddenly up close and personal with him again, and somehow it seemed awkward. I'd never experienced this feeling with Creighton. My mouth twitched. He skimmed his hands up my arms before one palmed the front of my throat.

I went still.

He didn't pull me to him, and he didn't tighten his hold. It wasn't painful. It was possessive.

"I can't read you. You're all over the place." His hand shifted as he said that, two of his fingers resting over my pulse.

I further relaxed, the little awkwardness melting out of me. He was the same. "This is just new for us. That's all. I don't know how I'm supposed to act. I mean, we're not boyfriend and girlfriend."

"We aren't?"

I frowned. "Uh . . ."

"Is that what you want?"

I blinked. "What?"

"What do you need? I could pretend to be the normal boyfriend, but you'd get angry. You'd know I was faking, so I'm being myself. But is that what you want?"

And that made me a little sad. It was a reminder that I would never get what was normal. And also sad at myself for making him think he needed to be fake for me.

"I don't want you to be anyone other than yourself."

Something flicked in his eyes. It was so fast, I couldn't place it, but then he was pulling me to him. I rested my hands to his chest, and without thinking, I maneuvered my hands so they were resting over his heart as well. Our lips met. It was sweet. Tender. Completely surprising.

He didn't deepen it, seemingly content to continue a gentle exploration.

It felt good. The warmth spread through me, and before long, I sank down into him. My hands twined around his neck, and I strained against him, wanting to get as close as possible. His other hand fell to my hip, sliding over it before moving to my waist. He slipped underneath my shirt, moved to my back, and he lifted me up once more to readjust us. As I was brought back down on him, I felt his hard-on, and I rolled over it.

I moaned at the pleasure that ricocheted in me. That felt so good.

My heart was pumping.

I asked against his lips, "Is it always like this? Or is it like this because it's you?"

He froze against my mouth. His hand tightened for a fraction on my throat. He lifted my head away from his and growled. "You're thinking about trying this with others?"

Some of the lust fell away. "What? No."

Oh.

I held still for a beat. He was pissed.

I lifted a hand to cup the side of his face. "No. Eight. I was wondering if this is normal? How it is between you and me." I shifted on his lap, putting some space between us. His hand remained on my throat, but his other rested on my thigh. "I've always heard that when a girl loses her virginity, it's sometimes not the greatest experience. You know?" My neck got hot. Of course, he wouldn't know. "Never mind."

His hand tightened as he pulled me back to him.

I rested my hands against his chest.

He didn't stop until my mouth grazed over his, and he said, "I'm aware that I can't give you a lot of experiences that others will have in their lives. I won't apologize for that. You made your decision last night, and I *know* you. You are thoughtful and methodical. You are not impulsive. You made a choice last night, and you chose me. To answer your question, does it matter? I have no intention of letting you find out for yourself. If you touch another man—"

I jerked away. "You'll what?"

He stared at me for a moment before he flipped us. Suddenly I was on my back and he was over me. His hand slid down my throat, pressing against my chest. He was coiled tight. All six three of him, as his hips bore down against mine.

"I'm waiting." I jerked my head up, almost butting against his. "You'll what, Creighton?"

His eyes were narrowed to slits. "I will gut any man who touches you. If he looks at you, I'll put him in a coma. If they think about what it's like to touch what is mine, I will make them regret it. Each." He growled. "And every single man because you are mine."

God. Fuck him.

That should've made me cold, but it had the opposite effect.

I wanted him all over again. My legs wrapped around his waist, pinning him to me. This wasn't smart. I knew that. Further giving into this hold he had over me, I was beyond caring.

I shoved at his shirt, panting. "Off. *Now.*"

He yanked his shirt off and tore at his sweatshirt on me.

As soon as both were off, he shoved his hand inside of my leggings, his hand finding my clit.

He breathed deep against my mouth before a groan tore from him. His mouth fell to my throat.

He was circling me before rubbing against my clit. "Are you sore?"

He lifted his head, beginning to pull his hand out.

I caught it and shoved it back. "I can handle it. Not the full throttle, but you know." I pressed his hand back between my legs to make sure he got my point.

His eyes darkened and he circled around my clit. "You're wet. That's for me. Isn't it?"

I was a wreck.

He saw me. He saw it all, and a cold triumphant look flared in his eyes before his mouth lowered to my ear. He said there, rough, as his hand moved back between my legs, "You don't know what you just gave me. This is mine, isn't it?" Two of his fingers slid inside of me. "This pussy."

I gasped, reaching for his wrist. Wrapping my fingers around him, I held on, but I didn't pull him out.

"But don't worry because I will treat you well. I'll make you moan and scream. I'll make you beg me to let you come as I draw out every climax that I'll give you. I'll give you *so many*. Your body already knows who it belongs to, doesn't it? You're going to just see me and your legs will weaken. How does that sound?"

He was plunging inside of me. It felt so good. *Sooo* good.

I knew the answer to my original question. I knew it in the back of my mind. This wasn't normal. This was because it was Creighton and only Creighton, and I opened my eyes, seeing him through the blur of what he was doing to my body.

He lifted his head, watching me back. His eyes were so dark and vast. A void was there, but I reached up, touching my fingertips to his cheek because that was my void now. All mine.

I was letting out a new monster, one I'd never seen before, but I couldn't think about that now. Not as he was wrecking my body with the type of pleasure that I knew was wrong to feel this good.

I exploded, my body arching up against him, and I cried out from the intensity of my release. It hit me hard, pounding through me.

Creighton watched, helping me settle back down.

One of my hands rested on his bicep, needing to touch him. The other went to his chest.

He remained above me. Our gazes were locked. He was searching me for something. I waited, until he pulled his fingers out, then he suddenly sat up over me. His legs were on either side of me, and he was breathing harshly. He put those fingers in his mouth, taking his time as he cleaned them up. When he was done, a smug grin curved over his face. "Thinking I just discovered a new favorite snack."

Air left me. *"Creight."*

My heart was still stampeding out of my chest. I was in a puddle, boneless and content at his feet. His next words should've chilled me.

"You're mine now, Blake. In every way."

They didn't. They sent my pulse soaring all over again.

This was so not good.

CHAPTER THIRTY-FIVE

BLAKE

I could hear voices when I went down to the kitchen. Nerves were pinballing around in me, but I paused going through the living room before entering. Marshall was sitting on the counter, a piece of toast in his hand, and he was swinging his legs to hit the backs of his heels against the cupboard beneath him lightly.

The scene was eerily similar to the other night.

Heath was making something at the oven. Palma was in a chair at the table.

The exception was that Levi was in the other chair across from Palma, and he was grinning widely as I entered. The others all ceased talking, but it wasn't because of me. Their eyes, almost as if they were one person, slid behind me to Creighton, who followed me.

I stood in the silence, taking in the rest of the room.

The coffeepot was gurgling again. The orange juice had been pulled out, along with a carton of almond milk. A full plate of French toast was on the table along with a bowl of scrambled eggs. I glanced at what Heath was making. Sausages.

He coughed, holding up his fork. "You want one?"

My stomach gurgled, and I winced. "Uh. I think I'm good. We have more toast?"

Palma was blatantly staring at Creighton, who had remained in the doorway. I already knew there was no reaction on his face, so I didn't turn around. Marshall jerked out of his reverie. "Uh. Yeah. I just put some in the toaster. You can help yourself." He held out the one in his hand. Rueful. "I've not stopped eating since I woke up."

A chair scraped against the floor. Palma shoved it back and extended her hand, bypassing me. "Hi," she said brightly, a wide smile strained around the edges on her face. "We've not officially met. I'm Palma, Blake's roommate." She waited, her hand out.

Creighton only stared at her.

Levi started laughing.

She shot him a look.

He shut up, or tried, grabbing a piece of French toast and bending over it, his big shoulders still shaking.

Marshall cleared his throat as he held his free hand up in the air. "Uh. I'm Marshall." His eyebrows pulled low, motioning to me with the last little bit of his toast that was left. "Blake's housemate . . ." He trailed off.

Creighton didn't respond to him either. He barely flicked Heath a look, who was watching the exchange, or nonexchange.

Heath coughed but readjusted so his back was turned to Creighton.

"Uh." Palma met my gaze, confused.

"If you're dating our roommate, you don't have to be a dic—" Marshall started to say, heated, but he stopped when Creighton looked his way. He visibly swallowed before popping the last of his toast in his mouth.

Levi was still chuckling. "Mom and Dad. Kissing in a tree. K-I-S-S—"

Creighton went around me, stopping just in front. "Shut up."

Levi just kept laughing. "It's a fucking riot and gross. Do we have to see *that*?" The last came from him as Creighton lifted a finger under my chin, tipping it up. He gave me a quick, but gentle kiss.

He shifted his hand to the side of my head, his fingers sliding through my hair as he shot Levi another glare. When he looked my way, his eyes softened.

He didn't say anything. Nor did I.

He went to the back door, and taking out his phone, he had just unlocked the screen when the door swung open from the outside. One of his men was there. No, a few of his men were there. Each nodded to him as he stepped out. They fell in line around him.

Levi hopped up to shut the door, flicking the lock. He gave the basement door a brief glance before returning to his chair and eating another bite of his French toast.

It was quiet for a second in Creighton's aftermath.

"Well." Palma shakily laughed. "He was more pleasant than at the diner."

Levi started laughing again.

"Dude. Can you, like, stuff it for a second? Not everything is funny this morning." Marshall shot him a testy look.

"Says you. I think this morning has been hilarious."

"Why are you here? To get in Palm's pants?"

Levi idly scratched at the side of his face before throwing Palma a smirk. "I mean, I wouldn't be averse to that." He winked at her.

Her cheeks pinked, but she was more focused on me. "You're good?" Her question was quiet.

I felt everyone's attention and jerked my head up and down. "Uh. Yeah." I coughed before motioning around the room. "Except for you know, this being slightly awkward."

"Is he going to be around more?"

The question came from Heath, who was peering at me. He didn't look upset, more curious.

Levi's laughter caught.

I went to Heath's other side where the toast just popped up and busied myself, buttering two slices for myself. "Uh. Yeah. I think so."

"Great."

"Marsh, stow it," Palma reprimanded.

"What? He's a barrel of fun, can't you tell?" He threw his arms wide, sitting up straighter. "I'm sorry, but am I the only one with their head still on their body or something? That guy is a criminal—"

"Watch it," Levi warned.

Marshall looked his way, but continued, "—and he's dangerous. And now what? He's dating our roommate? I'm not okay with him being here."

I wanted to shrink, right then and there. I wanted to disappear. "Look. I told you the situation—"

"The situation has changed, hasn't it? Were you fucking before?"

"Marshall!" Palma yelled.

"You're going to watch your tone," Levi said lowly.

Heath hit the side of the pan with his metal fork. "Marshall."

He quieted under their protests but shrugged and shook his head. He flicked his eyes in defiance. "I'm not okay with him being here."

I put the toast down on a small plate and faced him. "So you want me to leave, then?"

For the first time, uncertainty flickered over him. "I didn't say that."

"Dude." Levi was shaking his head.

Marshall shot him another dark look.

"I told you everything last night. If you're not okay with Creighton being here, then that means you're not okay with me being here."

"I—" Marshall scraped a hand over his jaw. Torn now. "I mean, why can't he just not come around?"

Levi began chuckling again.

"Dude, I am warning you."

"It doesn't work that way." Palma ignored the slight exchange between Levi and Marshall.

"What doesn't?" Marshall shrugged again, exaggerating the motion. He widened his eyes and spread his legs out farther.

He was settling in for a fight.

"They have a complicated and long history," Palma started, trying to be patient.

Marshall grunted, shaking his head. "This is our house. We should be able to say who can come and who can't—"

My phone buzzed in my pocket. I pulled it out to see a text from Creighton.

Eight: Do you need me to come back?

Me: Why would you ask that?

Eight: Levi said your roommate has an issue with me. He's your housemate. You decide. Do you want me to handle him?

Me: Of course not.

Eight: So you'll handle him? If he's making you feel bad, it's a problem. No one hurts you, Blake. In any way.

I scowled at Levi, who'd been watching me on the phone. He flinched. "Sorry."

The conversation that had continued now quieted in the kitchen. Attention went from Levi to me.

"What?" Marshall bit out.

I held back a sigh.

Me: He doesn't understand, but don't harm him in any way. I mean it.

Eight: Then he needs to shut up.

Me: Eight.

Eight: Quokka.

I couldn't suppress a growl.

Me: I'll handle him, but promise me you won't harm Marshall.

His response didn't come right away.

They were all watching me, and I picked up my toast, slipping into a chair on the other side of Levi when my phone buzzed. I hit the screen.

Eight: No one is allowed to make you feel bad. No. One.

"He's not wrong, you know." Levi had read it over my shoulder.

"Get back."

"Who's not wrong? Is that your boyfriend? What's he not wrong about?" Marshall raised his voice. There was an ugliness to him this morning.

Creighton was the alpha of all alphas, and sometimes guys who weren't used to being shut down so effectively and put in their place as swiftly as Creighton's mere presence tended to do, sometimes they didn't react the best way. Was that what was going on?

I caught the time and cursed. "I have to go if I'm going to make my class on time."

"You need a ride?"

I gave Levi a considering look. "Did he tell you to be another guard for me?"

"Guard?" Marshall echoed.

Levi happily beamed at me, fluttering his eyelashes a couple times. "Not officially, but he told me to stick around, and I don't mind giving you a ride."

"Your truck is here?"

"Uh. A vehicle is here. I don't know if it's my particular truck or not, but you know as well as I do that one of Creight's guys has some kind of vehicle close by."

One of. That meant there was more than the one usual watcher Creighton had assigned to me. Levi was here. How many others? I shook my head at Levi. "No. I'm good without a ride considering campus is just on the other side of the building."

"What?" He stared at me, blankly.

Palma snickered. "We live on campus."

"Oh." Levi considered that before grunting. "Good to know."

I really had to go. Creighton had brought my backpack down with him, and I spotted it on the floor in the living room. I went to grab it. As I returned through the kitchen, Heath held out a thermos for me. "Coffee."

I grabbed it. "Thanks." I tossed him a grin over my shoulder.

He gave me a small nod, before jerking his head in Marshall's direction, who was now glowering down at his hands that were in his lap. He'd gone back to lightly kicking against the counter underneath him. Heath commented, "I'll talk to him."

"Huh?" Marshall's head jerked up.

I only lifted up a shoulder in my response. "If you want, or I'll try again later."

I didn't catch what Heath's reaction was, instead being distracted as Palma stood up abruptly. She had been chewing on her top lip. "I have to go for a meeting this morning. I'll walk with you. Uh, one second though. I need to grab my stuff. You can wait for me outside, if you want. I won't be long." She took off, pounding up the stairs a second later.

Marshall had gone back to glowering at his lap. Heath resumed cooking. And Levi was unabashedly watching me. He waved another piece of French toast at me. "I'll watch over these idiots. I'll let you know if Boss comes to, you know, shoot *him*."

Marshall's look skewered him. "You're enjoying this too much."

Levi only tipped his head back, his grin never diminishing. "You're a delight."

Footsteps pounded back down the stairs and Palma rushed into the kitchen, her cheeks red and her eyes a little frantic. "I'm here. I'm ready. Let's go." She breezed right past me, opening the door first and stepping outside.

I shared one last look with Levi, who waved at me. "I got it covered here. Don't worry."

That did not reassure me.

I had just pulled the door shut before Palma pounced. "I think I made a big mistake."

CHAPTER THIRTY-SIX

CREIGHTON

IT Lead: Call me asap. Got your man.

I read the text earlier, but I'd been with Blake. Getting inside my vehicle, and once my driver took off, I called.

"Yo." The head of my IT department was named Gustav. He was a big Swede, always snacking on something, and I could hear the crinkle of whatever snack he was eating at that time.

"Gus."

"Hmm?" He tossed the food in his mouth and was speaking around it.

"Spit out the food."

He went quiet. "Hmm?" But I heard a spitting sound, and when he spoke next, he was clearer. "Sorry, Boss."

It was a common battle between us. He ate. Constantly. I asked him to wait while he talked to me, especially on the phone. "If you weren't the best hacker I knew, I probably would've shot you by now."

"Yeah . . . Sorry, Boss."

Gustav didn't think I meant it. He thought I was a "sweetie," thinking my obsession with Blake was a melting point for him. He also swore that I'd never hurt Levi and Lassiter as well, and by extension him.

I meant it.

Gustav had hacked his way into government departments, banks, and other countries for me. I wasn't altogether surprised when he already had the information for me a few hours later.

"What'd you find out?"

My phone beeped.

"I just sent you his picture and a file on him, but he's the guy in charge of the AI drone program."

The AI drone program that Lassiter told me was going to be launched in this city as a guinea pig sort of program before even being approved by the Senate and House. Because this was something that would most definitely need to be approved, or it would be automatically deemed a violation of this country's Constitution. They were already up in arms about so many other AI programs. Surveillance in drones would have people protesting on the streets.

Gustav was still speaking, "I went down the rabbit hole, and it looks like they're going to target certain territories in this city as a way to prove how effective they are."

Walden had met with the guy who was in charge of this program.

They were going to target my territories. Gustav didn't need to tell me. It made sense. Point to West and Walden on this one.

"I'm going to need you to corrupt the program."

"Boss?" He laughed, not believing me.

"Can you do that?"

He got quiet for a moment until he began speaking in a rush, his voice going up a notch, "I mean, yeah, but this isn't a program that's going to go away. This will happen. It's better if we—" He hesitated. "I don't know, do something else. But this is AI generated. It'll find me sooner than later. When that happens, we're all fucked."

"Gus."

He quieted, a hiccup coming from him. "Yeah, Boss?"

"Corrupt it. Keep an eye on it. I'm aware change is coming. I'm aware that we'll have to progress along with it, but you're giving me time. That's all. When they launch again, let me know."

"Oh." He laughed, weakly. "Got it. I can do that. I'll load in a virus so when they launch it, it'll eat its own data. That shit is a bitch to fix. It'll be down for weeks."

"Don't get cocky, Gus."

He coughed. "Uh. Not—yes, sir. Yes, Boss."

Maybe he was right. Maybe I wouldn't shoot him if I had someone better. He amused me too much. Then again, the person that would replace him might amuse me even more.

I ended that call and sent a text to Lassiter.

Me: I'm forwarding information on a man to you. I need a file on his children. After that, find his weakness. A mistress. Gambling debt. Whatever it is. I want it.

The world was changing. AI. Drones. Technology. I had an entire team of hackers at my disposal, but I wasn't forgetting that Ashton Walden also had a background in cybersecurity. Me, I was going to lean on my strength, and one of the classics worked for a reason.

A good old-fashioned threat.

Pictures of this man's children sent to him would motivate him to do what I wanted. If they didn't, I'd buy out whatever weakness Lassiter found on him. If he had a gambling debt, it would be mine, and I'd collect.

CHAPTER THIRTY-SEVEN

BLAKE

Housemate movie night. That was Palma's big mistake. She got the idea the night before, before the robbery and way before the shit hit the fan, and made everyone promise to attend.

We'd gone into the weekend, so that night and Saturday night, Levi and I ended up going to wherever Creighton was, and that meant one of his nightclubs or his buildings. It'd been nice and reminiscent of how it'd been in high school and my first three years of college. I studied, then hung out wherever the guys were. Sunday night, Creighton came to me, and he came to me every night since like our earlier routine. He'd come after I went to bed, wake me up, and would be gone by the morning. I wasn't sure how I felt about him being gone before I woke, but since that was the only time all of us housemates saw each other, I wasn't going to disrupt the peace.

Levi, however, had no problem disrupting the peace.

He never left, and we all came home that first Monday evening to find out that he'd cleared out the basement. He renovated it and put in a bed, and it was now his room. Levi moved in. Considering the fact that this was on-campus housing, I was certain he was violating some policy, but no one protested too loudly.

Palma thought it was hilarious.

Turns out she enjoyed having Levi around. She shared that she enjoyed his flirting, but also liked having him there because she knew he was there for my safety. I don't think she understood that Levi was more likely to *be* the danger than to protect against any danger, but she was enjoying his presence. I had to admit that I liked having him around too. He added comedic relief at times, and he also put Marshall in his place when he started to grumble about Levi's presence. However, that was only in the mornings because while everyone's schedule was usually busy, the guys had previously spent the evenings at the house. That stopped this week. The guys had taken to being gone and only coming in super late at night.

Palma wasn't having it. Not for Housemate Movie Night.

We were ordering Chinese food. Drinks were going to be made. And there would be movies.

I was excited. I was also nervous because Creighton was joining.

My phone buzzed just as I was getting to the house, and I let myself in through the front door. I pulled my phone out, saw it was Creighton calling, and stepped inside to text him back.

Me: One second. Just got to the house.

"Yo," Marshall hollered as he came down the stairs and headed for the kitchen. "Blake's here."

"Blake's here?" Palma asked from inside the kitchen.

There were other voices in there, and as I shed my coat and bag, Palma moved around Marshall, heading my way. Her cheeks were flushed, and her eyes were slightly dilated. The alcohol breath told me she'd been partaking before I got here.

"Hi." She was beaming.

"Hi." I softened. She hadn't enjoyed Marshall and Heath's absence this last week, so it was nice to see her smiling again. I nodded in the direction she'd just come from. "Who's all in there?"

"The guys. Plus Niko."

"Niko?"

She frowned, her eyebrows furrowing together. "Yeah. That confused me, too, but she showed up a half hour ago and announced that she'd be joining for the movie night. I have no idea how she even knew about it." Palma shifted a little closer, lowering her voice. "It's kinda funny, actually. She scared Marshall. He wasn't expecting to see her and then total high-pitch shriek. Funniest thing I've seen in a long time. She's just standing in there, against the wall and watching. The guys keep looking at her like she's an apparition that they can't believe they can see, you know? I've met her one other time. I forgot how pretty she is. But anyways, your boys are coming?"

"My boys?"

"You know." Her cheeks pinked even more. "Our sixth roommate and your man."

My body heated, just at the mention of Creighton.

I coughed, embarrassed.

"Oh my gosh. You're adorable when I bring him up. I mean, you're not blushing, but you get this whole sheepishness that comes over you," Palma gushed. "So Levi *is* coming, right?"

"I don't think anyone could keep Levi away, not if you told him there's food and booze." I gave her another assessing look before motioning for her to follow me upstairs after grabbing my bag. "What is going on with you and my foster brother?"

She tried to shrug it off, acting all casual. "I don't know. I mean, I don't mind having him around. You know that. He's here to keep you safe. I think that's sweet."

I guffawed, mostly because she'd already told me that part earlier in the week. "I call bullshit."

"What?"

"You know what. That's not the only reason you enjoy having him around." I bulged my eyes out at her.

She began laughing.

I led the way into our shared area. "Anything happen between you two?"

She groaned, pressing her palms against her forehead. "No. I wish!" She immediately blushed again. "This is so ridiculous of me. I'm acting like a schoolgirl with a crush, but I like him. It's just been flirting. He makes me feel nice." She straightened abruptly, her face falling. "Unless he's a flirt with everyone? Is he? Am I being stupid and getting my feelings involved when it means nothing to him? He is, isn't he? He's just a flirt, and I'm reading into things. Maybe I should back off. Put some distance between us. Never mind. Don't say anything. I'll do that. It'd just be smart of me." She groaned, pressing her palms to her forehead again. "Though, he's no Brad Grundle the fifth. He's *hot*. And funny. And"—she was growing flustered—"he's dangerous too. I shouldn't find that hot. I know that, but I can't help it. I'm being a stupid girl. I have to stop." She fanned herself before waving at me. "Okay, okay. You do what you need to do. Come down when you're ready. The guys ordered a ton of food so everyone can pick what they want. Oh, and the movies start soon. Do you want us to wait for you?"

I waved her to go on without me.

I needed a minute to myself, and after changing into some leggings and Creighton's hoodie from the first night we got together, I sent him a text.

Me: Call now?

He didn't respond right away, so I tucked my phone into his sweatshirt and headed downstairs. The food had arrived. The kitchen table had been moved so it was in the hallway that connected the living room, the extra sitting room, and the hallway that led to Niko's room. All the food was getting spread out on the table, along with a pile of silverware, dishes, and bowls. Palma and Marshall were in the kitchen making drinks for everyone.

My phone buzzed, so I pulled it out to read the screen.

Eight: No need. Omw. Levi's with me.

I didn't respond, but surveyed the living room. Niko, Palma, Marshall, Heath, Levi, Creighton, and I were all going to be attending this movie night. Seven people. We needed places to sit. The sectional could comfortably fit four people. That left three for the floor?

"Coming in from behind you."

I moved aside as Heath and Marshall were carrying a loveseat into the room. That's when I realized the sectional had been moved closer toward the front and closer to the stairs. The loveseat was put on the other end, closest to the kitchen.

They left and returned with two gaming chairs, putting them on the floor. Heath motioned to them. "So people have options."

Marshall returned, his arms filled with blankets. He dropped them on the floor in front of the sectional and loveseat.

"Should be plenty of room, but if this doesn't work, we'll have to get creative." Marshall winked at me before disappearing into the kitchen.

Some of my tension eased. He knew Creighton and Levi were joining, and he seemed to be back to his old self. That was good. Right? I hoped so. I felt Heath watching me. He was quiet, standing in the back, there to help. He wasn't wearing his normal leather jacket, but was wearing another pair of black ripped jeans that clung to his legs along with a longer black hooded sweatshirt. He gave me an awkward smile before averting his eyes.

"Here." Palma came into the living room, holding two peach slushy drinks. She handed one to me before asking, "What do you think Levi and Creighton will want to drink?"

"Um." The margarita looked good. "Levi will probably want one of those."

"And your man?"

My man. Warmth bloomed in me. "Um. Nothing, probably. Water?"

"Awesome. Coming right up."

Marshall came back into the living room and went to the food. He and Heath began filling their plates, and halfway through, Marshall glanced at me. "Might as well get some food and settle in."

That's when Niko arrived.

I took her in, not sure what I'd been expecting. She was a little taller than me. Slender. Long, sleek black hair that fell just beyond the middle of her back. Asian. Niko moved into the living room with a quiet confidence. Her eyes flicked to me, taking me in as I was taking her in. I couldn't read her, but suddenly I felt nervous.

"Hi." I started to hold my hand out, but she moved back a step, so I put it at my side again. "I'm Blake. Uh, one of your housemates."

She was wearing some sort of black dress where the top looked like an apron with thick straps and a choppy looking block that went over her chest. Underneath she wore a white lacy shirt that covered her arms. For her legs, she wore thick crocheted leggings. It didn't seem she was wearing any makeup, but she looked good. Comfortable too.

"I know who you are." Her lips pressed together.

She continued to stare at me.

"You two weirdos going to stand there and stare at each other or get some food?"

Niko scowled at Marshall but moved to get in line for the food. "Don't call me that. I'm more intelligent than you are."

Heath laughed. "Burned by our roommate."

Marshall rolled his eyes, but his top lip curved up. "I more meant that both of you are being odd. Just standing and staring. What? Hoping to become one with the wall or something? Get some food."

Palma came back in the room, gave both gaming chairs a perusal. "Good idea, whoever thought of bringing these down. Anyone else need another drink?"

Marshall and Heath had come around behind me, and as I moved forward, both settled on that end of the sectional. There was a little table on the end where two drinks were already sitting. Marshall picked up one and handed it to Heath. The other was for Marshall.

Niko eyed the food with a certain amount of disdain, but her plate was full when she was done. She took the other side of the sectional. Pulling out a bottle from a pocket in the front of her dress, she set it on the little table beside her. The liquid itself was green and looked rich in texture.

"Blake? You going to eat?" Palma started to fill her own plate.

"Yes." I put my drink aside and took a plate.

"Want to help me?" Palma asked me, indicating the other end of the table.

"Sure."

We picked up the table and moved it so it was directly behind the couch.

Palma was eyeing the sectional as I came around behind her. She gestured at the loveseat with her chin. "I'll let you and your guys figure out that seating." She claimed one of the gaming chairs, pulling it over so it was in front of the empty space on the sectional. She arranged one of the heavier blankets over her lap. When she was situated, she held a hand behind her. "Drink."

Heath smothered a laugh as he handed her the glass.

I followed suit, using the little stand that Niko was already using. She moved her drink aside to make room.

"So." Marshall raised his voice, holding the remote in his hand. "We had a debate earlier on what movie to watch, and we nailed it down to three. Everyone gets a vote between *Pretty Woman*, *How to Train Your Dragon*, and *Goonies*. Who wants to watch *Pretty Woman*? *Dragon*? *Goonies*?" He sighed as Palma raised her hand for all three. "Who doesn't have an opinion about what we watch?"

Heath, Niko, and I all raised our hands.

"Okay. Not helpful." He pretended to scowl, pointing the remote at the three of us who didn't care. "You chose not to have a vote, so you ended up voting by not voting. Don't complain to me later. Since Palma voted for all the options, that means I get to pick the movie. *Goonies* it is."

I hadn't dug into my food becausc I was enjoying this.

Marshall was in a good mood. That meant Heath was as well.

Palma was giddy because we were all here.

Niko was quiet. She kept glancing my way.

The movie started.

That's when the back door opened and Levi's voice thundered, "Honey! We're home."

The relaxed vibe in the room vanished.

CHAPTER THIRTY-EIGHT

CREIGHTON

Levi entered the room like a giant bowling ball, his personality running over everyone and everything in his way. A movie had already been chosen and was playing, but Levi bounced around the room, greeting Blake, then the Beauregard roommate. He jerked his chin up at the Nogoskeski boy and ignored the last roommate. Marshall Finch.

He gave the Yakuza roommate a look but chose to ignore her as well. She seemed fine with it, continuing to eat her food as if there'd been no interruption.

Blake hadn't touched her food, and I moved behind her, my hand grazing the back of her neck. "Are you not hungry?"

She moved into my hand, her eyes warming as she tipped her head back to look at me. "Waiting for you guys."

"Fuck yeah. I'm usually of the mindset that food is food, but this shit is good. Where'd you order from?" Levi's plate was overflowing. He put it on the floor by the empty game chair and went into the kitchen, coming back with two beers in hand. He offered me the second. I shook my head. I was reluctant to move away from Blake, enjoying the small touch even though I'd only left her bed twelve hours ago. It still seemed twelve hours too long.

"Oh. I made a margarita for you, Levi." Beauregard got up, going into the kitchen to show him.

The Finch boy was barely concealing his hostility, which was affecting everyone in the room.

Levi came back, noticed, and was half amused, though he would grow tired of the disrespect. He'd shared that both of the boys were largely absent over the week, so he hadn't had to deal with it in longer amounts of time. The Nogoskeski was also growing more tense, but with him, there was no concern. He would submit. He already had submitted the night they arrived at my fighting ring, and right now, he began giving his friend more and more looks.

A confrontation was coming.

It was just a matter of time. Finch would start it. When he did, Nogoskeski would be the first to rebuke him. That was a move Finch wouldn't see coming, and he'd feel betrayed. Which would add to the pile of humiliation that was coming his way because when he would say something, he'd find he was alone in his opinion.

I took the empty seat beside Blake, seeing she was wearing my hoodie again. I liked seeing her wearing my clothing. I liked it a lot.

She ducked her head, knowing what my reaction was about. A small smile toyed at the corners of her mouth. She liked seeing this effect on me. Well then. More sweatshirts would be left for her.

Levi sat somewhat in front of me.

I drew Blake's feet to my lap. She'd been watching me the whole time, a little tense, but she enjoyed that I was here. A roommate movie night with her boyfriend? I knew Blake was giddy inside, and I moved my thumb over her ankle. "Eat."

She liked this experience. Pretending to be normal.

She wasn't waiting for my permission to eat. That wasn't why she'd been holding off. She'd been asking in her silence if I was going to light the match to the gasoline her housemate was pouring into the room.

With my soft murmur, I let her know that I was here to play the good boyfriend part. I wouldn't antagonize the Finch boy. She relaxed right after, her smile softening. She picked up her fork.

"Did you just tell her to eat?" the Finch boy sniped.

The Nogoskeski boy hissed first. "Marsh, leave it."

"No." He jerked a hand in the air toward me. "He fucking told her to eat. She doesn't need permission to chew food."

Palma let out a sigh, holding her plate with both hands, her jaw tight. "Marshall. Stop it."

"No, you stop it, Palm."

Levi slowly put his plate down as well. I spared him a look, knowing he wouldn't launch his way into the argument on my behalf until I gave him the go-ahead. I moved my foot, touching his leg and holding it there. I wanted to hear how they would bicker. So far Marshall Finch was starting to get angry at being told to shut up by his own people. Blake was keeping an eye on me, but she knew I wasn't going to strike, so she was happily enjoying her food. I gave her drink a cursory look, seeing she was enjoying that as well.

"Don't snap at Palma," Heath said.

For a moment, I toyed with a theory about why I bothered Finch so much.

Did he want Blake? Was I in the way of him?

Maybe. A part of that seemed right, but it felt there was more.

Was it about being in control?

I was here. I took the power. It's just what was going to happen if I was in a room, and he sensed that.

That seemed to fit more.

He didn't feel in control, so therefore he was throwing a man-size temper tantrum.

Finch looked my way and jolted, seeing that I was staring at him.

He wavered in what he was saying, then finished, "—I don't give a fuck. No guy should give a girl the command to eat or not. That shit's not right."

Marshall Finch was red in the face. He wasn't going to let this go, not until he'd drawn me into the fight.

Nogoskeski was almost as red in the face, shooting me an alarmed look, his hand holding down his friend's leg. "Shut the fuck up, Marsh. I mean it."

"Is this what happens whenever you enter a room?"

The room fell silent because that question was directed at me, and it was spoken in Japanese and from the roommate they barely knew.

Her face was solemn, almost serene, as she waited for my response.

I waited a second before sending back, in the same language, "This is a pleasant surprise."

She barely reacted. "Why? You know the business my family is in. This is my first language."

"The surprise is that you would address me in it."

She raised an eyebrow, staring at me steadfastly. "You speak it fluently. Where did you learn?"

Learning languages came naturally to me. Almost eerily naturally. But I would never explain that I didn't quite understand how easy learning and speaking languages were to me, or how I wondered if having an eidetic memory had anything to do with it. Both items I hadn't even shared with Blake, who I was now ignoring as she was sending me a very searching look.

I skimmed the group and tipped my chin up to her. "Point to you."

She raised her second eyebrow in question.

We were still conversing in her language. I said, "A fight was going to happen, but with your one comment to me, you derailed it from happening and at the same time, forced something out of me that hadn't been known." I chanced a look at Blake, and knew as soon as we were alone she'd be tearing into me. Blake was the one that knew the most about me. I could see that she didn't like being in the dark.

Interestingly, Finch was calming down.

Ah. The fascination of covert maneuvers.

Because of her housemate's question, I was now the bad guy and Marshall Finch was able to settle back into his usual role of the "good boy." The sudden shift in dynamics helped him return to his normal place in the group, where it was comfortable. He felt a semblance of control again.

The Yakuza housemate had stewed at how I deftly used her presence in this house. I learned that most people didn't enjoy being used. Of course, most everyone used everyone for different reasons, even simple reasons such as feeling good about themselves, but they didn't like being told they were being used. This one was smart. She struck back how she could.

This entire conversation was a hidden fuck you to me.

I held her gaze until she began to grow uneasy. I moved my foot away from a weapon she hadn't taken into account.

I unleashed Levi.

CHAPTER THIRTY-NINE

BLAKE

"Languages aside, what the fuck's your problem?" Levi asked.

It took a beat before everyone clued in on who the question was for. Marshall scowled. "Uh. What?"

"You. What's your problem? You've been a bitch for a full week. I'm sick of it. You have a problem with me, with Creight, either say your shit now or shut your trap." Levi shifted forward, gesturing to me. "You don't think this comes on her? You think you can have a problem, but it's not going to bother Blake? You don't know Blake, if you think that."

"You know what? Fuck this." Marshall abruptly shoved up from the couch. "We're just going to fight if we stay here. Sorry, Palm. I tried. I really did, but I can't sit here with this"—he motioned to where we were sitting—"*trash* here."

I gulped. "Trash, huh?" I deflated.

Marshall froze. "I-I didn't mean you, Bla—"

He meant Creighton and Levi, but I was like them. They were mine.

Levi was right. No matter what, I'd get hit in the crossfire.

I jerked a shoulder up, my appetite gone. "It's fine. It's not like I haven't heard it all my life." I shoved to my feet, too, and began to leave. I got as far as three steps before a hand tugged on the back of my hoodie, stopping me. I was breathing harshly. The hand was familiar, so I didn't look back, just waited, and he crowded in. His heat surrounded me, his chest to my back. His voice was low as he asked, "Can I hurt him now?"

I knew Marshall hadn't meant me. I knew it, but others had. I was trash to them. I was beneath them. My family didn't want me. I didn't get to have a mom and a dad. No one adopted me. No one loved me. Kids were cruel, yeah, but most of those statements were spoken by adults and never in front of Creighton.

I drew in a shuddering breath.

He had protected me since he met me, and he was still doing it. I blinked back tears.

I knew not to weaponize him. *God.* I really did, but he was here.

I wasn't wanted.

I wasn't loved.

Except Creighton did. In his way, he did.

He couldn't love, but he was here. He was always here. At my back.

He was asking for permission to fight for me.

A pinching sensation began to push down in my chest, like someone was pressing a closed fist to my sternum and was continuing to push down, down, down until—I *broke*. A rough whisper escaped me. "Don't physically hurt him." After that, I fled.

"Blake!" Palma came after me.

I hurried to my room, but I knew I couldn't stay here.

You're overreacting.

What did you just do?

You're taking this too far.

My breathing was coming in hard, ragged, and I waited, prepared for an onslaught of comments like that, but they had no idea what it was like growing up *unwanted* from day one. Not one clue.

But fuuuuck.

Creighton unleashed Levi. I unleashed Creighton.

I shoved through into my room and began to pace, my hands in fists at my side.

Shit.

What had I done?

I needed to go back. I needed to call Creighton off, but it was too late. I'd already lifted the gate, and Creighton would not go back into the stall. He'd laugh at me if I went down there to try to harness him again.

He was an asshole like that.

The door was opened. Palma was there. She held a hand to her chest.

I shook my head as I continued to pace. "I know he didn't mean me. I know that." I flinched, not even wanting to imagine what was happening down there now. "Tell me Creighton's not actually killing him." I chanced a look at her, and stopped short.

She was pissed. *Pissed.* "Who the fuck cares. Marshall's been out of line for an entire week. He's like a little kid throwing a temper tantrum. He always wants things to go his way, and for once, it's not. Christ, Blake. Don't apologize. Marshall knew exactly what he was saying."

I swallowed. "What do you mean?"

She folded her arms tightly over her chest. Her eyes were glittering from her own anger. "Just that I don't care what your guy does to him. Marshall deserves it. It'd be good for him to be knocked down a few pegs." She eyed me in concern. "What do *you* need?"

I shook my head, not having one clue.

No, I did. I needed to go down there and figure out some way to stop Creighton because they really did not understand what I'd done.

I cursed, and pulled my phone out. I called Lassiter.

He answered almost right away. "Did he kill someone?"

A laugh escaped me because of course he'd answer that way, and of course his tone was accepting. Even hopeful. "No, but . . ." I needed to think about this. Did I really want to bring Lassiter into this? He was another weapon in Creighton's arsenal. I'd only told Creighton not to harm my housemate. I never said anything about anyone else. That'd be how he could get around me. Such a dickface.

"I need you to promise me something, even if Creighton gives you orders that go against it."

Palma's eyebrows shot up.

I waited, and as I did, the room seemed to shrink around me.

"Okay."

I frowned. That was easy. "Really?"

A dark chuckle came from the other end. "Yes, Blake. What do you need from me?"

"Don't physically harm my housemates."

"Done. Now what do you need from me? I'm already on the way to your place. What am I going to be walking into?"

I hesitated. "I don't know. I went upstairs. My one housemate was being an asshole—"

Palma bit out, "That's putting it mildly."

I continued to Lassiter, "I don't know what I need, to be honest. I just—"

"Got it. You need a distraction. I'll be that for you." He ended the call abruptly.

I looked at my phone, my mind racing.

"Who did you call?"

"Lassiter."

The voices downstairs went up another level in volume.

We both turned as if we could see through the door and down into the living room to see what was happening. Lassiter said we needed a distraction. I clung to that, knowing I'd have to process the events that happened tonight at a later time, but we were in the damage control phase. That meant getting Creighton away from Marshall.

"We need to go out."

Palma said, "Uh. Okay. Where do you want to go?"

I was thinking. Calculating. Not to any of Creighton's places. That'd be his territory. His men would be there. We needed somewhere neutral, where Creighton couldn't give orders and have thirty men do his bidding.

"Octavia." That was *perfect.*

"Didn't you quit there?"

I nodded, my excitement beginning to build. It was wonderful. Yeah, I'd been kidnapped from there, but what were the chances it'd happen a second time? And with Creighton present? It wouldn't happen. West and Walden wouldn't dare.

Octavia was *just* the place to go.

I smiled widely at Palma. "Let's go to a nightclub, and uh, Marshall can't come with us."

Palma's eyes were wide, unblinking. "I mean, duh. Of course, but are you sure that's what you want to do? I don't feel I'm totally following what's happening here."

She didn't. She couldn't.

I decided, just this once, to lay it out for her. "Marshall did the worst thing he could do. He hurt me. Creighton's killed men who *might've* hurt me." I waited, letting that sink in her head.

It didn't take long. She shuddered. "I have a question."

"Yeah?"

"That robbery last weekend. They took two of those guys out. What happened to them?"

My mouth dried up. "What do you think?"

Yeah. She was getting it now.

She whispered, "We have to go out."

"Now."

CHAPTER FORTY

CREIGHTON

I was the shark swimming, and Marshall Finch was the surfer who didn't know he was bleeding as he was swimming in *my* waters. I only got time to start circling him when Blake and Beauregard came down in a tizzy. Both were worked up.

Blake declared we were going to Octavia the same time Lassiter strolled in through the back door.

"Awesome. You're here." Levi whooped.

Heath's head reared back. "What the fuck? I locked that door the last time I went to get another drink."

Lassiter shrugged. Levi, Lassiter, and I each had our own fob for Blake's house. None of her housemates needed to know that information.

Blake took my hand, laced our fingers, and dragged me away as she shoved Lassiter in front of her. Levi was amused by the whole thing. "Right on. What's happening?"

"Normally we'd take the subway, but since you're here and you have all your guys, we can get a ride. Right?" the Beauregard roommate rambled as we hit the sidewalk. She took charge, directing Blake and me to one of my SUVs, and she, Levi, and Heath went to Lassiter's vehicle.

Finch followed to the door, but Beauregard had an exchange with him before she shut the door in his face. My gaze slid to Blake, who was looking out the window away from me. She was drumming her fingers on her knee, and I knew that if I reached over to feel for her pulse, it'd be racing.

She lifted the gate for me to go after Finch. Now she was trying to prevent that from happening. She'd changed her mind.

Oh, Blake.

She thought I would get distracted and change my mind.

He hurt her. Therefore, he was mine to hurt.

She would need to do better than this. Putting physical distance between me and her housemate would not work.

Twenty minutes later, she had kept with her mission.

She maneuvered us away from the rest of the group, and we were in a private booth in the far corner of the nightclub. It was set in the back of a short hallway with only two other booths before us, and both of them were empty. If Blake was behind that part, then I would be extremely impressed. As it was, I was still impressed because if she was still going for the goal of distracting me, it was working. For tonight.

She moved to straddle me.

I reached for her legs and felt the press of something sharp against my stomach.

She'd pulled a knife on me.

She was my soulmate.

Not that I ever questioned Blake's place in my life, but she just signed, sealed, and delivered that fact into my brain. She told me that I didn't have the capability to love, but whatever this intense burning inside of me, the feeling that would take me to my knees for her, if it wasn't love then I couldn't imagine how powerful that was because right now, she was my reason for existence.

She regarded me with determination and settled more firmly on my lap, sinking down on me.

I moved my hands to her waist, moving my fingers underneath my hoodie that she'd worn every night to bed until I peeled it off of her. There was a clean laundry smell from it, so she must've washed it today. I liked that she wore my clothes. It made me purr inside, and I waited for her to start whatever she was going to do. I didn't think she was going to pull my dick out and sink down on it, but I wouldn't stop her if she did. She had picked this booth to give us the utmost privacy. No one could see us unless they specifically walked over to see who was in this booth. No cameras were mounted on the wall, but knowing Mauricio and knowing how I had surveillance in my own places, I was sure a hidden camera was pinned on us. When we first approached, the bouncer held up a hand to halt our progression. Barely a second later, another man came out from the door and leaned in to share something with the bouncer. Both gazes went to me with a warning in them. I stepped away from the group and lifted my shirt. Knowing we were coming here, I'd already handed my gun to Lassiter. Now, whatever he ended up doing with it wasn't on me. Just as long as I didn't have a weapon and I wasn't recruiting within the nightclub.

I gave orders to Lassiter and Levi. Lassiter was supposed to get something from Spence, Octavia's manager, for me. How he did it was up to him. Levi's order was to keep an eye on the rest of Blake's group.

She was starting to let them in, and I didn't want anything to happen to them. For her.

I reached up to cup the side of her face, halting her in the mission she had in mind when she brought me to this private booth. She went still in my hand. Her eyes lifted, finding mine, and whatever she saw in my own eyes, I didn't know, but she licked her lips before her mouth opened slightly. "What are you doing?"

I gave her knife a pointed look. "I could say the same to you."

She bit down on her bottom lip, folding her head down, and rested her forehead to my chest.

My hand returned back to her waist, pushing up underneath my sweatshirt. It was warm in Octavia, but sometimes girls had different internal thermometers. As long as she was comfortable.

I felt her entire body draw in some air, as if she needed courage, and tipped her chin to me. Blake was giving me the feeling that we were two adversaries facing off across a boardroom.

I tugged her hips closer and rocked up into her.

She bit down on her lip again, one of her hands falling to my chest and her fingers splaying out. "Don't." Her voice caught as I moved her over me again, slower, intently. She could ride me like this. We could grind against each other until both of us came. Making out as if we were in high school would be fun.

She groaned and leaned back a little. "Creight."

I stopped.

Her eyes grew hooded, which I didn't like. I tipped her head up again, needing to see her. My thumb smoothed over her cheek softly. "What is this, Quokka?"

Pain flared over her features. "Don't. Don't call me that, Eight."

I didn't like that. "Why does that name bring you pain?"

She didn't grimace when I used it in the past. Once upon a time, she used to love it. Now it brought pain? I didn't like that. I shouldn't have pushed the endearment, but she called me Eight. I wanted my own name for her.

She shook her head. "I don't want to get into that now. I—" She raked her teeth over her lip again, bracing both of her hands on my chest. She pushed herself as far back as the table allowed. Her eyes were still hooded, but at this distance, she was more shadowed. I tried drawing her closer, wanting to be able to read her if we were going to hash something out, but she resisted. She gave a slight shake of her head. "No. I need this."

As I waited, I contented myself with pulling down the side of her leggings, just enough so I could smooth my thumb over her hip bone.

She shuddered, lust swimming in her gaze. She cleared her throat, and tried blinking away the desire. I repositioned my hand so my thumb tunneled lower under her leggings, but pulled it to cover my palm.

Her lips tugged down. "I know that you're going to go after Marshall."

I paused. That's what all this was about? For him? I wasn't a fan.

The hand still holding her knife to my stomach trembled. "I made Lassiter promise not to hurt him on your orders, so if that's what you were intending to do to get around what I made you promise, you can't. I'm going to make Levi promise too."

"I'd never give that order to them."

"Yes, you would."

I would. She knew me well. I grinned faintly. "Someone else, maybe. Not your housemate. His suffering is my Christmas present. Thank you ahead of time."

She huffed out an annoyed sound. "Don't thank me for that." Her grip tightened on the knife. She pressed it harder against me, and I knew it broke through some of my skin. I didn't think Blake was aware. "We came to an agreement once before."

She wanted to save people's lives. I remembered that with fondness.

"I want to do that again, but for Marshall instead."

The fondness vanished. "He's that important to you?"

"No." She held my gaze steadily. "But I don't like when you hurt people because of me. I can't live with that, Creighton. If we keep going how we're going, I need to compromise on some things, but so do you."

My hand shook as I tried to rein in my anger. "You would ask that of me? To not protect you? To not avenge you if someone hurts you?"

"You take it to the extreme."

"You can't put a leash on me."

"Compromise." She rolled her hips over me.

I stopped her and fixed her with a cold look. "Don't do that."

Her bottom lip fell open. "What?"

"Use your body to manipulate me."

"I'm—" She snapped her mouth shut and stewed. "That's not my intention."

I smoothed both of my hands around under her leggings, dipping down so I could cup her ass. A surprised sound squeaked from her as I lifted her up and then repositioned her, higher on me, *right* on top of my dick. "This entire exchange has been a manipulation."

"I—" She wanted to argue.

I waited, interested in how she could protest.

She closed her mouth. "I wasn't thinking of it in that way. I just knew that I needed to get you alone, and I don't want you to leave, so sitting on you seemed the best option."

I gave her knife a pointed look. "At knifepoint?"

She gave me an embarrassed look before closing the knife.

I palmed it from her.

She gave me a questioning glance.

"It's better if they find it on me than you."

Understanding flared. She leaned in, nipping at my lips. "But they're more likely to search you than me."

I growled. "They wouldn't dare."

Her smirk was triumphant. "Exactly."

I was enjoying this. This banter between us. I wanted more of it. I wanted to bicker with her until the day my heart stopped.

"I—" She cut herself off, then regrouped. Her shoulders rose and fell back. She straightened on my lap. "I need you to tell me what you're intending to do to Marshall."

I grew cold.

"Don't do that." She touched my mouth.

"Don't do what?"

"Look at me that way. With that icy smirk."

I blinked, shifting it away. She flinched again, and I cringed internally because I knew that instead I was giving her my "dead" look.

"That's even worse," she murmured under her breath.

My hand tightened on her ass. "You keep bringing up another man's name when you're sitting in my lap. And you *don't* want me to murder him?"

"Yeah. Okay. I get that, but please answer me. What are you intending to do with him?"

I toyed with my answer.

"The truth, Creight. Do that for me."

"I would do anything for you."

She scoffed, but the corner of her mouth tugged up. "Would you carry me over a mountain if it were in my way?"

"I would blow up the mountain for you."

She went still in my lap. "You're serious."

"Of course."

She remained still, holding my gaze for a longer beat. I didn't know what she was looking for. Whatever it was, a softness came over her, and her mouth gentled. "Where are my lines with you?"

"What do you mean?"

"I keep pushing and pushing, and you always let me. Everyone has a line. Where's mine with you?"

My gaze fell to her mouth. "It continues to surprise me that you don't get it."

"Get what?"

My hand returned to her throat, and I traced a finger up to the tip of her chin, raising it so I could see into her again. As our eyes met and held, her entire body trembled. "You challenge me. I never want you to stop challenging me."

I'd surprised her. "Why?"

My hand splayed out over the side of her throat before moving to the back, where my fingers sank in, anchoring her in a grip. "Because I need it. You stand in front of me, and you have a hook growing through my chest. You keep pulling me toward you. With each challenge and each yank, you are daring me to become a better man."

"A hook? Sounds bloody."

"The bloodier the better." I pulled her head back, knowing I hadn't given her the answer she wanted. "You told me I couldn't physically harm your housemate. My plan is simple. I'm going to torture him until he harms himself." Beautiful. Simple.

Physical pain would heal. Emotional pain could endure forever.

She blanched, and her mouth dropped open. She fisted my shirt in her hands. "*God.* No."

I leaned to her, my mouth grazing over hers. "He hurt you."

She flinched, turning away. "Only for a moment."

"No."

Her gaze returned at my vehemence.

I almost snarled at remembering. "Being called trash wouldn't hurt me. Or Levi. He knew that. He used that word to hurt *you*. You're the easier way to get to me. He knew this. He miscalculated, and he will learn that truth. Do not take that from me. I will never stand aside and let someone hurt you."

"Eight—"

"You wouldn't stand aside for me."

She stopped. Her eyes held mine. Those words got through to her. She was wavering.

Her hands lifted, taking hold of my shirt again. Higher up. They sunk in, fisting once again. "Yeah. Okay. I get that, but I can't handle that. I can't. Knowing you would beat him down until he harmed himself? I will not have that on me. Do not put that on me. You don't want me to ask you not to protect me or hurt back for me, then return the respect."

"What are you asking for?"

"Scale back. Don't go to the extremes you do. Not everyone is the same. There's a difference between someone robbing me and someone who said a word that hurt my feelings."

"Not to me."

She quieted, playing with her hands between our bodies for a moment before her shoulders slumped. "Yeah. I get that you don't see a difference, but there is one. In normal people world, there's a difference. A big one. In Creighton world, I get that harm is harm. You don't see the difference, but . . ." She took hold of my shirt and fisted it again. "I live in normal people world. I'm affected by what you do in normal people world. Not just for—my housemate, but for everyone that you would hurt on my behalf. You don't feel it, but I do. Everything you do to them, I feel. I carry that weight. I'm not saying never avenge me, just scale it back. Compromise. I can live with that. Learn the difference between a small slight and someone who's going to rob me, or do something worse."

A growl left me at the thought of either of those happening to her, but she was trying. This was important to her.

I angled my head to get a better read on her.

Then I saw it. This was *the* big obstacle for us.

I shook my head. "You are lumping two separate items together. A compromise on everyone who harms you versus scaling back on your roommate." I wanted to tell her she couldn't ask for both, but I couldn't go that far. I would lose her. "What you are asking is for one favor and then another bigger favor from me. What are you giving for both of them?"

She cursed under her breath, glaring at me. Her hand turned inward, and I could feel her nails through my shirt. I grunted, my hand pressing down on her thigh as I bucked up underneath her.

She expelled an annoyed growl. "How do I give you permission to hurt a friend of mine?"

"I'll run it by you."

"What?"

I let go of the back of her neck and skimmed my finger down her throat. She shivered in its trail. "I will present you three options, and you can approve one."

"And if I don't like all three of them?"

"I'll present three new options, but you will have to approve one."

She cursed again, her entire body beginning to shake in my arms. She had begun to move her hips over me. I could see she didn't know she was doing it. "Fine. What do you want from me in exchange for that?"

I considered her. I couldn't push too far with this request, but it would need to count. "I want to know why you don't want me to call you Quokka. You used to like the name."

Panic flared from her before she blanketed it. "What? No."

I caught the back of her neck again, but my touch was soft. "I am scaling back, for you. Give me this in return."

Her next curse was whispered, but she jerked her head in a nod. "Fine. Yes. I'll tell you."

The darkness in me shifted aside, knowing the void that was in me, the one that she seemed to fill when she was near me, a flicker of something good sparked there. That was her. Her tiny ray of sunshine that had somehow lodged itself in me and refused to leave. It was doing a little dancing jig.

I'd never tell, though.

She grinned at me, blowing out some air upward over her own forehead. "You make me sweat something fierce."

"Stop," I taunted. "You'll make me preen."

Laughter burst from her, and that dancing jig inside of me quaked before it exploded, growing triple in size. She was so goddamn beautiful, in every way that mattered to humanity. I loved her. I was sure of it.

I wanted to tell her my feelings.

They were there, pushing to escape, but I kept them locked up. She wouldn't believe me. I was obsessed. That's what she would say as she rolled her eyes, but then she'd stare at me as I was always staring at her, and I'd feel the connection between us grow once more.

It was only with her that I felt this link.

She made a mewling sound and moved for me at the same time I lifted my mouth.

She panted against my lips. "I need you."

"Then take me."

Her hand moved between us, and her hips lifted up enough so she could palm my dick through my jeans. I was ready to go. This entire exchange had been foreplay for me. I *needed* to be buried deep in her slick heat.

"Eight," she whimpered.

If this was my nightclub, I'd strip her bare in a heartbeat, but it wasn't. I didn't mind fucking on camera, but I knew Blake wouldn't want that. Scowling at where I guessed the camera was located and pointing at us, I stood from the booth, clasping Blake easily to me.

She made a surprised sound, but wound her arms and legs around me.

I began walking us out of there.

"Creight." She tried to look where we were going.

I recaptured her lips. "No. Stay here. I want your mouth."

As I came down the hallway, two of my men were waiting. Both straightened at seeing me. I said to them, "Home." They jumped to comply. I used one eye to keep track of our movements, and as I fell in line behind them, I saw Levi looking my way from where he stood with Blake's people. He'd been leaning against the side of their booth, but flashed me a grin and folded into the booth. He was reaching for Palma as we turned another corner.

My men turned down a side hallway. They were going to take us out through the alley door. Lassiter was exiting a closet door as we went past, a hand going through his hair to fall back to his side. He jerked at seeing us, then relaxed and lifted his chin to me. It was a signal that he'd gotten what I'd asked him to get for me. Right before we stepped outside, he waved his phone to me.

I pulled my mouth away from Blake enough to give him a nod back.

"What?" Blake had given into the pleasure between us, and I saw now that it had woven a spell over her. She let it. I was loath for her to clear it away and gently tugged her back to me. I nipped at the corner of her mouth. "It's nothing. Come back here."

A shiver trailed down her spine. She sank back into my hold.

Climbing into the waiting SUV, I growled at my men in the front. "Privacy divider. *Now.*"

A buzzing sound came next, and fucking finally.

Blake kneeled on the seat, lifting up as I made quick work opening my jeans. We both pushed our clothes aside long enough for me to find a condom and put it on. She sank down over me, and I let out a hissing sound because this was perfection.

She was perfection.

CHAPTER FORTY-ONE

BLAKE

Creighton was gone when I woke up. Not that I was surprised. I was wrung out, in the *best* way. There'd been talking, but honestly, not much of it. His phone went off around five in the morning, and I barely stirred. Since it was the weekend and since I hadn't gotten to sleep till late, I decided to sleep in.

When I stirred, I grimaced at seeing the time. It was past ten in the morning. That wasn't normal for me. But the house was quiet. Everyone else must've gotten back—I didn't know. I never heard them come home. They must've passed out or were still sleeping?

Padding downstairs, I fought back a yawn and went to get some coffee.

There was no coffee in the pot.

Marshall always made the coffee. First thing in the morning, he dumped out the old and brewed a new pot. He was a coffee snob in that way. Huh. I made a pot and waited long enough to fill a cup before I went back upstairs.

I felt a bit silly, but a part of me didn't want to shower. I needed to. I smelled like sex, only doing the minimal washing that was necessary after the last round. I smelled like Creighton. I liked smelling like Creighton.

I was loath to wash his scent off of me, but he'd left me a new sweatshirt, so after showering, I pulled on some leggings, a tank, and his newest sweatshirt. It smelled *all* of him.

I ran through what I needed to do today.

I had a paper due next week. There were a couple quizzes coming up. I needed to figure out what I was going to do for money. Time was even more precious with my added hours at the foster center, but I needed to get another job. I had a nest egg that I could rely on. I'd been able to build that up slowly through high school, summers, and the rest of college, but the move to New York had depleted a lot of that nest egg. It was only there because of Creighton's help, to be honest. He always made sure I had what I needed for food, school supplies, and some extra spending money. I tried refusing a couple times, but he'd show up, stock my room with whatever I needed anyways, and stalk out. After I left Miss Marcie's house, Creighton started to make sure the other foster homes were too scared of him to be anything other than polite to me. There'd been a patch of time before he started doing that, though.

Eventually, the last of my foster homes allowed me to do what I wanted.

New York was the first time I let myself think I could maybe have something normal. I was to the point now where did I dare let myself believe I could have both? Creighton *and* friends?

I couldn't change Creighton. I knew that. Would always know that. I needed to accept his limitations, too, but he said he would compromise. He said he would meet me halfway.

A flicker of hope was in my chest. A small one, but it was there.

Creighton wasn't going anywhere. I wasn't going anywhere. We could do this. And my friends weren't . . . Actually, I went over to Palma's room and tapped lightly on the door before opening it. She wasn't there. That was weird. Had they come home before leaving for breakfast?

I went upstairs to check the boys' room, and same thing. No one was there. The beds were a mess, so I couldn't tell if they'd been slept in or not.

Going back to my room, I checked my phone for any text messages.

Palma: Heeyyyy!! Where are you??

Palma: Your foster brother is so hot. Can I just say he's your brother? I know he's not by blood, but does it matter?

Palma: Where'd you go?

Palma: Oh! Your brother said you went back with your man.

Palma: Marsh is coming. Is that okay? You took off so I'm assuming it'll be fine.

Palma: Levi said it's all cool.

Palma: Get some tonight! I know you probably are. Have fun. I might get some with your brother. Gawwwd, he's so hot. Okay, okay. Ttyl xoxoxoxxoxoxox

Palma: I'm so drunk. Tonight is FUN

Heath: Heads up, Marsh is coming but your boy said you took off.

Marshall: I'm sorry for being a dickhead. Can we talk later? I don't like your man, but I'm getting that he and the boulder brother aren't going anywhere. I know I've been a dick lately. I don't really know why, but I'm sorry. Palma's really into your boulder brother so if he's just going to play with her, could you warn him off? I don't want her or you to get hurt. That's all.

Heath: Do you know where Palma is?

Unknown: This is Spence. Can you call me when you see this? Your friends were at my club last night and I just heard the lot of them were arrested. One of the guys got into a fight with some other customers. I don't know why all of them were taken in, but I'm sure we can figure it out. If we go down to the station together, as Octavia's manager, I'll see if the charges can be dropped. I'm reluctant to ask, but could we leave Lane out of this? His presence might tip the scale in a direction that might not be the best for your friends.

Holy shit.

Holy shit!

I had to reread his text because what the hell had happened last night?

There was no message from Levi, but there wouldn't be. He'd know I was with Creighton. Was this why Creighton got called away? My old boss's text was sent this morning at 7:23. The last text before that was from Heath, just before two, when the bar would've closed. All the other texts were around the same time, with Marshall and Heath's a few minutes apart.

I called Spence.

He picked up almost immediately, sounding frazzled. "Hey. I was hoping to hear from you by now. I'm heading your way. Are you around? I want to head in and see if we can figure this out before the club opens today."

"Uh. Yeah. I can be ready. I am ready, I mean. They were really arrested?"

"Yeah." He still sounded distracted. There were other noises in the background. Sounds from the street. "I made a call to a guy I know, and he said when they arrested the one guy, the others started protesting so much so they all were taken in. They were drunk. Shit happens. This happened in Octavia, so I'm sure I can get everything cleared away. It'd help if you come with me since they're your friends and you used to be an employee."

My head was swimming, and I needed to sit down. I gripped the phone tightly. "Yeah. Yeah. Of course. *Anything.* I just need to grab a few things."

"Good. I'm just around the corner. Come out to the curb."

"Okay. See you in a bit." I hurried to grab my wallet, sliding it into my back pocket, and grabbed my coat and slipped on my shoes. My heart was pounding when I stepped outside and sent Spence a text that I was outside. I looked around for whoever Creighton had watching me today, but I couldn't see anyone. I'm sure he was there, and for once, I was appreciative for their discretion. Spence asked to leave Creighton out of this, but no way would he be okay with me leaving without a tail. We *just* had a talk about compromise.

I didn't have to wait long before a truck pulled over in front of me. Spence was driving, so I went around to get into the passenger side. "Hi." My chest was tight.

He gave me a forced grin back, but got back into traffic before he could be harassed by other drivers.

"You know which station to go to?"

He nodded, checking his rearview mirror. His hands gripped the steering wheel tightly. Really tightly.

He looked more stressed than he should've. It wasn't like he'd been arrested.

I frowned. "Uh. Spence?"

"Yeah." He threw me a fast look. "I just want to get there. Get this done with."

Cool. Yeah. I got that.

I told myself to relax, except something was off. This didn't feel right.

I tried to tell myself to relax.

I was certain this wasn't the first time something like this happened at Octavia. And I was sure Spence was partially doing this so Creighton wouldn't use this in any way against . . . Well, against someone. I wasn't totally certain.

"Was there footage of the incident?" Was Levi taken in? "There would've been a really big guy with them. Did he get arrested too?"

"Uh. What?" He ran a hand through his hair, batting some loose ends away. He scowled. "Who are you talking about?"

"One of the guys with my friends. He—" Did I mention who Levi worked for? Would that help in this situation? I thought better of it. "Uh. Never mind. Do you know how many people were taken in? Was it all of them?"

He shook his head, still distracted. "I don't know. They're your friends. My night manager said they arrived with you."

"Uh. Yeah."

He nodded, more to himself. He kept nodding to himself. "Right. Right. We'll get this figured out. Don't worry. We're almost there."

I stared at him, and again told myself to chill. I wanted to know everything, but he was right. Just get to the station, and we'd go from there. More than likely there wasn't anything I could do, except be there. It would be all Spence, and he was going in to help me out. Help my friends out.

That's all I wanted.

Except as we kept driving, we began to head away from the main traffic roads.

My stomach began to shrivel up.

This *wasn't* right.

He turned down a street that led to a bunch of warehouses, and lead lined my insides.

He parked outside of one of the buildings and turned the engine off.

Yeah. Crap. This was most definitely not a police station. Why hadn't I acted on what my gut was saying?

I turned to him, ready to say something, anything for an excuse to get away from him, and that's when I saw the gun.

He had it pointed at me, from the other side of him. He clipped out, "Give me your phone."

Air punched out of me. "What?"

"Give me your fucking phone!" He pounded on the steering wheel with his free hand.

He was *furious.*

I jumped back from the sudden anger. I wasn't scared of violence, but this came out so abruptly. It was shocking. My throat went dry, and panic caked the inside of it. Slowly, going numb, I gave him my phone. "Thought Octavia was neutral?"

"Octavia is." He took my phone and opened his door roughly. Grabbing my arm, he dragged me after him, dropping my phone and kicking it to destroy it. I fell out of the truck and landed on the ground, seeing my phone was smashed to pieces. I was distantly aware of the rough pavement underneath me, but I was wearing leggings, so there'd be no blood trail left behind.

I fell to the side. My wrist was exposed. I scraped it against the pavement, needing to leave behind something. Blood. Skin. Anything. It was evidence that couldn't be erased so easily.

This wasn't the first time I'd been taken, or the second, or even the third. As the other times, I began to automatically shift into who I needed to become in order to survive.

By this point, I didn't care about the reason behind this kidnapping.

I was being taken. Period.

I was officially done being a pawn. If I survived this, I was going to declare my own war, and hell hath a fucking girl pissed off because this was the last time I was going to be taken like this.

I was shaking with fury, my blood boiling. Everything was rattling inside of me.

Spence barked at me, yanking me to my feet. "If you're looking for your tail, don't bother. I already took care of him."

"Took care of him?"

His laugh was bitter. "He might be alive, if he's found in the next few minutes. Let's go. Enough stalling." His fingers were going to bruise me. He didn't seem to care. He dragged me toward one of the warehouses, his gun still trained on me.

"If Octavia is neutral then why did you take me?" I tried resisting, but he just continued to drag me, so I fell down. I didn't care about how much I was cut up. Blood was really hard to clean. The more blood, the better trail I left behind.

He got to the door and snarled down at me. "I said Octavia is neutral. I'm not. Get the fuck up if you want to see your friends alive." He rested the end of his gun against my forehead.

So my friends had been taken? That was one answer given.

I needed more. "If Octavia is still neutral that means you're violating your employment. This won't go unpunishe—"

His growl was savage as he reached down and hauled me back up. "That's the whole point of this. Don't you get that?"

I gulped. "What are you talking about?" But I was up and standing, though my knees were shaking so much that I was swaying back and forth.

"I am done waiting for someone to actually do something to take out your boy. West and Walden ain't doing shit. If I need to get involved so other parties come to play, Mafia families bigger than West or Walden, so be it. No matter what, your boy's going to be killed, and that's all I want."

It was the first time I was seeing Spence in daylight, and he had pulled me so close to him. He wore colored contact lenses. "Your eyes."

He blanched as his hand tightened so hard on my arm, banging on the door. *"Shut up."*

"Why would you wear colored contact lenses?"

I ran through the reasons and landed on only one that made sense. Because he had eyes that would give away something he didn't want out there. Which meant he had eyes that would tell *me* something, eyes I knew. What did that mean though?

No eyes made a difference to me except another set of eyes I saw recently.

When I met Creighton's cousin months ago, he had the same eyes. The same gray color.

I did a DNA test on Creighton years ago and found out he had family in Maine. His mother was Taunti Worthing, who came from the Worthing Mafia family. Creighton took over those Worthing assets. It was a hostile takeover, from what I gathered.

The door opened, and Spence shoved me inside. "*Enough* talking. Let's get this over with." Two big guys moved aside, making room for us. They were in business suits, and each held a handgun. The bulges underneath their coats were more guns. I knew my Mafia types by now. These guys were foot soldiers.

Spence huffed. "Are they here?"

Both ran impassive looks over me, up and down, before one of them nodded to Spence. He gestured behind him. "Inside."

Spence continued to shove me in front of him.

I saw my friends.

For a split second, I'd hoped all of this had been a ruse to get just me. That my friends were actually fine, probably eating breakfast somewhere together.

My stomach dropped.

None of it had been a ruse.

Against the far well was a row of jail cells, and inside one was Palma, Marshall, and Heath. Levi had his own next to them.

Palma was pale, tears streaking down her face. Marshall was bruised up. One of his eyes was swollen shut, and his mouth was bloodied. Heath was similar. All three had their hands zip-tied behind them. There was tape over their mouths and around their heads.

My gaze went to Levi last and winced at seeing the state he was in.

He didn't have the same tape around his mouth and head. And he wasn't handcuffed or zip-tied, but it didn't look like it was needed. His jaw was physically hanging enough to the side so I knew it'd been broken. His face was one giant black and blue bruise with blood caked all over him. Both of his eyes were swollen shut. He was unconscious.

His shirt was half torn off of him with more blood seeping through. He'd been thoroughly beaten to a bloody pulp. I started to go to him, my heart tearing out of me, but Spence jerked me to him. His hands dug in even harder. "I don't think so."

The door slammed shut behind us. The two men came up behind us at the same time another door opened from the other end of the warehouse.

Four more men stepped inside, looking similar to the two guys behind us. Business suits. Guns in hands. Mafia soldiers. But behind them were another two men, and those two, I knew.

Tristian West and Ashton Walden had arrived.

CHAPTER FORTY-TWO

CREIGHTON

I was in Nightclub 3 when my phone rang.

Lassiter was also just walking into my office. I showed him my screen, and he gave a nod. He came inside, but shut the door and remained quiet as I accepted the call.

"Gus." The lead in my IT department. "What's up?"

"Uh."

Lassiter and I shared a look.

Gus was never uncertain. Eating. Excited. Nervous. Never hesitant.

"Gus," I said again, more assertive. "What's wrong?"

"Okay." He let out some air and plunged ahead, sounding out of breath. "We might—I mean, you—you might have a problem. You told me to corrupt the AI drone program, right?"

"Right," I said, dryly.

"Well, I was working on it last night. Or early this morning, depending on your definition—"

"Gus, get to the point," Lassiter snapped.

He was quiet, which didn't last. "Lassie? You're there? Awesome. That'll help, but okay, yeah. Getting to the point. So, anyways, like I said, I was working on the program, and I intercepted some communication about the program. I didn't want to miss anything, so I wrote a program to automatically scan for anything relating to it. I got an alert around four this morning. The communication itself was earlier between the guy in charge of the whole thing and another person. It took a little bit to identify the other person because he had all sorts of IP addresses to hide his identity, but I found him. The conversation was mostly asking questions about the program, what territories it'll patrol. Things like that."

"Gus!" I barked.

"Yeah. Sorry. Yeah. Right. Okay. The other person was Spence Calloway."

Lassiter's head jerked to me, growing eerily still.

"I know that he works for Cole Mauricio, so I was thinking maybe he was asking of behalf of Mauricio—"

"No." I shut that down. It was a waste of time. "You said there was an alert as of four this morning?"

He coughed. "Uh. Yeah. Calloway reached out to ask if the program was up and running, and he asked for a certain location too." He cleared his throat before speaking again, picking up speed, "The guy never responded, but the program *isn't* up and running. It's not set to start until next month. I got curious anyway and pulled up any security cameras in the area Calloway was asking about . . . Well. I checked your phones. It's more out of habit than anything. You, Lassie, and Levi were all in Octavia last night. Blake too. Then your phone and Blake's phones left. Lassie's left after a bit. Levi's stayed."

My phone buzzed. So did Lassiter's.

Gustav's voice got dramatically quieter, "You need to see what I found."

Lassiter said, "It's a video."

"A few different cameras, but I put the footage together."

I pulled it up and hit play.

Two vehicles pulled up to the back of Octavia. Their rear brake lights lit up as they reversed to get as close to the door as possible. The back door of the club opened. Spence stepped out, giving the vehicles a motioning wave before disappearing inside. The two guys both got out of the vehicles and disappeared inside the club.

I cursed at the sight of them.

"Who are those two?"

My voice grated over my throat. "Crispin and Penn Worthing. Two more of my cousins."

Lassiter's gaze went to me.

I cut my eyes to him. "You don't have to say it."

"You decided to let them live when you purged your family. What was your reason again?"

I gave him a look. "I thought they were useless. I'm guessing they aren't . . ." My words died as my cousins emerged from the club, each carrying a body over their shoulders.

"*Fuck*," Lassiter's curse was swift and quiet.

The first body was Palma. Over Penn's shoulder.

The second was Heath. Over Crispin's shoulder.

Both were placed in the back of the vehicles. Crispin and Penn disappeared inside again, coming back out, carrying Finch together. Crispin had him under his shoulders. Penn had his legs. They repeated, and the next time they appeared, they were carrying Levi's giant body. Spence Calloway was helping.

I hadn't seen this one coming. I expected this from West or Walden, not a club manager for Cole Mauricio.

"Find Blake's whereabouts," I clipped out to Gus.

Hearing his fingers typing, he said, "Already on it. I can't get a hold of Scooter. He's supposed to be watching her. His phone says he's outside her place. He's not picking up. But . . . Oh, fuck."

Lassiter lowered his phone, only focused on mine now. He migrated over.

"Boss . . ."

"Jesus fucking Christ, Gustav. Say it NOW!"

Another button was pressed.

My phone buzzed, just mine.

It was a second video. For a moment, one split second, I didn't want to hit the button.

As I did, it began to play out as Gus filled in the blanks, "While you were catching up on that earlier footage, I was already looking for Blake's phone. She got a text from Spence. I can send that to you, if you want, but I fast-tracked until her phone was turned off at this location. That's the video you're seeing."

The video showed a car turning down an alley, slowing down, and parking at the edge of the camera's lens. There was no movement for a bit, then the car shut off. The driver's door opened, and Spence Calloway got out, dragging Blake with him.

He kicked the door shut, then they were out of eyesight.

Lassiter's phone beeped.

I wasn't paying him attention. Blake was in danger.

I was about to tear the world apart.

My phone buzzed again. And again.

Gus said, back to business, "First text is the location. Second text is the time stamp. This happened—"

Lassiter was looking over my shoulder. He cursed. "Thirty fucking minutes ago."

I began for the door.

Lassiter didn't.

I glanced back once, scowling. "What?"

He glanced at his phone before shoving it in his pocket. His jaw tightened. "You know that thing you wanted me to get last night? DNA from Calloway because we couldn't find any information on who he is. Got the results back."

I already knew what he was going to say, but I bit out, "Fucking say it, Last."

"He's a Worthing." He paused, grimacing. "He's your cousin."

"He's going to be a dead cousin. Let's *go*!"

Lassiter ran for the door, close on my heels.

I was saying to Gus, "I want all of my men within a ten-mile radius to converge on that location. Send someone to check on Scooter. You got that?"

"On it, but . . ." He cursed again.

I was getting tired of the cursing. "Gus," I warned.

Lassiter darted around me. He was yelling orders to my men in the nightclub. I wasn't paying attention, only paying attention to whatever Gus was going to tell me as I shoved out of the door.

"A few minutes after they arrived, they had visitors."

"Who?"

Lassiter shoved out the door with me, and he jerked me in his direction. "I'm a faster driver." We got in his own truck. When I saw more of my men spilling out of the door behind us, I said quickly, "No. Only a few of them come with us. The rest stay. We have more of my men closer to that location who will be there. They'll need to stay and protect any assets here."

"Got it." Lassiter flung open his driver's door, getting inside, and at the same time was speaking into his phone, relaying my orders.

I went around to get in his passenger side. Gus still hadn't told me who showed up at the warehouse. "Gus."

"Right. I was just waiting—" He sighed into the phone from his end, his voice suddenly bleak. "Tristian West and Ashton Walden showed up, along with their bodyguards. They're heavily armed."

Panic swarmed up, an emotion I'd never experienced before. Anger was there. I knew that feeling, but this new one, panic alongside fear, was unsettling. I slammed Lassiter's passenger door shut. "Keep monitoring everything. See if you can find some way to get inside that building. We're on our way."

Lassiter was about to throw the truck in reverse when one of my men sprinted over, motioning for me to roll my window down. I did, and he handed me a bag. "Guns." Two bulletproof vests were next. He opened the back door and picked up a much larger, longer item. He got in with us, bringing a high-precision, long range sniper rifle. He had it wrapped in a blanket, but I knew what weapons I'd acquired.

He pulled his door shut and got to work. "Walden's got his own sniper. I figure let's even the playing field. Drop me off around the block, and I'll keep the front door clear for you, Boss."

Lassiter didn't wait for anyone else to say anything. He fishtailed out of there.

As we went, as my sniper reached forward and began to help put one of the vests on me, I was on my phone. I called in the man of mine in charge of guarding my four hostages.

"Yeah, Boss?"

"I will need you to bring the four Christmas gifts to a location I'll be texting you. You will keep them a block away and wait for my orders."

"Got it." He ended the call, and I caught Lassiter's disapproval.

I did not give one fuck. "If they don't leave by the time we get there, they will use Blake as a hostage. I will use any and all resources at my disposal to get her back and alive. You don't approve, I don't give one shit."

He huffed, but his disapproval lessened. "It's not that. You asked me to feel out the brother. I've been doing that. And the mom has cancer. Blake's there. She won't want you to harm those four, and you know it. Keep that in the back of your mind."

I fixed him with a look. A hard look, and repeated something I recently said to Blake.

"I'd rather she hate me and be alive than be *nice* and have her dead. You can stop sharing your opinion right fucking now."

He shut up.

CHAPTER FORTY-THREE

BLAKE

The other guys were guards, and as soon as they entered the warehouse, they fanned out. Two went to one side, and the other two took up position by the door. West and Walden were eyeing my housemates before looking at where I stood. They saw Spence's two guards, and all of them had a reaction. Disgust. Walden rolled his eyes.

Spence stepped forward. "I take it that you're acquainted with my brothers."

Brothers?

West's and Walden's heads pivoted our way, and I saw the surprise there for a split second before both saw me. And they stayed on me. A chill went through me at the cruel and cold smile that was pulling at Walden's mouth. "Please tell me you've brought us this gift. Please, *please*. I don't even give a fuck about who else you are, just as long as you tell me that Miss Green is here for us." His leer told me all the nasty ways he wanted to make me scream in pain.

West wasn't as fazed. His eyes narrowed on Spence. "You're a Worthing?"

Spence let out an aggrieved sigh. Very dramatic. "Finally. Someone fucking gets it. *Yes.* I'm a Worthing."

West took in Spence's two guards, who I guess were actually his brothers? Brother guards? Just brothers? Both were big, muscly, and didn't look super smart. Thick necks. I was stereotyping guys with thick necks. John Cena was smart, so not all guys with thick necks were stupid, but these two guys looked like morons. There was no articulate way to explain the look. Just, moron.

"Wha—huh?" It was one of the brothers, though both seemed taken aback. The one with dark hair was flabbergasted. They swung their gazes on Spence at the same time, who gave each a resigned look. His shoulders slumped. "Tobias Worthing got my mom pregnant, and forced her to give me up. I wasn't in the system. I was raised by my mom's neighbor. I thought I was one of hers until my own high school DNA test gave me a surprise. Nice little things, aren't they?" He bit out, glancing my way. "Identifying all of these little Worthings running around."

The two guys continued to stare at him. The dark-haired one's mouth hung open. "You're our brother?"

"Dude. Dad had an affair." The other nudged him with his elbow.

"Your father was Toby Worthing?" Tristian West had come closer.

Spence rubbed at his forehead, but made a show of focusing on West. "Yes." He cast me a dark look. "Creighton Lane killed him."

One of the brothers growled, low and guttural.

Spence seemed to pick up steam now that he said that last bit. His head perked up. He stood taller, straighter. "Before you ask, no. Cole Mauricio does not know who I am. I found out about my father five years ago. When my grandma, or who I thought was my grandmother, passed, I decided to come here. I approached my father, told him who I was, and it took a little bit, but after a while, he and I began a relationship. That ended two months ago." He sent another murderous look my way, and he glared for a full five seconds before lowering his voice, returning to normal level as he continued talking with Tristian

West. "I have been waiting for you or your partner to do something about Lane, and you still haven't. I'm tired of waiting." He motioned toward where my friends were locked up. "Lane took something of yours. Well, here's something of his. This is me, if you haven't figured it out, trying to speed this process up. *Hurt* the one person he cares about. That's the whole reason he took your people, am I right?"

What was he talking about?

I didn't have time to try and figure it out because as soon as he finished talking, Spence took a gun out and crossed the room, pointing it at one of the cells.

I opened my mouth. "DON—"

BANG!

I ended it on a scream and launched myself forward.

He shot—Palma screamed at the same time I did. A second bloodcurdling scream erupted from her, instantly making my stomach churn as Marshall dropped to his knees with an abrupt and violent thud. Heath scrambled, trying to go to him, but he and Palma still had their hands zip-tied behind them. Their tape was in place except Palma broke free a corner of hers. Her scream was too powerful, and a corner hung from her mouth, while the top of her lip was bleeding. Tears streamed down her face. She and Heath knelt down, but had to keep turning around to try and help Marshall.

Oh, god. Marshall.

I was caught by one of Spence's brothers, and I wasn't thinking clearly enough to get free from his hold. I tried jerking out of his arms, but he held tighter until my knees buckled. Marshall's wide eyes met mine. Shocked. Scared. Blood drained from his face. He tipped backward. His chest was heaving while blood pooled on his shirt, spreading around him.

This was me. Because I moved in with them—this wasn't just on Creighton. I should've gotten my own place. I shouldn't have made friends.

This was all my fault.

"There." Spence brightened, his cheerfulness like a dagger into my chest. "One down. Three more to go." He aimed at Palma.

"HEY!"

Tristian West was storming our way, his own gun up and aiming at us. Correction—at Spence. The other guard who didn't have a hold of me tried to intercept, but West growled at him. "Back the fuck up, Penn."

He raised his hands, his gun in the one hand, and backed the fuck up.

As soon as he was clear, West lowered the gun until it was resting against Spence's forehead. I could tell this was not how Spence thought things were going to go. His face was slack.

"What are you doing?" Spence asked, hoarse as his head moved against the gun's muzzle.

"You don't give us gifts and then kill one before you hand them over." West extended his other hand, palm up. "Keys. *Now.*"

Spence didn't dare move an inch. Slowly, he slid a hand into his front pocket and pulled out a key. He handed it over.

West took it, and held it behind him.

Walden snatched it up, whistling at two of the guys that came in with them. They went to unlock the cell where Marshall was bleeding all over the floor. As Walden's two guards stepped in and began to move Marshall, West spoke, "Lane took four of our people. *Four.* You're going to shoot another one, and that would've left us with only three as a bargaining chip. Three to four. You would've sabotaged us before we were even able to start negotiations with Lane. How do you think that would've gone over?"

Spence was so eerily still. Beads of sweat trickled down his forehead, and he swallowed again before pointing to me. "You only need her. He doesn't care about the others. Just her."

West's eyes skirted to me, hardened, and went back to Spence. He leaned in, and lowered his voice to whisper though everyone could hear, and that was the point. "*She* cares about them, I bet. Right?"

Spence wasn't following West's logic.

He pushed harder against Spence's forehead, enough where Spence flinched from the pain. "The thing you don't get is that Green, herself, is another player on the board."

I frowned, confused, but was distracted because the guards returned. They began to pull Palma and Heath out of the cell.

Palma screamed, "No! NO! Please."

I tried getting to her, and this time, the big oaf holding me wasn't expecting it. I launched free, and was across the room in a second. There were shouts behind me. I ignored them all and flung myself at the guard who was trying to manhandle Palma.

THINK, BLAKE!

Of course that voice in my head wouldn't sound like me. Of course it would bark at me, sounding like Creighton, and of course, I would adhere to it because dammit, it/he was right. I needed to think. Be smart. We could get out of this alive.

Walden's guard wasn't expecting me to know a few things, how to handle myself, so when I launched at him, he opened his arms to catch me. I let my body turn to dead weight, which he wasn't expecting. As I went down, through his arms, I grabbed his gun, completed a somersault on the floor. Shoving back up to my feet, I had his gun up and pointing at . . . Well, at everyone. I grabbed Palma and hauled her behind me. Heath helped, herding her too. They were trying to help each other with their tape and zip ties. The problem was that we were going farther into the cell.

There was still shouting.

I tuned them out.

The guard realized my mistake the same time I did. He lunged for the cell door, which would've locked us inside. I changed direction, going for the door.

I was going to be too late.

Except movement blurred in the cell next to us. A beefy arm reached through the cell, grabbed a hold of the guard, and yanked him back. The other beefy arm wrapped around the guard's neck, and my heart froze, for a full second, until a very bloodied and discombobulated face peered at me from behind the guard.

Levi woke up.

He couldn't talk. He could barely see, with only one eye opened, but he was trying to relay that he was okay. Or, no. He jerked his gaze from me to the door and back again. He was telling me to run.

There was a certain amount of resignation and acceptance, and sadness in his eye.

No.

No.

He was preparing to die.

I saw it. I read it. I didn't accept it.

I began shaking my head, but his eye jerked from me to the door and back again.

Heath shuffled to my side, saying quietly, "Let's go."

This was not going to happen, but I could already see that Levi was going to make it happen. My insides screamed in protest. They were wailing because I wouldn't lose a brother.

I *would not.*

He gave me one more meaningful look, grunting before he slammed the guard back against the cell.

Feet pounded on the floor.

They were coming to separate them.

Other guns.

I had two seconds to move.

One second to think.

One second to act.

With a snap, I knew what I was going to do.

One second—I shoved Heath and Palma out of the cell.

The last second, I raised the gun—they were all yelling.

I was the cash prize.

If something happened to me, Creighton would burn this city down. Knowing that, knowing I was not going to stand by and let Levi die for me—I touched the gun to my temple.

Everyone skidded to a halt.

The side door opened . . .

Creighton walked inside.

CHAPTER FORTY-FOUR

BLAKE

Creighton didn't stop moving. He walked in, saw me, saw the gun, and his eyes went black.

Without pausing, he took one step, put his gun to the back of one of Spence's brothers' skulls and pulled the trigger.

BOOM!

It wasn't a normal gun that he was using. The sound vibrated through the warehouse.

At the same time, Lassiter moved out from behind him, wielding a knife. He stepped up behind Spence's other brother and brought his knife cleanly across the front of his throat. He slit him, stepped back, and left him to fall as blood began gushing from his throat.

Everyone had been focused on me.

Now they turned, seeing who had joined us, but Creighton wasn't fucking around.

Spence forgot he had a gun and raised both of his hands, as if to stop what was coming his way. It stopped nothing. Creighton aimed at Spence and pulled the trigger, this time shooting through the front of the skull.

Three men were dead within a matter of seconds.

Creighton turned his gun on Tristian West next. He would've pulled the trigger a third time except while I'd been distracted, Ashton Walden, who I realized had already been heading toward me because he wanted to save his guard, stepped inside my cell and raised his voice, "Lane."

Creighton froze, seeing that while I had a gun to my head, so did Walden. He added, his voice low and calm, knowing he'd be heard clearly, "I wouldn't." As he said that, he took the weapon from my hand and put his own gun's muzzle against my head. He swiftly moved so he was standing behind me, his gun now touching the back of my head. Seeing he had Creighton's undivided attention, he whistled approvingly under his breath. "Now who's a good boy?"

Creighton's eyes went feral.

He was going to kill him. Creighton was a good shot, but not good enough to get off a shot before four other guns turned on him. I didn't want to math anymore. Even with Lassiter's help, it wasn't enough. I didn't want to lose any of them.

"Eight!"

He stopped, his eyes flicking to mine.

He was slipping. Seeing me with a gun to my head pushed him off the edge. He was free-falling. And now with Walden's gun taking its place, Creighton was almost to the bottom where he was determined to set everyone on fire if it meant that I'd be the only one to get out alive.

"Creighton," I whispered now. *"Stop."*

His eyes flashed, ominously dark. His face hardened. He had lifted his mask. He was letting everyone see the real him, and I cursed under my breath because I didn't know what he was going to do. He switched direction, and his gun was placed next to Tristian West's head. Right behind the ear. He said back, in a monotone, "Put your gun down, Walden."

Ashton sucked in some air, fury raining from him. Wave after wave of it. He growled, a short savage sound, before he yanked me against his chest, and repositioned himself so he could comfortably hold the gun against me.

I closed my eyes, saying a prayer, because he messed up in doing that movement. Walden didn't know it. West didn't know it. I knew it. Levi knew it. Lassiter knew it. And Creighton knew it. Because I was trained to get out of holds like this. It was extremely easy to do.

It was all down to me.

I held still and opened my eyes, meeting Creighton's. He was waiting, expecting me to slip out, and that's when he would shoot Walden.

I stayed.

He raised an eyebrow. "Quokka."

I shook my head. My voice came out soft. "No."

"Blake." His held a command.

"No." My chin lifted. "We're going to stand here, and we're going to talk this out."

"He has a gun to your head."

"You have one to his friend."

"Not the same."

"How is it not?"

Creighton's eyes flashed, but somehow they looked even more dead. Like a demon's. "Because I don't give one fuck about him."

I wet my lips. My throat was so dry. Desertlike dry. When was the last time I had any water in my system? I had coffee this morning and alcohol last night. Water during one of our sex breaks. I almost started laughing at the oddity of that thought. "They said you took some of their people."

He didn't reply. Which was a response in itself.

My chest lifted. "You and I made a deal."

"We've made a lot of deals."

My eyes flashed. "There's a specific one I'm talking about."

He didn't respond.

I growled. "You know which one I'm talking about."

He edged out, "That was *after*."

"Are they alive?"

He kept quiet.

Lassiter broke out, "They're alive." He jerked forward, ignoring Creighton's warning look. Lassiter raised his hands in the air, his knife still tucked against his palm. "They're unharmed, and they're close."

"Last." Creighton promised so many ways to die in that one word. "Shut up."

Lassiter's eyes flickered, his hands began to lower, but he looked up at me, stared, went to Levi, and lastly, his gaze fell to Spence's body. His hands lowered all the way after that, as did his shoulders. His head too. "You might not believe this, Creight, but I *am* doing this for you." He raised his head once again and moved to face him. "They will kill her. You took family members of theirs. Look at them. They're ready to die if it means bringing those family members back to their women. Blake is everything to you, but she's just a weapon to use in their arsenal against you. She dies, everyone dies. That part, they don't get, but I do. I know what you'll do, and you won't care about Levi or me. I love you too, you know. That's why I'm doing this." He abruptly turned and spoke, "They're in a vehicle one block over—"

Creighton's eyes flared, and he moved his gun, aiming it at Lassiter.

I ceased breathing. "EIGHT, NO!"

Everything happened so fast.

Creighton pulled the trigger, but Tristian West knocked him to the side. His shot went wide. Lassiter's eyes got big, paling at the significance of what Creighton almost did.

I lunged forward.

Walden released me.

I darted forward, had the forethought to slam the jail cell closed behind me, locking Walden and his guard inside. There was a thud from inside, and as I glanced back, out of the corner of my eye, a body had fallen to the ground from inside.

Levi was also on the ground, grimacing in pain.

But I was across the room, and as Lassiter shook his head, clearing it, he moved to intercept the other three guards that were three steps away from us.

Creighton and West were fighting, and not sure what to do, Lassiter yelled at me, "Guards, Blake."

Right.

A gun was on the ground. I swept it up and aimed at one of West's guards. Lassiter cursed, let his knife drop, and pulled out two guns from his back. We stood shoulder to shoulder, our three guns stopping the guards from getting any closer.

Walden had a gun, but I was hoping he wouldn't risk a shot into our circle. He could shoot his best friend.

There were three distinct thuds before it quieted behind us.

Then, a gentle hand touched my waist, pulling me against him, and once I was there, my arm faltered. The gun dropped—I was hoping the safety was still on, but I ceased caring. I turned around and molded myself against Creighton's chest. His arms wrapped around me. His head went to my neck, and he held me as we were both shaking.

And Lassiter stood there, guarding us.

I tipped my head, trying to relay something to him, but he shook his head. Once. Briskly and firmly. I saw the flash of hurt before he masked it. Creighton betrayed him. That was going to take time to undo, if it ever would, but—I was done thinking.

I glanced in Levi's direction. He was still lying on his side, his head resting on the ground, but he was watching us with his one eye open. Seeing we were okay, relief flared, mixed with pain, and I saw it happen, where he gave himself permission to succumb. He passed out.

Walden grated out, "Lane."

Creighton tensed before lifting his head.

I didn't look. I didn't care anymore.

Walden's voice was strained. "I already made a call. Our people are collected."

A fleet of vehicles were heard then, brakes squealing, as it seemed they surrounded the warehouse. Car door after car door opened and slammed shut. I tensed, except when the doors opened and they flooded inside, I knew we'd be fine. Finally. Creighton's army had arrived.

Walden cursed, but Creighton was speaking, "Let them go."

I lifted my head enough to say, "Marshall was shot. Walden's men took him outside. He might be . . ." I couldn't finish that thought.

Creighton gave a nod, and motioned for his men, telling them to go and look for Marshall.

He was found, and sped off to the nearest hospital.

Levi was helped next.

Palma and Heath were taken out after him.

We stayed in place as the other cell was opened.

I buried my head back into Creighton's chest, but heard scuffling. Walden's voice spoke up, coming to my right. Passing my right. "We have our people. You have yours. We can keep going, or we can meet at the table. I'll let you and your woman make that decision."

"Wait." I looked up. He and his guard were carrying Tristian West, who was alive but unconscious. Walden paused.

I asked, "Who did he take?"

Walden's eyebrows pinched together, confused for a moment.

I clarified, "Of your people, who did Creighton take? Who were they to your woman?"

His face cleared, and his eyes grew haunted. "To my woman? Two of her best friends. Molly considers them family. They were there for her when no one was." His eyes fell to his best friend. "And his woman? Her literal family. Her mom and brother." He looked as if he were going to say something more, but thought better of it. His mouth flattened into a line, and he met Creighton's eyes briefly before his own face turned into stone.

They carried his best friend out.

CHAPTER FORTY-FIVE

BLAKE

Levi was asleep in his hospital bed. They wanted to keep him overnight, but Marshall would be kept for a few days. I'd just come from Marshall's room, so Palma switched with me. She was in there with Heath, and I sank into her vacated seat with an extra sigh. Neither had tried speaking to me. I couldn't be mad about that because I understood. Of course they would blame me. They should.

I was tired. Not just physically exhausted, but my soul was tired. My emotions were fried. My thoughts were numb, except the only thing I could think and feel were the same emotion.

Betrayal.

He took four innocents.

Creighton broke my rule.

"Hey."

Lassiter was in the doorway. He paused, took me in, and closed the door behind him quietly. His eyes trailed to Levi before his shoulders seemed to deflate. "I'm leaving."

"What?" Panic sliced me. "Why—" I stopped because I knew. Of course I knew. Creighton hadn't just betrayed me. Suddenly, the numbness lifted, and I was feeling everything all at once. Shame. Anger. *Fury.* Guilt. And underneath all of that, sadness. "Are you coming back?"

I was losing another person I loved.

He was quiet for a long moment, his eyes downcast before he lifted his chin up.

I felt burned. Agony shone bright from him for a beat before he masked it. He struggled for words before he lifted up a shoulder. "I don't know."

Anger shoved forward, and suddenly I was *seething.*

Creighton did this. Lassiter got between him and me, and Creighton did this.

"Why'd you do that?" I couldn't keep the bitterness out of my voice.

He winced. "What?"

I scowled at him. I couldn't help myself. Everything was falling apart around me.

My roommate was shot. My other roommates were probably traumatized from being kidnapped because of me, because of Creighton. "You knew what he'd do. You gave away his bargaining chip and you—"

He tore himself away from the door, his hands fisted at his side. "Are you fucking kidding me?"

I flinched because he was right. He was so right.

I hung my head, the fight suddenly gone. A hollowness moved into my chest, spreading through me. I whispered, "I know. I know. I'm sorry. I—" I didn't want him to leave, not him either. Was this the beginning of the departures?

Lassiter was going first. Who was next? My roommates? This was a final line that was crossed, and I couldn't say that I didn't understand. I did. I got it. Who was after that? I gazed at Levi, wanting to think he'd never leave me, but everyone had a line. Eventually it would get crossed.

That's what Creighton did, because he only had one line. Me.

My lungs were burning.

God.

What was I going to do? What *could* I do?

"Look, Blake. I'm leaving, but I'm not leaving you. Okay? I'm not mad about what I did. I'd do it in a heartbeat because the asshole shouldn't have taken them in the first place. But let me be very clear here. I'm not mad he took them because that violates some moral rule you might think I have. I don't give a fuck that he took them. It was wrong that he took them because of *you*. You have morals and shit that the rest of us don't. Levi. Me. Creighton. We'll kill and maim and hurt whoever we need if it means we'll survive and the ones we love are protected." He gave his head a savage shake, biting out, "I didn't do that shit because of me. I did it for *him*. He loves you, but I love him. I . . . I need space. I'm not even mad at what he almost did. I knew what he'd do when I opened my trap, but it's final now. Hell. I don't know if that makes sense, but I don't give a fuck right now. I'll be back. Don't cry about this. Just, you know." He turned half away from me and gestured in my direction. His Adam's apple was moving up and down, and he closed his eyes as if he couldn't bear the sight of me. "You're the best of us. Stay that way."

Tears blinded me. I couldn't see him for a moment.

My throat hurt.

I blinked to clear my vision, letting some of the tears fall, and when I could see again, he wasn't there.

I'll be back . . . I replayed that in my mind. But would he?

Would he really?

He was gone.

And in a flash, I felt like I was back in Mr. Nathan's car before Miss Marcie's house. I was eight all over again. I was alone all over again.

The world felt too big, too oppressive, too heavy, and I couldn't get any oxygen.

A shadow moved from the doorway.

The back of my neck grew hot. The ache in my chest twinged. I knew without looking who it was.

He was there so soon after Lassiter had left, so he would've overheard, and knowing Creighton, he probably overheard everything.

I couldn't. I just couldn't.

I didn't want to see those dead eyes of his trained on me, with no remorse, no feeling, nothing except a vacancy that would never be filled.

I couldn't look at him. "I don't want to see you."

His voice came out low, "Blake—"

I raised my voice. "I don't want to talk to you."

"You're angry."

I whipped my head to his. "You're goddamn right I am. I'm *livid*, Creighton. I want you gone. I want silence from you." Jesus. That blank gaze of his. No soul. Nothing. Just . . . What did he have? An obsession with me? When would that go away? He'd never feel how I did, how Lassiter did, how Levi did. He'd never feel love. He wasn't capable.

I drew in a ragged breath, and something broke inside of me. It fell, and I could feel it withering to nothing until I was back to being numb all over again.

I welcomed it. I couldn't handle anything else right now.

I looked away. "You broke my rules."

"Blake."

The soft tone from him did nothing to me anymore.

"Leave." One last look. He wasn't the only one dead inside anymore. I let him see what he'd done to me. "I never want to see you again."

His eyes flared, but he left.

Good.

I sat there, my hand reaching for Levi's, and I was relieved.

I was also lying to myself.

CHAPTER FORTY-SIX

CREIGHTON

"I don't understand why we have to be here. With him." Ashton Walden sent me a chilling glare before he turned that glare on his best friend. "What are we doing, Trace?"

Tristian West ignored Walden, bypassing him to give me a nod and indicating one of the chairs. We had decided to meet in one of Octavia's basement rooms. Despite my cousin's recent act and murder, the club was still considered the most neutral territory for us all.

I gave Walden a considering look as I chose one of the seats.

Walden skewered me, going to the farthest seat away from me. "What the fuck are you grinning at me about, Lane?" He raked a hand down his face, cursing under his breath, pinning West with another chilly look as West took a seat somewhat in the middle. "Anything we decide here is going to be bullshit. I put a gun to his girl's head. No way is he going to let that slide."

I leaned forward. "I'll let it slide if you give me your sniper."

Walden's eyes widened, just barely before a wall slammed in place. "Fuck. Off."

"Ashton," West murmured, trying to convey some kind of message to him.

The two shared a look, communicating without words, until Walden cursed again under his breath and leaned back in his seat. He pulled out his phone and began typing on it.

West gave him a cursory look before facing me. He pulled his phone out of his pocket and read whatever was there before flicking an annoyed glance at Walden. His eyebrows pinched together. "Are you serious?"

Walden was back to glaring at him. "I said what I said."

West heaved a loud sigh and again made a show of facing my way. "We agreed to meet at the table. This room is metaphorically the table. Before moving forward, we all need to agree on a few terms. One, is the war done? Two, are you planning repercussions for what happened in that warehouse?"

Walden snorted.

West added, "Specifically, are you going to hold a gun to Molly Easter?"

Walden's woman. I studied Walden, saw how he tried to keep from squirming underneath my gaze. Since I'd walked into that warehouse, saw Blake holding a gun to her own head, I hadn't wasted energy in wearing my own mask. Dead eyes. That's what Blake called them. To me, it was just me being me. I was letting people see me, and most times, it made them uncomfortable. It should make them uncomfortable. But Walden wasn't restless because he was seeing the real me. He didn't give one fuck about my vacant gaze. He'd already seen the real me.

I murmured softly, "You're worried I'll do to your woman what I did to you."

He shoved off his chair in a heartbeat. "You sick fuck—"

I didn't react. I was expecting this from him, but so was West. He jumped up as well, getting in between, but he didn't just hold his friend back. He planted a foot and shoved him back into his seat. "He's baiting you. It's what he does."

I rather enjoyed seeing this interaction. I wanted to see more of it.

West was right. I said that on purpose. I enjoyed riling Walden up. He was like a windup toy, so obvious how worried, and he should be, but with Blake so angry at me, I chided him. "You can relax. For now. I have no plans on retribution."

West swore to himself while Walden bristled, snapping, "What the fuck does that mean? For now?"

I contemplated my response, but I didn't see the point in hiding the reason. "I'm sure you have your own plants to get information. They'll have reported to you that Blake isn't speaking to me. If I harmed your woman, I've no doubt that she'd never speak to me again. You, though. You are different. I can harm you any day and all day—"

"Enough!" West stepped between us again, his hands stretched out as if he could physically keep us apart. When we walked into this room, our guards stayed outside. Along with our weapons. Each of us was wanded down to ensure no gun or knife or any other weapon was hidden on our bodies. But that didn't mean we still couldn't fight. I enjoyed ripping heads off of bodies. It'd been a while.

"We agreed at the warehouse that we would hold at a standoff. I should not have to remind either of you."

A chilling look gleamed from Walden as he taunted me, "Creighton Lane. All alone right now. Buddy number one took a walk when you turned your own gun on him. Buddy number two is still recovering. Is he walking yet? And where's your girl? Oh, right. She iced you out, and that was *your* doing. You're used to hiding behind an army, and your personal army wants nothing to do with you."

My head tilted to the side.

Both went still at the first flicker of emotion on my face. It wasn't anger. It was curiosity. "That's what you think of me? That I hide behind my army?"

Walden frowned, his eyes flicking over to West before he settled back in his seat. My response surprised him. Or more likely, the lack of response. I wasn't angry. He'd been hoping to incite me, and it failed. He failed.

He replied, measured, "I mean, yeah. Why else do you recruit such a large army?"

"So I can control my environment." I gave both a new assessing consideration. "Is that not why you have your guards?"

Walden closed his mouth and shot West a look, who flattened his mouth before speaking for them. "We have guards for protection. Power." Both seemed conflicted by this new avenue of conversation. We'd veered into a direction they hadn't foreseen. West asked, cautiously, "Is that not the same for you? You recruit an army to ensure your territory, and you do with that territory as you please. We're the same, Lane."

"You do it for money," I said, and no, it wasn't the same as me.

I noted this before, realizing when I saw how much he cared for his friend and how both of them have loved ones. It was being cemented all over again. I did not recruit an army to ensure territory to make money. That's what they did. Power and money.

They used their guards to ensure their money. I used money to ensure the army.

West said, "We do it to control the city."

That too.

"To keep your loved ones safe from other families coming to harm them." I understood that aspect.

Both men shared another look before West said slowly, "Yeah."

So we were similar in one way at least. "I'm open to an agreement, but first and foremost, my men, Blake, and anyone Blake cares about will always be safe. That's nonnegotiable for me."

"What the fu—"

West stepped forward, cutting off Walden. "You will cease recruiting in our territories, and we can agree to that." His head lowered, more intent, and his eyes narrowed. He was now the epitome of a businessman, sensing a proposal was close. He just needed to suss it out, find the right terms, and present it to all parties, and we could have what they wanted so much. Peace.

"As long as my terms are always agreed to, yes. I will cease recruiting in your territories in this city." I wasn't concerned about other cities. Both the West and Walden families had always maintained they would only operate in New York City. As far as I could see, it wasn't that they lacked ambition. It was that holding onto this city was more important. No one could blame them. It was a treasure trove for our world.

"No human or sex trafficking," Walden spoke up. He was staring me down. "That's a nonnegotiable for us. And our loved ones are safe from you as well."

"How about we agree that neither party harms the other as long as we have this truce in place? If that's broken, then we're back to square one. I don't think any of us want that." West gave Walden a meaningful look, who settled in his chair again. "We keep the territories how they currently are divided. You keep what you've already taken."

"That's fine with me."

West turned to me, and his eyebrows lowered. He expected some sort of emotion from me? There was none on my face. At this point, I didn't know why he was surprised. "I don't care about peace like you do. I enjoy the fighting."

Walden snorted. "He only cares about Green. That's literally all, Trace."

"He's right. Blake's all I care about."

"Well, Miss Green made it clear that she cares about peace. She also cares that you couldn't go after our loved ones anymore—"

"That's not true. I can't go after anyone innocent or good. Just bad or guilty people. Those types are fair game. She won't be upset about that. We've talked about this. It's our form of compromise." Though, that wasn't altogether true anymore. I had to get her permission on how I could harm someone if they harmed her. And she wanted me to learn the difference between a small slight against her and a bigger slight. They made no difference in my mind, but that bothered Blake. Normal people world.

But according to those terms and what was being laid out, I could still go after Walden. Neither he nor West had included himself in the terms. Just their loved ones. I liked that loophole.

I said quickly, "I'm okay with those terms."

"I—" West opened his mouth, but shut it and gave me a blinking look of confusion. I had surprised him again.

Walden was the one who understood me the best, and he hated me. If he could string me up and take a butcher knife to my gut, he would. I respected that. West would never understand me. He was too human of the two. He could turn savage and ruthless, but he didn't have to. Walden did that for him. I hoped he appreciated his best friend for taking on that role for the two of them. Though, that didn't mean Walden was the most like me. No. He cared. He loved. In a way, I wondered if he cared and loved and felt more than West did. He was crueler, but if he'd been forced to be . . . If so, what would the repercussions from that be in the future? Would it erode their friendship? Would it build resentment between the two of them?

I'd gone back to studying them, and when a psychopath took on a questioning appraisal, it made anyone uncomfortable. The two glanced at each other.

I was making them uncomfortable.

Levi was indisposed for a few months. Lassiter, I didn't know when he would return to the fold. And Blake . . . That was a stay-tuned moment currently. So maybe I felt some sort of nostalgia for these two. Either way, if we were going to stop trying to threaten each other, I decided to offer them a gift. "I will help you protect this city."

They shared another look, this one longer than the others. They were uncertain about my offer.

I huffed, just a bit to myself. "It's my gift to you. If another criminal entity tries to push into the city, I will help eliminate the threat. I won't do it alone, though. You cannot ride my coattails. It will be a team effort. Partners, in a way. I will also promise that I won't use their attack to launch my own on any of your territories. I'll hold the treaty if either of you are weakened."

Walden grunted. "Good of you."

I tried for a normal-looking smile. Normal people world.

He winced. "Ugh. Don't. You've tortured me, remember? I've seen your true self."

Right. I relaxed, enjoying that. I let the mask fade again.

"Never mind. I can't decide what's worse. Put the fake shit back on."

I gave him a deadpan look.

"Okay." West broke in; his eyebrows rose as he took in our slight exchange. "We've come to an agreement. Correct? Loved ones are safe. Territories remain the same. If the city is under attack, all of us work together and we don't capitalize on it against each other. Are we all agreed?"

Walden scowled at West before he gave a reluctant and stiff nod. "Yeah. Fine. Agreed."

Both turned my way.

I was disappointed, but I hid that from them. It was small and fleeting. I thought there'd be more bloodshed. "I already agreed. Yes."

West's shoulders noticeably relaxed. He gave both of us an appraising and perhaps somewhat approving look. "Good. We've all agreed."

They seemed happy.

Blake would be happy . . . A sobering thought hit me because, no. Blake wouldn't be happy to hear from me. She'd be happy to hear about the peace, but not to hear from me.

She still wasn't talking to me.

I'd tried having my men trail her because that was our original agreement. But she wasn't even having that. She ditched them. She *kept* ditching them.

I checked my phone.

Her latest shift at the foster center was ending soon.

CHAPTER FORTY-SEVEN

BLAKE

"Satya, it's late. Is your ride here? Are you taking the train? I know you're not a fan of riding the train so late. We can send someone with you." The other staff member was frustrated. It wasn't apparent in his voice, but any foster kid was trained to hear the slightest intonation. This staff member was tired and stressed. I got it. We all had our problems, and I couldn't even really blame him for missing whatever was going on with Satya. She was fifteen and had started coming because she was friends with Cap from school. She was also quiet, so she got overlooked sometimes.

At first she only came when Cap and Malik were here.

Then, she began coming a few times when it was just Malik.

This last week she'd been coming alone. She showed up at different hours, but she stayed every day until we were closing. Tonight was the first night she wasn't moving fast enough for my coworker. I got why he was slightly annoyed. We couldn't do our last round of checks until everyone was gone. It was against policy.

The environment was theirs, and they were free not to feel rushed to leave for a reason. A lot of that was maintaining a safe place for them;

that meant free of everything, even the miniscule action that might be interpreted as "they don't want me here."

I got it. Shepherd, my coworker, I don't think he did.

He was a good guy, and his intentions were solid. He wanted to make a difference in social work, but I could tell that even though his family had been one of the good ones for fostering, he'd never been in the system himself. Some got it. Some didn't. I envied the ones who didn't.

And he wasn't getting it tonight.

Satya wasn't saying anything, but Satya never said anything. She was a good kid. Did everything asked of her. Followed all the rules, but her not leaving when we first said we were closing, that was enough to send off a red alarm.

I eyed her, not sure how to proceed at this moment. If I went by the book, I should be opening a dialogue between us. I was supposed to be asking if she felt safe to go home, etc. That would trip Shepherd's own alarms, but Satya knew how to lie and cover if she wanted. She was too smart. If I opened that conversation with her, she'd lie, and she'd lie convincingly.

She would probably even stop coming to the shelter because she knew Shepherd would be watching her closer than normal. And, well, I didn't have it in me to give a fuck about what the policies said to do.

I wanted to help her now, not in four months or four years, or when it would be too late.

With that decision made, I waited until she left and went over to Shepherd.

"Hey," I said under my breath. "Could you cover me? I just checked my phone, and my roommate had to go back to the hospital."

His eyes widened, and he stood up from where he'd been bending to pick up some of the puzzle pieces that'd fallen to the floor. "Oh, no. Yes. Of course. I got this. Go. Make sure he's okay. He's the one who was shot, right?"

I nodded.

He knew about Marshall.

He just didn't know that Marshall was currently with his family.

It was a good lie. Satya wasn't the only one who knew how to lie.

"Thanks so much, Shep. I'll owe you." I was already grabbing my coat and phone. My keys and everything else I needed were inside my coat.

The first week Creighton kept sending his men to trail me, and I'd meant what I told him. I wanted space. I needed space. That meant his little spies, too, so I'd taken to not bringing a bag with me. It was easier to ghost them if they decided to try and wait me out. That was last week. This week, someone was trailing me, but they stayed so far back that when I tried catching them, they eluded me. I never saw their face. There was no indication I was even being followed, but I knew my body. It was Creighton.

To his credit, when I started trying to catch him following me, he would leave me alone. It was always a mindfuck because sometimes I wondered if it actually was him following me or if I was just hoping it was him.

Either way, I didn't have a bag with me to grab, and as soon as I got outside, I was able to see Satya taking a right turn when she should've been going left. I hotfooted it after her.

I knew after the first block, she had no intention of going to her foster home. After five blocks, I started to get an inkling where she might be going, and I didn't like it. There were a couple vacant buildings in this area. Of course, they weren't really vacant. Just no one officially lived there. She ducked into one, and I cursed under my breath.

I paused, mentally preparing myself for what I was going to find in there.

Drug dealers, I'm sure. Other homeless people. People high. Any and all? Other people? A few gangs operated in this territory, but as far as I was aware, they all had an understanding with one of the three. West, Walden, or Creighton. I knew they were supposed to be having a meeting sometime, where I assumed they'd just finalize the standoff that had happened at the warehouse.

Still, I knew that wasn't a carte blanche for protection because it only worked if someone who was about to hurt me knew who owned the territory, and a lot of people didn't know. They were just getting by.

I was still going in. I needed to move before I lost Satya.

I was about to step off the block, cross the street to enter her building, when a hand grabbed my arm. My body instantly warmed, relaxing, as I was pulled against his chest. His scent washed over me, further fucking with my head because heat burst inside of me. My heart spiked.

He was here. Finally.

My mind caught up, and I rounded to shove him away from me. "Don't—" I didn't have time for this. "Don't you dare follow me—"

"Where?" Creighton didn't grab me, but he quickly shouldered me back against the nearest brick wall behind me. He loomed over me, his eyes almost glittering from the moon over us. He was all angry and sinister right now.

A sensation slid down my spine, wrapping around it.

He felt my body's reaction and paused, giving me a once-over, which only sent heat to spread through the rest of my body. It wasn't that I was aroused. It was the wrong time and place. It was relief because he still cared. And happiness because I'd missed him.

I instantly loathed my own body. Traitor.

"Into that warehouse? Because if you have the idea that you're going in there alone and unprotected, baby, you are sorely mistaken."

My heart picked up. I ignored it. "It's none of your busines—"

"*You* are always my business," he cut me off.

My eyes slid toward the warehouse, but I didn't think Satya had left. My gut was saying she was in there, and my gut further squeezed at the thought of who else was in there as well.

"Creighton, I—" The old exhaustion slammed over me. When he was like this, it took all of my strength to fight him. He was a wall, and he was immovable sometimes. But I had to get in there, and I didn't have the energy to fight him on it. Not on this.

Creighton gave me one of his usual stares, before he stepped away from me. "This is my area. There should be someone, at least one person, in there who's connected to me. If you get into trouble, you use my name. Got it? I know you can handle yourself, but if you get in a situation, just use my name. Your girl will need you. It'll save you time too."

What? He never gave in, not like this, not so easily, so quickly.

Or so reasonably.

I tried getting a read on him, but it was his usual flat affect on his face. There was nothing there to read.

He gave me more space. "I can see this is important to you, and I know you think I didn't listen to you the last time we talked. You asked for space. I'm giving you space." A third step away, and I had to bite down on my lip because part of me didn't want him to keep going. I wanted to reach out, grab hold of his shirt, and pull him back to me.

His hand lifted, cupping the side of my face before he touched his finger to my bottom lip. His finger smoothed over the dip in my chin. "Go, Blake." His hand fell away.

I watched it go, and ached inside.

Why?

I didn't have any more time to waste, and he knew it. He moved until he was in the shadows again, and I blinked, almost unable to see him at all now.

My heart hurt, but I crossed the street and went inside the warehouse.

Alarm and fear hit me hard, but I held them at bay, knowing I'd need to keep my head calm and clear in order to maneuver being inside. A guy immediately wafted over to me, his breath reeking, "Hey, ba-bee. Whatcha you doing here? Huh, honey? You here for a good time? You want a good time?"

The building was a vacant office of some sort. The front lounge area was where a few other homeless people were living. A girl was unconscious in the corner, a needle still in her arm.

I watched her chest and was relieved to see it rising at a steady pace. She was just passed out.

A hand waved in front of me. "Hey, you. Little girl. I'm talking to you." The same guy began to get closer, his voice rising. A little sharper.

I cut my eyes back to him. "Don't fucking touch me." I reached for my hip and held it there.

He tracked where my hand went. I didn't have a weapon on me. I used to and I should've, but I didn't want to take anything to the foster center in case it fell into the wrong hands. It'd been a decision I had debated long and hard about. When I made that decision, Creighton's men had still been tailing me. I never changed my habit.

But my fingers automatically curled what would've normally been there. This man would see that habit, and I was leaning on that, hoping he'd know I had some way to defend myself against him.

I let the guy get a read on me, knowing he wasn't going to take my tone personal. He was probably set in place to be the first wave of security in this warehouse, by whoever was his immediate boss.

It was a gamble if I used Creighton's name now. He might not know it, and if he did, he'd sound the alarm to go to his boss. That boss would take time to get here. There'd be a whole process they'd have to go through to verify I wasn't lying when I was using the highest boss's name because if I was, that was a crime meant for death. Of course, if I went that route, it'd take the time to deal with everything, but more than likely, I'd get the answers I needed about Satya easily. They'd lead me to wherever she was staying and give me any information I wanted to know.

But Satya could bolt before I got to her.

"You're not just anyone, are you, girlie?" He leaned forward, his crazed and drunken look falling away.

I was correct. He was security. It'd been his mask. He was very sober right now, giving me another assessment. "Who are you?"

"Look." I debated on what exactly to tell him. "I work at the center down the way. You know it?"

"The new one? The big fancy one?"

I hesitated before shrugging. "Yeah. A girl I'm worried about ducked in here. I'm not here to blow her situation. I just want to make sure she's safe." Now I was the one to assess him because if he lied to me and gave me some bullshit about how of course she was safe, she was with family, I was going to find a weapon here, and I was going to use it to beat him. And when I was done, then I'd use Creighton's name.

Maybe he read my intention or not, I didn't know, but a new emotion flickered over his eyes. He sidled away from me, waving behind him. "She's set up in one of the back rooms. As long as you don't mess with anyone, no one will mess with you. You got me?"

I clipped my chin up and down. "I just want to make sure she's okay."

He was already done with me and had turned. His hand rose again, giving another shooing motion.

I shooed.

She was in the fourth room, in what looked like had been an office.

She was kneeling on a sleeping bag on the floor, and sat up when I knocked lightly on the door. Her jaw dropped, and she had to blink a few times before she scrambled to her feet. "H-hi-whatareyoudoinghere?" Her face twisted up, and she blinked again, before her mouth curved downward. "Did you follow me?"

I didn't answer her right away, taking in the room.

She had a pile of books near her sleeping bag. One of those solar-powered flashlights. Her backpack was in the corner by her head. She'd been looking at her phone, and it was gripped tightly in her hand now. She held it up as if it were a weapon to keep me back. Sheets were strewn up to cover the windows, along with a blanket that had been clipped in place to hide the floor-to-ceiling glass so no one could look in from the hallway. A lawn chair was in the other corner, along with an empty place where another sleeping bag might've been. Some water bottles and food items were in a pile. Cereal bowls. Spoons. Napkins.

Crap. She was living here.

"Let me guess." I eyed her bag again, spotting something white tucked inside. "If I were to check your bag, you'd have a thing of toilet paper. Also guessing that's probably why we've needed to refill the bathrooms more lately even though we're not having more kids at the center."

She flushed, and she was going to spew.

I waved that off before starting to sit, then catching myself. "Do you—" I gestured to the bottom half of her sleeping bag. "Would you mind?" I didn't want to risk the floor.

"Uh. Yes."

I sat anyway.

"Hey!" Now she was standing over me, still clasping onto her phone.

A sadness came over me, blanketing me, and everything else, all my confused emotions at seeing Creighton, faded away. None of that mattered because right now, only this girl mattered.

Maybe she saw the change on my face, or who knows, maybe she was just sensitive and could feel the change come over me, but whatever she'd been about to say, she didn't.

I tried for a smile, but knew it was probably small. "Can you sit?"

She did, slowly. She kept watching me. "If you're going to call the cops—" she said, warily.

I waved that off. "Please. Gross. I hate them too."

A snort escaped her before she caught herself. When she did, her mouth went flat, and her eyes turned hostile. "Where I live is none of your business."

"Isn't it, though?"

She jerked upright, hissing. She was readying for a fight.

I ignored it. Her. The fight she wanted to spew, and I looked around her room again.

I let out a sigh.

"I did this, you know." My gaze caught and held on a row of stars, cut out and taped on a string. She hung them on the far wall. Those stars came from the center. I remembered seeing her at the craft table. She spent hours there, and I saw some snowflakes she'd cut out too. They were taped to the wall above the empty spot. A heart that she'd turned into a card, like it was a Valentine's Day card. That was propped so it was standing upright, also by that spot.

She loved whoever slept there.

"You did what? Narc on another runaway, thinking you were doing the right thing." She sneered. "Bitch, please."

"Bitch, yes please."

Her face went blank. "What?"

My gaze found hers again. "Bitch, yes please. If you're going to be rude, at least add the yes. Makes it snarkier. More sass. Nothing wrong with having more sass. I've had my own moments too." I motioned around the place. "And no, I meant that I've done this. *This.*" There were smaller items. A little wolf carving on the floor. "I had a good foster home when I was eight, but I had to leave when I was sixteen. Before that, I ran away a couple times. Before I was eight. And a few other times when I was sixteen." That was before Creighton found me, when he began threatening my new foster parents. Every time I was moved, he showed up and let the parents know how it was going to go for me. It was his form of Creighton's Foster Care Orientation.

I never had to run again.

He never asked why I didn't run *to* him. I wondered about that.

"You were a runaway before you were eight?"

I nodded. "Yeah. So I get it. I do." I pinned a look at her. "But I know your foster parents. I've met them. They seem like decent ones. Why . . ." I changed course. "You and whoever sleeps there, you two got separated?"

I lifted my head, making sure she could see my face. Read me.

She saw no judgment. Her shoulders suddenly slumped, and her head hung down. A weight fell from her. "Yeah. My little sister. They—" She let out a harsh breath. "I can't tell you why, but she couldn't stay where she was. I don't have much longer anyways."

"You're fifteen."

"I can do the thing where I file to get released early at sixteen from the state. That's a thing. Isn't it?"

Yeah. It was a thing. And she was going to try and get legal custody of her sister. I saw it all on her face. The hope. The desperation. I didn't know if it would work. I doubted it would, but she just gave me something to work with.

"You'll need a job."

Her head jerked up. "What?"

"You'll need a place to stay." I cast a glance around the room, shaking my head. "This won't work. You'll need *legal* housing. An apartment probably. You'll have to have a working bathroom. A kitchen. You can sleep in the living room, but she'll need her own room."

Hurt flared in her eyes. Her bottom lip started quivering. "Why are you saying this? You trying to mess me up or something?"

"I'm laying out what you'll need to do for the state to even consider giving custody to you. That's what you're planning, right?"

She didn't reply, but a sheen of tears told me I was right.

"Where's your sister now?"

"Her foster parents haven't reported her gone yet. She's still going to school. One of her classmates invited a few of the girls over for a birthday sleepover."

That was good. Real good.

"Your foster parents won't try and take her in?"

She snorted. "You were in the system. You know that's not how it works."

She was right. I knew it should work to keep the siblings together. That was probably the intent in the beginning, but a bed under a roof was more pivotal than keeping siblings together sometimes. A million different thoughts were going through my head, but I was going to school for psychology. I didn't know what graduate school I'd be doing afterward, and I hadn't intended to enter back into the foster world, but here I was. And here was a teenager who needed some help, some real help.

I could do that. Or I'd do what I could.

"You know who I am?" I asked.

She frowned, her thin eyebrows burrowing together. She was playing with her phone on the sleeping bag between us, turning it over and then over and then over. It was a nervous habit. She did the same thing at the center sometimes with whatever was in her hand. Pen. Pencil. Scissors.

"You're Miss Blake." She said it slowly. "From the center."

"No." I grinned. "That's not what I meant. I've caught the looks from some of you when the other staff aren't looking. I've heard the whispers." I leaned forward. "Do you know who I am?"

Comprehension dawned, and she nodded again, slowly.

"You know who protects me?" Whether I want him to or not.

Though a small voice reminded me that he backed away. He let me come into this warehouse by myself. He would've known the risks, and he still gave me space.

Some fear crept in her gaze. She lowered her head once more. "Yeah. I know."

Well, that was an easier stepping stone to start with—

She raised her head, determination gleaming back at me. Her chin was firm. "It's why I'm here."

I opened my mouth, surprised.

She continued before I could say anything else, gesturing to the hallway. "He's got a rule. You know that? No minor girls can be approached."

I closed my mouth on a snap. "What?"

"If we approach the gangs, the pimps, the dealers, that's different. But if we don't, we're to be left alone. Anyone who breaks those rules are, well, you know what happens. They don't show their face again. He did that. Neighborhood changed when he took over."

"Creighton did that?"

She frowned. "I don't know his name. They just call him Boss Lane or Boss Line. Something like that. The psychopath one, right? That's what else they say about him, but everyone knows who you are." She began grinning. "When I realized that you were the same Blake that's the Boss Line's woman, I almost shit myself. Crea thought it was so funny too. My sissie. I told her, too, when I figured it out. I had to sit down in the bathroom, right there in the stall. I was so shook up, I didn't even get to the toilet. Had to sit on the floor. Good thing I know you guys clean those floors or I would've shit my pants all over again."

Creighton protected the girls.

That was still rattling around in my head.

He did that for me. I knew he did. Or because of me. Because I'd been one of those girls.

He would've thought about it that way.

"He never told me," I murmured, softly.

She grew quiet, angling her head to the side. "He didn't? I'd think that'd be something he'd tell you right away. Make you feel good about it. You know?"

"No. Not Creighton." He wasn't like that. He didn't do anything for credit.

"Anyways, you think you can help me and Crea somehow?" She shrugged at me. "I mean, that's the reason you asked me if I knew who you were. Right? And why you told me you'd been a runaway too. You were doing all that to say that you can help us out? What are you going to do? You're going to ask your boyfriend to help us somehow? I bet he's got people everywhere. Bet he could grease the wheels and get my sister in my same foster home." She quieted, but her lip was back to trembling again. She sniffled. "You think he could do that?"

"I think." I needed to decide. To ask for Creighton's help or not. But what was I doing? Of course I'd ask, and Creighton wasn't spiteful. He would help merely because I asked him.

A new wave of gratitude swept through me, heating me up again. This was a new consideration for Creighton because a lesser man would have held this over my head, but he wouldn't. He would never do that to me. That's not the kind of man he was.

His obsession *was* unconditional.

I flicked a tear away and ignored how Satya got suddenly quiet, peering at me intently. I stood up, and motioned for her. "Grab what you need. I can't, in good conscience, let you stay here. Your sister won't come back until tomorrow, right? She'll go to her school?"

"At her sleepovers, I go and get her. We don't have school tomorrow. It's Saturday."

Of course. I'd forgotten because part of my world had been turned upside down since I entered a certain warehouse. "Can you go back to your foster home tonight? They were in the center four days ago and acted as if nothing was wrong."

"That's cause they left on a short trip. They got an old woman to stay and watch us, and she's blind as whatever can't see. One of the kids covers for me. I don't think the others will narc. You know how it is."

Sometimes narcing wasn't a bad thing, but I got it.

"You can sleep at your foster home tonight, and I'll talk to Creighton. Call me in the morning, and hopefully by then I'll have instructions on the next steps to take, but, Satya." She'd started to pack her bag, but paused. I said, "If you're in a situation where you think the only next step to do is come back to a place like this, please call me. I'm not a mandated reporter. You know what that means?"

She moved her head up and down, almost shyly this time.

"That means I don't have to report shit. Not yet. I'm more than okay with helping you with some back channels. Okay?"

Her tears welled up, and she had to blink a few times before they cleared, before she could speak again. "Cap told me who you were when you made sure Malik got home. It's why her and I decided to give the center a shot." She went back to packing.

I waited, thinking she had more to say, but no. She already said it.

Okay then.

I found some extra bags they had stuffed in a corner and began helping her pack. We put as many of their items inside the bags as possible. When I reached up to start taking down the stars on the wall, she stopped me. "Leave 'em for the next people. I can make more." She stood up, after finishing rolling up her sleeping bag. Our arms were full as we went down to the front door.

She didn't look around before she ducked outside.

I did, glancing over to make eye contact with the guy who'd approached me. He flicked his fingers, lighting up a joint, and the flare of the lighter illuminated his face for a second. His eyes were sharp, but he was from the streets.

Another city, another corner, and things might've been different between him and me, him and Satya. *But* we were in this city, in this corner of this city, and it wasn't. That was because of Creighton.

I stepped outside, starting to pull out my phone because if I was already going to ask Creighton for help, what would it hurt to ask for a ride as well? It was late, and I didn't want to travel on the train with Satya and Crea's personal items. Plus, that'd be a long-ass ride.

I didn't need to, though. I shoved my phone back in my pocket.

A black SUV was parked on the street, and one of Creighton's guys stood by the door. He nodded inside. "Boss called us in. Said you might need a ride."

I expelled a sigh because he hadn't given me space after all.

He just called in another watchdog for me, but as I bent down to climb inside, the guy added, "Just so you know, we arrived a few minutes ago. Boss said that'd be important information you'd want to know. He also said to make sure you know that we're not here for you." His eyes trailed to Satya. "We're here for her. We'll help her however she needs. Boss said to let you know that he won't have anyone killed, said you'd be real keen on that fact."

Well.

I . . . Okay then.

I was reeling all over again, and tried to sputter out a remark, but as soon as I climbed inside, he shut the door.

Satya laughed a little bit. "You should see your face. It's the same look Shepherd gets on his face whenever one of us girls starts talking about our periods."

CHAPTER FORTY-EIGHT

BLAKE

"So, it's done? The whole war thing that you never told us about."

We were at home, all of us, including Levi. He stayed in the hospital for a couple days, but he'd been sleeping in Palma's room ever since. She didn't want him in the basement in case there was a chill down there. She'd been quite the nurse to him, and Levi was eating it up.

I was in my room, studying since I had a big test coming up, before Palma knocked on the door.

Nodding to the bed, I said, "Hey. Come in. I need a break anyway."

She sat on the end.

"How's Levi?"

"Oh." A softness came over her, one that was showing up more and more regularly when Levi's name was brought up. I was happy for her. I was happy for Levi too. "He's good. Getting better. A few more months and his jaw will be back to being a smartass."

I snorted. "Only way Levi would not be a smartass was if he were . . ." I gulped. Wrong word choice there. I couldn't finish that statement.

"Yeah," she said quietly, clearing her throat. "Good thing it didn't come to that. For any of us."

The people who died were Spence and his two brothers. West was fine. Walden was fine. Their people were all fine. Levi had fractured ribs and a broken jaw. Marshall's family came up to take him to their home. As far as I knew, he was going to finish school online, at least for the semester.

"Have you been in contact with Marshall?"

She hesitated before nodding, then shrugging. "Just a phone call here and there. He's okay. Being shot, being—what was done to us—it's not normal. It can be traumatizing. You know?"

I almost laughed. "I've always been in foster care, but Miss Marcie's house was the first where I felt safe. Before her place, the family—that foster mom shot herself."

Palma gasped.

"I was in the room." My throat was burning. "She killed herself because her husband was doing things. To her. To some of the other girls."

"To you?"

"No." A small blessing. "The family before that, well, they put locks on our doors, and we were only allowed out when our social workers showed up. I was lucky. I got a good social worker. He recognized something was wrong and got me out of there."

"Did anything happen to either of those places?"

I wanted to tell her that my social worker helped shut them down, but that would've been a lie. They did get shut down, but it hadn't been anyone legally doing it. I didn't want to say the words. Add to the pile of bad things Creighton did for me.

I didn't feel bad about those casualties.

I tried, telling myself that maybe they would've changed. In the end, though, I just couldn't summon whatever emotion I needed to believe that.

"I'm glad." Palma surprised me. Her voice was hoarse. She covered her hand with mine. "Seeing your boyfriend in action, seeing who he's going up against, I know you're a good person. You don't like shouldering what he does to protect you, but you're not responsible for what another person does."

"I am if he's hurting others."

"But is he really? Levi told me about the rules you gave Creighton. Only bad. Only the guilty."

"He violated that when he took those four people."

"But he didn't hurt them."

"He was going to."

"But he didn't." She leaned forward, her hand gently squeezing mine. "The stories I've heard about him and that guy I'm seeing now, I don't think he's the same guy. I think he's changing. He's changing for you. That's what I think."

Yeah. Maybe.

He let me go into that office building alone. The following Monday, Satya and her sister came to the center. She informed me that her foster parents were able to take her sister in, said they got an emergency call Saturday morning that lined everything up. Creighton did that.

He hadn't followed me the last week either. I didn't think anyone else had either.

He'd been giving me space. He listened to me, actually gave me what I said I needed.

That was all in my head, just ruminating.

I missed him.

Fuck it. I really missed him.

"It's done, though?" Palma pressed her original question.

My throat grew thick with emotion.

Heath and Palma never got mad. At me. At Creighton. When I tried pushing it, apologizing, both shut me down. "It wasn't your fault." That's what they both said. I guess it was true. Sometimes I was so twisted up that I no longer could identify what was and what wasn't my fault. When I offered to move out, both shut me down on that too. Niko as well. She arrived at my bedroom that night and threatened me. "If you ever utter those words again, I will cut up all of your bags and shred them into tiny pieces. And I won't feel sorry about it. If I'm here, you have to be here." I hadn't seen her since that statement, but I figured she had her way to keep track of everything that went on with the rest of us.

So I never left.

And yes, the war was over. Levi kept me up to date. He told me the terms, but there'd been another meeting just a couple days ago about an AI drone surveillance program. It was set to launch in one more week, but Creighton's territory would not be surveilled. Since West and Walden's territories were already banned, that only left Staten Island. Levi said that the entire program was scrapped. It was going to be moving somewhere else. Creighton suggested Florida.

I nodded. "It's done."

"Just like that?"

"I think having my housemates kidnapped and my foster brother put in the hospital was enough."

Her cheeks pinked. "I know." She got serious again.

I steeled myself because I recognized the look by now. She was going to say something deep, something that would cut straight to the bone.

"Look, I don't know if you need me to repeat this, but just in case, I am. I'll say this as many times as you need to hear it. You are not to blame for any of this. The only thing might've been a heads-up, but you were trying to hide from it yourself. So it happened. It just did. You moved in. You're in love with a very scary guy, who does what he does, and because of what he does, all of that spread to us. I get it. Next time going in, we know now. Heath and me. We're prepared. We're ready. We aren't leaving. And by the way, Heath gets to see his brothers again. I didn't even know he'd been estranged, so I think that part of it is awesome." She paused, but I knew there was still more coming. I waited. She spoke, almost gently because she knew these words might be hard for me to hear. "I know your thoughts on the kind of guy Creighton is. You don't condone the lengths he will go for you, but I'm not you. I'm not as nice of a person as you are. I *am* okay with it. I care about you. And obviously he does too. So I'm okay with what he will do to make sure you're safe. I mean, Jesus, he did all of this because of you. Right?"

My insides hollowed out.

She was watching me keenly. "You see that, don't you?" She motioned around the room. "The war. Him pushing into this city. You told me that you began looking at this college two years ago. According to Levi, that's when Creighton began making steps for this war."

Her words were on repeat in my head.

I was the reason for all of this . . .

I *never* thought about the possibility that I was the reason he started down this path, but he only began to fight for control of the streets after I went to Miss Marcie's house.

He never said a word.

. . . I won't be able to guarantee your safety—

I was gutted.

He had done all of this for me, *because* of me. All of it. Since he was sixteen.

I began hyperventilating. I was the cause for so many deaths.

The pressure was suffocating me all over again. I couldn't be the reason. I just couldn't. Who was I? I was a no one. A foster kid. I was someone that was thrown away. I was tossed out like garbage, and then I met a boy when I was eight years old and he decided—Creighton's words jarred me.

I wasn't born with a soul, Blake. For fourteen years I was walking around, knowing something was different about me, but I didn't know what it was. I didn't care. Then one day a little girl gets out of this car and suddenly I got something in my chest.

My lungs stopped. They just completely stopped.

He'd told me. He had. I just hadn't realized the ramification of how completely he meant what he said.

I met a little girl when she was eight years old, and suddenly I understood the world. You gave me the world. You gave me everything . . .

I wasn't worth any of this, much less this responsibility. How could I process this?

Creighton was obsessed with me, but to be the reason for all of this? It wasn't right.

I had so many conflicting emotions swirling inside of me. Unworthiness. Resentment. Regret. Who was I? I kept coming to that feeling. I was a nobody to the world.

Except to Creighton, a voice kept whispering in the back of my head. I wasn't a no one to him.

"You okay?" Palma was asking. I heard her voice in the distance. My heart was pounding, thumping loudly in my chest.

He was capable of anything, literally anything. He could destroy the world, and I was either the motivation or the reins holding him back.

My vision began to blur at the edges.

Palma was talking, her voice droning in the distance, until she grew clear again and I heard, "—It makes sense. It's almost simple. We just want our loved ones safe. He wants to make sure the world is safe for you, so he controls the world you're in. It's beautiful, in his twisted way."

Christ. It was.

CHAPTER FORTY-NINE

BLAKE

"Miss Green." Tristian West approached me on the front steps of the center, dressed in his business suit and a nice custom-tailored jacket. He looked like the epitome of a young wealthy entrepreneur. His driver shut his back door, but remained standing on the side of his SUV. Still in guard mode. I knew his name by now. Pajn. I gave him a nod before greeting his employer.

"Mr. West."

A brief chuckle left him. "How about we just use our first names? Tristian. I'll call you Blake? Is that okay with you?"

I lifted up a shoulder. I wasn't really sure what was going on here. I looked up and down the street, but didn't see anything out of the ordinary. "Are we at war again? Is this the first offensive being launched?"

Another brief chuckle, but it sounded more forced. "No, Blake. We have an understanding. Lane with Ashton and I." He gestured behind me. "I'm not sure if you're aware, but I was previously approached to see if I wanted to help invest in this facility."

"What?"

"Imagine my surprise when I realized you were one of the volunteers."

"Are you going to do it? Invest?"

"I already have. Let me correct myself, I'm the reason it's up and running."

Oh. I was stunned. He would've needed to already have invested before—"Are you the reason I was asked to volunteer?"

The slight grin faded from his face. "No. My investment in this place has nothing to do with my other business."

"It's not a moneymaker. Why invest?"

"Did you know that Molly was also in foster care?"

I frowned.

"Ashton's better half, as he would say." He shrugged, his eyes trailing behind me to take in the center. "It was the right thing to do. I have a plethora of ventures. Places like this, plus others. Legit businesses as well. I'm sure you can imagine. Lane runs the businesses the Worthing family used to have, plus a good amount of his own. He does well. He has his hand in multiple pockets too."

My mouth flattened. "You won't be able to use me to control Creighton, if that's why you're here."

"That's not why I'm here." He gestured behind me. "They're having a Christmas event. Of course it's a big fundraising event as well, but I'd intended to bring Ashton and Molly. Ashton doesn't know about my involvement with this center. I'm not sure if you're aware, but Lassiter has been showing up lately."

He was ping-ponging around, and the last was a surprise.

I missed Lassiter. And the fact that he knew something about my brother that I didn't, pain sliced me.

"They're rebuilding her bowling alley. He's been around. He and Pialto have—they've grown close. I don't know the exact nature of their friendship."

That felt like another stab in my chest. Lassiter was getting close to someone?

"Pialto and Sophie are coming to the Christmas event. They know it's meant to be a surprise for Molly. I'm assuming Lassiter will attend with them in some form or fashion. Jess's mother and brother are also attending. The center is a good foundation for all of us to come together and move forward. With Lassiter and Pialto, your volunteering here, I'd like to invite everyone to the party. Your housemates. You." His mouth dipped down as he added, curtly, "Lane."

I almost laughed at the contempt he couldn't contain, but the rest, it did feel like he was sincere. Or he was trying.

Lassiter.

I missed him.

I also missed Creighton.

I swallowed a knot. "If Last is attending, we'll be there."

"Excellent. I'll let the board know. You can look for the invitations in the mail." He was getting ready to leave.

Nerves suddenly hit me. "In the warehouse, you mentioned that I was also a player on the board. What did you mean by that?"

He stopped short, surprised. "Because you are. I wasn't talking about just the power you hold over Lane. Though you do. That power can't be ignored. Your boyfriend is like an assault rifle, and you're the pin that either turns him into a killing machine or you can keep him as just a pile of metal. But no, that's not all I was referring to. I meant you as a player. In a similar kidnapping situation, my wife wouldn't have reacted as you did. She would've gotten free, but she might not have done it as fast. She would've raged. She would've yelled. She would've stolen someone's gun and shot her way out of that building. Molly would've been sweet until she flipped a switch she has. After that, I don't know the destruction she would've left in her path, but I know there would've been a trail. You, though. You shut down. You quieted. You just did the work, like a professional. No fuss, no ripple. You were there, and then you weren't. It's your natural default setting. And knowing that, I feel reassured letting the war stop where it has, letting Lane remain operating in my city."

I was dazed at all of that.

"Creighton once told me that I'm bad at what I do."

I almost laughed. "That sounds like something he'd say."

"He was right, in a way. This business is dirty. It's cruel and cold and ugly. I am not a bad man, but what I do *is* bad. I get that. There might be a time in the future where Ashton and I decide to go legit, and there will no longer be any West or Walden Mafia business, but that's not today. Or tomorrow. And until that day happens, I'm okay knowing that your boyfriend is another threat in this city. It's like we had a wolverine trying to break into our house. Ashton and I decided to open the door. The wolverine is now *in* our house, but you know what else? If anyone tries to get in, they have to get past that same psychopathic wolverine because it turns out, he is lethally protective of the ones he loves. I can work with that."

Psychopathic wolverine. How appropriate.

CHAPTER FIFTY

BLAKE

It was dark by the time I got back to the house.

I stopped short in my bedroom, seeing Creighton on my bed. He'd stopped having me followed, so either I was still being followed or . . . "West messaged you? A heads-up that he invited us to the center's Christmas party?"

He moved to sit against the headboard. "A heads-up call. I think he'd rather work with you than remain civil with me. Is that what you two talked about? Are you and West going into business together? You want to off me and take over my network?"

I moved to my closet and pulled my shirt off over my head. Dropping the rest of my clothes, I tugged on his hoodie. No matter this recent time apart, I still slept in it. This one or the other five hoodies I'd liberated from him.

Padding barefoot to the bed, I crawled on top of it before hesitating, and then I just went for it.

I'd missed him.

I settled over his lap, straddling him.

His hands went to my hips, holding me in place, but he continued just to watch me. "This is a surprise. The meeting must've been *very* informative or very *boring*. Which was it, Blake?"

Oh yeah. I heard the bite again. He was pissed. "You're trying to start a fight with me."

"I've stayed away. I pulled my men from following you. *I* stopped from following you. I helped that girl and her sister for you. Now this? Now I'm getting a call from Tristian West that he had a conversation with you?" His hands tightened on my thighs for a moment. "If you're upset that I've come to see you and you're about to stick a knife in me, give a guy a little warning. I'll try and keep my body relaxed so you can stick it all the way through."

I closed my eyes, rested my forehead against his chest, and breathed him in.

God. I loved his scent. Pine trees and just him. I said there, "You're not funny."

"Not trying to be." His hands smoothed out over my legs again. "What is this, Blake? I need the full rundown on what West talked to you about and if you want me to leave, I'll go after that."

Shaking my head, I lifted it to better see him. I didn't want that.

As I did, some of the tension left him. His face softened. I didn't know Creighton's face could soften. He raised a hand to cup the side of my face, ran his hand down my chin. His words came out soft too. "Is this the final goodbye? Have you decided to leave me? I moved heaven and hell to keep you safe from them, and the second the war is called off, you have a nice little chat with Tristian West. From a battle perspective, it's slightly genius. From a personal perspective, not a fan."

I took his hand in mine and settled back on his lap. "Stop." My other hand slid down the front of his chest, and I ignored how his hands moved up underneath his hoodie on me. My heart skipped a few beats. My body began to heat up. "He showed up at the center when I was leaving. Said some things, but the gist is that he wants to move forward with all of us being civil."

Creighton still wasn't happy, eyeing me. "He said 'some things.' What things?"

Fisting the front of his shirt, I pulled him toward me, off of the wall. I began to lean in, intending to kiss him, but I remembered that I couldn't. Not just yet.

Except . . .

Screw it.

I gave in.

I bit his bottom lip, ignoring his groan. "He was informative. Very informative."

"Still not liking this conversation, but I'm enjoying *this* part of it." His words were a cold challenge, but his eyes were molten.

I rocked over his lap, closing my eyes, because that felt good. He felt good.

I grinded over him a bit more.

His hands helped me, moving my body over him, and I was starting to forget he was annoyed with me.

He pulled back. "We need to talk."

I growled briefly, but stopped and slumped over him. My hands went to his chest, toying with his shirt. "I know. I'm sorry. I knew when I came home that I'd need to talk to you about what West said, but . . . I wanted to talk to you. If anything, I wanted to thank you for helping with Satya and her sister."

"That's it? Just to thank me?" His hands went back to touching me, kneading my hips. "You were giving in? Just now? Or was this a onetime thing and then what? Back to telling me to stay away from you?"

"No." I shook my head. That wasn't fair to him. "I—" Okay. Let's do this. Really do this. I moved to the side of the bed beside him, and positioned myself so I was facing him. My legs crisscrossed, and I pulled a pillow to my lap. Sinking my hands in the front pocket of his hoodie, I let out a sigh. "I wanted to talk to you. I wanted to see you, but I needed time away to figure out what I was thinking and how I felt about things. Marshall was shot. My housemates were kidnapped. Levi is still healing. Lassiter is . . ." He was spending time with someone who wasn't us, and I couldn't talk to him about Pialto. "You took four innocent people."

He cursed under his breath. "I didn't kill them. Scooter's fine, by the way."

"Who's Scooter?"

"Never mind. I didn't kill Walden, West, or either of their women."

"Like that makes it better?"

"No." He sighed. "I've already told you that you can't put a leash on me."

"Rules were no one good and no one innocent."

He looked away. "There's a lot of good people who do bad things."

"I know." I leaned forward and cupped his face, turning him to see me again. "You and I have already come to a compromise. You not killing Walden after he put a gun to my head, that's huge progress."

His eyes burned, and I was seeing how much it pained him not to do whatever he wanted to do against Walden. Then, he blinked, and some of the burning had faded. "I'd already taken him and tortured him prior. I've tried reminding myself of those memories. I wish I had taken video and I could replay it as much as I wanted."

My eyebrows went to my forehead, because that was morbid. "Uh." I waved that off. Different topic for a different day. "I just needed space, and you gave it, and thank you. So West told you about seeing me, huh? That must've brought him such joy. Being the one to tell you before you were told by anyone else."

He ran a gentle hand up the side of my face and tucked some stray hair behind my ears. "I got him back."

I opened my eyes again. "What'd you do? And please tell me it's not sending us into another war. Marshall already got shot. If Palma gets shot, I think Levi would revolt. So that leaves Heath, and I don't think his brothers would be happy with you."

"West's brother-in-law is going to work for me."

"Wha-what?" I blinked a few times. "His brother that you kidnapped?"

"His wife's brother, and yes, I've been eyeing him. He wasn't a part of West's network. I approached, offered him a position in one of my clean businesses, and he took it."

I blinked a few more times because that was kinda genius. "So you still ended up taking one of theirs after all." I grinned, slowly. "I like it."

"They took one of mine."

Ah. I said faintly, "I wondered if you knew about Last."

He watched me for a few seconds in silence. I wasn't sure what he was looking for, but then he let out another sigh. Reaching over, he took my hand in his, pulling it to his lap, and laced our fingers together. "My shot didn't go wide because West knocked into me. I wanted it to go wide. West jumping when he did was cosmic timing."

"What do you mean?" I leaned forward, my free hand resting on his knee. "Why would you—" But I thought about it. There was only one explanation. "You did that to push him away?"

He shrugged, looking away, but I caught the flash there. It was something I'd only seen on his face when it came to me. Pain. A little bit of regret. He was feeling that about Lassiter. He cared. He did, about Last. About Levi.

He really was changing.

"Eight," I whispered.

"He fought me on Pialto, so I knew there was already some interest there."

A different thought came to me. "When did you learn Japanese?"

At my question, his eyes went flat again. Dead. My hand along with his fell with a thud to his flat stomach. "The first time I met someone who belonged to the Yakuza."

"Are you serious?"

"Heath Nogoskeski was already in this house. There was a fire at the previous place Niko was living in. I had her transferred here. No one could move on the house unless they wanted to risk giving the Yakuza an excuse to launch their own push into the city as well. I had her assigned here as an added form of protection for you."

"You orchestrated that?"

He wasn't looking at my face. His gaze had fallen to our hands. He went back to tracing over our fingers.

"Hey." I caught his chin and lifted it up. "Palma said they had another housemate who had to go back home. Something about a sick relative. Did you have a hand in that too?"

"I didn't orchestrate her mom getting sick, but I did help open up their doctor's schedule so they wouldn't have to wait months to get the bad news."

I wasn't surprised anymore. "Were you behind the fire at Niko's original place?"

His eyes flickered at me, but he didn't comment.

I sighed, knowing what that meant. "What else should I know about?"

"Nothing major, but there's a few things. Small things."

My head was a mess. I knew he was capable of things like this, but to hear it all laid out, hearing that there was *more*, my mouth was suddenly so dry. My stomach dipped.

I had to ask. "Did you start this war because of me?"

He stilled, and for a second, his eyes blazed.

"Did you?"

"Two years ago, I saw a pamphlet for this school on your desk."

I growled. "That's not an answer." Why wasn't he answering me? It wasn't like him. But then I thought about what he just said. I really thought about it.

Two years ago . . .

He was right. The pressure had been getting to me, of living in Cincy, everyone knowing who I was to Creighton, everyone just knowing who Creighton was. There'd been a fair at our college, and I walked through, idly picked up the brochure, but there'd been nothing idle about it. I remembered thinking how far away New York City was from Cincinnati. Thinking there were probably other Mafia families who operated there, and since it was New York, maybe Creighton couldn't get to me as much. I had a thought that I could hide in the shadows, hide from him, hide from everyone.

Then he hanged my date the next year, and the decision was made. I started the process.

He'd been watching me. Waiting. Now he let out a soft sigh. "You wanted to get away from me. I knew that. I chose not to let you. I didn't know where you were going to go, but I knew you were going to go somewhere. I made plans. I hadn't just made the decision to push into this city. I started by taking over surrounding cities first."

I was horrified. "On the off chance I decided to go somewhere else?" Him taking over meant death. Bloodshed. "How many people have you killed because of me?"

His eyes went full-on black. He moved in a flash, grabbing me and twisting so I was on the bed beneath him. He loomed over me, but lowered his head so he was a few inches from me. *"None."*

I gulped. My hands were shaking. "Creighton—"

"None." He let out a curse and ran his nose over my jawline before dipping down to my neck. He inhaled me, one big breath, and then lifted his head to hold my gaze again. "You need to get this through your head. You are not responsible for anything I choose to do. My choices, Blake. Mine. You can agree with them. You can hate them, but they are not yours. They are mine. Now, did I decide to start a war for you? No. I decided to push into a territory where you might attend college because I wanted to make sure the territory was safe for you. When I did that, when I made the decision to do that, I was met with resistance from the current territory holders. I did that. Me. You had nothing to do with that."

I said weakly, "But if I hadn't decided to come to this city, you wouldn't have pushed your way in, and the people who died wouldn't be dead."

A new tenderness came over him.

He closed his eyes once, bent his head so his forehead rested on mine gently, and murmured, "I have minimal memories of my mother.

A few. I don't know if I loved her, but I didn't hate her. My last memory of her was the night she overdosed on street crank. My first kill was her pimp. And if you think when I found out she had a whole family who did nothing to help her, that I *wasn't* going to do something about them? I was going to wreak havoc on the Worthing family. You coming to New York just meant that I wasn't going to destroy all of their assets. I'd simply take them over instead. But no, Blake. Again. You have to stop trying to take responsibility for decisions *I* make."

Did that help? Hearing all of that?

Somewhat.

He let out another soft curse and moved us again, but this time he slid an arm underneath me, and lifted me. He reversed our positions so he was sitting against the headrest and I was on his lap.

I sank back on his legs, knowing what he was saying, and hearing the words, but I couldn't accept them.

He ran a finger along my cheek again, sliding down to trace my neck until he cupped the back of my neck. "What's battling in your head? Let me in."

I drew in a ragged breath. "I'm the reason you took over Cincy. You started to do that after you met me—" A sob choked me. Those are years and years of death, all at my doorstep. All because of me.

He exhaled a long and deep breath. "You need to listen to me very clearly."

I blinked back the tears and met his gaze.

"When you moved into Miss Marcie's house, a particular network set up shop. Their specialty was kids for sex trafficking. They started taking kids in the neighborhood, and yes, one of their recruiters saw you, and his eyes lit up. I dug out his eyeballs that night, but there was a picture of you on his phone. He'd already sent it to his employers. They were going to move on you. I started tracking them down, and I took them out. I realized I was *good* at doing that shit. Death and destruction. I took over the streets, then the city, because I didn't want other little kids to get targeted. There's rules in my territory. You recently learned some of them, but yeah, I run that territory, and yes, I do bad shit there. But I also keep them safe for people too. You're so horrified at the people who died, but you don't realize a lot of people are alive. If you insist on taking credit for the bad shit, take credit for the good shit too."

A pressure was on my chest, pressing down.

I clung to his wrist, the one he had cupped around the back of my neck as if he were anchoring me. As if I needed my own touch on him to keep me grounded. I didn't want to slip away, but the implications of what he said, the thought if I'd been taken? I knew it was true. I remembered more than a few older men giving me looks that made my skin crawl, and then they'd be gone the next day, and I remembered being relieved. I felt safe.

Creighton did that too.

"Creighton," I choked out, a tear falling from my eye. "No one cared about me before you came along."

He cursed, dragging me to him, and he caught the tear, wiping it away. "What are you talking about?"

Another tear fell. And another. "What you did for me? The good and bad. I'm not worth it. I didn't deserve it. I don't deserve it. I—" My chest was there, caving in. Just so much pain. It was paralyzing. "I'm not worth this."

"Blake." My name came out hoarse, broken, from him.

I'd never heard that sound from him.

A new tenderness was there, as if he were seeing me for the first time. A new gentleness. A new warmth. He was Creighton, but he wasn't. He was staring at me as if he loved me.

I asked, my throat hurting, "You're looking at me like—"

I reached up to touch his face.

He caught my hand, squeezing. "I'm looking at you like I love you because I do." His eyes flared, hot. "Of *course* I love you." He let go of me, and his hand slid into my hair, fisting it. "I've not told you because you wouldn't believe me. I'm not so black and white, Blake. There's gray in me. I can feel emotions. I love you. I know I do. The problem is if you'll accept that or not. Before this conversation, I don't think you would've. It's not just obsession. It's love. I love you."

My chest cracked under the pressure, except there was an opening there. Light streamed in. Rainbows. Warmth. That was love. I could feel it. Love in a place I didn't think I ever deserved to feel before. I was feeling it now. I whispered, "I believe you."

"Do you?"

I nodded, pressing my fingers to his wrist again, moving so I could feel his pulse. It was skyrocketing.

"I'm not worth this, though."

He leaned close again. His other hand went to my hip. "You are what's invisible to the eye. *You* give me a glimpse of what a normal person thinks and feels. You are that window for me. You are the bridge that helps me understand what makes someone love another person where they would give them the world if they asked. All just to make the other person smile. That's what you give me. If that's love, yes. I love you, Blake. When you entered my life, your soul was so big that it filled me as well. You share it with me. I'm just the selfish prick that takes it when I can." He kissed me, long and slow and cherishing. "You are worth *everything* to me."

Was I?

I didn't think I was, but good came from Creighton's destruction too.

I would remember that.

I had no words after that. He'd taken them from me, and left all these emotions in their place. Except four little ones.

My voice broke. "I love you too."

EPILOGUE

CREIGHTON

A month later

Blake was upstairs getting ready for this event. Since she'd been invited, she began talking more about how she hadn't been able to experience the city. Hence, she now wanted to do the tourist experiences so she could say she'd done them. And I knew she was loving this "normal" way of life, so I had no problem doing my part for her, being the normal boyfriend.

That meant dates. Lots of dates.

We went to Broadway one night. Then we went to Ellis Island. Saw the Statue of Liberty another day. We took a trip to Times Square. Walked through Central Park. Passed through Canal Street. Chinatown. Little Italy. Toured the Metropolitan Museum of Art. Saw a show at Café Carlyle. Got cheese at Zabar's. Did a culinary tour at the Chelsea Market.

I was tourist-ed out.

Blake was in heaven.

"Boss, my man." Levi came over, thumping me on the arm before he poured himself a drink. "You ready for this?"

I eyed him, waited until he settled with his drink in hand before I reached up and tipped the drink out of his hands. It fell to the ground, and he glared at me. "Asshole."

"I won't repeat myself about you calling me Boss."

"But you are my boss—" He'd begun to bend down to pick up his now-emptied glass when a burst of feminine laughter came from the top of the stairs. He paused for a second before grabbing the glass, or he would've.

My foot kicked it away from him, and he glared at me again.

"Such a dick." Levi picked up his glass, tossed a towel on the floor where the liquid spilled, and filled another drink. He came back to settle beside me but had moved out of my immediate reach. He only got one sip before the girls came down the stairs. "Whoa."

He straightened upright, a dumbstruck expression coming to his face, and when I looked, air left my lungs. I only had eyes for Blake.

She was beautiful every day, but this, how her silk cream dress molded over her body, with a slit up one leg—she was *stunning*. Her brown skin shimmered, and her hair was sleek, falling down past her shoulders.

Blake was everything.

She bit her bottom lip at my approach. A shy and self-conscious look hinted in her depths, but I cupped the side of her face and whispered over her lips, "Beautiful. Absolutely magnificent."

Her hands went to my arms. She squeezed them lightly. "Really?"

I nodded, knowing she could see how serious I was. "You are a gift that I will never deserve, but too selfish to give back."

She clutched to me as my mouth sealed over hers.

I could kiss her forever.

I would kiss, and taste, and savor every touch like this. I didn't want to go to this event. There'd be civilians there. My former enemies. Academic types. Blake said her professor would be there as well.

"Are we ready?" Heath called from the door.

Levi and Palma moved to follow.

Blake held me back. "You'll behave tonight?"

"That means no killing? Walden will be there."

She pushed a finger into my chest. "No maiming. No killing. No slicing. My professor will be there. People from the center. Malik said Cap is even coming. Satya, too, with her sister."

I'd recently met Blake's favorite four that utilized the center.

"I'd never harm them." I took her hand and began leading her out of their townhouse, stopping only to grab our jackets. They'd be needed since Blake insisted we be "normal" for this event. That meant traveling to Rockefeller Center by train.

She laced our fingers together. "You know that's not who I meant. Just, be fake tonight. You know. Be civil. Normal people world."

"Normal people world is overrated."

She laughed shortly, squeezing my hand. "True, but wear the fake persona mask tonight. Don't scare my kids."

Her kids? That's how she considered the kids who utilized the shelter? I searched her face to see if there were any hints of resentment, but I found none. Just warmth. She was happy. I don't know if the shelter was perfect for Blake, but *she* was perfect for the shelter. I wasn't surprised.

I remarked, "Never. However, I will do no such thing when it comes to Walden."

I was fully aware she was doing some of this because of me, going into her studies and continuing her work with the center because she hoped to help me learn how to have more empathy. It was about her, but about me too. Maybe one day that would happen. It would make her happy. Myself? I didn't care. I followed her rules, and I began to feel other sensations inside of me, so maybe she was correct. Maybe there was a way to help people like me grow as a person? All I knew was that I'd begun to change for her and I'd continue except I would never let another rule over me. Or rule over Blake.

I would always ensure her safety. Even if that meant I would sacrifice myself.

I didn't think other psychopaths would make the same decision.

Her smile softened, knowing that I meant what I said. She rested her head against my arm for a moment. "Thank you."

I pressed a kiss to the side of her temple.

Once we got onto the subway, silence came over the train.

Blake didn't want to attend this Christmas event pulling up in a slew of private vehicles. Said that wasn't "normal poor college student behavior."

I already knew I had men working on this train. They hadn't been notified ahead of time. The group settled at the end of the car, and I leaned back, holding a post with one hand. My other curved around Blake, keeping her anchored to my side.

Conversation began to pick up, but quieted among our group as one of my men approached. He had eyes only for me. "Sir?"

I lifted my chin behind him. "We'll be going to the Rockefeller. Move to the next car."

He clipped his head in a nod at my command, and soon the rest of my men all went to the other subway cars. Instead of continuing to work, they stood guard at the doors so no one else could come onto our individual car. This was routine for wherever I went, and for the most part, Blake's housemates had grown accustomed to this treatment. They continued their conversations.

The other civilians noted how I was treated. They watched me. One raised her camera to record me, but I looked at her. She squeaked, her eyes bulging out, and she fumbled her phone, dropping it to the floor. It rolled all the way until Levi stopped it. When she came over to take it, he said something to her.

Her eyes went past him to me, and she nodded quickly before returning to her seat.

She didn't try to record again.

Blake sank into me. "Some things will never change."

I glanced down at her. "Do you want that?"

She considered my question, tipping her head up to meet my gaze. She shrugged. "No. I love you. You still have to be you. I fell in love with you, not a version of you."

She did indeed.

She looked at me, saw my monster, then claimed my monster as hers.

BLAKE

It was a couple hours into the Christmas party, after Creighton had to step out to take a call, that I slipped away to the bathroom. It was when I was returning, going down a hallway toward where the larger group had congregated. Hearing a sudden burst of voices, I glanced over, but I almost did half-heartedly because I didn't even know there was a door beyond the women's bathroom. It was a side exit, and I'd realize later that the door was camouflaged, and how sneaky was that, but I recognized the two big guys just coming in from out of that door.

Those were Ashton Walden's guards. Elijah and Derek.

Right behind them, dressed in a business suit with a phone pressed to his ear, and looking distracted was Ashton Walden. My knee jerk reaction was panic, because of old habits. I was alone. Vulnerable. They could grab me, but I remembered the war was done.

I shoved that fear away and stayed put.

They had to go past me to get to their table. They had enough people at this Christmas event so their group was at one side of the banquet and we were on the other. That'd been done on purpose. I doubted my professor or the head of the center was aware of the dynamics, so I had to guess that Tristian West had orchestrated the seating arrangements. Either way, we'd barely interacted.

The two guards began to pass, but once Walden saw me, he stopped short.

He eyed me before he said into his phone, "I need a minute. Do me a favor, Molly? Let Trace know that I'm about to have a face-to-face with Psychopath's Girl? Thanks. No. I'm okay. I don't need you to come and She-Hulk out." He put his phone away and fixed me with a contentious glare. "Taking lessons from your stalker boyfriend?"

I was confused. "Are you implying that me standing here is stalking you?"

"If the shoe fits . . ."

"Yeah. Uh. No." I gestured three feet away. "Girls' bathroom. Not a stellar stalking hideaway. But kudos to you for thinking I'd want to stalk you if that were the case." I tipped my head toward his guards. "They're super stellar at their job then? Going right past me."

He rolled his eyes. "Or maybe you're just that unremarkable? They skip right over anyone who's inconsequential."

"You realize who you're saying that to, right?"

He narrowed his eyes. "What? The great and infamous—"

I stopped him before any more stupidity came out of his mouth. "I grew up tossed away like garbage. I was put in the system, and different homes were forced to take me in. You know. *That* world. That's where we are right now. This event. That's who you're talking to. I just wanted to give you a reminder that I'm a human being. I'm a person. I am used to people taking one look at me and hating me instantly because I dare to breathe the same air they do. And just so we're on the same page, I am not going to disappear to make you happy. In case you keep going down that avenue." I didn't say the rest, but I was feeling it. Right now, at this event, I didn't want to take any more of his shit.

I was tired of those types of insults.

I might've been garbage to others, but Creighton only needed one look to decide I was the world to him. That's what mattered.

He grew quiet before sighing. "I hate your boyfriend. That's the only reason behind my antagonism. No other reason."

Fuck's sake. My grin twisted up, and I eased some of the sudden seriousness. "Didn't you hear? I'm the pin that either turns Creighton into an assault rifle or keeps him null and void. Nothing unremarkable about that, now is there?"

"It's more than just one pin."

"Whatever. I'm important."

"If we're going to exchange jabs, I'd rather not unless I get permission to use knives on you, and in that case, after you." He stepped to the side and indicated the door.

"Such a gentleman," I deadpanned.

"Only if there's a lady around." He made a show of looking around, craning his neck. "Do you see one? For what it's worth, I've never thought you were garbage. I've always known you were the linchpin to that psychopath." He motioned between us. "Can we share these types of insults? I'm not familiar with the rules for us, what will or won't set off that psychopathic wolverine."

"You know." I kept my tone casual and stepped toward him. "Creighton and I discovered that security tend to search him for weapons, but not me." I wagged my eyebrows up and down.

His face got hard. "If you were going to stick me, you wouldn't have waited to corner me outside the women's bathroom, and didn't you just remind me about where we're at tonight? At an event for *foster* children." His dark amusement vanished. "What do you want, Miss Green?"

Sadly, our fun needed to come to an end. "Jake Worthing and Sawyer Matsen. You put a ban on them from coming back to this city. I want you to lift the ban."

He stared at me, long and hard. Then laughed as he began to walk away.

"Hey!" I got in his way. "I'm talking to you."

"No." He glared at me, widening his eyes. "You're attempting to start another war. I couldn't have heard what I just heard because if I did, either you're trying your hand at being a stand-up comedian or again, you want a war to start that would begin with you and me. Right here. With that request." He hissed, his control snapping. "You must be attempting to fuck with me. If so, don't bother. I'm not a cheater."

A growl was rumbling in my throat, working its way out from frustration. "Sawyer—"

"Are you forgetting what they did to you?"

"I like Sawyer, and I like her family. They're nice people. They've been texting me. She should be able to visit her family here."

He lifted his head, pinching the top of his nose, and muttered swift curses under his breath. "You're certifiable. Just like your boyfriend."

"Listen—"

"No!" He cut me off. "How about that? Just, *no*. No. Leave it alone." He began to go around me.

I let him get until the end of the hallway before I said, "Her paintings weren't destroyed."

He stopped, but didn't turn around. Not right away. He stood there, his back tense and his shoulders rigid before I heard another expletive leave him before he looked back. He'd been mad before, but this time, he wasn't steady. Had I pushed him too far?

I said, speaking calmly, but knowing I had a torpedo of nerves inside me, "Molly's bowling alley and Jess's art gallery. Creighton burned both of them down because you went after me. That's what happened, right?"

His eyes were primal. "You have used up all the good graces I have in me for you. If you don't get to the point, I swear that I will find the knife you have on you, and I'll use it to start this war myself."

Jesus Christ.

I kept on, ignoring his griping, "The paintings were moved. Creighton didn't have them burned. He also had some personal effects saved from your woman's bowling alley. Things he thought might mean something to her."

"You're lying."

"I'm not. He told me."

He scowled at me, trying to read if I was lying or not. He seethed. "If you're fucking with me—"

"Why would I? Don't forget he did that because of what *you* did to *me*."

"I really *really* hate you and your boyfriend." He pulled back. "Fine. You want the ban lifted on Worthing and his woman? It's his funeral. There's history there with him and the rest of us. Some of it isn't good. Most of it isn't good. Not to mention, he's your boyfriend's cousin. If we don't kill Jake, there's a good chance Lane will for fun."

"The ban needs to be lifted, and you have to promise you won't use it as bait to go after him or Sawyer. You've not met her aunts or her mom yet. You might be scary, but you've got nothing on them."

He didn't reply, just continued to scowl at me.

"Do we have a deal?" I held out my hand. "I'll tell you where the paintings are and the rest."

He looked at my hand as if it was diseased before he sighed and shook my hand. "Joke's on you."

I tried to yank my hand away, but he clamped down on it and used it to reel me in closer. "You don't like me and mine, but with the ban lifted, I can let you know now that when Sawyer's aunts were here, I did meet them. They also met Jess's mom, and guess who all became fast friends?"

I sucked in some air, horrified at his implication.

"That's right." Walden laughed cruelly in my face. "You just opened the door for those same aunts. Once they're here, you're the one who gets to deal with them, not me. See you at Sunday brunch."

His parting words burned me.

I couldn't. Not Sunday brunch.

Oh no. They were going to love Levi.

"What was that about?"

I screamed, whirling around, and screamed all over again. "Lassiter!" I launched myself at him, wrapping my arms around him. I'd been trying to give him space, tried not to stare at the "other" side too much, but Creighton said there was a chance he'd come with Pialto.

He went rigid before he slowly forced himself to hug me back.

I stepped back, all smiles, because this was good. Him saying hi to me. This was a good sign. "Hi. How are you? What's new with you? Any new friends or more than friends? You don't have to answer that—"

"It's not serious."

"Oh." I took him in again, really took him in and saw the exhaustion between the lines. He wasn't doing well. But this was Lassiter. He wouldn't open up to me like Levi or Creighton. If he was here, he was here for a reason. "What's not serious?"

"I know Trace told you about Pialto and me, but it's not serious. We're friends. Sophie too. They've adopted me. Kind of. Molly as well. You'd like her. You'd like *them*."

I snorted. "Walden's camp? I doubt—"

"No. You would." That hurt look was still there.

I reached up, touching the side of his face, wanting to rub it away if I could've. "He did it to push you away."

He laughed softly. "You think I don't know that? I know he did. West didn't hit him that hard." He expelled a sudden breath, closing his eyes. His shoulders loosened. "I haven't been with them the whole time. I went back to Cincy for a bit. Visited my old house. A lot of things have changed. Heath's brothers are running things there for Creight now. They're doing a good job." His gaze trailed behind me, searching. "I might need to stay away for a bit longer. I'm not ready. I'm not quite over him."

"Okay," I whispered. I didn't want my brother to hurt, and he was hurting, and I couldn't stop it from happening. "I'm here for whatever you need. Okay?"

He continued to stare at me as if he were seeing someone he didn't recognize, until all of that went away. The wall slipped, just a bit. "Thank you, Blake. You look happy."

I nodded, unable to speak. Sudden emotions were clogging up my airway. I pulled him to me for another hug. Before I let go, I whispered, "I don't give a fuck about blood. You're my brother."

He suddenly hugged me back before he coughed, and stepped away. He couldn't look me in the eyes, but that was okay. His hands squeezed my arm one last time before he slipped away, going through that camouflaged door.

"Everything okay?"

The timing of it all. I had to laugh.

Creighton had come to stand on the other end of the hallway.

I turned back in the direction Last just left. "Yeah."

He'd been here. He said hello. That meant something.

Things were going to be okay. I'd felt it before, but I accepted it now.

I rested my head against the wall and smiled at my man. "Can you take me home?"

"Happily."

"Why don't you want me to call you Quokka?" Creighton asked me as soon as I finished taking off my dress and changed into sleeping shorts and one of his hoodies. He hadn't changed, waiting for me on my bed, and I was okay that he hadn't changed.

And of course he was calling in his favor tonight.

Hoping to stall, I gave him an appreciative look, skimming my hand down his front. He was still dressed in business pants, a button-down shirt, and a tie. All of it had been tailored so it molded to his body, accentuating just how lean, but built, he was. Creighton did work out, and I knew he lifted weights, but he did it more as an activity to spend with Levi. It looked good on him. For some reason he had also put on a baseball cap with the brim pulled low. I think he pulled it out when we were in public or traveling, like we had earlier on the subway. As if that could camouflage his hotness. I scoffed at that in my head.

That was my favorite look on him, and I might've salivated a little bit at the sight of his square jawline. The guy was blessed, and sometimes it wasn't fair, but with the looks, I wasn't going to complain because I was the one that got to touch him.

I flipped his tie over his shoulder. "I like you like this. Though, I like your usual outfit too. Jeans and a Henley or sweatshirt. Joggers if you want to be comfortable or look like an athlete. Plus this." I tapped his hat.

He grabbed my finger before I could tap it again and pulled me against him. He was trying to scrutinize me underneath the brim. "Quokka story. Enough stalling. It was a favor."

Right. Right. I restrained from rolling my eyes. "Okay. It's stupid. I'm almost embarrassed about it, but—" I took a deep breath. "Okay. Here goes. I know you started calling me a quokka because that day we watched a documentary about them."

"You remember that?" He pulled me to sit on his lap, his hand falling to my thigh.

I nodded. "I was ten."

"You weren't feeling good."

I rested further against his chest. I reached down for his hand and began tracing his fingers. "You'd already left the house for the streets. Miss Marcie didn't approve of what you were doing so you didn't come around that much anymore. But I'd been sick and feeling horrible that day, and you came."

He brushed some of my hair from my forehead, still watching me with those dead eyes, but his touch was tender. "You were a no-show at school. I got notified, so I went to the house to see if you were okay. No one was there to take care of you."

"Miss Marcie had to leave me alone because she had some meetings at one of the other schools all day."

"I know. I messaged her, said I could stay with you." He smoothed some of my hair back, tugging it behind my ear. "She'd never let me do that for another kid. Not that I would've asked, but she knew it was different with you."

"When you saw how sick I was, you went and collected all of the stuffed animals everyone had in the house, which doesn't seem sanitary now. I'm surprised I didn't get even more sick, but you dumped all of them in my bed and crawled in with me."

His mouth strained. "I was on top of the covers, and the door was open."

"I know. You had someone bring an iPad to the house. You let me use it that whole time I was sick, but that day, we watched all of these animal videos. I loved the one about the quokkas. The smile they make. They're adorable. And then I read all about them, and I used to think how cute they were, and you started calling me Quokka, and I thought it was the best ever."

"What changed?"

I grew tense because this was the part that was embarrassing. I began idly drawing a circle on the back of his hand. "I—some of the girls at school found out about it, and they only cared because it was your nickname for me. They began to tease me with all the bad things about quokkas. That I was stupid to wish I had a quokka as a pet because they were illegal to have and that meant I needed to go to Australia to have one. That they only looked cute, but they were really a rodent. I don't think that's true. I looked it up later. They're marsupials. They said other stuff. I couldn't touch one because I'd make it sick and I'd kill it. I had the touch of death. They teased me about that stuff, but it was *all* the time, and after a while, it got in my head. It went on for a full year."

"When did they say this stuff?"

"In class so you wouldn't have heard about it. I knew you had older kids on your payroll by then, but none in my class. I always sorta worried what you would do if you ever found out they were saying that stuff to me."

"You were bullied." He tilted my head up.

"I was being teased." I relented at his look. "But yes, it was hurtful enough. I got those girls back eventually. We played volleyball the next year in gym, and I made sure to spike the ball at every one of them. They were horrible."

He cupped the side of my face, moved his thumb over my cheek. "I'm sorry they did that to you."

"Yeah. Well." I wanted to shrug it off, but I couldn't. They'd poisoned that endearment for me.

"Wolverines are ugly."

"What?" I laughed, confused. "Random much?"

"Hmmm. And they're sometimes called a skunk bear because they give off a bad smell when threatened."

"Uh. What are you doing?"

"And they cheat, in my opinion. They're polyamorous. I am not a cheater."

"No . . ." Where was he going with this?

He reached for my free hand and held it up, playing with my fingers as I'd been fiddling with his. "They're weasels too. Glorified weasels. Their scientific name means 'the glutton,' which is appropriate because even if they're only twenty-two pounds, they're willing to fend off wolves or a bear for its meal. The name fits, right?"

My laugh came easier. I felt lighter in my chest. "Again. What are you doing?"

"Ah. There it is. Made you smile."

I fell silent. He said that with such seriousness.

"That day you were sick, you laughed the rest of the afternoon. That's not nothing. You hadn't smiled in seven days. You smiled that day. You laughed that day. Even if it's a silly animal like a quokka that did that, I don't care. Those little girls were cruel. I wish I had known because I would've done something about—"

I groaned, sinking my whole weight against him. He was so earnest and being nice and looking so good, and my resistance crumbled. "You suck. You know that?"

"You'll tell me the next time someone hurts you?"

I straightened away from him.

"Eight?"

"I don't like that you were hurt and you didn't tell me. I can guess the reason you held back, but, Blake, I want to know." He tipped my head up to meet him. "I am working on the compromise between us, but you are everything to me. Knowing you were hurting and never told me, that destroys me."

He was being so serious right now.

My heart almost couldn't take it.

Tears welled up. I confessed, "I don't understand why you love me so much."

He went still.

I couldn't look at him. "You did everything for me, and I just don't get it. I'm not worth it—"

He growled, low and savagely from the bottom of his throat. "Don't even fucking finish that statement."

Pressing my forehead to his chest, I whispered the next words because I needed to get them out of me. I just had to. They wrung themselves from my throat. "Somedays I feel like I'm no one. Then I look at you and I know that I'm everything to you, and I . . . I still don't understand it. There's a level of responsibility I need to take for what you've done because of me, but then I stop and think about what you would say to that. What you *have* said to me. I know you said that only you're responsible for your actions. And I get that. I do, but it's hard to feel it. You know? Then there's the whole other layer underneath it all, that you have conquered cities for me, and I—" The words caught in my chest. Alongside the love, the pain, and the disbelief. "I don't deserve it."

I tipped my head to look at him. His eyes were so black, but there was emotion reflecting back at me. Real emotion. Pain. Love.

My heart surged. "Creighton?"

He blinked. The emotions were still there, but they were less heated. "I know it'll take you a while to accept that you're worth everything. I know that, but it's the other way around, Blake. *I'm* not worth feeling that love for you, but I do, and the way I see it, as long as you're willing to let me love you, I'm going to show it. And you are wrong. You are worth *every* life I've taken. You are worth every life I've saved. I love you. *Please* start accepting that."

I pressed my lips to his. "I will. I'll start accepting it."

"Promise?"

I nodded. "Promise."

Some of his tension left him. He slid a hand up my back, to the back of my neck, and into my hair, where he cupped my head. He tilted my head back so he could meet my eyes better. "I've not asked about your talk with Walden tonight. I'm growing. See. You're having a marked effect on me. That should make you smile." He waited, so serious.

I smiled, feeling raw.

His thumb touched the corner of my mouth. "There it is. I like seeing it."

I cocked my head to the side. "You're really not going to ask?"

He shook his head and leaned in again. "Nope. You didn't kill him, so I won't be going to war again so soon. But besides your smile, you know what else I *love* about you?" He dropped his forehead to rest against mine. "I *love* when you're naked."

A heated shiver went down my spine. "Have I told you recently that I love you?"

"You have, but you can say it again. I like hearing it."

I reached up on my tiptoes for him and pulled his head down to meet me. "Well, I do."

He evaded my lips. "I want you to say it."

I was a girl on a mission, so I ignored him and latched my mouth to his.

He sighed against my mouth, "I love you, my little Quokka."

"Yeah, yeah. I love you too, my psychopathic wolverine."

ACKNOWLEDGMENTS

I want to thank all the editors, proofreaders, and *everyone* from Montlake who helped bring Creighton and Blake's story to life. Thank you for your patience with me as well. Thank you to my agent as well.

Thank you to Deb and Tami for the support, listening, and assistance. You two are always there if I need anything, and I truly appreciate it.

Thank you for the readers in my reader group, Tijan's Crew! I always say it, but you have no idea how much support I draw from your posts, comments, and likes.

Thank you, thank you, thank you.

And as always, thank you to my eleven-year-old pup, Bailey.

We've been through a lot, you and me, Bubba.

ABOUT THE AUTHOR

New York Times bestselling author Tijan writes suspenseful and unpredictable novels. Her characters are strong, intense, and gut-wrenchingly real—with a little bit of sass on the side. Tijan began writing after college and was hooked right from the start. Since then, she has written multiple bestsellers, including the Fallen Crest series, *Ryan's Bed*, and *Enemies*.

Tijan is currently writing many new books and series with an English cocker spaniel that she adores. To connect with the author, visit her website (www.tijansbooks.com) or follow her on Facebook (www.facebook.com/tijansbooks) and X (@tijansbooks). You can also check out her Instagram at www.instagram.com/tijansbooks. Tijan is managed by the Park, Fine & Brower literary agency.